(*Im*)perfectly
Happy

(Im)perfectly
Happy

sharina harris

KENSINGTON BOOKS
www.kensingtonbooks.com

KENSINGTON BOOKS are published by

Kensington Publishing Corp.
119 West 40th Street
New York, NY 10018

All Kensington titles, imprints, and distributed lines are available at special quantity discounts for bulk purchases for sales promotion, premiums, fund-raising, and educational or institutional use.

Special book excerpts or customized printings can also be created to fit specific needs. For details, write or phone the office of the Kensington Sales Manager: Kensington Publishing Corp., 119 West 40th Street, New York, NY 10018. Attn. Sales Department. Phone: 1-800-221-2647.

Kensington and the K logo Reg. U.S. Pat. & TM Off.

ISBN-13: 978-1-4967-2563-9
ISBN-10: 1-4967-2563-8
First Kensington Trade Paperback Printing: May 2020

ISBN-13: 978-1-4967-2564-6 (ebook)
ISBN-10: 1-4967-2564-6 (ebook)
First Kensington Electronic Edition: May 2020

10 9 8 7 6 5 4 3 2 1

Printed in the United States of America

To my masterminds—this one is for you!

This book could not have been written without the support and friendship of my mastermind group and best friends. I also thank my mother, Pamela, for taking the time to answer all my questions about public defenders. And extra-special thank you to my critique partners: Connie, Mary, LaShon, and Pamela. You've made me a stronger writer and I so enjoy our Saturday mornings.

AUGUST

CHAPTER 1
M-Day—Raina

Today was a good day. And not because Ice Cube was rapping on the "oldies" station, the name some disrespectful person in radioland had given 90s music. Today was the big "M" day—*moving day*—and the biggest day I'd ever had.

I breathed in the freshly painted walls and looked around the room, taking in my new home. I wanted to explore: push buttons, open and shut cabinets, play with the thermostat, and revel in the fact that my mom wasn't here to yell at me for running up the bill.

I toyed with the wood blinds that covered the windows in the living room and peered out. The neighborhood was quiet, neat rows of cookie-cutter houses, even-spaced rosebushes and even-height trees. Even the kids who skipped rope in their driveway were quiet. Everything seemed perfect.

This was the complete opposite of the run-down apartment complex on the outskirts of Atlanta where I grew up. Ten-year-old me would've been ecstatic at the upgrade, but thirty-two-year-old me was waiting for the other shoe to drop.

My boyfriend Cameron and I were moving to our four-bedroom, two-and-a-half bath home in the 'burbs of Atlanta, though technically it was Cameron's house. Thanks to my poor decisions in college, I had no power and bad credit. Free pizza for credit cards. Damn, I'd been greedy, stupid. Stupid and dependent on a man.

And I could tell from the excitement that made Cameron bounce with every step and the light that ignited his already warm eyes that he was just tugging me down the path of adulthood. Suburbia. Everlasting commitment. *Marriage.*

What in the hell have I gotten myself into?

My palms were a soupy mess, I wiped them on my shorts, while my heart pounded against my chest.

The screechy squawks of packing tape being ripped off cardboard and the sound of occasional grunts coming from Cameron, who was unpacking boxes and shifting furniture, forced tendrils of guilt down my spine. He was grinding away getting things done while I sat motionless, alternating between Disney Princess happy and trembling like a frightened kitten.

My phone buzzed, and I grabbed it from the pocket of my cutoffs. Nikki's name flashed across the screen.

I pressed the answer button, but before I could greet her, she said, "How's your scary ass doing?"

"I'm good. Just getting things organized." I lied easily to my best friend from college. And like all best friends, she knew I was full of shit.

"You're a damn lie."

"What's up, Nik?" My annoyance was clear in my tone. "You know I'm busy."

"The girls and I were talking . . . and anyway, I volunteered as tribute."

The girls she was referring to were my two other best friends from college, Sienna and Kara. We were always up in each other's business, so I wasn't surprised they'd gotten together to discuss God knows what.

"Volunteered for what?"

"Volunteered to talk some sense into you. We know you have cold feet about moving in with Cam."

What did they think I would do—run away from home? I squelched down the flare of irritation that prickled my skin. My friends meant well, but I wasn't in the mood for the *all men aren't like your daddy* lecture. I knew that already. Otherwise, I wouldn't be doing a bunch of domestic shit like buying mulch and analyzing a dozen gray paint samples with stupid names like Mole's Breath.

A roll of sweat trickled from my neck onto my chest. I used my hand as a fan. I was pretty sure the sweat was from the heat, not anxiety.

"Hellooooo, Raina? You still there?"

"Yes." I modulated my tone to my late-night radio personality I used for my job. "I'm perfectly fine."

"Sure you aren't. And don't take on that bougie-ass radio therapist tone with me. You're talking to a friend, not a caller from your show." She smacked her lips. "Anyway, can you talk?"

I looked at my guy, who was whistling as he drilled studs above the fireplace to mount our big screen TV.

"Not right now," I whispered.

"Good. You can just listen. Cam is a great guy, and this is a good step. You've been together for six years, and he's been more than patient with your crazy ass. Who else would propose three times, get rejected, and then buy a house with you?"

"First of all—" I stopped myself when I caught Cameron's attention. His eyebrows crinkled, and his eyes scanned me. I knew he was checking to see if everything was good. I gave him a smile and thumbs-up. "It's Nikki. She's just wishing us good luck."

"No, I'm not. I'm convincing your crazy-ass girlfriend to calm down," Nikki yelled over the phone line.

He nodded. Thankfully I was far enough away that he couldn't hear my opinionated friend.

"Tell her I said hello." He loved my friends, but Nikki was his favorite. The way we bickered and teased each other, we were more like sisters than best friends. Cam had often joked that we needed our own reality show, but today I wasn't in the mood for the Raina and Nikki comedy hour.

"Hell, he should just do the James Grayson plan and knock you up." The former wild child was referring to her husband, whom she'd married after an unexpected pregnancy.

"Shut up." Instead of using my usual sharp tone when it came to Nikki's craziness, I lightened it up and added a fake, airy laugh. I put my hand over the receiver and returned my attention to Cameron, who was still focused on me. "She's so crazy. Let me just step outside real quick and then I'll help unpack." I blew him a kiss and he caught it. "Be right back."

"Hello? Raina. Raina," my friend said in a singsongy voice while I made my escape out the door, down the porch steps, and a little past the curb near our mailbox.

"Shut up, you psycho. Say what you need to say so I can get back to unpacking." I whispered despite my distance from the house.

"So you aren't zoning out? Thinking about an escape plan or comparing Cam to your bum-ass daddy or comparing yourself to your mom?"

"What if I am?" I challenged her. "I'm just being smart."

Naïve women like Ma gave second and third and fourth chances to men who didn't deserve even one. I liked to think I was different, but it turns out that Ma's dark skin, oval face, and Coke-bottle shape weren't the only things I'd inherited. And like her, decades-old daddy issues were firmly shackled around my ankles, and attempting to loosen them had just tightened them more.

"There's nothing wrong with being smart, but he hasn't

given you or us any red flags. And you know I can sniff out crazy."

"Yeah, but people change."

"True. And if he changes for the worse, you'll deal and I'll break his knees with my bat. Unwind the bubble wrap you've got tight around yourself and live a little."

"Why, thank you." I rolled my eyes. "What would I do without you?"

"I honestly don't know. But as your bestie godmother, I'm here to save you from your damn self."

"Ooh-wee, Mommy! You said 'damn,'" I heard Nikki's little girl, Bria, say in the background.

"Don't say 'damn,' precious. And I wasn't cursing. I was talking to Raina about a beaver building dams in her new neighborhood."

"Oh, can I meet him?"

"No, baby, he's rabid."

"Rabid?" Her little girl sounded alarmed. "What's rabid?"

"He's crazy. Sniffs his own butt."

"Speaking of being a damn lie . . ." I muttered.

Nikki must've covered the phone because what she said was muted.

She got back on the line. "All right, girl, I've gotta go, but before I do, I'm gonna give you a dose of your own medicine and tell you the deal. Just because you're living together doesn't mean you have to get married or have kids anytime soon. Just enjoy this new chapter in your life and move forward one day at a time. Okay?"

I instantly felt soothed by Nikki's words. I could do this, and it was sound advice. The very same recommendation I'd given out myself to my listeners.

As a radio host, I've heard my share of heartbreaking stories. There are a lot of crazies who call in. But there's a pattern in the female callers—women who turn away good men due to their past scars. I could change, and I had to—for Cameron and for myself.

I sighed. It was heavy, yet cathartic. "You're right."

"I know I am." Nikki softened her tone. "And you're welcome."

"I didn't say thank you."

"You want to and I accept. Anyway, I gotta go make the kids their lunch. Talk soon."

"Yeah, okay. I'll text y'all after I get settled. Kiss your babies for me."

"You've got it. Bye, girl."

I ended the call and returned to my new home. The movers had neatly lined up our boxes against the walls in all the rooms. I walked to the middle of the room, sat on the floor cross-legged, and began unpacking lamps, books, and pictures. I was interior-design challenged, but even I got excited thinking about decorating my first home.

Cameron finished installing the mounts. He wiped the sweat from his forehead with the bottom of his tee. "Hey, what's that?" He jerked his head toward a small, flat package near the couch.

I pushed myself from the floor and rushed to hide the gift that was meant to be a surprise for Cameron. I slid it behind another box with my foot.

"None of your business." I gave him a sly smile, and my voice had an edge of mystery that I knew made him curious.

"We live together now. What's mine is yours." He'd lowered his voice an octave in the way he knew was panty-dropping. If he didn't drop his Barry White act in 2.5 seconds, I was liable to jump him.

He tossed me a smile that melted my insides. Cameron's gaze drifted back to the box.

"Hey! Don't look over there." I stretched my arms high and

waved them in the air. Cameron's gaze went from my hands to my neck, and then lower.

I dropped my arms and covered my chest. "Quit staring at my boobs."

"I wasn't staring at your boobs. I was staring at your heart."

I smiled. "Yeah. I've been told I have some sexy ventricles."

Cameron pointed at me. "Stop distracting me with your boobs and your brain. Tell me, what is it?"

"Okay, I'm done teasing you. You know it's yours. Open it." I clapped my hands. He was so going to love my gift.

Cameron stepped over tools, boxes, and bubble wrap and headed straight for me. He grabbed me by the waist and gave me a smile that tripled my heartbeat. His six-foot-four frame always made me feel small and protected.

"What?" I licked my lips and held my breath.

He tucked a strand of hair behind my ear. "I'm glad we're doing this."

His warm breath tickled my neck. I shrugged in a way that I hoped looked playful. "No big deal. The condo was getting too small anyway." Despite my playful tone, my voice croaked and my mouth twitched. I turned away to hide my conflicted expression, which I imagined made me look like a deranged clown.

I took a big gulp of air and suppressed the urge to drop my head between my knees. My lungs shrank and I inhaled and exhaled deeply until I didn't have to concentrate on breathing again.

His strong hands stroked my cheek and traveled leisurely to graze my bottom lip. His honey brown eyes, tinged with worry, peered into mine. "You okay?"

I closed my eyes, trying to shut off the panic, and nuzzled into the warmth of his calloused palm. He didn't ask more questions because he knew the answer: I was freaking out. Despite it all, his hands remained steady and sure.

Cam was my giant teddy bear and had always been that way since the first day I'd met him. It was summertime and I was out at a concert with my girls—swaying my hips and sipping my drink—when something had brushed against my skin and zapped me. And it wasn't the hot Georgia sun. The source was a sight to behold—a beautiful black god built like a linebacker with large, strong arms, a thick neck, and chestnut-brown skin that seemed like it had been perfectly baked under the sun. The crooked, cocky smile he'd given me highlighted his chiseled jaw, which was covered by an expertly cut five o'clock shadow. Despite all of this, his bright brown eyes were what had drawn me in like a moth to a torch.

Despite his tall, bulky frame, he walked over with the fluidity of a panther. He asked for my name, and when he said "Raina," there was so much intensity to it that I knew this wasn't just going to be one night.

I smiled at this memory and kissed his hand. Firmly rooted back in the present, I was confident that I'd made the right decision.

"I'm okay." I breathed in deeply, this time successful in feeling calm. I reached for the package and gave it to him. "Open your gift."

"Okay, baby." He winked, then grinned as he quickly did away with the tape and pulled the red and black jersey out of the packaging. Cam's smile morphed into a comical "O" expression, and his eyes bulged when he saw the Sharpie marks scrawled above his favorite football player's number.

"How did you . . . ?" His voice was unnaturally high.

"Let's just say Mr. Jones is a fan of my show."

"Baby." He reverently laid out the jersey on the sofa and pulled me close. "This," he swiped my mouth with his tongue, "is the best gift," he nibbled my lips and kissed me deeply, "ever. Kinda puts my gift of cigars and Scotch to shame."

Reaching beneath his shirt, I caressed his warm skin. "How about we bust out the cigars tomorrow?"

"Sounds good. I want to get my entertainment system up and running, and I know you're going to the attic. Go ahead and get your *Murder, She Wrote* on before you go to work."

"Gah." I thumped his chest. "Don't remind me that I have to go in."

Work paid the bills but taxed my soul. I didn't want to be in radio broadcast. I was supposed to be a *New York Times* best-selling author by now.

Twenty-year-old Raina would be disgusted with my life. What happened to the girl who formed a Mastermind group with her friends in college? We swore to each other that we'd follow our dreams, keep each other on track.

He squeezed my shoulders. "I'm not going to lecture you right now, but you need to think about quitting that damn job. You know I have your back."

And be a kept woman? No, thank you.

Cam raised a hand before I could comment. "Go upstairs. Write. Take a nap. Then go to the-place-that-must-not-be-named."

I journaled before and after my radio shows. It helped me channel the frustration I felt after some of my callers asked for advice. Instead of giving them a good kick in the pants, I had to coddle them. If I told listeners the truth about their messy-ass decisions, my ratings would plummet. But in my journal, I could tell them exactly how it is and the root of their issues. I could be the real me.

Cameron leaned down and kissed my forehead. Despite the ninety-degree, sweaty-balls heat Georgia's infamous for, he still smelled like my Cam: spicy and woodsy and solid. He was all man and all mine. I grabbed his plain gray tee and inhaled deeper. He didn't comment on this—he was used to it, and I think he liked it.

"Okay, off I go." I started up the three flights of creaking stairs. My flip-flops slipped on the freshly shampooed carpet. Reaching the top, I tugged the thin white cord to pull down the attic steps, and the creak and groan from it unfolding sounded like a waking dragon.

I took a deep breath and smiled. The smell was like opening an old book. Despite its musty smell, the last owners had modernized the space and included a daybed and a set of built-in shelves above a desk. It was exactly how I envisioned an attic-office but was too untalented and lazy to execute. While I loved yelling at the doomed couples on HGTV, I was not a DIY girl.

The hardwood floors were a mix of light and dark wood, and the ceilings were higher than usual for an attic—so high, in fact, that I could jump and not touch the vaulting. I admired the tall, wide, and recently polished bookcase left behind by the previous owners. My fingers easily glided along the shelves.

I spotted the rocking chair Cam had catty-cornered near the window. I'd badgered my mother into giving me my grandmother's rocking chair, tugging on her sense of legacy in passing down a fifth-generation item. I loved that damn chair and had penned all my worldly knowledge, angst, bad poetry only a teenager could understand, sitting in it. I moved the rocker near my desk and parked my ass in the chair. A faded Polaroid picture had been propped on my desk.

"Cam," I groaned. "You pushy SOB."

The faces of my closest friends stared back at me. We'd been friends since our freshman year at Emory University. At our college orientation, we gave each other the black people nod. You know, the slight chin dip that conveys, "Yes, I realize there aren't too many of us around and if I see you running away from something I'll do it, too, no questions asked."

I slid my thumb across the Polaroid and read the caption on the bottom of the picture. "The Brown Sugarettes Mastermind

Group." We were still close, just older and sadder adult versions.

Sienna's gorgeous smile caught my attention first. She was a few inches taller than my five-foot-six height, modelesque, and a second-generation immigrant from Kenya. Beside her was Nikki, who rocked a choppy asymmetrical bob with gray streaks. With her brown skin, she looked like the punk version of Storm in *X-Men*. That woman was all the way rock-and-roll and even snarkier than me.

Surprisingly, she had become the saddest version of herself in our adulthood transition. Her streaks were replaced by a respectable shade of dark brown, and while she still rocked shorter locks, the edge had disappeared, replaced by a suburban mom hairdo.

Nikki had two sweet kids she adored, but she'd confessed to me that if she had a do-over, she would've waited ten years before becoming a mom. She'd wanted to be a musician, and she was so damn talented I was willing to bet she could still go for it even now.

My attention drifted from Nikki's face to mine. My hair was shorter then. I'd chopped off my relaxed hair right after breaking up with my college sweetheart and decided to grow dreads. They were now past my bra strap. At the time I chopped off my hair to be defiant. My ex loved my long tresses and would stroke them after we made love. I'd wanted a separation from the silly girl who'd fallen for the player.

Beside me was Kara, wearing her signature smirk. She'd most likely just finished kicking someone's ass on either the tennis or basketball court. Kara's always been my opposite: highly competitive and singularly focused. What can often make people with single focus dangerous is how they can swing between genius and lunacy. Fortunately, Kara's steadily in the middle, and her competitive, type-A personality kept us on track and boosted all of us to do our best.

The Mastermind group had been my idea. I was bitching to my friends about being snubbed by an exclusive writer's group on campus, despite my excellent grades and recognition from professors. The next day, there was an episode of *Oprah* about the law of attraction. I'd been fascinated and read anything about it. After a few books, I noticed a theme about meeting up with other ambitious people for support.

We were all highly motivated, and although our goals were supremely different, we were still able to help each other.

We hadn't talked about our group or met since a year after graduation. But this picture staring at me, with our hopeful, yet confident smiles, churned my insides. What happened to us? Was I the only one who felt like a failure?

I pulled the phone from my pocket to send a group text for a get-together soon. After a flurry of messages back and forth, we decided to meet at Kara's place in a few weeks. A decade later, it was time for us to face our dreams.

But for now, I needed to write and then get ready for tonight's show. Deferred dreams could wait. Work could not.

An hour later I walked through the double doors of the radio station. "Hey, Greg." I waved to the security guard. I waited for his usual greeting of "Evening, Raina," and he didn't disappoint. I hustled past and gave him a slow, exaggerated wink while I waited for the ancient elevator to shake, rattle, and close.

A few fans of *Raina's Fireside Chat* called me the black Delilah, I guess because we're both famous radio hosts who heal the lonely, despondent, and brokenhearted with a perfect song. I love Delilah, and I used to listen to her on the cheap radio I'd won from selling the most candy in middle school, but I never wanted to *be* Delilah.

If I'd stolen my persona from anyone, it was my late Grandma Jean. *You broke? Stop spending all your damn money on smokes. Need to lose weight? Put the fork down and walk your ass 'round the neighborhood. Your man cheating on you? Leave his lying, no-good ass.*

She came from the school of the Old Testament and an eye for an eye. *So before you leave his no-good ass, burn some shit up.* Grandma's wisdom would be too explicit for radio, so I'd polished up her Southern colloquialisms, added a dollop of kindness, empathy, and occasional sternness, and suddenly I was the friend whispering encouragement in your ear at one o'clock in the morning when sleep wouldn't come. I'd created my own style.

But I'm not sure how I got here. I'm sarcastic, moody as all hell, and just as acerbic as Grandma Jean. She didn't believe in twisting herself in knots over a man or anyone, for that matter. Nor did she believe in the institution of marriage—she kicked out my grandpa when Mama was a teenager and never looked for his sorry ass since. Those were her words, not mine. She ingrained her sense of independence, self-contentment, and self-awareness in me, and I wouldn't be the woman I am today without Grandma Jean.

But you wouldn't know it from my current occupation. The pseudo radio therapist was someone I made up. I'd played around with different personalities on my college radio station as a joke. I got a call from a scout after college, and now the joke was on me because I'm stuck.

My producer, Rhonda, gave me a nod through the window panels, signaling the show was about to start. I scanned my small studio no bigger than half a dorm room. My U-shaped desk included a computer and all of my necessities. Green tea, because it made me wise: check. Fuzzy socks, because the GM at the station, who didn't give a damn about his staff's comfort, blasted cold air all year long: double check and a toe wiggle. A notepad for when I was inspired to write between commercial breaks: checkity-check-check. And last but not least, my handy whiteboard, also known as my sanity. Some nights I played hangman with myself. If my producer was in a bad mood, which wasn't often, she'd join the game. The magic phrase that pays never changed: "Kill Me Now."

I know, how millennial of me. Some of my callers were sweet, and I affectionately named them my raindrops. But a good majority were the cause of their own problems, and they wanted a song to magically fix it.

"Sure, Noah from Buckhead. I'll put in your request to play 'Ain't No Sunshine' for your wife, even though you got caught banging your secretary." Some callers got the full K-I-L-L at once.

My producer's pale fingers jutted in the air. "In three . . . two . . ." The "one" was silent.

I pulled in a breath away from the mic and then leaned in. "It's midnight, and you're listening to the smooth sounds of WBXL radio. I'm Raina, and I can't wait to hear from my raindrops today. Before we kick off our calls, I want to read you an email I received last week from one of my listeners." I pulled up the email on the computer screen.

> *Dear Raina,*
> *My name is Elise. I'm twenty years old and my grand-mother is dying. Nana raised me when my parents aban-doned me. My first memories are of my grandmother reading to me, teaching me how to can fruits, sew, and cook. Best of all, she encouraged me to dance. I love danc-ing and I'm good at it—I'm currently attending Juilliard.*
>
> *I called Nana and I visited home every chance I could afford, but it hadn't occurred to me that her voice had got-ten weaker. She told me to stay in New York the few times I insisted on visiting her, so I could save my money. After a while, I realized I was being put off and decided to go home. When I saw the oxygen tank, I knew she was dying.*

The problem is, she refuses to let me take a leave of absence from school. She made me promise to stay and says it doesn't make sense for me to stop my life to watch an old woman die. Against my better judgment, I've returned to school. But with every pirouette, extension, and plié I take, I feel heavy, guilty. I want to leave school. How do I get her to see that it's the decision I want to make without upsetting her?

Conflicted and brokenhearted,
Elise

My throat squeezed shut, remembering Grandma Jean's death. One moment she was watering her plants in the backyard, the next she was dead of a heart attack. I didn't know which option was worse, the unexpected suddenness of someone being here today and gone tomorrow or knowing your loved one has limited time left. This poor girl was alone. At least I had my mother. I pressed my fingers against my eyelids.

Keep it together, girl.

I cleared my throat. "Grandmothers are precious. My grandmother passed when I was in my early twenties, and it was devastating. She was my rock like your Nana is yours. I can feel the agony pouring from your email . . . but, Elise, I think you've already made your decision. Go home. Take care of Nana. Don't let her sway you. Stand your ground and her anger will pass. I don't know if you're religious, but I do believe in heaven, and Nana sounds like a pretty sure bet to get her wings when it's her time. I also want to remind you to enjoy your grandmother. Read her stories, sew by her bedside, do the things she's done with you.

"When she passes on, know that you're never really alone. She'll be there when you walk down the aisle and when you give birth to your children. And when life gets too much, give me a call or email. I'll be praying for you, Elise. Be strong. Be brave. I'm going to find a special song for you and Nana."

I played the song already queued, "I Hope You Dance."

I took a deep sip of tea, hoping the hot liquid would eliminate the painful lump rising in my throat. I remembered when my neighbor's dog had died and I had cried as hard as his owner because I'd loved that damned dog. Grandma Jean held me up and dried my tears with an old handkerchief she seemed to use for every occasion, whether it be swatting a fly or spit-shining my face.

"Whatcha crying for? We all gonna run out of birthdays. We pass on from here and on to the next. No sense in crying about it."

My producer gave me the okay signal, and I forced myself to relax. Rolling my neck, I sent a quick prayer up for Elise and then geared up for the barrage of callers.

I glanced up and waved to my broadcast assistant who fielded our calls. After placing someone on hold, she looked up, waved, and smiled broadly at me. She was brilliant, and my favorite—I was willing to bet she would host her own show in a few years.

I waited for my call tag, which sounded so soulful and deep, like a cross between Toni Braxton and Anita Baker. I'm still proud someone thought enough of me to sing my name for seven full seconds.

"I'm back, raindrops, and I'm so excited to hear from you. We have . . ." I listened for Jamie to give me the name. "Rudy James from Woodstock. He's from the OTP. That's 'outside the perimeter,' for those of you new to Atlanta. How are you, Rudy?"

"I . . ." A deep voice sighed. "I'm good, Raina. I'm just a little emotional today."

I nodded and gave him a "mm-hmm." I'd practiced and perfected that "mm-hmm" over the years so it sounded soft, warm, and comforting, like homemade apple pie. Cameron wasn't impressed by my trademark psychoanalyzing sound, and it was banned from our home.

"And, well, I'm thinking about Jeffrey."

I perked up. Tonight could be two-for-two for being able to help people who *actually* needed advice.

"Tell me about Jeffrey. Who is he to you?" I asked.

"I have this anxiety, you know? It sometimes bubbles in my stomach. When I'm away from him I freak out. But when he's near me, God, when he's near, I feel like I can take on anything. But I have this deep-rooted fear. I'm afraid he's going to leave me."

I slid to the edge of my seat, waiting for him to dish.

"Like Mr. Miyagi," he whispered, like saying the name caused a fracture in his soul.

"Mr. Miyagi?" I scrunched my forehead. "Like from *The Karate Kid*?"

"No. Mr. Mee-owwgi. Anyway, can you find the perfect song for my cat? Show him that I love him and that I don't want him to ever leave me like the others."

I flopped back in my seat. *Jeffrey is a cat. A motherfucking cat.* This was too much. I narrowed my eyes at Jamie, who clutched her stomach while silently laughing. She was no longer my favorite.

I tried to hide my disgust and keep hold of my professionalism. "I'll find something for your cat. Jeffrey, right?"

"Yes, Jeffrey. Named him myself. Pick something good, okay? He meows on most of your picks, but last week he was pretty quiet."

Well, fuck me, Jeffrey's disrespectful ass didn't like my songs.

A part of me wanted to defend my honor, but I'd grown tired of this cat soap opera. "I have something that Jeffrey will like. Best of luck to the both of you, and I appreciate you listening."

I typed a message to Jamie and requested "What's New Pussycat?"

Grabbing the marker while Tom Jones lulled Jeffrey to cat-nap land, I drew an upside down "L," the post for a stick man to hang from. Next, I drew the head, the body, and the arm.

A red flashing light signaled the next caller, and this time, Jamie preemptively covered her mouth and clutched her stomach. *Great.* I cradled my head and massaged my temples. Tonight was going to be a long one.

CHAPTER 2
The Nose Knows—Kara

"Dried green apples. Lime and melon and mango. Ripe." I swirled the glass and dipped my nose to sniff and sleuth out the golden liquid's history. "Green pineapple. Freshly cut grass. There's definitely a green theme here."

"Cut out the commentary and focus, Kara. Go with the system."

Dipping my head to acknowledge my crotchety mentor, I continued my practice exam. "The wine is clear, bright. Medium intensity." My fingers wrapped around the stem of the glass. I inhaled the aromas and took a deep gulp. I swooshed the wine, using my taste buds to take it all in. After forming the story, I spat the wine into a plastic container. "This wine is dry with a chalky note. This wine has flowers, white flowers," I clarified quickly, knowing that Roddy would chew me out after the practice exam. I took another swirl and spat. "No evidence of oak. Green herbal notes. Medium acidity. Nicely structured. This wine is from a cooler region, possibly somewhere in France." Pausing from my assessment, I took another sip. "This wine is from Northern France, the Loire Valley. Sauvignon blanc. Produced in 2012."

Taking a deep breath, I moved on to the trio of red wines, utilizing my deductive tasting techniques.

Roddy grunted and nodded his bald, shiny head in approval. "Nicely done. But I'm not surprised. You've got a good nose, and you've already passed the service and theory portions of the test." He folded his arms across his chest and leaned away from the table. "Have you been practicing blind tasting outside of our meetings?"

With everything else in my life, I was Superman, but blind testing was my archnemesis, my kryptonite, and I acted like a weak-kneed, nose-bleeding swooner when it was waved in my direction.

I knew the theory, *in theory*, but it always tripped me up during my exams. "Yes. I've got my taste cards in my purse." I patted my slender crossbody Coach bag that mostly held my three-by-five notecards.

"Good. Study with Eduardo, Claudia, and Martin. They're hungry and talented and will make good partners. You'll be ready to take the test next year."

Pretending to pluck lint from the pristine white linen table, I avoided his keen blue eyes. Kevin, the head server for Pie Squared, a five-star Italian restaurant, milled about the tables, setting up to open at noon.

"Hi, Kevin." I waved at my colleague.

Kevin smiled and looked as if he was coming over, but after a quick glance at Roddy, the slender waiter pivoted.

Wuss.

"Kara," Roddy leaned closer, lowering his eyebrows to a father-knows-best stare, "tell me you are taking the Master Sommelier Exam next year."

A bitter black coffee taste blasted my mouth. I couldn't blame the tannins from the wine, it was the fear of the test— this Herculean task had bested me three times over. "I . . . I'm not sure if I'm ready."

Roddy's beet-red face moved closer to me. This time I leaned away.

"Then why in the hell are we here practicing? Why did I get up from my warm bed and warmer wife, drag my carcass downtown to quiz you on this shit? You think I have time for a wishy-washy somm who's afraid of her own shadow?" His voice rose with each word.

I wasn't prepared to go to blows with my mentor, but I wasn't going to let him chew me up and spit me out like the rest of the trainees either. This man made Gordon Ramsay seem like Father Frank, my sweet old Catholic priest.

Gearing up for battle, I mentally played "Eye of the Tiger" and dropped my voice to sound cool, firm, and confident. "Roddy. I've taken the test three times already, with two years in between. I'm just being cautious and giving myself time to prepare." I gave him the small, practiced smile I usually gave to my know-it-all wine patrons and reveled in my quick win. He couldn't argue with logic.

"What's in your head, girl?" He tapped a wrinkle on his forehead. "What happened to that young lady who practically harassed me to hire her because she'd read in *Wine Enthusiast* that I was the best and she refused to be taught by anyone less than the best?"

I didn't need his lecture. I wanted to swipe a bottle of wine, take it home, and not spit it back into a bucket. But when Roddy was on a roll, he was on a roll, and there would be no victories for me today. I could not win this battle.

Roddy's meaty hand slapped the table. The glasses clattered from the force. "And who was the young woman who bet me a thousand bucks that she would become an Advanced Sommelier in a year?" His voice rumbled like an old Chevy engine.

That was easy money. I was young, cocky, and thought I could take over the world. Now I was an old worrier, if you considered thirty-two being old. That was all before I'd buried someone I'd loved. That Kara was fun and energetic—now I checked the weather, listened to podcasts and NPR, and thought about hitting fifty and taking advantage of AARP discounts.

He didn't wait for my answer. "And who was featured as one of the top ten sommeliers on the rise?"

I shivered remembering the photo of seven white men, two white women, and my token black ass grinning in the middle. The photographer for the magazine had forced me to smile. *Can't be black and unhappy.* And of course the interview questions they asked me and only me were about diversity in the industry and not about my experience as a wine expert. *"Why don't more black people pursue this career?"*

"Oh, I don't know. After trying to catch up from four hundred years of enslavement, Jim Crow laws, segregation, and other forms of inequality, some of us don't quite have time to think about tannins and acidity."

The editor didn't print my quote. It's not that I thought my career was unimportant, and I loved doing what I do, but let's be real; I wasn't saving lives, just food pairings.

Roddy, however, believed wine was life, and although I was feeling a bit spicy today, I thought it prudent not to share my negative experience with my mentor. "Yes, that was me." I raised my hand. "Top ten sommeliers on the rise. And I'm still right here, Roddy."

"No, you're a damn ghost! And you have been ever since your mother, God rest her soul, passed on."

A sharp pain struck my chest. I knew this. Since my mother passed nearly two years ago, I lacked motivation, creativity, and zest. Being a sommelier required storytelling, and one needed to have a certain *je ne sais quoi.*

I was uninspired, boring, sad, and not at all like myself. But today wasn't the day for an intervention. My raised hand turned to a stop sign. "Don't go there, Roddy. Too soon."

But he kept going. "She died. You didn't." He lowered his voice and dropped the usual boom to his version of gentle. But it wasn't enough. The floodgates were about to open.

"Don't." I lowered my voice to subzero temperatures, but despite my reproving tone, my voice still shook, and my eyes and nose burned.

"Right." His eyes softened but his tone did not. "Kara, get your head out of your ass. Find that competitive spirit you *used* to have, and for God's sake, take that damn test! And do not, under any circumstances, ask me to help you study when you have no intentions of doing anything with your talents."

I faltered. I wanted to agree with him, and tell him that I was taking the test. But I just couldn't take the snickers from my colleagues. I freaking hated to lose. I especially couldn't handle the disappointed look on my husband Darren's face when I told him all the sleepless nights of blind taste tests, thousands of flash cards, the endless study sessions with my quirky group, and buckets upon stained-pink wine buckets were for naught. And it wasn't just that. I'd lost faith in myself once I didn't have Mama, my number one motivator, to whisper encouragements in my ear.

"Roddy I . . . I . . ." My throat closed shut. I exhaled and steadied my voice. "'I will let you know what I decide."

"What a fucking waste." He rolled his eyes and stood up. "Stay outta my sight for a while." He stormed away, muttering something about pansy-assed millennials.

Master somms could be divas, and he was one of the greatest.

My thoughts drifted to my mother. She was originally from the Virgin Islands, and a devout Catholic who raised her daughters to be proper Catholic girls. Not a curse word came from these lips and not a sin confessed that wasn't absolved by Father Frank. I was all that and more before Mama died.

A warm, soothing feeling, like being wrapped in a fleece blanket, came over me, and my mother's soft voice whispered in my head. *You want anything, sweet pea, you pray real hard to God and you work your butt off, too. Guaranteed, there isn't anything you can't do or ask for that He won't provide.* I shucked off the blanket and shucked off the memory as the too-familiar feeling of bitterness soured my stomach and burned through my chest. I hadn't only lost faith in myself.

I lost faith in God.

And I didn't need to serve a God who took good people away before their time.

God didn't provide for things that counted. Win a marathon race, sure. Close on your dream house, of course, my child. Save Mama from the cold hands of death . . . not so much. I'd prayed on my knees until they were sore that Mama would beat cancer.

I banged my head on the table and got a commiserating shoulder pat from the now-brave Kevin, who whispered, "It's all good."

I gave in to my earlier desires and bought a bottle from the wine shop on-site at the restaurant. I wasn't working tonight and planned to take full advantage of it.

Roddy had put me in a black mood, so I needed to go dark. Black cherry, blackcurrant, blackberry. And violets. The color purple and sometimes violets signified death, and maybe I wanted my dreams of being a master somm to rest in peace. It wouldn't be the end of the world if I never achieved the master level.

Advanced somms still made good money. Seventy thousand dollars was nothing to sneeze at—it was enough to buy a spacious home for the kids Darren and I had yet to create, and enough to go on our annual friends' trip, as well as my girls' trip. There was no shame. Roddy wouldn't make me feel ashamed.

There was no going back to the failure-is-not-an-option girl I used to be. A lot had changed. Back then Mama was alive and cancer-free. Dad hadn't swallowed his grief in a daily forty-ounce bottle, and my sister Tracey wasn't dating a deadbeat I was sure I'd seen throwing a chair on *The Jerry Springer Show* last year.

The only good and steady thing in my life was Darren. Quiet and unassuming, he was a true nerd who preferred gaming to going out, anime marathons to movie nights, and reading random Reddit threads rather than a book. I used to be the fun one in our relationship. I was the one who would bungee-jump from a cliff or challenge someone to a race in a crowded parking lot. But then I grew up and had to put away my childish things.

I lifted up the bottle of my hubby's favorite bourbon that I'd picked up from the store on the way home.

"Thanks, babe." Darren hugged me and then poured his bourbon into an empty decanter on the bar. "How was your meeting with Roddy?"

I shrugged my tired shoulders and placed my newly acquired wine treasure on the rack. "Same ol', same ol'." I sighed and leaned against the kitchen counter. "So get this, he wants me to—"

"Take the test," he finished for me.

"How'd you know?"

Tilting his head, he stroked his goatee. "Why else would you be meeting with him?"

"To stay sharp."

He shook his head and moved away from the bar. "Okay, Kara. So . . ." Darren ventured carefully, "Are you going to take the test again?"

On the surface his tone was casual, but I could tell he was anything but. His muscular forearms bulged with veins brought on by a clenched fist barely hidden under his crossed arms. The tightness in his cleanly shaven jaw also gave him away.

He swallowed, and I lowered my gaze, noticing his Adam's apple against his dark chocolate skin bobbing, once, then twice.

Tension and stress and aversion permeated the air.

I could darn near taste his displeasure, which was no surprise. The master's exam was not for the faint of heart, with a pass rate of less than ten percent. Here was the reality: Roddy was the only master in Georgia. Less than fourteen percent were women. None were African American women.

Ten years ago I had dreams of breaking the mold. My passion was deep, bold, and full-bodied. The optimism was over-ripe citrus. But after failure number three, not to mention being thousands of dollars poorer after paying for each test, I lost the taste.

Darren didn't enjoy the journey of nasty spit buckets and nerdy wine experts staying at our place until the wee hours in the morning. My months of burning the midnight oil, studying theory and flash cards, and having various mixtures of wine on my breath and a permastained red tint on my tongue weren't good for a relationship. We didn't kiss or have sex much during exams.

"It breaks my heart when I see that devastated look in your eyes." Darren's words after the last failed test about a year ago echoed in my head.

I took a deep breath. "What do you think?"

He shrugged. "Give it another go."

"What?" I jerked back my head. "You think I should try? Remember, this is attempt number *four*."

"Yep. Not gonna lie. I'm not a fan of how obsessive you become, and I hate your study partners." He did a mock shiver, and then smiled. "But . . ."

"But what?"

"It's what you love to do. You get this . . . I don't know . . . this gleam in your eye when you talk wine. It's damn sexy. But . . ."

"But what? What's with all the suspense? Just tell me already!" I slapped his shoulder.

He grabbed my hand and pulled me closer to him. "All right, all right. Don't take this the wrong way, but for the past year or so you've kind of lost your mojo."

"My mojo?"

"You don't compete anymore." He moved us to the dining room, near my Wall of Winning. He wrapped his arms around my waist, then pulled me back against his chest.

"Three years ago you won the tennis championship for our neighborhood. Two years ago you placed second for the Peachtree Road Race."

"Should've won first place. Stupid leg cramp."

"Right, and then the Bron-tasms won the kickball tournament. You led us to victory, team captain."

I chuckled at the team name that I had chosen in honor of my favorite basketball player, LeBron James. "Good times."

"Great times. But you don't enjoy these things anymore. You gave up."

"I've been busy." My voice was a note too high to give my defense credence. I shrugged out of his embrace. "But I'm still active. I run, I hike, I play tennis, just not competitively. It's not healthy to be that aggressive."

"Yeah, for normal people, but for you, it's different."

"So I'm not normal?" I asked, crossing my arms. Irritation slithered across my skin. What the heck was he getting at anyway? We didn't have these types of conversations. Darren had never been this pushy. It was the reason why our relationship worked.

"Hell, no," he said with zero remorse. "But that's what makes you, you. And that's why I want you to take the test again. For yourself . . . and for the promise you made to your mom."

I rolled my eyes and stomped to the sofa. I sat, stretching my legs on the couch before my too-honest-for-his-own-good husband got any ideas of sitting beside me. "Why does everyone keep bringing Mama up?"

"Roddy?"

"Yes. He said I'm a ghost." I frowned and crossed my arms. "Am I a ghost?"

Darren settled on the leather ottoman in front of the couch. His eyes scanned me over. "You're . . ." He hesitated, probably assessing my crossed arms and clenched-jaw body language to mean "woman on edge."

"You're not a ghost, but she haunts you. Sometimes I think you wanted to . . . to go on with her." His tone was loving, but there was a deep sadness lurking in his eyes. It wasn't sadness for me, but for himself.

I was dragging in the moving on with my life department. I knew that I needed to heal, but I hadn't done much to move forward. I did a few counseling sessions, but if anything they just cut open my wounds. My family and I didn't talk about Mama. In fact, we rarely spoke these days. I swallowed the hot, painful lump in my throat. I would've completely lost it if it weren't for my husband.

Darren had nursed me back to health after Mama died, becoming my rock. He took me out on dates, forced me to eat, to comb my hair, and encouraged me to be a productive member of society. I relied on him so much that I was scared it would drive him away. When I told him this, he reassured me, told me that no one or nothing could push him away, that he'd always be by my side.

And I needed him because my cheerleader was gone.

Carla Kennedy, Mama, had been my support system all my life, even when Darren and I were married. She had been my best friend, my confidant. We went on trips together just the two of us, and we had inside jokes that were three decades old, often feeling like we lived in our own orbit.

I reached for Darren's hand and whispered, "I miss her. I

think of her every minute of the day. Sometimes, though, I forget, like when I see something ridiculous happen on *The Real Housewives* and I pick up the phone to call her, and then I remember and I'm devastated all over again."

"Your mom would want you to live. She'd want you to pass that test. You know that."

Moving closer, he pulled me into his arms, settled me on his lap, and hugged me tight. "You can do anything you put your mind to, Kara." His words were so sincere. Flutters of butterflies attacked my chest, and I felt warm, secure, and loved.

Immersed in the moment, I touched his face. This was a mistake. He clutched my hands, kissed my balled fists and playfully shoved them away.

The butterflies disappeared.

"And I'll support whatever decision you make." His voice was tight and tense.

The last statement wasn't filled with the same warmth as seconds before. I was glad Darren couldn't see my eyes because he could always read me. I nodded against his chest and squeezed tighter. After years and years with someone, you know the things you shouldn't do. Seven years later, I still didn't know why my husband hated when I touched his face. No idea why he flinched, as if expecting something hot and heavy to attack him.

Pushing down my pain, I smiled and settled for a kiss on the lips. "Got any new games?"

He went on describing a new game about an attorney who solves mysteries for his clients. It seemed boring, but I feigned interest.

"Cool. I have a Jack Reacher book that's calling my name. Why don't we hang out on the couch tonight?"

He smiled, this time a fraction wider, most likely relieved that I hadn't call him out about the flinch. I wasn't the only person with ghosts.

* * *

It was Friday night, and I was preparing for our girls' night. The vibrating phone buzzed against the marble countertop. I dashed to my cell, clicked the answer button, and then cradled the device to my ear as I rushed back to arranging the cheese and charcuterie platter.

"Please tell me you aren't calling to cancel our girls' night," was how I immediately greeted my best friend, Sienna. The woman was on a mission to get her fiancé, who was also an attorney, reelected to a city council position. Between visiting nursing homes, kissing puppies and babies, and grand openings and closings, I hadn't seen my best friend in a month.

Her rich laughter flooded through the receiver. "No. I told Keith that I could either be indisposed for the night or I'd be disposed of for good once you and the ladies caught up with me. And you'd be the ringleader."

"Damn right," I agreed.

"What's the murder weapon of choice?" Sienna asked.

"A bottle of Cab."

"Motive?"

"You canceled on girls' night? Obviously I'm a woman scorned."

"Nice," Sienna had started this game with me years ago when she was in law school.

On the surface, Sienna seemed to be all positivity, kindness, and light. But she certainly had a slightly morbid sense of humor. As a public defender for the city of Atlanta, she needed the balance, otherwise her clients—hell, the world—would feed on her warmth and drain her dry.

Her fiancé was already doing an excellent job of that. Sienna proudly wore oversized rose-colored sunglasses when it came to Keith. She thought he was the second coming of Martin Luther King Jr. who would save our city from poverty, drug abuse, and gang violence and achieve world peace.

But what Sienna didn't see was that Keith was pretentious, third-generation black wealth, who liked the sound of his voice, and was in lust with his looks and in love with anything in a skirt. How Sienna didn't notice his wandering eyes was beyond me.

My best friend cut into my unkind thoughts. "I'm calling to let you know that I'm bringing salsa and guac. But it's the store-bought kind. I didn't have time to mix and mush."

My hands froze from arranging the tray. My breath rattled in the receiver.

"I know you have that ridiculous no store-bought food policy, but some of us work seventy hours a week defending the rights of our citizens. And even more hours helping to win the city council position."

The election was over a year away.

"You're not even the one running."

"Yeah, but Keith is. He needs me. He told me I was a key component of his reelection campaign."

More like his I'm-down-with-the-black-community card, because prior to the election he hadn't formed real relations with the black populace in his district.

"Fine. I'll see you in an hour. Just do me a favor and put it in a nice container."

"Of course." Sienna's tone straddled the line between amused and offended.

"All right. See you soon."

"Byeeeee!" Sienna clicked off.

I'd Swiffered the floors, wiped down the counters, and lit a few vanilla candles for atmosphere. Bending over to my free-standing stainless-steel wine cooler fridge, I selected two white wines for Nikki and Sienna. Earlier, I'd chosen the reds for Raina and myself from the wine cellar Darren had built in the basement a few years ago.

I scanned the kitchen and living room. Everything was in

place and quiet, but in a few minutes, my home would be filled with raucous laughter. It had been a few months since we all hung out.

When the doorbell rang I jumped from the couch. It was probably Sienna. Raina and Nikki were always notoriously late. Nikki had an excuse with the kids, but Raina was just . . . Raina.

Peeking through the blinds of my front door, I was surprised to see Nikki. She knocked. "Hurry up, Kara! It's muggy as hell out here!"

"Yeah, yeah, don't get your panties in a twist." I opened the door and Nikki rushed in like a whirlwind. Surprisingly, tonight she wasn't in her Stepford mom gear of pearl necklace, pencil skirt, and pumps with an all-hair-in-place bob. Not that I didn't prefer the look on her, but anytime she was in PTA mom mode, she was in a bad mood. Instead, she wore beat-up jeans, black Chucks, and a hoody. Her bob didn't have the typical middle part—she'd probably raked her hands through it, something she did when she was frustrated.

Nikki drummed a catchy beat against her thighs. "Girl, where's the wine?"

"Take a load off. I'll pour you a glass of Pinot Grigio."

"My favorite," she trilled in a musical voice.

"Don't I know it." The girl kicked back wine like a toddler with apple juice.

"You can turn on the TV. I know Raina won't be here on time, and Sienna has stuff going on with Keith."

Ever the hostess, I poured my friend a healthy portion in a large wine glass that would make even Olivia Pope from *Scandal* envious.

Nikki smacked her lips and reached for the glass. "Gimme!"

"You're starting to talk like Junior," I said, referring to her son. "And how is my handsome man, by the way?"

"He's a demanding diva, just like his—"

"Mother?"

"Moi?" She shook her head and gave me her best duck-face impression. "Why, I'm the most down-to-earth person you've ever had the pleasure to meet!"

Despite her joking, Nikki was unpretentious and came from humble beginnings. It made her role of being a stay-at-home mom and the wife to a husband who earned well over six figures and worked with Atlanta's rich and famous a challenge that Nikki hadn't quite mastered.

The doorbell rang again. This time, Raina stepped through the door.

"Hey, girl." Raina pulled me into a hug. Her light, flowery perfume tickled my nose. I took a step back and surveyed my gorgeous friend. "You look cute." I pointed at her off-the-shoulder white romper. I was tempted to ask where she got it from, but it would be a waste. I was more of a pressed slacks and blouse type of girl.

Raina patted the turquoise wrap covering her head and struck a pose. "Thanks, boo." Raina greeted Nikki and then turned back to me. "Where's Sienna? She's usually the first person here."

"She's running a little late, probably from some fund-raising event with Keith. Anyway," I shooed her toward the couch. "Go, sit. I'll get you a plate of nibbles and a drink."

After a few minutes, Sienna arrived with her store-bought dips.

"Sorry I'm late. Keith had this thing, and I needed to show my face and be the doting fiancée that I am. I couldn't miss it." She rushed into the kitchen, her heels clicking against the hardwood floors, and opened the cabinet.

"What do you need?" I asked. Even though Sienna had

been in my home a million and one times, I didn't like people messing up the order of my kitchen.

"I'm looking for your cute little bowls for the guac and salsa."

I nodded to the lazy Susan on the counter. "I figured you wouldn't have time to get the containers. Kick off your heels and relax. I'll pour you some Chardonnay."

Sienna kissed me on the cheek with a loud smacking noise. "You are the best!" She leaned against the counter and reached down to take off her navy blue pumps. I raised my eyebrow and nodded toward her conservative shoes. Never, in the fifteen years that I'd known her, had she ever worn boring footwear. She'd always sported ankle-and-neck-breaking heels in bright, bold colors.

"Election season. I have to wear these two-kids-and-one-on-the-way heels." She shook her head. "I mean hello, I can still be fashionable. Look at Michelle Obama." She brandished her shoe in the air.

"I don't disagree with you. But if they're not your style, don't wear them."

She sighed and then pasted on a smile. "No, no. I'm just being a brat. It's fine." She waved her hand as if swatting a gnat. "I don't want to put Keith in jeopardy, and image is everything. I'm five ten in my heels, and that means Keith and I are nearly the same height."

I shrugged as I scraped the dips into the bowls. "I'm sure you aren't the first tall woman Keith has encountered. He can deal."

Or not. I'd prefer not so she could find someone else. Preferably not Ben Carson's doppelgänger. Sienna had made a lot of sacrifices. Recently she began sporting a fifteen-inch weave instead of rocking her natural hair that she usually wore in a short, curly fro.

Sienna made a noncommittal sigh.

"Girl! Get your ass over here and say hello!" Nikki yelled from the couch.

After pouring Sienna a glass, I grabbed mine and walked into the living room. Nikki was in the middle of blasting some of the moms at her kids' private school.

"I swear they're cornering me."

"Who?" I asked, settling on the couch beside her.

"Sandra, Meegan, fucking Lynette." She growled and gulped the wine.

We'd named them the Witches of Eastwick, and although Nikki had a flair for dramatics, she was right on the money about them. They made *Mean Girls* look like child's play. If you didn't participate in baking fund-raisers with homemade dishes, and come to every event and PTA meeting, then you were deemed a "bad mother." The only reason they sniffed after Nikki was because her husband, James, was a tax attorney for celebrities and big-deal CEOs.

"I ran into Meegan at the bookstore. I was trying to find something for Junior's story time, because if I read that damn green pork and egg story again I'm going to stab myself in the eye with a fork."

Sienna, our resident vegetarian, gagged. "Green pork? What are you teaching your kids?"

"She's talking about *Green Eggs and Ham*." Raina shook her head.

"Right." I nudged Nikki's shoulder. "What happened?"

"So anyway, she struts up in her tight little skirt and says 'Nicole, you haven't signed up for our bake sale. All parents are required to this year.'"

"What do they need now?" Sienna asked.

Nikki snorted. "I dunno. Probably a chocolate fondue fountain for fucking recess."

"Damn, those kids are spoiled." Raina shook her head. "Your kids excluded, of course."

"Oh, they're spoiled, too. It's a struggle to keep them grounded. Especially when James is putty in their hands."

"He's putty in your hands, too," I added. And it was true. That man adored Nikki.

"Yeah, yeah. So anyway, she's all pushy giving me this *gotcha* look, as if I'm gonna sweat anything this chick says to me. So, I tell her I'm bringing air pudding and wind pie."

We all crack up laughing.

"The worst part," Nikki continued, "was that she really thought it was a dessert! Of course I kept going on and on about it being a special recipe handed down from my great-great-great-grandmother." She took another sip of wine. "Anyway, her dense ass smiled and told me she'd tell the others about my contributions. She must've done it because her henchman, Lynette, emailed me last night and told me that it wasn't funny and I needed to support our children. Blah, blah, blah . . . the children are our future. And she had the nerve to copy James in the email like I was in trouble with my dad."

"So are you bringing something?" I asked.

"I just said it." Nikki smirked. "Air pudding and wind pie. Now . . . who wants more wine? Screw it." She waved her hand. "I'll just bring over the bottles."

"Finish your drink first, Nik." I rolled my eyes. She had a good five ounces left.

"Yeah, and it's just a matter of time before I'm done." She looked at Raina and Sienna, then shrugged. "Why's she trippin'? She knows the deal."

"She," I pointed to my chest, "is sitting right here."

"Girl, just get the wine." Nikki smacked her lips. "You know you don't want me poking around in your kitchen."

"Fine." I sighed. "Why don't I bring you a big straw and you can just pop it in the bottle?"

"Ohh." Nikki rubbed her hands together. "I actually would be down for—"

"Joking. We may not be in public, but you will act like you have some decorum." I stood and then retrieved the wine bottles, placing them on my wood serving tray.

Nikki leaned over and grabbed her favorite Chardonnay. In her other hand, she had a large straw—the kind that was meant for Big Gulps from highway convenience stores.

"What in the hell is wrong with you?" I shook my head, equally irritated and amused.

"I keep straws in my purse." Nikki shrugged. "It's a mom thing."

"Aww. I so miss your shenanigans, Nik." Sienna sighed. "How long has it been since we hung out?"

"Four score and seven years," Nikki replied between sips.

Sienna patted Raina's knee, giving her a sunny smile. "I'm glad you texted us. Between my job and Keith's campaign, life has been crazy."

Raina nodded and bit her lip. "I actually have a proposal to make." She paused. The only thing moving was her gaze, which drifted from Nikki to Sienna and then finally to me. Her eyes bounced from scared to determined. After her dramatic pause had run its course for ten whole seconds, she whispered, "You ready?"

"Girl, yes. Just tell us." Nikki waved her hand in a get-on-with-it motion.

Raina rooted through her large purse and produced a tattered blue notebook. She raised the book in the air, still silent and with serious eyes.

A rush of adrenaline blazed a path from my toes to my head. I recognized that notebook. We'd written our goals and what we'd accomplished. It had been my idea to create a points system and award the winner every semester. Back then, I had no doubt I'd be a master sommelier by thirty. I swallowed around the knot that had formed in my throat. Was the universe trying to tell me something or torture me?

"Well, this is a blast from the past." Sienna's voice was low and careful.

"Girl no . . . just . . . just no." Nikki's voice shook with emotion. "We aren't doing this. I refuse."

"Just hear me out." Raina slapped the notebook on the ottoman. "We all know what this is. We created our group years ago and we fell off, which sucks, but I think we should reinstate it."

Nikki groaned. "That was years ago. Things change. Why are you bringing this up now?"

Quite honestly, I wanted to ask the same question.

Sienna piped up. "We promised to hold each other accountable."

"Yeah, when we were barely twenty. We didn't know what we wanted out of life." Nikki's voice was high and pinched and stressed.

Nikki was usually a straight shooter, but I could taste the acrid lie. She wanted to be a professional musician. Nothing had changed and nothing could take away her talent. Not her husband or her kids or her lack of confidence.

Raina shook her head. "Nikki, you are so talented. You could still go for it. But you're gonna have to put on your big girl panties, and most of all, don't lie to yourself. You know you aren't happy with washing clothes and keeping house."

"Being a stay-at-home mom is—"

"Sucking away your life force."

"Damn, girl," Nikki muttered under her breath as she folded her arms across her chest.

Classic Raina, the queen of duality. She was a like a Sour Patch Kid. First she's sour, then she's sweet. I think she used most of the sweet at her job that she ironically hated and for Cam, whom she actually loved but was too afraid to admit it.

"And Sienna," Raina tapped Sienna's shaking legs, "you

wanted to go to law school, pass the bar, and become an attorney. You've done all of that. You have just one more goal: running for office."

Sienna tugged at her skirt with an uncertain smile. "Yeah, and now Keith is on city council." She shrugged and cleared her throat. "I'm helping his campaign. It's the n-next best thing."

Raina shook her head. "But is it?" Her voice was full-on Raina, the radio therapist. "I'm just saying that you deserve to have your own thing. Your own piece of happiness."

"I can't run against him, Raina." Sienna's normally soft voice grew hard.

"No. But maybe do something else. Run for a school board position. Just something to consider, okay?"

Sienna nodded without her usual enthusiasm.

Raina tilted her head and moved on to her next victim: me.

"Kara." Raina cleared her throat. "It's great that you are working in your field, but don't you want to pass that wine test?"

My cheeks heated from her direct question. "Of course I do, but it's not that simple. I've tried three times."

"Then try again. Didn't you tell us a few months ago that you were practicing with Roddy?"

"Yeah, well, Roddy is pissed with me. He thinks I'm not living up to my potential."

Raina bobbed her head. "I'm not picking on you, but girl, you used to run around like a My Little Pony on crack. If you weren't working, you were zip-lining, BASE jumping, or climbing a pile of rocks. I know that things changed since—"

I squared up my shoulders, squinted my eyes, and scrunched up my face in a don't-screw-with-me look.

Raina raised her hands in the air, a sign of surrender. "Sorry," she whispered. "We're here for you, girl, and you've been keeping things in." Her voice was genuine and a touch worried. It was the tone she used for her raindrop callers who had legitimate issues.

I relaxed and sighed; I knew it was over-the-top. "You aren't wrong. And it seems like this week is tell Kara how it is." I recounted my conversations with Roddy and Darren.

Nikki leaned and gave me a side hug. She knew how it felt to lose a parent. Her dad had died when she was younger, and from the reverent way she talked about him, I knew they were extremely close.

"Look," Raina leaned back into the sofa, "I know I'm coming off as aggressive, and you can go around and take turns on how I haven't done anything with my life. But I realized something the other day: We're living scared. We used to be fearless and confident."

I found myself nodding. I'd been thinking the same thing, and I was tired of this new version of me. I wasn't weak. I didn't lose, and if I did, I came back swinging.

Nikki jumped up from her seat. "Well, fuck me, this is sad." She waved her hands. "Why'd we have to go there? This is like . . . fuck, like a smack in the face."

There were a lot of talented people in the world, but Nikki was magic. Her soulful, scratchy voice was the perfect mix of blues and rock-and-roll. She always claimed that black people owned it before and she planned to take it back. I wanted that for her. Looking up at Sienna's and Raina's sad eyes, I knew they wanted it for her just as badly as I did.

"Maybe we can do this." Sienna spoke up. "I'm a lawyer, and sure, I'm not running for office, but my husband-to-be is. I can still accomplish my goals to make the world a better place, and I intend on doing it." She pointed at Raina. "And who's to say Raina won't ever be a writer, or Kara won't be a master sommelier, or you a singer? We're in our early thirties. We're still young."

"Oh yeah, I'll pack up my kids, tell my hubs to quit his job that supports us all, and take them on tour with me. That'll be great."

"Sit down and stop pacing the floor, Nikki." For the first time during this conversation, Raina sounded unsure. "Take a seat. Let's just . . . chill out." She took a deep gulp of wine and leaned back, tapping the glass stem.

Everyone was quiet. Sienna sat still, her eyes unfocused on the television. Nikki patted a complicated beat on her thighs. I wasn't the only one facing my demons today.

I looked around the living room, taking in my Wall of Winning decorated with plaques and trophies and ribbons. I've beaten the odds before—this test was difficult, but I could overcome it.

Maybe it was the wine, but Raina was starting to make sense. I'd been living in fear of my own shadow for the past few years. I needed to grow a pair and get back in the game.

I lifted my eyes to meet Raina's. I grinned. Her eyes sparked with recognition. She knew I was in. Her smile was bright as the evening star.

I cleared my throat. "Let's do it."

"Yes!" Raina pumped her fist in the air. "Sienna?"

Sienna nodded. "Yes. I'll . . . I'll have to change my goals. I'm helping Keith right now, and I need to focus on him. But maybe I can do more things for his campaign and be a part of his key staff once he wins."

"Love it." Raina bobbed her head. "Nikki, what say you?"

Nikki laughed, a vacant, lifeless laugh. "I'm sooo *not* in. I tried, remember? I failed."

"You didn't fail!" Sienna yelled. "You got—"

"Knocked up. And my band left me in the dust. James went to grad school, I had another kid, and staying at home made more sense. Life happened, my dreams ended."

I stood and hugged her. I wasn't a hugger, but I knew she

needed it. "Then let's reform your goal. You don't want to leave your kids at home. I get it. But you could start off slow. You can write songs and compose music from home, right?"

"Right, but I want to be on stage. I miss it."

"Then do some gigs, start small."

"Who's going to take care of the kids when I go to these nightly gigs?" Nikki waved her hand, but her eyes were different. There was longing there.

It was clear she wanted to go for it, so I pushed the pedal. "I'll babysit for you. You know that."

"Me too." Raina and Sienna chimed in.

"And hello, grandparents!" Raina quickly added.

"I guess I could try—"

"She's in!" Raina interrupted and went straight into boss mode. "We're meeting every week, come hell or high water. No excuses, and we hold each other accountable. Agreed?"

"Agreed," we all said back to her.

"Let's make a toast," Raina lifted her glass, and we followed suit. "To finding our happiness!"

CHAPTER 3
Not-So-Darling Nikki—Nikki

I was up to counting a gazillion sheep, and those wooly ass-holes still hadn't helped me get to sleep. And who in their right mind would be comforted by a sheep's creepy and judge-y eyes?

It wasn't the sheep's fault. I blamed Raina. And since she'd dropped the bomb on us reactivating our group over a week ago, I'd been downing warm milk and whatever bullshit remedy that came up on my Google search.

Bleep! Bleep! Bleep!

The alarm clock reminded me of a tractor-trailer backing up to unload its wares. I usually needed something loud and ob-noxious to wake me up, but not today. Rolling over, I swiped the sleep system remote from the nightstand and adjusted the bed's setting to a flat position. I hadn't adjusted it much—just enough so that James wouldn't give me an "I spent too much money on this bed for you not to use it" speech. It's a bed, a soft one with a softer pillow. I hadn't always had the luxury. My father was a traveling man, and a music man. He gave me my talent, or according to my mother, my curse.

I sighed heavily as I wrestled to shut the steel door in my mind, that led to the past. During all this, James had remained sound asleep. No surprise there. Lucky bastard. Not even the loud racket from our kids could wake him up.

Shuffling out of bed, I quietly navigated around, picked up my robe from the chaise lounge, and zombie-walked my way to the kids' rooms. Per my usual routine, I veered toward my daughter Bria's room first.

My baby was sound asleep, clinging to her overstuffed teddy bear. She'd be turning nine in a few months. The thought of her getting older plucked at my heartstrings like a bass guitar. When I first found out I was having her, I hadn't reacted well. James had just been accepted into his MBA program and my band was finally starting to get a decent following. I had all but decided to have an abortion. I sat by myself in the parking lot, and despite James's protest, I was determined to go through with it.

Then I felt it—a flutter. It obviously wasn't a physical manifestation from my baby, but something else. Like her soul was stirring. After I felt it, I knew I couldn't abort the baby. I was twenty-three years old, a college graduate, and the baby was made in love. Things could've been a whole lot worse. I turned the ignition on, drove away, and never looked back.

"Wake up, Bria-bree."

My mini-me smiled and lifted her arms in the air. I bent over and gave her the hug I knew she wanted.

"I had the best dream, Mommy."

"What were you dreaming 'bout, baby girl?" I pulled at the blankets that James had tucked tight around her body.

"People were shouting your name. And you were singing, but not around the house, in a big, big place."

My heart thudded and I furrowed my brows, trying to figure out how she knew about my old dreams of singing on a stage.

"I, um . . . yeah, baby, that's a good dream. You go and get ready while I wake up JJ."

"Okay, Mommy, but what should I wear today that's different?"

Much to my chagrin, the kids attended private school. Navy blazers, knee socks, boring-ass black shoes, and an ugly-as-all-hell red Pilgrim's bow. From the day she could form words, Bria had always been about self-expression. She wanted colorful streaks in her hair like Mommy, which I changed years ago to a respectable brown. She wanted cool, funky shoes and loved cartoon socks. But when we enrolled her in private school at age six, my normally even-keeled daughter had a tantrum. I didn't want to stifle her like my mother had done to me, so I promised we would find fun ways to rage against the private-school machine by pushing the envelope for the uniform.

"I'm thinking we can use that vintage red and navy blue polka-dot headband." I tapped her wrist. "And let's debut the red bangle bracelet we found at that shop in Little Five Points."

Bria flicked her index and little fingers. "Rock on, Mommy."

"Rock on, baby. And remember, if you get caught, pretend like you don't know anything. And if you get in trouble, you need to—"

"Call Mommy," she said in a voice that told me she knew the drill. After doing this for nearly three years, we'd only been caught twice. When a teacher or principal called, I'd feigned ignorance and assured them that this wouldn't happen again.

Our decision made, I pulled out Bria's accessories box from her closet and laid out the headband and bracelets on her dresser. I walked next door to wake up my son.

JJ loved his sleep, and there were no sleepy smiles, hugs, or kisses when I woke him up. Lots of waahs and *I don't wanna, Mommys* greeted me in the morning.

After getting him dressed, I kissed him on the head. "Okay, baby boy, let's get you some breakfast."

I wasn't much of a cook. I could do the staples, and thankfully my kids weren't food critics. My husband just appreciated the effort. Breakfast was the easiest: an omelet for James and oatmeal for the kids.

After the kids were fed, I herded them to the car. I connected my phone to the Bluetooth to play my music through the car speakers.

"Any song requests?" I asked the kids.

" 'Midnight Train to Georgia'!" Bria shouted. I smiled. I'd been humming the tune last weekend while cleaning, and she'd wanted to hear the song. Bria had then fallen in love with Gladys Knight and the Pips. My girl had good taste, just like her mama.

" 'The Wheels on the Bus'!" JJ yelled. He then followed up with a demanding, repetitive chant.

That fucking song. I definitely hadn't hummed *that*.

"Fine. We'll listen to 'The Wheels on the Bus,' " I said, hoping to shut my four-year-old terror up. In the rearview mirror, I saw Bria pouting. I blew her a kiss. "We'll play Gladys when I pick you up later today."

She folded her arms across her chest. "Mrs. Figueroa is picking us up today."

"That's right." I nodded. "We can do a fun singing session when you get home, 'kay?"

"Okay." She nodded reluctantly.

I scrolled through my list to find the dreaded song. Despite the composition's simplicity, I tapped my fingers against the steering wheel and hummed along. The damn song would probably be in my head for the remainder of the day. If the songwriter were still alive, I'd make her go round and round.

I dropped JJ off first and then headed toward the elementary school. As I pulled up, I noticed Sandra, Meegan, Lynette, and some other new recruit talking outside on the curb. Like me, they were dressed in pearls, heels, and a skirt. I taught my girl about self-expression, but here I was looking like a suburban Barbie clone because I had a fear of embarrassing James if I dressed like a bum.

I illegally parked my car just beyond the curb to walk Bria into school. Lately, she'd been complaining about some little boy calling her names in the hallway. She hadn't pointed him out yet, but I was determined to find the little asshole and figure out if he had a crush on her or if I needed to find someone to kick his ass. I wasn't above bribing a husky fifth grader.

"He's not here, Mommy," Bria whispered to me as we walked down the hall. I guess I wasn't as sly as I'd thought.

I kissed her forehead once we arrived at her homeroom. "'Kay, babe. I'll see you later."

The PTA warlords were still idling on the curb. They whispered among themselves and then tried to wave me down.

"Sorry ladies, I've got this thing I'm late for." I gave them a two-finger salute and rushed to my Range Rover.

I pulled into the graveled parking lot of Rev and Go, a coffee shop in East Atlanta, after I dropped off the kids. I'd contacted my old classmates to see if they had any openings in their bands. No one had a vacant spot for a lead singer/guitarist, but someone's uncle was interested in adding music to his coffee shop.

So here I was, strapped with a guitar I hadn't touched in a year up until a few weeks ago, nerves and attitude jumbled up into all 140 pounds of me. Okay, lies, 147 pounds, but who's counting?

Despite my internal battle, I strolled in like I owned the bitch because I was a rock-and-roll goddess, and goddesses didn't punk out at the finish line.

I noticed a man with blond hair with sprinkles of gray. He

wore a purple T-shirt that displayed a colorful sleeve of tattoos on his forearm.

I gave him a chin jerk. "I'm looking for Eric Scott."

"You've got 'im," Eric responded in a gravelly voice. "Are you Nikki?" He looked me up and down. I knew what he was thinking. Dressed like an extra on *Mad Men* in my hot pink cardigan, blue flared skirt, and kitten heels, I didn't exactly blend in with the locals.

"Yup." I extended my hand and we shook. "Dana tells me you're looking for a musician to play in your shop once a week. Any preferences for music?"

Eric shrugged. "I heard you were good. Wow me."

"Right here?" I looked at all four customers in the café.

"Yep. They're regulars, so I'll want their approval."

"Let me grab my amp from the car." After I wheeled it in, I noticed the group of customers clustered around the front with Eric in the center.

"Up here, Nikki."

"All right." I moved my guitar to the front and strummed the opening of "Purple Haze" by Jimi Hendrix, one of my favorite electric guitarists. I took them on a psychedelic experience, minus the narcotics. Two of the regulars popped from their seats, dancing and darting around like wood nymphs.

My performance was met with loud claps and whistles from the group and the staff.

"So, Nikki," Eric said with a shit-eating grin. "When can you start?"

For the last few weeks, I'd been living my double life as a mom by day and musician by night. No one had been the wiser.

I felt like hot garbage, lying to James. But every time I tried to tell him, my mouth dried up. My tongue would get thick like

I was having some allergic reaction. My feet got all tingly, and I had to slam them against the floor to regain feeling.

Not to mention, I'd sweat like a hooker during Communion. One time I'd been sweating so bad, James asked if I'd been running.

There were reasons, legit reasons why I couldn't tell him just yet. Like the one time when, for our four-year anniversary, we went to this shitty all-inclusive resort in Jamaica. The food was crappy, so we drank too much and screwed like bunnies. It was fun until he drunkenly confessed that he was happy his wife was no longer a musician because music took too much time and he liked me being home. He passed out.

James was usually so careful with me, with his words and his actions. I knew he didn't realize what he'd said. So I buried it deep, pretending to be perfectly happy.

He hadn't realized that I'd written him a song and planned to sing it for him.

He hadn't realized that my heart had dried, fractured, and crumbled into a million pieces. Because for once in my life, my soul mate hadn't realized what fed my soul.

So I quit. Put up my guitar. Buried my lyrics in the closet and the music in my heart.

I became a good little wife and kept house. I could tell it made James happy. He stopped giving me nervous looks when an epic guitar solo came on the radio because I stopped strumming the chords in the air.

And he no longer did the weird head bob thing when I launched into a tirade about good music.

Or maybe he stopped because I stopped. And it was the day that music died.

And my perfectly happy life worked until Raina's big-ass mouth and terrible ideas made me feel again.

But things were different now. Bria was pretty mature for her age. Junior was practically potty-trained. And as soon as I grew a spine, I could ask Mama to help out.

I can do this. I am doing this.

I dropped my babies off early this morning, and after swapping my pearls for my guitar pick necklace my father had given me, and the skirt and blouse for stonewashed jeans and a tee, I connected my laptop to my television.

The gig thing was sweet, but there was no way I would be discovered in a coffee shop.

The easiest way to do it was to reach out to my old band. They already had a hit song, courtesy of moi, and I was sure I could write a few more if given the chance.

Davey, the drummer, used to send links to their new songs, but for the last few years, I'd ignored him. I couldn't any longer. If I wanted to pitch the idea of writing a few songs for them, I had to see if I could fit into their new brand.

I pulled up YouTube and searched the band's name, Tattered Souls. Some super fan had created and shared a playlist.

My fingers froze and hovered over the keyboard. A band of steel wrapped around my chest; my lungs, hot and burning, ignored my inhales.

Breathe. Breathe. Breathe, dammit! My body finally obeyed my silent commands and a deep gush of oxygen rushed into my body.

"This is a terrible idea." Despite my reservations, I pressed play. "You can do this. Just fold clothes and listen to your old band."

Somewhat relaxed, I turned my attention to the fresh basket of laundry near my feet and a four-pack of Riesling minis on the table.

I tapped my feet along to the upbeat tune as I folded clothes. The song wasn't bad but I could tell from the simple rhythm and bubblegum lyrics, they were chasing the Billboard

Hot 100. I hadn't heard the song, so I guessed they hadn't reached the top charts yet. The catchy rock tune ended and was replaced with a solo guitar. The A-minor chord reached into my chest, pulled out my heart, and owned it. The strums were long, angsty, and achingly familiar. I tossed the clothes on the sofa, eyes now focused on the laptop.

My band, my fucking band, playing my fucking song I'd sold them a few years ago. It was right after JJ was born. I'd written it for Trent Masters, my ex and former bandmate. It was about seeking redemption and absolution. I'd written the song for my daddy.

I'd written the song for me.

Trent's soulful blue eyes stared at me from the screen. I bet women loved him. They always had, which was why our relationship had been so volatile, finally crashing when James barreled in and stole my heart.

Trent had the voice and face of an angel, but despite all his talent and looks, I had been the leader of the band. I felt a hot weight land on my vocal chords. I couldn't speak, couldn't breathe as my ex twisted my heart. The song ended and the band became a blur behind my misty eyes.

After downing a mini-bottle of wine to cool the heat in my throat, I grabbed my laptop and googled Tattered Souls. In a matter of seconds, the website popped up as well as a list of their tour dates. They'd be in Atlanta next week. Without thinking twice, I purchased a ticket—with my own credit card, of course. I did not want to hear James's shit. The seats were cheap, so I splurged on a good one.

What's the plan, Nik? I jumped from my couch thinking through what to say to them. I could reach out before the concert. No. I didn't want them to know. I just needed to see them live first. I wasn't all that sure if I wanted to join the chaotic rocker lifestyle again.

"Okay," I whispered to myself as if I were concocting an evil plan. "Go to the concert, call Davey afterward, get a drink with the guys, and go from there."

Now I just needed to figure out an excuse for going to the concert by myself.

My hands shook as I gave my phone to the venue attendee to scan my ticket.

The burly, bald man smiled at me. "Great seat. Enjoy the show."

Enjoy the show. That was yet to be determined, but one thing that would help was a big dose of liquid courage. I made a beeline to the nearest bar. No sissy drinks for me. This girl needed bourbon.

Booze acquired, I walked down the aisle, all the way to the second row, center stage, of course. I was frugal by nature, but not when it came to music. After thirty minutes and some shuffling behind the stage, it went dark, and the venue became electric. Hoots and hollers and screams filled the air. The lighting snapped back on and lit the band on the stage: Davey on the drums, Ethan on electric guitar, and Drew on bass.

Trent was front and center. He looked good. *Really good.* A few strands of his long hair were just over his left eye. The rest of his dirty-blond hair was tied at the nape of his neck. On entering, I'd noticed more women than men. Needing more booze, I threw back my bourbon, neat and straight. The brown liquid blazed a fiery path down my throat, and I welcomed the pain and the distraction. The lights went out again, and smoke billowed up.

Discordant chords shrieked from the sound system. Davey slapped his sticks against the snares, counting the rest of the band into the song. They were damn good and I swayed my hips to the tune. Like a dog on a metal chain, Trent's voice yanked at my attention and kept me hostage. Pain and pleasure filled me up to the brim as I listened to song after song.

The show was nearly over and the lights flipped on. The music was now subdued, and Trent gave the crowd a sexy grin. My heart slammed a series of tri-pl-et beats against my chest. I knew the plan. They still had the same old shtick: Invite a hot girl on stage, make her panties melt as they sang a rocking ballad to her, and then later, for Trent and maybe Ethan if Trent was feeling charitable, screw her brains out.

"I'm looking for . . . someone. A special someone to come onstage."

The crowd went wild. Well, the women. Scratch that, some of the men, too.

Trent's eyes scanned the crowd, and I wondered what he was thinking. Would he see me in the second row? A busty redhead sat a few feet to my left, and I knew for sure that she would catch his eye. She was attractive, wearing a tattered Tortured Souls tee slashed in all the right places and a miniskirt showing off legs for days. Yep, just his type.

I was never his type. I was tall, curvy, with big lips and a bigger butt. I remembered how he would always say there was something about me. Something that made a man want to be *my* man and I would always stand out to him, like a beacon of light. I snorted now, just as I'd done then. He'd always been a shit poet.

His eyes lit up when he spotted the redhead. *Called it.* His lips curved into a smile and he lifted his hand from the guitar string, ready to pick his latest victim. I rolled my eyes and folded my arms across my tee. His eyes moved on from the redhead and his blues clashed with my browns.

"Well, I'll be damned," he whispered. But it wasn't a whisper because he was mic'd.

"Nikki fucking Hardt." He said a little louder. But I was Nikki Grayson now.

The slow and steady rhythm from the drums and cymbals slipped a beat. Guess I'd surprised Davey as well.

"I'll be damned," he said again. This time he waved. "Get your ass up here."

I shook my head and looked away, as if averting my eyes would make him go away. What in the hell was I thinking—strutting my ass to the second row of seats, center stage of all places? I'd tempted fate, testing his old promise to always notice me in a crowded room.

"Aww, my girl's acting shy. Let's give her a round of applause to encourage her."

I rolled my eyes and shook my head again.

"I'll stand here all night and beg if I have to." He lowered his voice and moved the mic closer to his lips. "You know that I will." His tone held a promise, just like the one he'd used in the bedroom. Just listening to him made me feel like I was cheating on James.

I spotted the security guy at the end of the row and nodded. A few women, including the redhead, gave me curious, envious looks as I made my way toward the stage. They didn't realize I was saving them from a world of pain. Trent was a god in the bedroom, made you feel like the most important woman in the world, and just as you were soaring off his declarations of love, he'd drop you. It was like he fed off the bitterness. The pain wasn't as sweet if the tears weren't real. Pain and pleasure always came in a package with Trent. I leaned into the ugly memories, covering myself with them like a barbed-wire armor, and marched onstage.

The crowd was quiet now. The rock god has gotten his way, and they were waiting for what happened next.

Trent handed his guitar to me and nodded at the roadie behind the stage. Something happened and the mood had changed. There was a shift in power. He had gifted me with temporary rock god status and I decided to pretend, just for one night.

Feeling bold, I began the chords to the song I'd written for them. I knew they were saving the best for last; it was their hit song I'd written to sing the panties off of some woman. But not tonight. Tonight, *I* would make the hairs on the back of the crowd's neck stand up. *I* would give them goose bumps. And I didn't need to sell my sex appeal, I just wanted to make them feel. Trent had corned the market on rock-and-roll, but without me, they didn't have any soul.

The band played the song, and my voice floated to the mic as Trent harmonized effortlessly beside me. Walking closer to the mic, I poured my entire being into the crowd. I felt it again—that warm feeling spilled from me and into the crowd, and like glue, it stuck us together until we were one.

Like a succubus, I fed on the crowd's energy. I tossed back my head and hit a high note I hadn't tried in a while. I was a little rusty, but my voice sounded like a vintage record. The second time I hit the note, it was pure and clear. The cobwebs of lost dreams were cleared away. My thoughts drifted to my travelin' man daddy, who let cocaine get the best of him. He loved his family—loved my mom and loved me harder. But the music, and the ups and downs, and the disappointments were all too much for him. Mama said it was like he had a gun to his head and each day, his finger slowly inched against the trigger until it popped.

And it did.

I was sixteen when Daddy died. And the following years weren't so sweet. Mama had stopped the piano and guitar lessons, but by then it'd been too late. The drug that was music had slipped into the next generation and coursed through my veins. I guess some of Daddy's vices lived on, too. With my heart and soul, I sang the lyrics and prayed that Daddy had found his peace.

A sunken face trapped between white lines.
The pale warden keeps me closed in a cage I've made.
Can't trust promises from a dead man
The dead tell no tales
Can't trust promises from a dead man
But my intentions have always been pure.
I'd love you, but I'd kill you
I'd love you, but you'd hurt
I'd love you, but I'd break you
Send a prayer to the reaper
As my body turns to dust.

I squeezed my eyes shut on the last word, but my ears were flooded with thunderous applause. I cracked my eyes open and saw someone in front of me wiping away tears.

Trent wrapped his arms around me and yelled, "Nikki fucking Hardt. My girl wrote this song for us a few years ago. She used to be in the band, and we haven't been the same without her."

I jerked my head to face him, surprised by his humble admission. They were talented, they didn't need me, but I had needed this.

"Good night, Atlanta! Thank you!" Trent waved to the electrified crowd and hurried us off stage. Davey, Drew, and Ethan, my boys, rushed to me with hugs and kisses on the cheek.

A short, plump brunette with dark, calculating eyes was staring at me.

I offered her my hand and gave her a smile. Guessing by the frumpy skirt and heels, she was either their manager or worked with the record company.

"Nikki."

"So I hear," she purred. She circled me like a shark. My

hackles rose. I wasn't sure what she wanted, but it didn't feel good. And I wasn't one to be intimidated.

"Well, boys," I turned my back to her and faced the band, "I've gotta get going." I glanced at my watch. It was a quarter till midnight, much later than I'd expected. "Are y'all still in town tomorrow? I'd love to grab a coffee or drink so we can catch up."

And get you to let me rejoin the band.

"Whoa, whoa, whoa!" Davey jabbed a drumstick in my face. "Are you insane? We're hanging out *tonight*. And you need to explain why you dropped off the face of the earth after you had Junior."

An army of fire ants bit my insides. Davey and I were as close as siblings, and even after I dropped out of the band, he would visit and hang out with James and the kids. But it had become too painful to hear about the gigs, even in passing. Like it was a damaged limb, I had to amputate my old life. "Sorry, Davey, but I gotta get back to the kids."

"The kids are asleep. Text your man and sit your fine ass down." He gestured to the seat.

"All right. I'll . . . figure something out." By that I meant I'd lie my ass off to my husband and tell him that I was having a late night with the girls. He trusted me and wouldn't mind it. Fuck. Now the fire ants had spread throughout my entire body.

Three days had passed since my reckless night. I felt scared. But I also felt so alive, reenergized.

It was like an ugly part of me had awoken, and now it wanted to play. I'd become obsessed with the band. Davey demanded my new number, and as promised, I texted him pictures of the family. It hadn't felt like three years had passed.

Trent was another matter. I hadn't given him my number, but he found it anyway. I had been staring down at the phone for half an hour, in half disbelief over what Trent had sent me.

Someone posted a video of the concert when you were onstage. People are demanding you come back to the band.

I snorted and fired off a text. He was so full of shit.

People? What people?

He sent me a link to the video. He did not lie. The video had half a million views and endless comments asking who I was and if I was joining the band.

My hands shook. What if James saw the video? What if someone recognized me? I'd been lucky so far, but as my mother always said, what was done in the dark always came to light.

Wow. That's crazy. ☺ I'm flattered.

And I was seriously flattered, my fingers were still shaking. Trent quickly fired a text back.

My band manager Julia (you met her the other night) wants you to meet with the record execs. Possibly write a song or two and add it to our tour. Are you in?

My heart jackhammered in my chest. Shit was getting real now. This was beyond coffee shop crooning.

Unless he was pulling my leg. I would seriously beat the shit out of Trent if he was lying. He had to be playing me because this didn't happen—dreams didn't come true like this.

But what if they did? Only one way to find out. I wrote:

You're kidding. They don't want me.

They want you. I want you. Ask Davey if you don't believe.

Davey immediately followed up with a text.

I'm sitting beside Trent. All of it's true. Especially the thing about Trent wanting you, so don't go there ;)

The winky smile at the end made me smile.

Davey was not a fan of Nikki and Trent together. We were explosive. Davey had been over the moon when I'd found James.

Of course. I'm a happily married woman. Not sure about the music thing. I'll get back to you soon.

I needed to talk to my girls. Luckily, we were scheduled to meet for our Mastermind group in a few days.

CHAPTER 4

First Lady in Training—Sienna

"Mr. Porter." I folded my arms across my chest and paced the floor of the holding room.

"Yes, Ms. Njeri."

I stared at my client, who was dressed in a neon orange jumpsuit. His large dark hands were cuffed, feet shackled, and his eyes were cast on the stainless-steel table in front of him. "What did I tell you to do?"

"To go to work, go home, and keep my nose clean."

I nodded, my irritation slightly soothed by his contrite tone. "That's what I said. Because when one is currently on the docket for possession of marijuana, one must keep their nose clean until the plea bargain has been negotiated." I stopped pacing the floor. "But here we are, at the county jail, just days later." I waved my hands in the air. "I could've gotten you off easy with a plea bargain. Probation for maybe a year, and if you'd played nice, we could've had the misdemeanor stricken off your record. But, Mr. Porter, you're making it hard for me to do my job when you get locked up for assault."

"I'm not one of those guys, Ms. Njeri. I'm not a criminal," he whispered. His voice sounded hoarse and earnest.

I settled into the chair in front of him. "Then who are you?"

"I'm a husband, a father. A son, a . . . a brother. And when my little sister stumbles into the house, shirt torn, lip busted by her deadbeat boyfriend, it's my job as a big brother to make sure that idiot knows she is protected. And that she's loved and is to be cherished." His chocolate eyes were determined. He showed no remorse.

I wanted to reach over and squeeze his hand. Scratch that, I wanted to give him a hug. I knew he was a good guy with extremely bad luck.

"I know you aren't a criminal, Desmond. I get why you did what you did, but I . . . sometimes you need to take a step back and think of an alternative. Like calling the cops on the guy instead of going to his house." I balled up my hands and lifted them. "And using your fists."

His lips quirked. "Duly noted, Ms. Njeri. I just wanted you to know what kind of man I am. I know you got a lot of people coming and going that don't care, but I do. I see the looks in the cops' eyes, and the other folks that work at the jail. They think I'm just another nigga."

"Don't say the N-word," I quickly scolded. "If you don't want them to look at you that way, don't say things that make them feel okay to label you as such."

He smiled, but I didn't. I hated the word, even though it was a part of some of my friends' and family's vocabulary. I didn't want to give people the excuse to ever use a racial slur. Hearing us say the word made people who weren't black feel comfortable to say it as well.

"You were the first person in all of this to look me in the eyes and ask for my story. You're a good woman."

I shrugged, this time smiling. "It's my job."

He shook his bald head and gave me a small smile. "Sure, it is. But you care."

Standing, I smoothed out my skirt and reached for the manila folder. "Let me see what I can do."

"Do you think you can get me out?" His voice was shaky, just above a whisper, sounding vulnerable.

"I'll do my best." I didn't want to lie to him.

My heart stalled when his eyes dimmed. He nodded, looking at the wall.

"You know why they call me the Gladiator?" I asked, walking toward the door.

"Why?" he responded, eyes still averted.

"Because I'm a warrior and I'll fight to the bitter end for my clients, like my own life was on the line." I didn't wait for his response, just pushed open the door, ready to work my black girl magic.

My dogs were barking. And my shoes, although cute, had pinched my toes. Limping into the townhome I shared with my fiancé, I pushed the door open, kicked off my heels, and yelled, "Keith, I'm home!"

A caramelized sweet-and-spicy scent greeted me in the foyer. I followed my nose to the kitchen. "Please, God, tell me it's Pad Thai from Thai Village."

"The name is Keith, not God, except in the bedroom, and yes, I got us some takeout from your favorite place."

"Did you get the—"

"Prix-Pow with the basil sauce. Veggies only, of course."

"Thank you!" I went straight for the brown bag and tore it open. "I'm starving. I didn't get a chance to eat lunch today."

"Yeah, I figured." Keith ran his hand over his baby face. "You need to take better care of yourself, sweet cheeks."

He was right. I was ten pounds lighter than I was in law school, but with a caseload of fifteen to twenty per month, I was overworked. I didn't have it in me to not give my clients the defense they deserved. Everyone deserved a chance.

"I know, I know." I broke away from the food and gently

tugged his red and blue striped tie. "I appreciate you taking care of me."

He kissed my lips and squeezed my ass. "And I always will, baby. You know that, right?"

I wiggled my ring finger. "Oh, I know. This is forever. Till death."

His kissed my fingers. "Till death."

If the ladies were here, Raina would roll her eyes, Nikki would snort, and Kara's eyebrows would be to her hairline. Unlike me, they weren't into second chances.

A few years back, right after law school, he'd cheated on me with a paralegal at his firm. The woman had reached out to me on Facebook and sent me a bunch of dick pics. I was devastated. My friends had rallied around me, calling him everything but a child of God.

But no matter how much he'd ripped me to shreds, I couldn't let him go. Or rather, he was determined for us to stay together. Over the past few years, he'd been the perfect boyfriend and now fiancé. He cooked, cleaned, cared about his fellow man, despite his very privileged upbringing. His parents were rich attorneys and had made their fortune in Florida. They were the most disconnected black people I'd ever had the displeasure of meeting. And admittedly, some of that had rubbed off on Keith.

When I first met him in law school, I'd loathed him. Despite what my friends thought, I wasn't blind to Keith's faults. I knew he was slightly arrogant like his father and a bit imperious.

After two years of fruitless efforts of asking me out, I had finally snapped and told Keith that he was a self-serving, know-it-all jerk. But then he'd said something that had given me pause. *"I know I can come off a little brusque. But just give me one hour. One hour of your time to prove to you that I'm worth it. Everyone deserves a second chance, right?"*

It was something Baba, my father, had always said. When he was a young boy in Kenya, he'd been caught stealing. Mr. Ochieng, the shop owner, threatened to call the police, but after some pleading, and the explanation that he only wanted food for his family, Baba convinced the shop owner that he would work off his debt. My father worked at the shop and eventually used the money to pay for college. Years later when Mr. Ochieng died, he left my father a nice inheritance, having no children or heirs of his own. My father had used the money to move to America, and days later, he met my mother, who also was born in Kenya.

So, I was a softy for second chances, and if it weren't for second chances, I wouldn't be alive. My Baba's story is what had made me to want to make the world better. I wanted to help instead of condemn, because you never know others' circumstances.

It's true that Keith had squandered his second chance when he cheated a year later with a friend of a friend. And that time, I didn't tell my friends. I couldn't stand to see the look in their eyes or hear their well-meaning words. Keith loved me and he'd promised to never do it again, and this time, I raked him over the coals. It took three months for him to get back in my good graces, and for the last four years, we'd been solid.

"Let's eat." Keith broke into my thoughts. He scooped my dinner to put it on a plate. "Go sit down. I'll bring your dinner and a glass of wine."

"Thanks, sweetie."

"So what poor soul did you save today?" he yelled from the kitchen.

I sat down at the dining room table and then massaged my feet. "My clients aren't poor souls. We all can't work for the rich and fabulous."

Keith was an intellectual property lawyer in tech. Atlanta

was booming in the tech scene, and so business was booming for Keith.

"You could always come work with me."

I shuddered and Keith chuckled.

"I know you'd wither away and die if you were stuck reading contracts and litigating all day. But it pays."

It sure did. I took home nearly half his salary. And not to mention the salary he took home as a city councilman.

"How did the fund-raiser luncheon go?"

"It was good." He scooped up rice with his chopsticks. "Would've gone a lot better if you were with me."

"Sorry." I twirled my noodles. "I had to bail out a client."

"Hope they were worth it," he mumbled.

"Of course he was. Every client deserves—"

"The best legal representation. I know, I'm sorry, baby. I just missed you. You know you're the best at coaxing people to write a check. And Chris, as great as he is, is not a people person."

"Ah, Christopher. I will crack that nut one day."

His campaign manager-slash-consultant was a challenge. He was brilliant, and the strong, silent type. Thanks to Chris's brilliance, Keith had won his first election by a landslide. Now Keith was the incumbent, but for some reason Chris hadn't fully committed to working with us again and I couldn't figure out why.

"So he's working on the campaign?"

Keith shrugged. An annoyed look marred his handsome face. "Still hasn't committed."

"I'll talk to him, maybe squeeze in a dance with him at the Mayor's Ball in a few months."

"Don't worry about it, baby. You know just as much about campaigning as Chris. Hell, he even said it himself."

"Really?" I asked, oddly pleased. Chris didn't seem to like

people and *really* didn't seem to like me. But he was astute and thoughtful and, when no one was looking, kind. I was determined to win him over.

"I wish I could help more, but running a campaign is a full-time job, and the PD office has me swamped."

"I know it is, sweet cheeks. I just want you to focus on being my first lady. In four years or so, I'll run for mayor. Then governor."

Running for public office used to be my dream, but if I ran, I know it would be too much of a strain on our relationship. I pushed the thought away.

I leaned in and kissed him. "I would be happy to be your first lady."

His phone buzzed against the refurbished white wood table. He swiped his phone, answered it, and walked away. I heard a few groans and mumbles, something about a meeting with a client. He didn't sound all that pleased.

He bent over to kiss my forehead. "Speak of the devil. Chris is out at dinner and wants me to meet a potential donor."

"Nice! If he's calling about donors, then he must be interested in running the campaign."

Keith shrugged. "Yeah, hope so." He checked his phone, shook his head, and stuffed the cell into his slacks. "Okay, let me get out of here, baby." He turned toward the door.

"Beg if you have to!" I yelled at his retreating back.

"Have you figured out what you want to do for the Mastermind group?" Raina asked me as she passed around the agenda at our inaugural meeting, hosted at Kara's place.

I shrugged. "I'm still thinking it through, but I really enjoy helping out with campaigns. And with the city council election coming up soon, I think I'm going to get even more involved this time around."

Raina shook her dreads and returned to her seat. "Sooo . . . you want to base your goals off your man's dreams?"

Irritation swarmed in my chest. I drew on my patience. "No. I enjoy campaigning. I like the strategy, fundraising and I—"

"Then do it for yourself." Nikki jumped in. "Look, I'm all for supporting your man. Hello," she did a Vanna White wave toward her body, "I busted my ass and worked two jobs while James was in grad school, with a newborn, so I get it. But you've always wanted to run for office. What's changed?"

Kara brought over a tray of wine and settled beside me. "Shitting on Sienna's goals isn't part of the agenda."

Nikki snorted. "And color me impressed that Raina created an agenda."

"Girl, you know I didn't create that. Kara's type-A ass sent me the agenda last night."

I chuckled into my wine glass. Kara was a bit of a stickler for rules and order.

Raina clapped her hands as if to call the meeting to order. "Let's talk about our accountability structure. I suggested we meet once a week, we can Skype most times, and maybe meet in person once a month."

Raina paused, I assumed to get our feedback.

"Works for me." I pulled out my iPad, which contained some notes I'd jotted down the other day. "I do have a suggestion about the meetings. When we were in college we met for hours, which made sense because we lived together and had more free time, but I think we need to add more structure. We could give ourselves ten to fifteen minutes to discuss what we're doing, what works, and what we're struggling with. And we can provide each other with feedback and resources."

Nikki raised her hand as if she were in the classroom. "Question. We're all over the place as far as expertise. It's not like you guys can tell me if my voice is flat or if a song isn't flowing well."

I sipped my wine, placed it back on the tray, and put on my defense attorney hat. Nikki was trying to slip herself out of this group, and it wasn't happening on my watch. "I think it's a good thing. We have diversity of thought. Just because I'm a lawyer doesn't mean I can't help you brainstorm through an idea outside of law. Sometimes having someone who isn't in the weeds is helpful. And like I said, we're also sharing resources that will ultimately help in our personal development."

Raina threw me a smile. "Thanks, girl. Now, let's go around and share what we want to achieve, the timeline, and how we plan to do it. I'll start."

Raina discussed outlining a historical fiction novel about a former slave's journey to finding her kids.

I clapped my hands, excited by the synopsis. "I like it, Raina. Sounds like a tearjerker."

"Thank you, Si-Si. I'm going to start the outline this weekend." She pointed to Kara. "You're up next."

Kara squeezed her hand around a notebook. "Well, I'm gonna go for it again. Hopefully the *fourth* time is a charm."

"You know that's not the actual saying, right?" Nikki smirked.

"Shut up." Kara rolled her eyes, used to our friend's ribbing.

"Darren is on board?" I asked. I knew the last time she'd tried, it had caused some tension. As much as I wanted to be upset with my friend's husband, studying for the master's exam was stressful for the significant other as well. I'd lived with Kara a year after college, while she'd been preparing for the advanced test. Kara had spit buckets and wine stains everywhere. I shuddered at the memory.

"He says he'll support me and that he just wants me to be happy. The final test is in the fall of next year, but I've already been studying, so I'm not behind. I may have you guys help me with blind taste tests. But mostly I have a few partners I'm working with. It'll be crazy busy the next few months, so it'll be good to do some Skype meetings."

Raina nodded at me. "Okay, Sienna. Give us your update."

"We've already discussed what I'm doing. I'm going to get with Christopher, Keith's former campaign manager, to see if I can shadow him."

"With his fine ass," Nikki muttered not too softly into her wine glass.

"Yaaaas!" Raina fanned herself. "Those Michael Ealy eyes and Goldilocks dreads. He can get it." She shivered.

"He can more than get it. Homeboy can have lifetime access to the uterus." Nikki pointed to her own to further drive the point home. "Well . . . he could get it if he didn't have those crazy eyes."

"Oh, Lord." Raina shook her head.

"I'm serious. Black men with light eyes are usually crazy as hell."

I rolled my eyes at the Nikki-ism. The woman had a backwoods theory about everything. "That simply is not true, Nik."

"Yes, the hell it is. I'm telling you, men with light eyes are straight up touched."

"Touched?" Kara tilted her head. "What does that even mean?"

Nikki lifted her fingers to tick off her points. "Touched in the head. Not all the way there. Boiling bunnies crazy." She snapped her fingers. "You remember Mark from school? Gorgeous green eyes, fine as hell, but we found out later that dude was running over squirrels and wearing women's panties."

I shook my head. "He did not run over small animals. Now, the women's panties thing may be true." My sorority sister had told me one time he'd bent over and pink thong panties rode up his back. With sparkles. "That doesn't make him touched. That just means he likes to wear women's underwear."

Nikki continued as if her points were valid. "I'm telling you, don't trust the light eyes or men who don't have facial hair."

This time, the other women nodded, including Kara, who was typically the sane one of the bunch.

"No, ma'am." I shook my head. "That, too, is factually incorrect and is not gospel. Case in point, Keith doesn't have facial hair."

"Exactly," Raina muttered.

Nikki snorted. "Girl, please. Just because you use your lawyer's voice doesn't make it true either."

Kara shrugged her shoulders. "I'm not sure if Chris can help, seeing as he doesn't speak."

I smiled. Leave it to Kara to stay on track.

"Keith mentioned the other day that Chris thought I did really well last time. And yeah, he doesn't seem to talk, or care for me, but I think I can turn it around."

"If anyone can, it's you," Nikki agreed.

Raina twirled her fingers in the air. "All right, Nikki. You're in the hot seat. What do you have for us?"

Nikki grabbed her glass of wine and gulped. "I, uh. Well, you know, I want to be a singer and songwriter. And, well . . ."

Raina rolled her eyes. "Duh. Tell us something new."

"Okay. I kinda sorta looked up Tattered Souls the other day and saw they were performing. So I . . . I went to the concert."

"With who?" Raina looked offended. They'd always gone to concerts together.

"By myself. I told James we had a girls' night."

"Cheese and crackers, Nik," I admonished. "You lied to your husband?"

"Yeah. That's not the interesting part." Nikki gulped her wine again and then took a deep breath. "Trent saw me in the crowd and convinced me to come onstage. Long story short, there's a video floating on the internet of our performance.

Their record company wants me to write a few songs. Trent even hinted at a reunion of some sort."

We were all quiet. Even Raina didn't have something to add. On one hand I was excited for my friend. Not only did she have the gumption to reach out to her band, but she performed and killed it. Although Nikki pretended to be rough and tough, she was a softy on the inside, and she needed the boost in confidence about her talent.

Writings songs was fine; however, being in the band meant being around Trent Masters, and he was bad news. And with Nikki's incredible talent and Trent's manipulative nature, it was only a matter of time before they gave her an offer. The other girls and I used to call him Hurricane Trent. He blew in and jumbled Nikki's emotions with lots of rain and pain. She didn't need him to be successful, but knowing Nikki she went that route because it was the easiest path.

Nikki squeezed her eyes shut. "Guys. Say something."

Kara answered her quietly. "Do you want to go on tour with them?"

Nikki drummed her fingers against her lap. "I dunno. But that's not on the table. For now, I want to write. I can't lie . . . it felt *so* good to be onstage. But I don't know if I can drag my family into that crazy life."

Kara nodded. "Okay, when does the record label expect an answer?"

"They didn't say."

Kara tapped her chin. "How about joining a band locally? Or something else around Atlanta."

"I have a gig at a coffee shop called Rev and Go."

"Damn, girl." Raina snapped her fingers. "You aren't playing any games. Go, you!"

Nikki smiled. "I can't let y'all asses outshine me." Her smile slipped. "Do you really think I should drop Tattered Souls?"

"I get why you'd want to work with them." Raina tilted her head. "But let's be real, James is gonna lose his shit at the thought of you traveling to God knows where with Trent."

"True. Very true," Nikki conceded. "I'll stick to writing the songs for now." Her voice was high pitched and rang untrue. It was the same tone so-called eyewitnesses from the prosecution's side used in court. Whether Nikki admitted it to us or not, she'd made her decision.

"See, this Mastermind group is helping already." Raina smiled. "Now we just have to get Sienna off Keith's nuts and doing her own thing."

DECEMBER

CHAPTER 5
'Tis the Season of Giving—Raina

I opened up the family-size bag of potato chips, dumped it into the white plastic bowl, grabbed a paper towel roll, and hustled back into the living room. We had another Mastermind meeting, and this time, it was at my house.

My friends were gathered in a semicircle, armed with magazines, poster boards, scissors, glue, and booze.

Kara frowned at my whack snack display. "Please tell me you have dip, and no, hot sauce doesn't count."

I placed the paper towels on the table. "I think you know the answer to your question."

"Do you have any fruit or cheese?"

"Nope and nope. Well, I do have cheese slices and the squirtable cheese."

Kara's expression went from mildly irritated to supremely pissed. My friend did not play with food.

"I don't know why you even asked." Sienna munched on a granola bar. "That's why I bring my own food when we have girls' nights at Raina's."

"Hey, now! The chips are just the appetizer. I ordered a pizza, wings, and I even got a veggie pizza just for you, Sienna."

Sienna looked relieved. "Oh. Well, that was thoughtful of you."

"I try."

So I wasn't the best hostess. Nothing was homemade and I never had bottled water, per Kara's bougie-ass preference, or vegetarian options outside of the occasional celery and carrots that came with our wing order. And to Nikki's great disappointment, I don't know how to mix a cocktail to save my life.

Whatever. Hospitality wasn't my calling, but I could damn sure whip up a vision board party, which was what the meeting was all about. I'd read somewhere that visualizing your perfect life and putting it in a high visibility area was a powerful way to attract your dreams. Not that I particularly believed in laws of attraction, but it wouldn't hurt to have a daily reminder and focus on what I wanted out of life.

After I dumped the bowl of chips on the table, I sat on the floor and selected a cutout of the most recent *New York Times* best sellers list.

Nikki pasted an ad for *American Idol* to represent her singing career, while Sienna arranged pictures of interlocking wedding bands, a baby nursery, political ads, and the Obamas.

Sienna looked at my facial expression, the one I hadn't realized I was wearing, and laughed. She knew what I was thinking. There would be no weddings or babies on my board.

Kara sipped on the wine she was wise enough to bring while cutting out words from a magazine. She looked at my board. "Nothing for radio?"

"Hell to the no." I shook my head. "I'm so over that job. Did y'all hear my show from last Tuesday?"

Kara and the others shook their heads.

"Some little girl, and yes, I said little girl, because a real woman wouldn't do this, confessed to being a side chick to some married woman who's in the closet. Homegirl spilled all the tea, told me her lover's name, occupation, everything. Hell, if I hadn't stopped her she would've blurted the woman's Social Security number." I waved my scissors in the air. "Then she had the audacity to request R. Kelly's 'Trapped in the Closet.' I'll be damned if I play that pedo's music on my show."

Sienna reached for her drink. "You can't be serious? God, some people are just awful."

Nikki paused mid-cut. "I deleted all that bastard's music from my playlists. I'm not exposing my babies to that pee-wielding pervert."

"You have the craziest callers." Kara plucked a chip from the bowl.

"Yeah, well, that's the reason why my job isn't on the board. Enough about that." I dismissed the topic. "Does anyone have progress reports?"

"I do." Nikki leaned in and waved at us to get closer. "So the gig at a coffee shop . . . they want me to perform every other Saturday now," she whispered.

"It's okay. Cam can't hear you downstairs." I pointed toward the downstairs stairway.

"What? That's awesome!" Sienna said at full volume and gave Nikki a high five. "Can we come see you?"

"Yeah. I'm on every Thursday starting at four o'clock, Saturdays at five. Don't tell the menfolk, of course."

"So you haven't told James about the gig? And have you made a decision about the band yet?" Ms. Bucket of Cold Water, Kara, asked.

"I haven't. I'm still figuring things out." Nikki jerked her shoulders. "Anyway, who's next?"

I took the heat off my best friend. "Well, nothing as exciting as Nikki, but I signed up for an online writing class."

Kara went next. "I joined a wine study group."

Sienna's shoulders drooped. "Nothing for me. Christopher hasn't responded to my calls or emails. But I'll likely see him at the Mayor's Ball." Her lips thinned. "He can't avoid me forever."

"Or you could find someone else," I suggested. "He isn't the only campaign strategist in Atlanta."

"He's the best, and I want him." She sprinkled glitter on her board and avoided eye contact.

"I bet you do want him," I mumbled under my breath.

"You want that *D*." Nikki snickered.

Sienna tossed a glue stick at Nikki. "Shut. Up. You know what I meant."

"Sure we do." Kara surprisingly joined in on the fun.

Sienna bit down on her lip, I could tell she was wrestling to remove the smile on her face. "I hate you guys."

I reached over to hug my friend. "Aww, we know you love Keith too much to think about another man's penis. Now, y'all need to hurry up and finish. I've gotta go in early for work tomorrow."

"Are you serious? I'm not even halfway done," Sienna protested.

"And this is why we will never have a meeting at Raina's house again." Kara pointed at me. "Agreed?"

Nikki, Sienna, and Kara all nodded together. "Agreed."

I should've known today was going to be a clusterfuck. We had our boring-ass Monday-afternoon meetings for the entire station. No amount of caffeine or free coozies or donuts could make up for my getting approximately two hours of sleep.

Usually we started the meeting several minutes behind schedule because one of the hosts for the popular morning and midday shows would try to out-diva each other with crazy requests or stories about their listeners.

Before I could even step foot into the meeting, Colin, one half of the morning show, stepped into the elevator with me.

"What up, Rae-Rae?" He lifted his fist to give me a bump.

He received the silent treatment and the side-eye for several reasons. One, Colin was a middle-aged white guy. Thanks to Facebook, I knew he enjoyed country music (nothing wrong with that, I used to get my Shania Twain on), hiking, and brewing his own beer. I also know the closest contact he's had with anything black was his Moleskine hardcover notebook he carried around like a security blanket. *So, no, Colin, you may not bump fists with me, and you may not call me Rae-Rae.* In the interest of keeping my job, I exercised my right to remain silent.

Colin cleared his throat and then turned his attention to the elevator door. He moved on to the subject of his wife and dog. I decided to contribute to that conversation because, honestly, his wife was nice and his dog had been friendly when he brought them to our last company picnic. Also, this was my way to silently teach Colin about how to converse with black people.

I should log this under my volunteer hours.

The elevator dinged and I rushed from the enclosed space. After the painful ninety-minute team meeting, I crashed on the sofa in the back, since my show would start in two hours, and tried to take a nap. I couldn't sleep because again—the cheap-ass owners refused to crank up the heat. I guzzled down Earl Grey tea, donned my happy cat fuzzy socks, and geared up for my calls.

It was two weeks before Christmas, the most emotionally exhausting time of the year. During this season, I was extra sensitive and attentive. When I was a radio host in college, a freshman had called in. Her entire family had died on the way to visit her at college, and she wanted to be with them. I talked her off the ledge and we still emailed each other, even to this day. She is now married with two kids.

The holidays reminded people of those they lost, of what they didn't have—the opposite of the reason for the season. I had to be on my A-game because one bad piece of advice could send someone jumping from a bridge into I-75 traffic. I even abstained from playing hangman from Thanksgiving until the New Year.

Which bought me to my caller. "Hello, raindrop!" I greeted my listener. "Who am I speaking to?"

"Bradle—I, um . . . mean Daniel from Midtown."

More like Bradley from Buckhead, but whatever.

"My family left me, Raina."

"I'm so sorry. Do you want to talk about it, or put in a request?"

"Both. And I'd like to request 'Please Come Home for Christmas.'"

We got that request a lot, usually from douchebag boyfriends. Massaging my temples, I prayed for patience. Perhaps he was different. "Tell us your story, Daniel." *And prove me wrong.*

"I just want my family home. I've got a boy and a girl, and my wife took them away from me. I want to win them back. I want my wife to love me again. I sent her an email, told her I planned to call you tonight. I'm hoping you can help me."

"I can't guarantee anything, but you have my ear."

He sighed and continued. "I just wish my wife would've given me a chance to explain. She didn't have to involve the kids and take them away. Hell, I didn't mean anything by it. *She* didn't mean anything to me. I just needed to blow off some steam."

Cheater. Called it. In my peripheral vision, I caught Jamie with her two fingers in the shape of a gun, pretending to blow her brains out. Her auburn strands swished from the dramatic action. She and I were on the same page on cheating, especially after she caught her boyfriend of two years with another woman. Rhonda's face was blank, serene even. I shouldn't be surprised—the woman only cared about advertising dollars. Damn, I wish I had my whiteboard.

"She was just an indiscretion."

"Daniel," I interrupted, gentling my tone. "Sounds like a bunch of excuses to me. If you want to win your family back, try apologizing. Own up to your mistakes."

And keep your dick in your pants! I refrained from saying the latter. The FCC would *so* not approve.

"That's what I was getting to, Raina." His voice sounded clipped.

"My apologies, Daniel. Please continue."

"Right. So, here goes. Baby, I'm sorry. I'm sorry for cheating on you. I never should've touched our HOA president."

"Good," I managed to choke out.

"Whew. That felt good, Raina."

"I'm glad. Thank you for calling and good luck with—"

"I have some more confessions."

"Well, I can't absolve you from anything, so maybe you should speak to your wife—directly."

"No, no. I'm sure she's listening. If not, I'm recording us. Baby," he deepened his voice, sounding like the B-version of Mike from Boyz II Men during the begging bridge break. "I'm sorry for screwing that girl from my trip. I'm sorry that I messed around with your old college roommate, but most of all, baby—I'm sorry for giving you herpes."

"What!" I yelled. "You gave your wife herpes? There is no cure for herpes, Daniel."

Rhonda was waving her hands in the air. Jamie's blue eyes widened. I had no fucks to give. None. There would be no gentle raindrops, but a thunderstorm.

"I know. I know. I mean, we both have it now, so we might as well stay together, right? So, anyway, if you could play 'Please Come Home for Christmas,' the R-and-B version because I need to put a little soul into it." He chuckled.

The asshole chuckled. My temperature spiked, which was a feat, given the cold radio station. He was talking, but I wasn't listening.

All I remembered was the countless nights my mother cried herself to sleep when she thought I'd dozed off. Or when we scrimped and struggled while my father had another family. Cold nights when all we had were blankets and each other. We were so poor, my mom had to move us in with Grandma Jean, and they did not get along. My mother and I were in the same position as Daniel's family.

I hoped that motherfucker was lonely for the rest of his life.

"Sure, Daniel from Midtown. I'll put in your request to play 'Please Come Home for Christmas,' even though you gave your wife and mother of your kids an STD. Herpes, after all, is the gift that keeps on giving."

Rhonda waved her hands and mouthed *Go to commercial.*

I couldn't. I was on a roll, and this raindrop was gonna learn today. "Oh, and Daniel's wife, if you're listening: Please don't come home for Christmas, Martin Luther King Jr. Day, Valentine's Day, St. Patrick's Day, Easter, Memorial Day, Labor Day, Halloween—"

"Wait a minute, now," he yelled.

"No, Daniel. You are the worst of the worst. And you have the audacity to call my show, like I'm some sort of Catholic priest, to confess your dirty-ass deeds and give a shitty apology to your wife? Nuh-uh, partner. You need to own the fact that you've forever altered your family's life. You—"

A commercial blared from the headset. Rhonda had cut me off.

Damn. I rocked back in my seat. I cussed on the air.

"I mean, what were you thinking, Raina?" Rhonda ran her fingers through her platinum blond hair as she paced the floor.

I was seated on a lumpy paisley couch, half shocked and half proud of what I'd said. "He called in and asked for my opinion and I—"

"No. Oh, no, no, no. You do *not* get to turn this around. He didn't want your opinion, he wanted you to *listen*. To say a soothing word or two and play a darn song! That's your job, and you've done it beautifully, well . . . up until now." She waved her hands. "Now we're going to have the owners and the FCC up our behinds."

"We?"

Rhonda tilted her head as if I were on something. Something *real* strong, by the looks of her deep frown.

"Yes, *we*. I'm the producer. And my job, along with Jamie's, is tied to yours. But you didn't think about us, did you? It's one thing to play your immature judgmental games silently, it's a whole 'nother thing to say what you think."

Clasping my hands together in prayer, I gritted my teeth. *Say what I think.* That's been the issue. I'd always censured myself. Always said what people wanted to hear, but *not* the right thing. I was tired of giving piss-poor advice. Tired of pretending people weren't awful. Tired of excusing bad behavior. I had a bullshit meter and, apparently, it had a low threshold. "Look, Rhonda. You're right—"

"I know I am."

"I'm not finished." I raised a finger for silence. "You're right about me not being thoughtful regarding you and Jamie. It wasn't fair, and I didn't think about you two. Honestly, all I could think about was that an immoral man wanted me to excuse his behavior. I know my brand is to be sweet and kind and nurturing. I don't know if you've noticed, but I'm not that person."

Rhonda's lips twitched. "Never occurred to me." She sat on the couch beside me. "Look, I know you aren't the Raina we've marketed you to be, but no one forced you to do this, and there's nothing wrong with the job. Do you know why people love you?"

"Because I kiss their asses?"

"Because you listen. Some people don't have a friend or a listening ear. Or someone who won't judge them for their choices, however bad they may be. Your voice and your words give them hope." She exhaled, a long, frustrated, worried exhale and leaned back, head cradled on the top of the sofa. "Maybe I'm being Pollyanna, but your work, our work, is important."

I grabbed her hand. She looked up in surprise, her blue eyes bright with emotion.

"I'm sorry, Rhonda." I twisted the bangles around my wrist. "I don't want you or Jamie to feel like I don't value you."

I tried to move my hand away, but she held tight. "So, what's the next move? Should I pack my bags and prepare to never work in a top market again? I'd make a cute hobo."

Rhonda shook her head. "I honestly don't know. Best case scenario, you'll have to apologize to Daniel and the listeners. Suspension is pretty much guaranteed."

Damn, that sucked. I'd just bought a house with Cam, another thing I hadn't considered during my rant. He was a pilot, a captain at that, and could afford taking care of the mortgage by himself. My savings had been wiped from the down payment. I really should've let Daniel, the herpes wielder, go.

"Worst case is that I get my ass fired, right?"

"Right."

"Right," I repeated, my voice weak and unsure. Suddenly, I appreciated the job I never wanted.

"If I get suspended or fired, let Jamie step in. She's sharp and has a great sense of humor. Just let her be herself and not the old Southern grandma shtick I had going."

Rhonda nodded.

"Okay, I'm gonna go. I'm sure they'll make their decision by tomorrow, but I plan to get knockout drunk, so call me if I need to stay sober."

"Roger that," she said in a voice that belied her jealousy of my plans.

* * *

"If it makes you feel any better, I'd never give you herpes." Cameron wrapped his arms around me after he slid into bed.

I lifted my head to look at the time: eleven a.m. Right after I left the studio, I'd called him, but he was still in the air. He must've heard my rambling voicemail, chock full of tears, curse words, and lamentations about my soon-to-be-jobless status.

"You're taking the whole thing in stride." I heard the sleepiness in my voice and cleared my throat.

"It's not so bad."

"Not so bad?" I snorted. "You didn't hear what I said."

"Yeah, I did. I had a layover and listened on your station's radio app." He pulled me close, my back flush against his chest.

"You were right to say what you did." His mouth was near my ear. "The guy was an asshole, and if the station can't see that, then they don't deserve you. They deserve a robot. Someone willing to push a button to generate a nice response to dumb shit."

Warmth spread in my chest and traveled to my stomach at his praise. "Why, Cameron, are you trying to seduce me into falling in love with you?"

"Nah. I'll settle for a blow job, though."

I chuckled and rolled away so I could turn to face him. I cupped his stubbled cheek. "What am I going to do with you?"

"Funny, I was going to ask you the same thing." He grabbed my hand and kissed the center of my palm.

The ringing phone interrupted our intimate moment. I rolled over to the nightstand and looked at the screen.

"Rhonda," I mouthed, as if she could hear me.

"Pick up. Face the music, babe."

I shrugged and feigned nonchalance. But honestly, my heart was flopping around like a seal at Sea World.

"Hey, Rhonda. What's up?"

"Hey, Raina. You know why I'm calling, so I'll get right to it."

"Okay."

"The top brass are pretty pissed. They wanted to fire your ass, but I came prepared with the numbers from the show and how we've diversified our listeners. They compromised. Do a nice apology. Ninety-day probation, and Jamie will cover for you. Non-paid, of course."

Fuck. I needed the money. "Thanks, Rhonda."

My tone must have been not-excited because Rhonda followed up with, "You have a job and you have a loyal following. Be grateful for that."

"You're right. Thanks for pointing out the silver lining."

"Don't thank me, thank your listeners. Apparently, we had a huge social media storm between last night and this morning. Check your Twitter and the radio station's Facebook page. People are eating up what you said. Especially women."

"Wouldn't I tick off my loyal listeners if I apologize?"

"You aren't getting out of that apology, Raina." Rhonda's voice was hard.

I know I was pushing it, but I'd rather drink castor oil than apologize to that grimy asshole.

"You need to apologize for the delivery of the message, but not the message itself. You know what, I'll craft the apology. You just read it like a news release or a promo."

"I can do that."

"You have no choice. Now enjoy your vacation and stay out of trouble."

I ended the call and took in Cameron. He'd scooted his back against the leather headboard, arms crossed and eyebrows wrinkled.

"What is it?" I asked. "I know you heard the call, but it's not all bad. I'll be back in action in three months. I don't have a lot of savings, but I—"

"It's not about the money, babe. You hate that job. Now all of a sudden you're acting like you can't live without it."

I pushed myself up to sit beside him. "We just bought a house, Cam, and we need the money. It's called adulting."

"You need to take this time to figure out what makes you happy, not go back to the same rat race."

I shrugged. "Not being poor or jobless makes me happy."

Cam didn't respond. Just gave me his trademark stare downs.

"Okay, fine. I know what makes me happy. Writing. I'm still fleshing out my characters."

His biceps flexed against his crossed arms and he shook his head again. What the hell was up with him? I'm not trying to be a starving artist.

"You've got a ready-made book. You write in your journal every day after work. It's what you really want to say to your listeners who need to be called on their shit."

He's right. I repeated the sentiment out loud.

"Of course I'm right. Take this time to clean up your notes and write. You can edit it so you won't get in trouble with the station. Make it about personas, like the cheating spouse or the clueless friend that lets a girl or guy run over them."

"Right," I said again. "That's actually a good idea."

"Babe, you got the full package when you got with me."

My mind whirled with possibilities. The great thing about writing nonfiction was that I could write a proposal first. If I had a few bites from publishers, I could snag an agent. I already had an audience in a top market and a solid following online. The big issue was, my listeners wouldn't be my new audience. They loved the fake Raina. But, according to Rhonda, I got a lot of praise from women on social media. Maybe they could be converted.

"There's smoke coming from your head. What are you thinking about?"

When I quickly told him my plan, he grunted in approval.

"Yeah, I say you check it out. See if it becomes viral, if it already isn't. If you decide not to return, you can introduce your audience to the real you."

"I'm not ready to quit my job just yet. Let me do some research, write a proposal."

"Good plan. You can brainstorm some ideas with your lady group."

I rolled my eyes. "We're not ladies. We're masterminds!"

"My bad." He twined his finger around my dreads.

My mood rose from the lower pits of hell to cloud eleven hundred. I could do this, I could really become an author.

I moved away from the headboard, put myself between his legs, and gave him what I knew was a sexy smile. "You have a choice. Eternal gratitude or blow job."

His eyes ignited. "I think you already know the answer."

I did. I stroked him, just the way he liked it, light squeeze, slow and measured. My man liked to be wined, dined, and seduced. Lowering my mouth, I took a lick at the answer.

From the intake of breath and grip on my hair, I knew I'd guessed correctly.

CHAPTER 6

Not My Kind of Movie—Kara

White jasmine, my favorite scent, filled the air. Candles, all white, from large, fat pillars to small, round tea lights covered the kitchen counters and living room table. The candles, no longer solid, were a waxy soup surrounding nearly extinguished wicks.

Date night. "Ahh!" I smacked my forehead. The heady fragrance weighed down my guilty conscience like solid gold bricks.

Yanking my phone from my purse, I tapped the screen to check the time, but the phone was off. It was off because I'd powered it off. The study group had a no cell phone rule, and as the new kid on the block, I had to follow the rules.

Claudia, Eduardo, and Martin had been studying together for months, and they only let me join because my mentor had asked. But I should've just silenced my phone. None of them were married and on their spouse's shit list because they'd been neglectful. The other night, I'd woken up Darren as I muttered mountain ranges between Sonoma and Napa. Sad thing, I was sleeping when this happened. Darren shook me awake and told me to chill the hell out.

Sanity was slipping away, and I feared if I didn't pass this the exam time around, I would turn into Gollum and wine would become "my precious."

My mind wasn't the only thing slipping away. Something had changed between me and Darren. He was no longer supportive and often complained when I went through my flash cards while in bed. This was the fifth or sixth time I'd flaked on him. For five months, I'd been working and studying, tasting and spitting nonstop. And in the process, I'd ignored Darren. There was a long, wide, tall invisible wall, and I was pretty sure if I kept at this, I'd never be able to scale it. This wasn't about five months of regret; this was about three years. I had convinced him, and in the process, myself, that this time around would be different. I wouldn't become this obsessed monster that didn't have the time to talk.

I looked around downstairs. Darren wasn't here.

No, he was here, either in our room or in the basement. His car was in the garage. Based on the sounds coming from upstairs, I made an educated guess. It was time to face the music. Dropping my heavy purse, leaden with notes and a half-empty bottle of wine that I needed to dissect—not now, obviously—I walked the green mile upstairs and took a sharp right to our room.

Darren sat in bed, his back against the headboard, Nintendo 3D-whatever in hand. The light was off, and he didn't move when I opened the door. The light from the screen and from the computer monitor wedged in the corner of our room illuminated his face. The playful sounds from the Super Mario game didn't detract from the heaviness in the atmosphere.

I turned on the light and leaned against the wall. He squinted his eyes a bit but still focused on the game. This was bad, really bad. Darren was a lot of things, but he was rarely frustrated or angry with me.

"Darren, I'm so sorry about tonight. I promise I—"

"Don't promise," he whispered. Finally, his brown eyes settled on me.

Licking my lips, I thought of something I could do to fix this mistake. Maybe I could cancel tomorrow's study session and we could reschedule. "I can cancel tomorrow's study group. We can do date night tomorrow?"

"No."

"No?"

He paused the game. Silence flooded the room as his angry gaze burned my skin. "No. I hired a sushi chef to come over tonight. You didn't answer, so I told him not to come. If you're hungry, you can eat the rest of the pizza I warmed in the oven."

I didn't like this feeling. I was hot all over, like I was wearing a fur-trimmed jacket while drinking an enormous glass of Pinot Noir.

Tears pressed against my eyes, but I blinked them back. Tears wouldn't help. I needed to fix this, fix us. But I didn't know how. "Tell me what to do, and I'll do it."

"Keep your word," he said, resuming his game.

I opened my mouth, but then I shut it, remembering what I'd learned when I joined the management team right after college. Underpromise and overdeliver. He needed action, but for now, he needed space.

"You're mad," I stated the obvious.

He didn't respond.

"Shit. You know I'm no good at this. I'm sorry I get obsessed with these tests, but it won't be forever."

Still, he didn't answer.

"I'll sleep in the guest room." I needed space from my guilt, from the heavy atmosphere in our bedroom. I moved toward the drawers and picked up a few things. This time the tears did fall, but it was okay. He was looking down and my back was facing him.

Heat warmed my back, and my body trembled. A strong,

corded arm wrapped around my waist. I leaned back, my head cradled against his chest. His other hand gently moved my hair to the side. His woodsy, clean scent muddled my senses. Then he kissed my neck, so gentle, so reverent. Tears splattered against my chest. This was us. We didn't need the words.

Soundlessly, I turned to face him, stood on my tiptoes, my hands against his abs, and leaned in for a kiss. Soft and sweet, but then it turned to more. Hungrily, we devoured each other's lips. He tasted of Merlot, and I didn't know if it was left over from the tastings I did earlier, but I wanted more. I needed the fuzzy, buzzy feeling to make me forget my regret. Groping my bottom, he lifted me into the air and then dropped me onto the bed. While he undressed and caressed me, I promised myself to study less and be a woman of my word.

I was running on fumes, studying and working and trying to be a decent wife. A few minutes ago, I was on my way home, but I rerouted to Sienna's apartment. Tonight, the group wanted to do a show-and-tell to showcase what we'd been working on and provide critiques of our work. I didn't have much to show for these days, just a stained tongue, bags under my eyes, and a bad attitude.

I sighed, remembering that Sienna's townhome had limited parking and since I was late, I would most likely have to drive around the neighborhood to find parking. Today must've been my lucky day, because I found parking near the back, right by her apartment. I rushed inside to find the ladies were already there, gabbing about a show I was too tired and too busy to watch.

"Hey!" Nikki yelled, wine sloshing from her glass.

"Watch the couch!" Sienna yelled from behind me as we neared the den area.

Nikki rolled her eyes. "Girl, it's leather." She reached for a napkin and patted the seat dry.

"Now that you're here, I've gotta bone to pick with you, Kara," Raina shouted from the sofa.

I wanted to say "get in line" but instead, I shook my head and settled on the couch. "What did I do this time?" It didn't take much to set Raina off.

"Why in the world did you like my ex's picture on Facebook?"

I tilted my head. I didn't even realize I'd done it. *I must really be on fumes.* "What picture?"

"The picture where Fernando is hugging his pregnant wife from behind. You can't miss it. They both had their shirts off, looking like they'd struggle-swam in a vat of Palmer's Cocoa Butter. The butter in a tub, not the squeezable lotion."

"Because that level of detail is important," Sienna deadpanned from the kitchen.

Nikki nodded as she sipped her wine and then smacked her lips. "It is. It's a different level of greasy."

"So why did you like his photo?" Raina pressed on. "Answer correctly or I'll get Nikki to bring out Louella."

Louella was a bat that Nikki had been carrying around in her trunk since forever.

"Why are you still his friend?" Nikki asked, in the same demanding tone.

I massaged my forehead. Was she seriously grilling me about Fernando? "You guys know I'm rarely on social media, and I didn't realize we were still friends. As far as liking his pic, I didn't realize I did. I must've clicked on the image by mistake. I don't even remember what it looked like."

Raina pulled out her phone. "Oh, I can show you, since your *like* came up on my feed.

"News flash, we don't *like* anything from that greasy bastard," Nikki said in a singsongy voice.

I sighed long and hard when Raina sat beside me. "Please, don't."

Ignoring my request, Raina shoved her phone in my face. Fernando and his bride did indeed look overly lubricated.

"The caption reads," Raina cleared her throat, "'A strong king needs his queen.'"

"Aww, that's kinda sweet," Sienna cooed, placing a snack tray on the table.

Oh, goodness. Wrong move, Sienna. Wrong move.

"Kinda sweet?" Raina squeaked. "Since when has Fernando been a king? That negro was a dirty, broke-ass pauper when I met him. As far as him doing this black-and-white greasy-ass picture concept, his ashy ass was using some watered-down, dollar store lotion until I upped his game."

"That's a little harsh," Sienna admonished.

"Harsh, but it's all the way true," Raina returned. "I spent four years"—she spread out the fingers on her hand and wiggled them—"four long years dealing with his shit and then two years after we broke up, he gets married and all of sudden he's a family guy?"

Fernando was the worst, so I was happy she dropped his sorry ass right after college. What I didn't understand was why she was still upset. I decided to ask. "Why are you upset? You've got Cam, a wonderful guy. What's the problem?"

"The problem," Nikki stepped in, "is that she wasted years on him. All along he already had a queen, but he didn't appreciate her."

I waved my hands in the air. I was tired of getting beat up. "Fine. Duly noted. I will never again like your ex's photo. As a matter of fact," I grabbed my phone and swiped open the app. "I'm deleting his friendship." I searched for his name and did so. "There. Now, can we get started?"

"Oh, she's feisty today!" Nikki laughed.

Raina stood to turn down the television and Sienna sat in the now vacant spot next to me.

"All right. Let's kick off the show-and-tell. I'll go first."

Raina smiled in her seat, eyes glowing. I focused on her, noticing the glow everywhere. That radio suspension must've been good for her. She was never this happy.

"I went to a literary networking event last week and met a few editors. I told them about my concept, and two of them have asked for a proposal. As you all know, I've already gotten started on the proposal, but I still need a professional, like a freelance editor, to review my work."

"Why don't you send us what you have?" Sienna suggested.

"Yeah," Nikki bobbed her head. "This is show-and-tell."

"I'm way ahead of you ladies. In your in-box, you'll find my outline. Can you give me feedback, in say, two weeks?"

We all agreed. Nikki jumped from her seat and pulled out a guitar from behind the couch. "I've got a new song. The band and I negotiated that I'd write a few songs and maybe even cut a few tracks. The studio agreed and plans to release a few singles to test the waters."

Nikki played the song, and it was absolutely beautiful. Lost in her own world, she tilted her head back as she strummed her guitar. The song was haunting, about a second chance at love, forgiveness, and loving someone through the tough times. Nikki did sad songs well. It would be a hit, no doubt.

Everyone clapped after Nikki finished her new composition and put away the guitar.

"That was beautiful, Nik," Sienna complimented.

Nikki snapped the guitar case shut. "Yeah, the band loves the song and we're going to record soon."

"So when are you going to tell James about the band?" I asked.

Nikki widened her eyes. She still hadn't told her husband

and continued to sneak around. She snapped on us when we encouraged her to come clean.

"Like I've said a million times, I'll do it when I'm ready."

I shook my head. "Nikki, you're being ridiculous! Just tell him the truth. It's only going to get worse the longer you wait."

"Right. Like I'm going to take marriage advice from someone who barely speaks to her husband."

My shoulders squeezed together. "What are you talking about? I do speak to my husband."

I glanced at Sienna. She'd been the only person I told about my troubles with Darren. I should've known not to tell my chatterbox best friend.

"I'm not the one who flaked out on date night like nine or ten times." Nikki's tone turned nasty.

"Four times." My snitch-ass best friend came to my defense. "But let's not get into a fight. Following dreams can be tough on relationships. But, Nikki, Kara's right, and we've all been telling you to talk to James. It's your choice—"

"Damn right it is."

Sienna sighed. "And, Kara, sweetie, you know I love you, too, but Nikki is also right. You've gotta find balance. You can't rightfully talk about Nikki."

I knew I was wrong, but I was irritated. Here I was, exhausted as all hell, while my well-rested friends told me about myself. "Fine. I'll go home and speak to *my man* right now."

"Wait, we aren't finished." Raina raised a finger in the air. "Don't get all pissy because Nikki dished it back. Let's just finish the meeting."

"I'm sorry, but," I swung the purse strap across my shoulder, "I've gotta go cater to my man." I bowed my head in submission as I paraphrased the popular Destiny's Child song. "I'll see y'all in a few weeks."

I stormed out of the house, so unlike myself, and didn't rest until I reached my car.

Maybe it was a good thing I was leaving early. I could surprise Darren, maybe even cook him something nice to eat.

I hyped myself up on being a better wife and squelched down the feeling of being a terrible friend. I'd apologize to my friends later.

When I returned home, I had a pep in my step. I promised myself I'd cook Darren a nice meal, seduce him, and give him a little sumthin' sumthin'.

I opened the door and was not surprised when I didn't find him in the living room. He was most likely in his man cave in the basement. "Darren, I'm home!" I yelled as I stomped down the steps.

I didn't hear him respond, but someone else did. A chill slid over my skin, so intense goose bumps broke the surface.

I heard a moan. A long moan followed by, "Right there, Daddy!"

The chill became a tundra, yet my heart sped. I gripped the railing. This couldn't be happening. Not to me. Not to us. An electrical prod shocked my system. I stumble-ran the rest of the steps and nearly toppled on the slippery carpet. I flung open the door.

"Aha!" My chest heaved as my attention darted around the room.

There was my husband, stroking himself to two women on dual computer monitors.

His face flitted between shock and embarrassment.

"What in the hell, Darren?" I stomped to his computer monitor as he scrambled to pull up his pants, which were pooled around his feet. "Is this what you do while I'm busting my ass for exams?" I scanned his computer.

After he halfway fastened his pants, he tried to close down the screens.

"Oh hell, no." I slapped his hands out of the way and took a look at the damning evidence—a screen with clips of women with big asses. On the other monitor was an email from his old college buddy. The email was a picture of a woman in nothing but a Santa hat. His friend asked if Darren had been naughty or nice. Darren responded that he'd be a bad boy for her. *Son of a bitch!*

"Oh, really?" I swung my head and seared him with an angry look. "You're so bad now?" I yelled, but tears were next. I could feel the stinging tide of emotions rise. This wasn't the man I married. I wasn't so naïve that I didn't realize men and women watched porn, but to share pictures—naked pictures of women with his friends, his *married friends*—was the final straw.

"Who are you?" I backed away from him. Well, I tried. My legs were gelatin.

He stood, still fumbling with his pants. "I'm sorry, Kara, I—"

"You do this with your friends?"

"Yes. I'm sorry. We just do it for fun."

"F-for fun?" The anger was rising again. "You share pictures of women. Probably saving it to your hard drive and saying nasty, degrading things? That's your definition," I pointed to the screen, "of fun?"

He was silent, but his eyes were pleading. Usually his warm brown eyes tugged at my insides, but I was empty.

"Are you . . ." I cleared my tear-clogged throat. "Are you cheating on me?"

"Never," he whispered, as if it were a vow. "I would never cheat on you, Kara. You're my everything. I love you."

"I'm obviously not your everything. Y-you have this secret life where you jerk yourself off in a dark room and share dirty pics with your boys. I don't know you."

"You can check my phone, baby." He grabbed the phone from his desk. "Right now. Check it and you'll know I'm not cheating. I go to work and I come home. Yeah, sometimes I blow off steam with the guys, but I never meant to hurt you."

He raised his palms in the air. "I swear to you that I'll never do it again."

I ignored his outstretched hand. "Blow off steam? You mean perving on other women." I shook my head. "I bet you hook up with these women and then—"

"That's not true and you know it. I'm always home."

"How am I supposed to know?"

"Yeah." He folded his arms across his chest. "How *are* you supposed to know? You're never home, but I am. I make sure you have a meal waiting for you every night when you come dragging from work or studying. I give you a fucking massage until you fall asleep, tucked to my chest. I clean the house because you never have the energy to do anything. And when you cancel on me, I roll with the punches because I love you." He punctuated each word. "And, yeah, maybe I was wrong for sharing pictures and watching porn. But we haven't had sex in two months. Every time I try to touch you, *my wife*, you roll away and say 'maybe tomorrow,' then fall asleep."

His razor-sharp words sliced into me. Yes, he was still a fucking perv, but he was right. I was never here. But damn if I was going to admit it. I was tired of getting knocked down today.

"Sleep down here tonight with your," I squinted at the screen, "Big Booty Brazilian Bitches." I wasn't calling them bitches. That was the name of the porn he'd been watching. I turned to stomp back upstairs. He tugged my hand before I could turn the corner.

"Kara. Stop. Please, let's talk about this. We obviously have some issues to work through."

We? I felt as if I'd been smacked across the face. "Sure. The issue is my husband watches porn and objectifies women. You want to solve *our issues*, stop watching porn and swapping pictures with your friends." My tone was venomous and sarcastic, I'm sure it would've made Raina and Nikki proud.

"It isn't that simple and you know it. We need to fix this, fix *us*. I'm willing to do whatever it takes, but please, baby, let's talk it out."

I jerked my arm away from his hand and took a step back, thinking through my wish list. "Stop watching porn."

"Done, baby."

"I mean it." My voice was low and harsh. "Cancel your subscription and delete your files. Whatever it is you've got going on."

He nodded.

"Stop sharing pictures with your friends."

"Of course, baby. I can do that, too."

I wanted to roll my eyes. I didn't believe a word he said. "I also want us to go to counseling."

"Counseling?" he asked, his voice sharp.

"Yes. You obviously have a problem. And this is a deal breaker. I can't be with someone I don't know, and it's obvious that I. Don't. Know. You." I waved toward his setup of lotion, tissue, and hand sanitizer. At least he had the decency to clean his hands.

"Baby, you know I how I feel about counseling."

He was a man of few words, who hated to talk out his feelings. I knew this, and still, I pushed. I was feeling vindictive and pissy and hurt. Mostly hurt. "I thought you just said whatever I want."

"Fine, baby. You're right. I'll do you one better and find someone for us. That's just how serious I am about our marriage."

He leaned down and tried to kiss me. I smushed his face.

"Not happening. And I meant what I said. Sleep down here tonight."

Turning the steering wheel, I pulled my Camry into the ghost town of a parking lot. Darren had been a man of his word, and within a week, he'd set up an appointment with a therapist. I turned off the ignition, checked my appearance, and relaxed. I tried to, anyhow. I was ten minutes early, by design.

I needed to get myself together before I got my head examined. The office block included a row of buildings, brick and rectangular and off white. For some reason, I'd imagined it would be more secluded in the outskirts of the city, with a wraparound porch and a golden retriever who licked away tears when you cried.

Darren's Camaro slid beside my car. He parked, looking in my direction with a slight smile. I turned my head away from him and frowned. For the last few days, it'd been hard to be nice, to find the good in him and in our marriage. No, not just our marriage—my life. I was suffering from good old-fashioned depression, and no matter how many Disney movies and reality television shows I'd forced myself to watch, I couldn't get back to me. Being mad at my husband, not having him to lean on, not having *anyone* hit me harder than I'd imagined. I reclined my seat and opened the door.

Darren stepped out of his vehicle and waited for me near the back of my car. "You ready for this?"

"Are you?" I quickly snapped back.

The small flicker of optimism in his eyes faded.

I needed to calm down. "Sorry. Yes . . . I'm ready, I guess. Just anxious. I don't know what to expect, you know?"

"Right." He dipped his chin. "We're in this together. I want us to work this out, get over this hump."

This was more than a hump, this was Mount Everest. I decided to keep my commentary to myself. "Well, let's take the first step."

We walked through the doors, and I was surprised again by the setup. The office was kind of new-agey. Near the sign-in sheet was a mini rock waterfall, illuminated by LED lights. The speakers near the desk played zen music—sounds of waves crashing with pan flutes above the sounds of nature at a respectable volume. A eucalyptus mint scent wafted throughout the office.

After we signed in, we took a seat in the lobby. Before Darren could make awkward small talk, I closed my eyes and pretended to nod off. What was the protocol on things to do when waiting for a marriage counselor? We couldn't hold hands. That would be confusing to me, him, and the counselor. We couldn't chat it up about the weather.

I didn't have much time to mull over what Miss Manners would do because our names were called.

"Mr. and Mrs. Jones?"

I opened my eyes. A short, black man with a bald peanut-shaped head gave us a smile.

We both stood and stretched out our hands to shake. I didn't need Miss Manners to tell me that.

"I'm Dr. Harrison. Nice to make your acquaintance. Come on back." He led us through a long hallway lined with doors on either side with name plaques that displayed PhD and other letters behind the names.

He opened the door to a cozy, comfortable room, like an office in corporate America. "Please, come in." He moved to a chair near a desk and motioned us to sit on a love seat.

Was that done on purpose? I bet some couples couldn't stand to be in the same room with each other, let alone on an intimate couch. I examined my seat choice and decided to sit a few inches away from the end. Not too close, yet not so obvious in my desire to sit far away from my husband.

Dr. Harrison started off with a few softball questions, who we are, what we did, the crazy weather. Finally, after a few minutes of small talk, he clapped his hands together.

"So. Why are you here today?"

Darren swallowed, squared his shoulders. "We're here because of me, Dr. Harrison."

I snapped my attention away from the doctor and to my husband.

"Last week, my wife caught me watching porn and . . . and I also exchange pictures, dirty pictures, with my friends."

"Mm-hmm." The doctor steepled his hands, and I wondered if it was a requirement to say "mm-hmm" if you were a counselor. Raina did that a lot on her show.

"How did that make you feel, Mrs. Jones?"

"I was upset, obviously. I never knew he did stuff like that."

"Stuff like what?"

"Watch porn. Share pictures and make these lewd comments about women. It hurts me because I know I'll never look like those exotic women he obviously has an obsession with."

"It's not an obsession, Kara." Darren shook his head.

"Then what is it? A hobby? A fetish? What?"

Dr. Harrison raised a hand. "Not that I'm making an excuse, but sometimes men do watch porn," he said in the most condescending voice ever.

Yes, I knew people watched porn. One time, Darren and I even watched. I was tipsy, but it was fine. I knew it was a regular thing for Raina and Nikki to do with their guys. But what pissed me off was that I didn't know he did this by himself. It wasn't something sexy or new for us to try. When I saw his little setup, I realized that porn was something he sneaked off to do. I felt like I married Darren's representative, and it hurt like hell that he felt like he couldn't be himself around me.

"Yes. I get that. Some of my girlfriends do, too. I'm not so much mad about the porn as I am about the stupid pic exchange and the nasty comments. Hell, most of his friends are married to beautiful, loving women. Why aren't I, *we*, enough?"

Dr. Harrison nodded, his eyes squeezing shut as he listened.

"Mr. Jones, Darren. Why was your screen up?"

Dumb follow-up question, but okay. I'd see where he was going with this.

"I thought I was alone. Kara's been busy lately with studying."

"Oh," Dr. Harrison grabbed his notepad. "You're in school? I thought you were a sommelier?"

"I am, but I'm studying for the master level. It requires a lot of my time to do so. Studying is like preparing for the LSAT in my field."

"Got ya." He turned his attention toward Darren. "So, you thought you were home by yourself. Have you been doing this more since Kara has been focused on her studies?"

Darren nodded. "I guess I've been frustrated, too. The canceled dates, we rarely have sex, and I . . . I just needed a release."

"I get that." Dr. Harrison lifted his pen in the air. "I do. But you have to be mindful of your wife, protect her."

I smiled and glanced at Darren. Dr. Harrison was a smart guy.

"If you're going to do stuff like that with your friends, don't make it so easily accessible. You have to protect her from those types of things. I know guys like to do stuff like that, but she shouldn't have to *see* you do that."

Scratch that. Dr. Harrison was fucking dumb.

"Wait, what?" I furrowed my brows. "Are you telling my husband to hide things from me?"

His large brown eyes focused on me. "I'm asking him to *protect* you."

"By lying. We don't lie in our marriage, Dr. Harrison," I bit off angrily. Why I needed to tell a marriage counselor this was beyond me. And what made it worse was that we were paying him $120 an hour to fix us.

"FYI," I looked at my husband. "Don't lie to me."

"I won't." Darren eagerly nodded.

"My apologies, Mrs. Jones." The counselor's voice wasn't as contrite as I'd have liked. "Let's move forward. Darren, I'm so concerned about the root cause for this type of behavior. Why didn't you speak to your wife about your frustration?"

"Because . . . because—"

"He doesn't express how he feels," I finished for him. "He's always had a hard time with opening up."

"Why is that, Darren? I want *you* to answer the question."

"My family." He squirmed uncomfortably in his seat, adjusting his jeans and then his jacket. "My parents died in an accident. I was a toddler, so I barely remember them and I was raised by my grandparents. They were affluent, and I had all the things I wanted in the world, but we just didn't talk that way."

"Were they affectionate? Did they tell you that they loved you?"

He shook his head. "No."

"Can you define what love means to you? What love is?"

He shrugged. "Sometimes I . . ."

"Sometimes, what?" Dr. Harrison encouraged.

"Sometimes I think I don't know what love is."

Blood drained from my face. Porn, throwing away his freaky-deaky stash was what I'd thought we'd be discussing. I stared at my husband, willed him to look at me, tell me to my face that he didn't love me. But he stared straight on, chest heaving as if he'd just run a marathon. I licked my lips, swallowed. My mouth had gone dry, heart pounded like gongs in my ears. "What does that mean? Y-you don't love me?"

"Of course I do. I'm just confused right now."

Tears clawed like an unyielding beast up my throat. I couldn't see anything in front of me but blurred lines. Tears dripped from my eyes and settled on my lips.

Dr. Harrison stepped in. "I think Darren and I should do

some one-on-one time. Then after a few sessions, we can go back to marriage counseling."

I nodded, grabbed my jacket, and rushed out of the office. My husband, the man I thought I would love forever, didn't know how he felt about me.

God, I wished it was only about the porn.

CHAPTER 7

Cappuccino, Anyone?—Nikki

The small crowd of forty clapped after I'd finished my set. I smiled, took a bow, and exited stage left on the platform I was pretty sure the owner's kid had made in wood shop class.

Being on the makeshift stage wasn't the same rush that had electrified my bones when I performed onstage with Tattered Souls at the Tabernacle. But Rev and Go had a lot of charm. Hard Rock Café meets crazy corner coffee shop. A mixture of high and low tables, high-back chairs, comfy couches, and framed autographed pictures of musicians, artists, and sports stars. The East Atlanta neighborhood had an eclectic crowd of business professionals, someone's eccentric aunt or uncle who probably sculpted nude models, and "retired" trust fund kids.

It wasn't *my* neighborhood. Don't shit where you sleep, Daddy used to say. So, I booked a recurring gig thirty miles away from home while Mama stayed with the little ones.

"Woo! You rock!" A deep voice snagged my attention.

I smiled at the silver fox with a salt-and-pepper goatee. "Thanks, man."

I gave him and his group of coffee buddies a quick wave and weaved through the tables to the front of the house. Slapping my hands on the counter, I leaned over to bug my favorite barista. "Give me your strongest drink, Jonas."

He was facing away from the stainless-steel cappuccino machine. "Triple shot espresso?"

"Not quite. Hot coffee, a little sugar, fresh creamer, and, oh, whiskey, if you have it."

He snorted and turned to face me. The lanky recent college grad gave me a smug smile and smoothed over the side part in his chestnut hair. "No alcohol, just the freshest ground coffee you've ever had the pleasure of tasting."

"Joking." I patted my back pocket with my bedazzled flask. "I've got the whiskey."

Jackie D. Tennessee. The same brand Daddy loved. I didn't smile at the thought, or at the memories of Daddy's sweat-soaked clothes smelling of stale cigarettes and rubbing alcohol. He'd squeeze me too tight, but I didn't complain. I was just happy he was home.

"Love you, baby girl," he'd say, trying to whisper, but his voice boomed in my ear. His breath was a combination of bile and booze and honey.

Goose bumps darted down my forearms. *I'm not like him.*

James or my babies would never see me like that. The key was greasy food, like a burger and fries, and hydration. A shot or two never hurt anyone. It was the benders that were dangerous.

Jonas pushed the coffee to the side table and motioned toward a waiting customer. After he gave the customer her beverage, he turned to face me. "You're gonna get me fired one of these days," he mumbled as he made my "virgin" Irish coffee. "Eric is gone, but you still need to go out back."

After six weeks of performing at Rev and Go, Jonas and I had a routine. He'd caught me sneaking booze near the corridor between the bathroom and the employee break room. Whatever I'd concocted had been so terrible, I coughed and sprayed the floor with my failed experiment. He shook his head, made me clean up the mess, and gave me a lecture about alcohol on the premises and how Eric, the owner, would can my ass if he ever found out.

The following week Jonas crooked his finger toward me to follow him to the employee break room, opened his work locker, pulled out a thermos, and gave me the best Irish coffee I'd ever tasted. Since then, he'd told me he'd make the drink, I just needed to bring the whiskey.

"Thanks, Jonas." I tipped the mug in his direction.

"No problem. You've earned it. I've noticed we've got a bigger crowd since you've been playing for us. People are sticking around and ordering food. Eric even mentioned looking into getting a license to sell beer and wine."

"Oh, wow."

"Yeah." Jonas smiled and pointed to the red and white flyers with my picture and name. "You're our star. I had a few customers mention they'd come from Macon to see you. You're generating some buzz, Nikki."

My heart slapped against my chest. This was good, really good. But I didn't want them to depend on me. What if one of my kids got sick, or if James caught on and wanted me to quit?

"Th-that's cool. I'll start the last set after I finish my drink." I rushed to the back exit and flung open the door. I didn't realize how hard I'd been breathing until I saw puffs of breath dotting the cold air. Shit. I leaned against the brick wall while my mind raced. Grabbing the flask from my pocket, I dumped the whiskey into the mug.

I felt sick to my stomach. This was getting out of hand. Sooner or later, I'd have to come clean. The lies I'd told my mom and James continued to pile. James thought I was either doing PTA stuff or hanging with the girls. Mama was so happy that I'd invited her to hang with her grandbabies, she hadn't noticed, which had been surprising. The lady was as sharp as a finely honed tack. Nothing usually got past her.

Just last week, I'd written two songs for the band, and somehow they'd convinced me to sing on the tracks. Now there were flyers for Rev and Go.

When I signed the ninety-day contract for the coffee shop gig, Eric had something in there about using my image for advertising, should I gain a following. I quickly signed it, excited that someone wanted to pay me to sing. I should've let Sienna review it first. Damn. Just one misstep and everything would be crashing around me like dominoes.

I had to come clean, and I would. Soon. I just needed another week of this to myself. I needed this high, this unfiltered emotion. Something that belonged to me. I didn't have to run it by Mom for her to shoot me down, or see James's nervous fidgeting, like I'd leave our family for music. I didn't have to worry about how I would eventually be a bad mom when this came to a head.

And it would. Sometimes you just know when things are going to happen. The stars were aligning, and I knew it was my time to shine. What I didn't know was if I was ready for the spotlight.

I chugged the rest of my drink. The liquid stung the back of my throat, the perfect stimulus for me to get out of my head, pull myself together, and sing my heart out on stage.

I tapped my fingers on the steering wheel as I waited for the other cars in front of me to pick up their kids. As I finally reached the curb for pickup, my daughter ran to the car, pigtails flying behind her, with a bright orange sheet of paper in her hand. "Mommy, Mommy. Guess what?" She peeked through the passenger-side window.

"Get in the car, precious, then tell me the good news."

Bria swung open the door and hopped into the SUV. She swallowed, inhaled, and opened her mouth, but then shut it.

I was about to pull away from the curb, but instead I shifted the gearshift back to park. Cars honked behind me, but those impatient fuckers would have to wait. "Spit it out, Bria-bree."

She leaned over and shoved the paper into my waiting hand. I scanned it. The first ever talent show hosted by the school, at the top of the next school year in the fall. The grand prize was $300. Nothing to sneeze at for elementary school students.

"Very cool." I arched my brow into the rearview mirror. "You want to do this?"

She bobbed her head. "Yes, Mommy. And I want you to finish teaching me how to play guitar."

A smile broke free on my face. I'd been teaching her little by little, like Daddy had done. Just a few chords, easy songs to learn on guitar like "Wonderful World" by Sam Cooke and "Three Little Birds" by Bob Marley. I needed to figure out an age-appropriate song that didn't suck. God, I hope she didn't want to do any bubblegum pop songs that would likely be featured on a Kidz Bop album.

Unbuckling my seat belt, I hopped out of the car to more honks, opened the back seat door, and hugged my baby. "I can definitely do that, sweetness. When we get home, we can make a list of songs you want to learn."

She squeezed back. "No, Mommy. I want us to make a song together. It's gonna be epic!"

My baby was full of surprises today. "Sounds like fun! We can brainstorm what type of songs we want. Love songs, a song with a good message, oh, or maybe a song about having fun."

A long honk broke our Hallmark moment.

"Yeah, yeah. Go around me." I waved to no one in particular and hustled back to the driver's seat. I quickly shifted the gears to drive and pulled out when I noticed the volunteer pickup person was striding in our direction.

"Mommy, yuck!" Bria shuddered.

"What are you yucking about?"

"I don't wanna sing a love song. I want a song that means

something. Maybe something with a message about doing good things? Like when you, me, Daddy, and JJ volunteer at the soup kitchen during the holidays."

God, my daughter was the best. *Better than her lying-ass mama.* "That's good, baby. We can talk about it after dinner."

"What's for dinner?"

I shrugged. "Your grandma decided to cook a spread for us today and I was shooed out of the kitchen. She's at the house now."

"Yay, Grandma! I love it when she cooks."

"Wait a minute! My spaghetti is pretty darn good."

"It is, Mommy. But you can't be great at everything."

"Oh, yeah? What am I so great at?"

She put up her fingers and ticked off the points. "Singing, piano, guitar. And you're a great mommy, of course. Much cooler than the other moms. Everyone says so. Even Dina D'Garzo and she hates everybody."

Her compliments warmed me. I had an awesome family, and I wasn't quite sure what I did to deserve them.

When we arrived home after the short drive from the school, Southern home cooking greeted us. If my nose served me correctly, I smelled baked chicken, some sort of fried cornbread, and sweet potatoes.

"Hey, baby," James greeted me, with his namesake cradled in his arm. He leaned down to kiss my cheek and then settled our son on the floor.

"How was your day?" He pulled me close and gave me a better kiss.

"Gross!" JJ yelled.

"Eww!" Bria echoed.

"Settle down, children." James shook his head. "There is nothing wrong with showing the woman I love affection."

"Facts," I told the kids and gave my husband a deeper kiss.

Warmth spread throughout my chest as I pulled away. No need to get too hot and heavy in front of the kids and Mama.

"So, how was work? Is that noob pop star still giving you trouble?"

"Nah. She's good, now that I provided her with a few charities she can cut a check to, to keep her taxes lower."

He grabbed my hand and pulled me up the stairs. "Mom, can you watch out for the kids for a minute?"

"Sure, hon!" my mom yelled back.

"Got a surprise for you," he whispered.

"If it's the same surprise you've been giving me the past decade, the cat is out of the bag. I got two kids out of your *surprises*, and I already know you're packing."

He stopped on the landing of the stairs, threw his head back, and laughed. "God, I love you." He bent over and kissed me again. "And no, it's something else." He directed us to his home office. In two steps, he reached into his desk, pulled out a piece of paper, and gave it to me. Sheesh. What was it with my family pushing pieces of paper in my hand? I read the slip of paper. It was a travel itinerary to . . . I squealed. "We're going to St. Lucia?"

"Yep. Just you, me, and the beach. No kids allowed, and a sexy bikini is all you'll need."

I jumped him, wrapping my legs around his waist. "We're going to St. Lucia!" I screamed.

His strong arms wrapped tightly around my waist. He kissed my neck and then trailed kisses along my ear. "Told you I'd always take care of you."

My heart stuttered as I remembered his promise. We had been happy, in love, but dirt-ass-poor while he was in grad school full-time. I'd just found out I was pregnant, and I'd freaked.

James, however, was typical James. Cool, calm, happy.

When I broke the news of our expanding family, a flair of possession lit his dark eyes. He scooped me into his arms and made love to me.

Slowly. Lovingly. He worshiped my body and whispered so many promises that I couldn't help but believe. One of the promises he'd made was that he would always take care of me: mind, body, and soul.

"What brought on this surprise?" I slid down from his arms, but he still held me close.

"I noticed you've been busy with the Mastermind group and the PTA. I know being a stay-at-home mom is tough." His eyebrows creased. "You're always Mom, but I get to go to work, talk to my peers, then I crash after dinner. I want us to have time to ourselves, too. I'm sorry if I've been neglecting you."

"Never." My voice was hoarse, altered by all the damn guilt weighing me down. I'd been sneaking around, playing my gigs, making music, and my husband thought I was tired, unhappy, and ignored. My fingers grazed his face, traced a path from his silken eyebrows down to his thick, full lips to the beard that covered his milk chocolate skin. "You're perfect, James. Absolutely perfect. Marrying you was the best decision I've ever made."

Worry dropped from his face, replaced by the dangerous smile I fell in love with when I spotted him in the smoky crowd all those years ago.

"All right." He titled my chin and gave me a quick peck. "Let's go downstairs before our spawn give your mother a heart attack."

"Set the table for me, Nicole. Dinner is almost ready." Mama continued to stir the pot over the stove.

"Yes, Mama."

"And don't forget to wash those babies' hands."

I inhaled softly and rolled my eyes.

"Save the 'tude, young lady." She didn't look up, and I was still amazed at how she knew when I was rolling my eyes, sucking my teeth, and giving her 'tude, as she liked to call it.

"Fine, Mama." I hustled out of the kitchen and set about doing what I was told. Sure, I had a sassy attitude when it came to my kids, husband, friends, and frenemies, but I was damn near a pussycat when it came to Mama.

Even before Daddy had passed, she was always the authoritarian figure, while my dad tried to figure out ways to sneak around her to get me what I wanted. After Daddy died, it was hard to joke around with Mama. We were poor and brokenhearted. There wasn't much to smile about.

"Dinner is ready!" my mom yelled from the kitchen while I arranged the table setting.

A stampede thundered from overhead. Could be the kids or James. They all loved Grandma's cooking.

Everyone rushed the dining room table, but after Grandma gave them a look, they all slowed. Even JJ. My husband grabbed the booster seat and pushed it up for our son.

Mama settled on the opposite side of me. Her peach blouse fit nicely against her curvy figure and chocolate skin. She was beautiful, but I looked nothing like her. I took after my daddy; my skin tone was on the lighter register since my father was biracial.

"Let us pray." Mama bowed her head and stretched her hands. I grasped a hand, while James took the other. She squeezed my hand twice as she'd done ever since I could remember. Never with anyone else, just me.

"Dear Heavenly Father, thank You for giving me the strength to prepare this food for my family. Thank You for my handsome son-in-law who takes care of his family like a *real* man should."

I rolled my eyes. Sounded nice on the surface, but I knew she was throwing shade at Daddy. The man was dead, for God's sake.

She took a deep breath. "I also want to thank You for my beautiful and smart grandbabies."

"I not beautiful!" JJ shouted. "I hand-sum."

"Excuse me, Lord." Mama giggled. She never giggled with me. "My beautiful granddaughter and *handsome* grandson. And thank You for my child."

Not talented, gorgeous, accomplished? She needed to take a page from *my child* on compliments, but whatever. I decided to give my eyes a rest before they got stuck in the back of my head. The woman was throwing the entire shade tree at me today.

"In the name of Jesus, we pray—"

"Amen!" We all joined in.

After a few minutes of eating, my husband started our usual conversation.

"How was school, baby girl?"

Bria grinned, still chewing her food. "Great, Daddy!"

James motioned her to swallow and she complied. "I'm gonna join the talent show and Mommy is gonna finish showing me how to play the guitar!"

My mother's fork clattered against the china dinnerware. Her eyes drilled holes into me. "You're what?"

My heart dropped. I did not want to have this conversation with Mama around. She was like the mom from *The Water Boy*, but instead of foosball being the devil, it was music.

I cleared my throat. "Yes, Mama, I am. Bria is a natural."

"Babies, close your ears," she said to my kids.

Used to our sparring, they ducked their heads and covered their ears. James, however, looked pissed.

"You want her to end up like Stanley? Your father was a *natural,* too. And so were you." She waved her fork in my direction. "And look how you ended up." She then pointed to my wine glass.

"Kids. Leave the table." James's voice rang clear. He helped JJ out of the seat.

JJ protested. "But, Daddy, I hungy."

"I know, son. I'll come get you in a minute. Count down from one hundred."

He ushered both kids out of the way and then returned to the dining room table.

Standing by his chair, he pivoted his attention to my mother. "Daniella. You know I love you. I appreciate all that you've done for us, especially when we were struggling financially in the early years of our marriage. But I won't stand for you coming down on Nik. Bria is *our* daughter. She loves music, and she has always had a curiosity. You remember when Bria hopped in Nikki's lap whenever she played on the piano or crawled on top of Nikki when she strummed the guitar? If *our* daughter wants to learn music, then she will learn, and learn from the best." He turned his attention toward me, his eyes blazing. "My wife."

James and Mama had a stare down, and neither blinked.

Well, I blinked because I was a softy, and I tried and failed to hold back my tears. I loved this man. I didn't think I had room in my heart to love him more, but there it was. The proof was in the loud *kathump* of my heart, the way time had slowed, and swear to God, I heard Minnie Riperton singing the la-la-la-la-la chorus from "Lovin' You." If Mama's stuck-up ass wasn't sitting there with a just-sucked-a-lemon facial expression, I'd jump across the table, strip James down, and give it to him like the kids were gone on vacation.

"Now," he continued. "I'm gonna go get *our* babies, and we are going to have a nice dinner, understood?"

"Understood, James." Mama's shoulders stiffened. "I understand my opinion is not welcome."

"It's welcome, but you don't do it in front of our kids. Especially when we've had this conversation before."

I reached for my wine glass, gave my mom a victorious smile, and saluted. This time, she rolled her eyes.

After James put Mama in her place I was walking on sunshine, so much so that I was humming when I gathered the laundry to fold upstairs in our room before I went to bed.

The lights were out, save the small glow coming from his phone. That was strange; it was only just after nine o'clock at night. James usually didn't lounge in bed until eleven.

I flipped on the lights. "Are you against light now, Edward Cullen?"

One of his hands braced his forehead as he stared at his cell. He jerked his head up, eyes narrowed to slits. "Nikki *Hardt*." He spat out my maiden name. "The newest member of Tattered Souls."

The laundry basket slipped from my hands. "I-I, that's not true. I didn't join the band."

"Yeah, I thought so, too." He rose from the foot of the bed. "When someone anonymous, probably from the PTA bunch that you've pissed off, sent me this email, I thought surely this is a lie. Surely my wife of ten years wouldn't sneak around with her old band, old *boyfriend*," he spat out the word, "and lie to *me*." He slapped his chest.

"But then I heard the leaked song, 'Yesteryear,' a song where you literally moon over the old relationship with your ex-boyfriend for two verses."

I swallowed. That song, that *fucking* song. I knew it would get me into trouble. And I hadn't even written it. Trent and someone else from the label had penned the tune. They swore it would be a hit. It was a damn good song, but not worth my marriage.

"I didn't write that song, James. And I didn't mean any of the words. It's just a song."

"But you're recording with them. Hell, I saw a fucking video with you and Trent singing to each other from a few months ago. Fuck! Nikki . . ." His voice grew hoarse. "All this time. All this time, I'm thinking you're tired and drifting away from me, but it's not me. It's you." He jabbed a finger toward me. "You and the music and that damn band."

"Baby." I strode to him, made him sit down on the leather footstool near the bed. My hands cupped his face. I touched my forehead to rest against his. "I'm sorry. I was scared and stupid. I didn't think you'd approve of my joining the band. I haven't . . . I just cut a few tracks. And, well, since I'm putting it all out there, I have a coffee shop gig."

At the news, his head jerked away from my hands. "Damn, Nik. More lies?"

"That's all, handsome man, I swear."

He snorted. "It's e-fucking-nough." He stood again and paced the floor. "Stop with this hiding shit."

"I-I promise not to sneak around. I'll never lie to you again."

"The coffee gig is fine, but . . . but you can't see Trent again. The other dudes are fine, but Trent has never respected our relationship. He's always tried to get in your pants."

I slumped on the seat, my heart dropping to the floor. I'd been teetering on what to do about the band, but now that James was taking it away from me, I wanted them. I had to try. "Babe, the coffee gig is sweet, but the big money will come from the band."

"You don't need the band, Nik. You never did."

"Yes, I do. And now with the track leaking, it's a matter of time before buzz starts. I can't leave them hanging."

"Can't leave them hanging?" His deep voice somehow

squeaked. "What about your family? Are you gonna leave us hanging?"

"No, don't do that." I shook my head. "I've always sacrificed for this family, from day one."

"And I haven't? I don't love my job, and still I knock out the mortgage, utilities, the car note for your fly-ass Range Rover, private school, clothes. All with a smile on my face because that's what adults do."

Firewater burned my chest. How dare he? Yes, he was the breadwinner, but I sacrificed my body, my *dreams*, for our family. "We've both sacrificed, and I refuse to go back and forth with you on who does more, but I need . . ." I raked my hands through my hair. "Something that's just for me. I need to be more than a mom and a wife. I need the music."

"It's a fine time to have a revelation." His hands clenched at his sides. "When we have a mortgage, small kids and one barely potty-trained, and we're in our fucking thirties!"

"Stop using our kids and my age against me."

"I'm telling you—"

"And I'm telling *you* that I'm dying!" I shouted over him.

He stopped pacing and jerked as if he'd been shot.

I pressed forward but didn't step closer. "I need this, James. And you owe me. I love them, God, do I love our kids. I love you. Nothing is sweeter than a smile and a kiss from you, handsome man. I love the life that we've built together, but, still, I . . . I need more. I'm not running away, I'm just asking for more time."

"So, what?" he whispered. "You want to go on the road? Leave us? You hated touring when you were younger."

"Just a few months, tops. We'll start in the top of summer, be back by fall. I need to try, just to see—"

"You've made up your mind already, *Hardt*." His words sliced at me more finely than a block of Calphalon knives. He used to call me "Hardt," my maiden name, before we got married. He jerked open the door and slammed it shut.

Not how I'd planned it. No, that's not true. I didn't have a plan, other than to keep up the lie. Now I was paying the price. I was suffocating and bleeding and scared.

I shook, like a junkie needing a fix.

Like Daddy.

I thought I'd scraped the bottom of the barrel of pain when Daddy died, but I was wrong. To numb the pain, it was either play my guitar and sing my heart out or . . . or numb it with something stronger. A shot or maybe a few. I wouldn't get sloppy drunk like Daddy. Drunks were the worst. I loved Daddy, but I could hold my liquor much better than he did.

Walking to my closet, I rummaged through my purse for my flask.

The red-hot whiskey burned my throat but soothed my nerves. The warm liquid stung but then loosened my chest. I could breathe again, and the bleeding from my heart clotted. Gripping the flask, I had no fear. I could do this. There were plenty of musicians who were parents.

"He'll come around," I whispered, then took another deep gulp. James loved me. Our love would never die. With those comforting thoughts, I curled up in the corner of the closet and drifted away.

Chapter 8

I Think It's Going to Rain Today—Sienna

"Sienna?" Keith's voice teetered between agitation and indulgence. My head jerked as I focused my attention on him.

"Smile, beautiful." He gave me a practiced megawatt smile and nodded toward the official photographer of the Mayor's Ball.

A bulb flashed. White spots danced in front of my eyes. I grabbed the back of my seat, blinked until I could see, and scanned the spacious ballroom again. I was so nervous the butterflies in my stomach felt like buzzards picking at my insides. Tonight, I'd planned to harass Christopher.

He'd been a slippery fish—avoiding my calls, never responding to my emails or texts. He was a rude one, but he was the best, with over a decade of serving as senior advisor to senators in Washington, DC. I would be darn lucky to snag him. Before tonight ended, I was determined that he would a) work with Keith again and b) become my mentor. Not to mention I was starting to feel like a dud compared to my friends, who'd already made major strides in their goals.

"Don't worry, sweet cheeks. He's here. You'll find him."

A grin broke across my face. "How did you know?"

He wrapped his arm around my waist. "I just know. And being the confident man that I am, I won't even get offended that you're more focused on another man than me. You had that same tenacity in law school when you were determined to get the internship with the Newton Law Group."

I'd been a terror back then. But after the summer internship, I knew I could never work for corporate, aka the dark side of the law. "Well, I'm doing this for you."

He gave me a *yeah, right* look.

"Okay, for us," I amended.

"I know, sweet cheeks." He leaned in and brushed his lips against my ear. "Did you notice that we're just three tables away from the mayor? Much better than last year."

I patted his knee, remembering how offended Keith had been when we sat toward the back of the room last year.

Servers floated around us as they elegantly cleared off the entrées and quickly replaced them with thick slices of cheesecake. "I'm sure Mayor Edwards will pop by after dessert."

Keith pointed past my shoulders. "There he is."

Thinking it was the mayor, I slowly turned my head. My heart sped when I saw him, like a bull spotting a bright red flag. *Christopher.*

Long, brown dreadlocks were tied behind his head, his piercing blue-gold eyes scanning the room as if on the lookout for someone. His perusal stopped, eyes widening and nostrils flaring when he saw us.

I waved and grinned. He dipped his head and grimaced before pivoting on his heels and marching in the other direction.

I yanked the linen napkin from my lap and tossed it on the table. "What's up with that?"

"All right, party people, it's time to dance!" the DJ announced. The diva that is Diana Ross's sultry voice floated over the speakers, singing, "Ain't No Mountain High Enough." I could see Diana's smile, see her shimmy with all the confidence in the world, telling me to *"Go get him, girl!"* I didn't shimmy but instead squared my shoulders and stood.

"Where are you going, sweet cheeks?"

"To go get him." I stormed away before Keith had the chance to dissuade me or tell me not to embarrass him.

The place was huge. Three hundred people jam-packed, and Chris had effortlessly dodged me. "Dammit. Where is he?" I stretched my neck, even stood on my tiptoes. After ten minutes of fruitlessly circling the room, I wanted to give up. Plus, Diana was no longer cheering me on. Discouraged, I made my way back to my seat when I got a whiff of smoke. *Smoke! Chris loves to smoke!* Terrible habit, but the man was a chain smoker. He was most likely puffing his poor lungs away outside.

Turning on my heels, I rushed to the entrance of the renovated warehouse and turned a sharp right. My heart revved again when I found him leaning against the brick wall near a silver cigarette bin. *Gotcha!*

"Christopher," I said on a sigh. I tried to calm my heavy breathing, still out of breath from speed walking. Grabbing my arms, I attempted to rub away the cold. My strapless black dress was not appropriate for winter weather, even in Georgia.

"Sienna." He dragged in a long puff of smoke and then exhaled. A thick white cloud billowed between us. Waving my hands, I stepped back and coughed. Probably just as he wanted, to create a divide between us. I still didn't understand what his damn problem was with me.

My recently manicured nails dug into my palms. "Why have you been avoiding me, Christopher?" My voice was sharp and imperious, like a teacher berating a student.

"I don't want to talk to you."

I stepped closer, so close if he breathed deeply his chest would touch mine. It wasn't appropriate to get in a man's personal space, but I had to know. "Why don't you like me?"

He snapped his head back, narrowed his blue-gold eyes. The flash of blue in his eyes showed his surprise. Perhaps he was surprised by my audacity. But if he really knew me, he'd know I could be bold when needed. The blues in his eyes gave way to gold, reflecting twin pools of anger. "I don't dislike you. I feel *sorry* for you." He took a step back and smoked away from me.

Sorry for me? Embarrassment and pain seeped down to the hard concrete lot. Why feel sorry for me? I had a damn good life, thank you very much. A fulfilling career, a wonderful family, a great guy, and the best friends in the entire effing world.

A flame ignited in my stomach. Each puff he carelessly smoked stoked the fire in my belly. "Why?" I bit off, crossing my arms so tightly it pushed up my breasts.

His eyes dipped to my chest. He swallowed. "You're the living and breathing example of Little Miss Sunshine. You're so determined to block out the bad, you don't see what's going on around you." He stubbed his cigarette and tossed it in the bin. "You think everything is *perfect and wonderful and lovely*." He mimicked my voice, making me sound like a silly cartoon character.

"I don't think everything is perfect and wonderful and . . . and whatever the hell else you said." I waved at him.

"Lovely," he sarcastically supplied.

"I don't. I'm a second-generation immigrant. My parents both came from humble beginnings, yet they were able to provide for me and my seven siblings. We were rich in love but not much else. If I wanted something that wasn't a necessity, I worked my ass off," I growled.

"Sienna—"

"No. Be quiet and listen." I jammed my finger just above his rib cage, and my finger nearly broke against his granite chest. "Now, where was I?"

"You worked your ass off." This time the sarcasm was gone,

and his already deep voice had gone deeper. The disdain had left his eyes, replaced by something else I was too worked up to analyze. Whatever it was had siphoned away the red-hot anger.

"Yes, I did. I graduated number one in my law school class. And you know what I d-do now?" My teeth were chattering. I needed to wrap this up pronto before I became a Popsicle.

He shrugged out of his black tuxedo jacket and flapped it around my shoulders like a cape. "You're a public defender for the city of Atlanta." He stepped closer to me, or had I stepped closer?

"D-damn right. Which means I don't get to ch-choose my clients. Some are guilty, some are innocent, but all deserve a fair trial. Someone to look them in the eyes and let them know that they aren't the sum of their mistakes. That they are worth something. Sometimes I'm their last hope, and yes, I'm their Little Miss Sunshine. I do it for them." I jerked my thumb back, pointing to no one in particular, and then pointed to my chest. "I also do it for me. Because if I let the dark bleed through, I won't be any good to my clients or to the community. I'll be just another shitty lawyer shuffling through cases, treating my clients like a number. Just another shitty person who doesn't care about the welfare of my fellow man."

This time, he stepped closer. I was pretty sure it wasn't me.

"You want world peace, Miss America. It's admirable, but I'm not the man for the job."

Despite his asshole response, I laughed. "I don't need you to teach me world peace, Chris. I want you to teach me how to win. I want to help Keith when—"

"I'm not convinced Keith is the right man for you." His voice was gruff and as bitter as the cold weather. He took a deep breath. "I mean . . . I don't think Keith is going to be the man to make major changes for the community. He did okay in his first term, but he hasn't kept most of the promises he made."

I nodded. "You're right. He hasn't addressed the traffic problems, the pothole on Greenwald, or the stop sign needed on MLK Boulevard and First Street; and he takes forever to respond to emails. I'll make sure he upholds his promises. Keith is a good man." I rubbed my chilly arms again.

"If you say so."

"I do." My eyes bored into his. We were in a stare-off, and now that I had his very warm jacket that smelled of cognac and tobacco, I could stare at him all night. *Not because he's good looking, but because I want him.* For my mentor. Nothing else.

"Fine, woman," he growled.

"Yes!" I pumped my fist in the air. "You won't regret it."

"I'm already starting to." He cracked a small smile, and the victory tasted even sweeter. *I got Christopher Lucas to smile.* After a few short seconds, he dropped his smile. "I'll stay on for a few months, see how it goes. You'll be my second, and I'll teach you everything I know. But if I find something I don't like, I'm out of here."

"I'll be the best mentee you've ever had. You'll never have a reason to quit on me. I promise." I stuck out my pinkie to seal the deal.

"Put away your damn pinkie, woman. I'm not worried about you."

I rolled my eyes. "Look, I'm not sure what you have against Keith, but he's committed and focused. Trust me."

"Fine, sunshine." He pushed off the wall. "Let's get you inside before you freeze to death."

Rain in Atlanta equaled chaos. People thought we'd lost our minds back when our city turned into the real-life version of *The Walking Dead* after three inches of snow—we'd really lose our big-city street cred if they realized that we were just as bad with rain. My foot stayed glued to the brake. Every couple of minutes, I inched forward on I-75. Nervous energy swarmed in my chest. Today was the worst day for rain or for me to be late.

My Bluetooth-enabled cellphone interrupted my streaming podcast. Christopher's name flashed across the dashboard.

"Hi, Chris!"

"You're late."

I glanced at the dashboard. I had a minute. Technically, I wasn't late. "Not yet." But I would be by at least twenty minutes.

"I saw the traffic. You will be, sunshine. Thought you pinkie-swore you'd never let me down."

Technically, we hadn't pinkie-sworn. "I distinctly remember you swatting away my finger; therefore, nothing I promised the night of December eighteenth is binding in a court of law."

"Because pinky-swears are binding in a court of the law." He laughed. It was a little rough, a little rusty, and it warmed me like a shot of tequila. Like the liquor, his laughter was dangerous.

"Where are you, sunshine?"

"Um, not far, about two miles, but traffic is atrocious. I'm sorry, I'm not normally tardy but—"

"It's fine. The coffee shop is full. I think people are trying to wait out the bad weather and gridlock. Seats are all taken, and everyone looks comfortable. We'll need to meet someplace else."

I rolled my eyes. "Then why did you give me crap about being late?"

"Because you are late. It's 7:01 now."

"Fine, Christopher. Let's meet at Keith's office, the one he has for city council off Trinity Avenue. I'm less than a mile away from the exit, and it's only a few blocks from where you are, so you'll probably get there before I do."

"Fine." His voice grew deep and cold. "I'll wait outside for you."

The podcast I'd been listening to blared through the speakers again. He'd just hung up, no *see you soon* or *goodbye*. The man was moodier than a hormonal teenage girl in the throes of PMS. I attempted to call Keith to let him know about our meeting at his office since traffic was slower than molasses, but he didn't pick up.

Fifteen minutes later, I finally pulled into the employee parking lot for the building. After I crept my yellow Bug up the slight incline to the lot, I parked my car and pushed the electronic park brake.

"Keys, check. Purse and notebook, check. Umbrella." I reached into the back seat and grabbed my bright yellow umbrella. I rolled my eyes. Chris was going to get a kick out of the color. I looked down at my outfit, a polka dot navy blue and white blouse with a bright green skirt. God, I looked like a walking rainbow against a storm cloud.

I opened my door and dashed across the lot. As promised, Chris stood outside, below the faded green awning, smoking a cigarette. After Chris and I became *real* friends, I planned to persuade him to quit. If I could convince my stubborn Baba, my father, to stop smoking, Chris didn't stand a chance against me.

"Hey!" I retracted my umbrella once I hit the dry zone under the awning. "I'm going inside. Just come in when you've finished."

He nodded and exhaled. "Be there in a minute."

I waved at the cloud of smoke that wafted toward me. "Okay, I'll set us up in the conference room. Yay!"

He lifted his eyebrow and shook his head.

Dang it, why did I have to say "Yay"? "I mean, excellent! See you soon."

I propped my umbrella against the front door to the office.

Rap music boomed from the back of the building. Keith was usually a classical music type of guy. If he was feeling the need to turn up, he'd listen to smooth jazz.

"Maybe I'm finally rubbing off on him." I couldn't wait to tease him about being a closet rap fan. Bobbing to the beat, I walked toward his office.

I yanked open his door. "Hey!" The smile on my face slipped, tumbled, and splattered on the floor.

Shock rooted me to the spot. I couldn't move, could only stare and stare and stare as my fiancé fucked his office coordinator in rhythm to the song "Truffle Butter." The song was so loud they still hadn't heard me. Keith and . . . and Patricia— yes, that was her name—were facing the back window, away from me.

I closed the door. A chill settled over my bones, a chill I didn't think anyone or anything could warm. God, Chris was still outside. Thank goodness he hadn't witnessed my moment of shame.

One step, two.

I walk-shuffled toward the front door. Keith's empty promises echoed inside my head. "I'll never cheat on you again, sweet cheeks."

Three steps, four.

"I was young, immature. I've got a good woman, and I'll be damned if I hurt you again." *Five steps, six.*

I pushed the door open. Something wet hit my cheek.

"Sienna?"

I looked down at my feet. I couldn't remember what number of steps I'd taken. "Ten, I think," I whispered low to myself.

The cold overwhelmed me. My teeth chattered and clattered like a china cabinet during an earthquake.

"What's wrong? Let's get you inside." He reached for the curve of my arm.

"No!" I screamed, rushing into the rain and toward my car. *Eleven, twelve, thirteen, fourteen.*

"God dammit, Sienna, slow down." Chris grabbed my arm, swinging me around.

I was cold. The car was warm. I could think in the car. I'd be safe in the car. I wiped the water from my eyes, trying to focus on Chris. "W-we . . . we can't go in there."

Chris wouldn't listen. Instead, he pulled me back under the cover from the building. "Why the hell not?"

I couldn't say it. A tsunami of pain drowned me. I struggled to control the ache, struggled to breathe. "K-Keith's in th-there."

His face morphed from irritation to confusion to understanding. "He's not alone," he stated simply.

"No." My voice cracked.

The storm that raged around us mirrored his eyes. "Let's get out of here."

He went for my umbrella, but I walked away into the rain. I tilted my head, hoping to wash away the pain. It wasn't soft and comforting. It was cold, relentless, hard. Suddenly, the rain had stopped. My eyes cleared and I blinked at the swatch of yellow that filled my vision. Chris's warm body stood behind mine. No, the rain hadn't stopped, but it had been blocked by my silly bright yellow umbrella. Grabbing my hand, he led us to his sports car, opened the door, and buckled me in. He rushed to his side of the car, shook out the umbrella, and placed it in the back seat.

I opened the window, grabbed the umbrella, and tossed it outside. I wasn't feeling like Little Miss Sunshine today. Buying a sensible color umbrella had just been added to my to-do list.

Thankfully, Chris hadn't said anything. After he swerved like 007 out of the parking lot, he punched a series of numbers on his phone. "Jax. Need a favor; a pickup," he grunted. "No, a car . . . yellow Volkswagen Beetle." He did some sort of man chuckle and gave me an amused glance. "Yeah, no shit. I'll send you the coordinates." He waited for a beat or two. "No keys, but you'll figure it out. Get it to my place by tonight, soon as possible." He nodded, although Jax couldn't see him. "Good."

He ended the call. I felt marginally better. Apparently, I wasn't the only person whose calls he ended abruptly.

Chris didn't speak after his call, and there was no music, just the sounds of the windshield wipers and heavy raindrops. Heat blasted through the vents. Oddly enough, I could feel the air, but it still didn't cut through the freeze that blanketed my body.

Some time later, we pulled into a gated condo community. He opened the passenger-side door and unbuckled my seat belt. Grabbing his umbrella—it was blue, by the way—he guided me out of the car and marched me upstairs to an elevator bay.

Thirty-something floors later, Chris opened the door to his home. He waved me in, and I took a few steps, remaining in the foyer, conscious of my wet skirt, shirt, and shoes. Tilting my head down, I twisted my hair around my fingers. My long, fake tresses clumped together, and no amount of coaxing would bring any semblance of order to the wet mop on my head.

Chris stomped into a room, I assumed his bedroom. Seconds later, he returned with a plain white shirt, basketball shorts, and a plastic bag. "Bathroom is down the hall to the left."

I nodded and went about getting into something dry. *Can't get sick.*

When I returned to his living room, a mug sat on a silver tray. Chris had settled into a recliner chair, but the drink was in front of the love seat. "Chamomile tea." He waved toward the mug. "Drink up."

Hands shaking, I grabbed the cup and took a sip. Usually I blew before I drank, but I was desperate to feel. A splash of warmth hit my tongue, but not the sting I craved.

"Drink more. You're shaking."

I drank more, even though I knew it wouldn't help. Keith's face popped into my mind. The look of ecstasy on his face when we made love. Then my warped brain shot over to the scene with him and his office manager, going at it like animals. I couldn't see his face, but his head was thrown back, and his moans formed a heartless symphony that looped in my mind.

"Sienna?" Chris had moved closer. He lifted his hand, and his calloused thumb wiped a tear from my cheek. I hadn't realized I'd been crying.

A fierce expression took over his face. His lips turned up like he was ready to maim someone. His eyes were full-on golden and his body vibrated with raw power.

"You knew. That's why you didn't want to work for him."

He nodded.

"Of course." I sighed and relaxed into the butter-soft leather couch. "You wouldn't want to be associated with a scandal."

"No. I wouldn't want to be associated with a dumbass." He stared at me so hard I began to squirm.

"What?" I asked. "My hair doesn't look that bad, does it?"

He cracked a small smile and sighed. "No. Even drowned in the rain you look . . . nice." He cleared his throat. "You changed your hair after Keith got elected."

I curled my fingers into my palms, an effort not to tug at my knotted hair. Keith had suggested the change, saying it was his fantasy to run his fingers through my hair. He couldn't do it with my coiled fro.

I would not be sharing that tidbit with Chris. He already thought I was pathetic.

"That's why I didn't understand you." Chris's deep voice broke the silence. "When I caught him, he told me you and he had an understanding. That you were willing to turn a blind eye as long as he didn't embarrass you in public."

I jerked my head away as if I'd been slapped. *How many people has he told the same lie?* Tears freely slipped down my face. That was why Chris had pitied me. He thought I was one of those women who didn't care, that I was just about the power and fame. Or that I was too stupid for words and had let Keith run over me. An iceberg settled over my heart, encasing it so solidly that I couldn't tell if I had a heartbeat any longer. I was afraid it would never thaw.

"I'm so cold, Chris," I whispered, shivering. "I can't seem to get warm."

He pulled me into his arms, surprising me. From the way his eyes had widened, he'd surprised himself. The cold eased. "Just a matter of time. Those rays of sunshine will break through."

I shook my head.

Five years. Five whole years. I should've left the second time around. Should've been stronger. By this time, I could've been happy, been healed by now.

I wrapped my arms around his torso, sank into his chest, and breathed deep the menthol scent that clung to his clothes.

Rolling over to snuggle Keith, I cuddled closer to his chest and placed a quick kiss on his neck. I rubbed my hand down his hard, flat stomach. My man must've been hitting the gym harder these days, because his abs were like hard ripples under my fingers.

A throat clearing stilled my movements.

Oh, no.

Oh, no, no, no, no.

I yanked my hand back as if I'd slammed it on a hot iron. Sitting up, I grabbed the nearest pillow and pressed the fluffy shield against my braless chest. I didn't have much in the boob department, but a girl still had pride.

Chris had remained still. In fact, he was propped against his black leather headboard looking as cool and calm as a balmy breeze. His upper body was bare and buff. And good God, his body looked as delicious as it felt. If I hadn't been in the throes of heartbreak, I'd have appreciated the chocolate eye candy.

"Morning, sunshine."

"I thought I was sleeping on the couch?" I smoothed down my unruly tresses.

He shook his head. "After the day you had, you needed a good night's sleep. In a bed."

"Right. And why are *we* in bed together?"

"It's my bed." He scratched the stubble along his jaw, looking slightly amused.

"Ooookay. I'm going now." I rolled out of his humongous bed. Had to be a California king, which he needed for his six-foot-four frame.

The basketball shorts he'd let me borrow nearly slipped down my waist. I pulled the drawstrings and tied a bow.

"What's the plan?" His eyes danced. He looked amused at my fumbling.

"Plan?"

"Yes. What are you going to do? You didn't go home last night, and Keith blew up your phone with calls and texts."

"He did?" I asked, scanning the room. "Where's my phone?"

He reached over to the side table and pulled my phone from the drawer.

I tried to pretend I wasn't mesmerized by his core muscles and broad shoulders.

"I turned it off."

My shoulders bunched. "Kind of high-handed of you."

"He called twenty times before I turned it off. Sent you multiple messages. Messages and calls make noise. You needed to sleep." He stretched out his arm with my phone in his hand.

I walked to his side of the bed and took the phone. "I don't have a plan." I shrugged. "I'll give him back his ring and stay with my parents until I get my own place. Simple as that."

"Do you need me to follow you home? Take your back?"

Warmth crept up my neck and flooded my cheeks. *Keith made you feel warm, too.*

I squared my shoulders and loaded the competent counselor's voice in my arsenal. "Thanks, but no. He has a thing with the Atlanta Press Club this morning. Won't be back until after two. I'll pack my stuff in the meantime."

"So, he gets the house? Why can't he leave?"

"Technically, it's his home." His parents had given him the keys a few years ago when he turned thirty.

Chris nodded. "Your car is outside. Call me when you get settled."

The arrogance and demand in his voice made me roll my eyes. "Okay, Christopher. I'm going to use your bathroom and then go. I'll wash your clothes and return them."

He gave me a small smile. "No need. Looks better on you."

Rushing from the room, I hid the small smile on my face. A flutter of appreciation filled my chest. *Was he flirting with me?* I opened the door to his guest bathroom and leaned against the sink, staring at my reflection.

My eyes, droopy and sad, were tinged with pink. My normally nice stature was saggy, and my rat's nest hair was the cherry on top of my hot mess sundae. There was no way Chris had been flirting with this wreck staring back at me. He barely liked me. Worse, he *pitied* me. And right now, I was pretty damned pitiful. Turning on the faucet, I splashed my face with water and scrubbed.

I wish I could scrub away the stupid. Sliding my tongue against my teeth, I grimaced when I felt a light scuzz. *I need toothpaste.* I rooted around the drawer and found what I was looking for. The toothpaste had been rolled, twisted, which forced me to squeeze until the nearly empty tube pushed paste to the top.

Nearly empty.

That's me. Somehow, I'd allowed a man to twist and roll me into his desires, and when he'd used me up, simply sling me into a drawer, forgotten.

Nearly empty. I had nothing else to give. And I didn't want to give anything away.

Fuck Keith and fuck men. I was done, and if it wasn't battery-operated or my fingers, nothing would penetrate me. I turned on my phone, deleted all texts from Keith, and messaged my girls.

Keith is a lying piece of shit, and I'm leaving him. I need to pack my stuff and go. Meet me in an hour?

My phone rang like I knew it would. Nikki's name flashed across the screen.

"Girl, what happened?"

"I caught Keith banging his office manager." My voice sounded deceptively calm, despite the new surge of anger rolling through me. I opened the bathroom door, grabbed my stuff, and walked out of the condo.

"Oh, baby, I'm so sorry. The kids are with my mom and James is upstairs working. I'm so there. Keep your head up, okay?"

"Okay." I nodded, even though she couldn't see me. "Oh, and Nikki?"

"What's up?

"Bring Louella."

My besties all showed up within an hour. I'd already started packing my clothes. Keith could have the furniture and the bed he'd probably used to screw other women.

The ladies had rallied around me. Kara had even forgone wine for margaritas. I was feeling nice, easy, and loose after my fourth one.

"Okay, ladies." I knocked my fist on the granite island counter-top. "Hear ye, hear ye!"

"We're listening, honey." Raina's voice was soothing, kind. Her eyes were understanding and sad. I didn't need sadness. It was Independence Day, and I was officially an independent woman.

"No sad face, Raina! And don't use that tone you use with your drippity-drop listeners."

"My listeners are called raindrops," Raina gently corrected and shrugged when Kara sent her a shut-up look.

Raina raised a hand in defense. "Or whatever. Drippity-drop works, too."

"That's right! Besides, I'm happy—no!" I snapped my fingers. "I'm static!"

"Ecstatic," Raina cut in again. This time Nikki gave her a look above the rim of her margarita glass. "What?" Raina asked, tone defensive. "Friends don't let friends use poor grammar."

Kara walked up next to me. "Sweetie." She rubbed my shoulders and gave me a hug. "What do you need us to do? I see you have your clothes packed. Raina bought boxes. Nikki's got the tape. We should get you packed and out of here before Keith returns."

I drank the last of the margarita in my glass and wanted more. Shaking the nearly empty pitcher, I looked at Nikki. "We need more margaritas, stat!"

"What time is Keith coming back?" Kara followed me around the kitchen while Nikki and Raina sat at the counter that bled into the living room.

"Sheesh! Relax, Kaaaara!" I bopped her on the nose. "We've got until two-ish."

Kara looked at the watch on her wrist. "That's great. We've got four hours. Plenty of time." She walked away from the kitchen and up the stairs. After a minute, she returned with a piece of paper. "Do you think you can step us through what you want to pack?" She looked around. "Not sure what's yours and what's Keith's."

My head swam. She was talking too much. I needed more margaritas. Why couldn't we drink? Oh, and maybe some edibles. We hadn't done that since college. "I just want my clothes and that painting over there." I pointed to the gift Baba had given me for our housewarming party. Keith hated it. Said it looked too urban. Should've known then he was a bastard.

"You know Baba hates Keith. Said he's too slick. Said I needed a man's man."

"Amen to that!" Nikki lifted her glass.

Kara wrote down the painting. "Anything else? No towels? What about your books?"

I shrugged. "My books are at my parents'. Keith said my bookcase didn't fit in with the décor. Plus, he didn't think it was appropriate to have all my romance novels out for everyone to see."

"Good riddance," Kara growled. "He's an asshole."

"He is," I quickly agreed. "Now, for the important part. Nikki, where's Louella?"

Kara tilted her head. "You can't be serious. Why do you need Nikki's bat?"

"To break shit."

"This isn't a Beyoncé video, Sienna." Kara shook her head. "You can't go around smashing things with bats."

Nikki walked out the door and a few seconds later returned, bat in hand. "Didn't think you were serious, but I brought her just in case."

"Nik!" Kara shouted. "Do not give her the bat."

Nikki sashayed to me, gave me Louella, and winked. "Go crazy, girl."

I did a couple of practice swings, and Kara backed away. "You're an attorney. Hell, Keith's an attorney. He could press charges, and you could lose your license to practice law."

"He won't. Keith's a fraidy-cat when it comes to negative publicity. He'll be a good little boy. Probably try to pay me off for my silence during the election." I stepped away from my worrywart friend. "What should I break first?" I asked no one in particular, scanning the room.

"The television?" Raina suggested. "Guys act like fucking babies over their TVs."

"Good idea!" I moved toward the TV mounted on the wall. Lifting the bat in the air, I swung with all my might. The television cracked and splintered, like a ripple in the water, but permanent. "Yes!" I jumped in the air. "Asshole." I hit the television again. "Piece of shit, mother-effing, I mean, *fucking* scumbag of the earth asshole-fucker!"

Raina leaned and cupped her hand to Nikki's ear. "We need to step up her cussing game."

"We'll have a Samuel L. Jackson fest in a few weeks," Nikki whispered. "He's the master."

"Thinks he's"—*whack!*—"God's gift to women." *Whack,*

Whack! "He's not even that great in bed. I taught him all the tricks to please me." I swung harder and harder. "You think I don't want a guy that fucks me so good I take his ass to Red Lobster? He ain't even worth a Big Mac at McDonald's. More like the value menu."

"Oh, Lord. Now she's quoting Beyoncé lyrics," Kara whispered and waved her hands wildly. "Somebody stop her!"

"With his McPick two for two-buck ass," Nikki yelled, and Raina gave her a high five.

"No." I shook my head. "Sadly, he's not even worth two items from the McDonald's value menu."

"With his not-even-a-dollar-ninety-nine ass!" Raina shouted.

I spun around to continue my work of art while Raina and Nikki encouraged my shenanigans in the background. I took another deep breath and swung. Small pieces of the television screen fell to the floor. "Stupid, lyin' piece of crap . . . liar!"

"Damn right he is," Nikki agreed. "Keith lies more than a possum in the road."

"Guys, you're not helping!" Kara screeched, but I noticed there was a thread of laughter in her voice.

"Fine," Nikki sighed. "I suppose we aren't helpful." She cleared her throat. "Sienna, honey?"

"What!" I was tired of my friends interrupting my anger fest. Especially Kara. She should understand and support me, not be a freaking wet blanket. "Let me guess. You're gonna say this isn't me. That I'm above this and shouldn't stoop to his level. Well, you know what? I'm tired of being the nice one. Nice girls finish last." I marched over to a vase, swung, and destroyed it. My body shook with rage. "And this isn't the second time he's cheated on me. This is the third, well, to my knowledge." I wiggled three fingers in the air. "I didn't tell y'all about the second time because I knew you guys would think I was stupid. Well, I'm not stupid, and I'm going to break every piece of breakable stuff in this house." I pointed the bat at

Nikki. "*And* I'm gonna run against him for city council. I'm going to destroy his stuff and his career!" I lifted the bat in the air as if wielding a sword on the battlefield.

"Oh, shit!" Raina whispered. Kara looked at me with wide eyes and slowly walked back to the couch.

Nikki shook her head. "Nice speech, but I was just gonna tell you to put your hips into it. You don't want to throw out your back. Shoot, we aren't in our twenties anymore." Nikki nodded to the TV. "Please, continue."

And I did.

APRIL

CHAPTER 9
Judgment Day—Raina

The prison sentence was over. I slid on my stunner shades, hopped into my car, and hightailed it to my morning meeting at the radio station. I was so damn ready to work. Scratch that, I was so damn ready to make *money*. I'd written my book proposal, and in a few weeks, I expected to hear back from the publishers I'd pitched.

But writing proposals and pitching nonexistent books didn't pay the bills. So, as much as I'd enjoyed being creative, being broke wasn't cute. Sure, Cam and I had a great time since my schedule was much more normal. We hung out with friends and family, and frequented festivals in Atlanta, but I was living on a stipend and at the mercy of my boyfriend.

I swiped my parking deck pass and released a breath when the bar lifted. After I did a happy dance in my seat, I tried, but failed, to park in my reserved space.

What in the hell?

If looks could kill, the blue Nissan Sentra, owned by Jamie's just-got-out-of-college ass, would explode. *She must be feeling herself.*

During my forced semi retirement, I listened in on a few of her shows, and they were solid. She was genuine, and gave great advice. I was proud of her, but I still wanted my damn space back. No worries, I'd kindly let her know to move once things were back to normal. Until then, I had to park in the back of the deck. Way, way back—absent light and people and heat. After I activated the alarm, I rubbed my hands together for warmth and from excitement as I thought through how I would spend my next check.

Don't be stupid, Raina. Save for the first few months, then you can get those Louboutin sandals this summer.

Plan in place, I strolled into the lobby of the building.

"Hey, Raina!" the security guy greeted me.

"Hey, Greg. How's it going?" I pointed to his polyester pants. "How are your knees?"

"Oh, I can't complain." He patted his leg. "Got my replacement coming up soon."

"I hope that knee replacement doesn't make you lose your weatherman power," I teased, as he often predicted rain when his knees ached.

"Ha-ha. We'll see."

"All right, Greg. Talk to you later. Gotta go grovel to the big bosses!" I made a sad face that I knew would bring a smile to his face.

"You'll be fine. You've been missed."

I rushed to the elevator, my skirt swishing around my ankles. Once the doors slid open to the office, I strode to the front desk. "Hey, Sheila!"

A grin spilled across the receptionist's chestnut-brown face. "Hey, lady! It's been so boring without you around. Glad you're back."

"Girl, I'm happy to be back! A sista has bills to pay."

"Right!" Sheila laughed and then leaned over to grab the phone. She cleared her throat and transitioned from homegirl to professional. "Mr. Rossi, Raina just arrived."

My heart petered at the name. I knew I'd be meeting with

Rhonda and Franklin, the pain-in-the-ass GM, but I didn't realize the station owner would make an appearance.

Sheila gave me a smile and wink. "I'll send her back." She replaced the phone on the cradle. "Go on back to conference room F."

Nodding, I concentrated on walking to my destination and breathing. The breathing part was difficult. It felt like someone had pricked a small hole in my lungs and slowly let the air seep out, giving way to quick, panicked breaths. Rounding the corner, I finally arrived. The pristine glass doors gave me a glimpse of my sentencers. Seated on the same side of a rectangular table were Rhonda, Franklin, and Tony Rossi, the owner.

Pushing open the door, I walked into the room and put on my warrior face. "Hello, everyone." I sat on the opposite side of the table. Bottles of water and cups as well as bags of my favorite green tea were placed in the middle of the table.

Has to be a good sign, right?

Hands shaking, I grabbed the hot water decanter, poured the liquid into the plastic cup, and then settled into my seat.

"Good evening, Ms. Williams," Tony greeted me. Tony's slicked-back hair brushed the collar of his gray sharkskin suit. A small round emblem pinned to his tie matched his glinting pinkie ring. All he needed was a cigar and two broad-shouldered guards to complete his made-man persona. But instead of hardened soldiers, he had soft civilians.

Franklin, the GM, had on his usual uniform—a blue button-up shirt with a lanyard that held his employee ID. He looked like an asshole assistant manager at Kmart. Franklin, who never liked me, cleared his throat and simply said, "Raina."

Rhonda fidgeted with the antique-looking bracelet on her wrist. Her face spasmed between drug-induced happy and drug-raid nervous.

I dunked my green tea bag into the water.

"Let's get right to it, shall we?" Tony smoothed his tie. "While we appreciate your hard work, we," he gestured to Rhonda and Franklin, "feel it's best that you part ways with the station. You have to understand that you put us all in a tight spot when you verbally attacked a loyal listener."

My cheeks blazed. "He cheated on his wife and gave her an STD."

"It's not for us to judge." Franklin's voice was hard. "You had a job to do, and you screwed the pooch, girlie."

"Raina," I replied back, my voice tight.

"Huh?" He twitched his head like a cocker spaniel.

"Not 'girlie,' Raina. And this *girl*, as you love to call me, brought you thousands of listeners, major sponsorship deals, and an offer for national syndication. Now you want to drop me because I told an asshole the truth?"

"The decision has been made, Ms. Williams." Tony's squinty brown eyes held no remorse.

I squeezed the cup in my hand so hard the lid popped. They made me drive twenty miles to get fired? Hell, they could've called or sent an email. And fucking Rhonda could've given me the heads-up. I shouldn't be surprised that her by-the-book ass hadn't bothered to call.

I threw a poisonous look at my ex-producer and took a deep breath to control the angry pulse thundering in my ears.

"We aren't leaving you empty-handed." Rhonda finally spoke up. She smoothed the sleeves on her wrist. "If you sign a confidentiality agreement, basically that you'll not post anything negative about the station or the nature of your resignation—"

"Resignation!" I tilted my head back and laughed. It was hollow, hurt. Damn, but I hated to depend on people. I focused on my hands gripped around the cup, willing myself to keep it together. I would not cry. Not in front of Tony, who viewed me as merely a line item to cross off his to-do list. Or Franklin, who had never believed in me since day one. I used to take great pleasure during our Monday morning meetings when they announced the growing stats from my show. And I damn sure would not cry in front of Rhonda, who barely looked me in the eyes. She knew this was bullshit.

Rhonda slid the manila folder in front of me. I opened the packet and scanned the documents. Blah, blah, blah. Can't discuss my forced retirement, can't sue, no negative posts on social or other channels and . . . My eyes stopped and focused. They didn't want me to discuss my experience as a host on the show for four years. Damn, I couldn't sign this. My entire book was based off the bullshit stories from my crazy listeners.

After I reshuffled the papers back in order, I tapped the paper stack against the oak table. "I won't be able to sign this."

Rhonda bit her lip. "You do understand that this is the only way you can get your severance? We're offering a month's pay."

The hell you say! I slid the pages back to Rhonda. "First of all, I've been working here for ten years, and you're offering me pay for one month? I mean, do you think I'm that stupid?"

Franklin rolled his eyes and mumbled, "Yes."

"Oh, go fuck yourself, Frankie."

"Classy, Raina." Franklin folded his arms across his chest. "Keep it up and you won't get a red penny from us."

"Oh, you'll be giving me lots and lots of pennies. You see," I cleared my throat, "what you should've done is had me sign an NDA when I started, but you were green, just like me, and you didn't think I'd be as popular as I am."

An angry red flush spread from Franklin's neck to his face. Tony looked mildly intrigued and gave me a look a panther would give a mouse.

"Since I've been working here for ten years, brought in major sponsors—you're welcome by the way"—I gave them all a gracious Ms. America smile—"I deserve far more than a red penny. I think I deserve one year, just a tenth of the time I've invested in this station."

Franklin snorted. "You expect us to pay you for a year? You're out of your mind."

"Let me make this clear. Jamie's good. In a few years, she'll be great. But she isn't there yet. My listeners are loyal, and they will boycott your ass. So, if you want me to keep my trap shut about the nature of my . . ." I turned to Rhonda. "What did you call it? Resignation, right? Yes, so if you want me to keep my silence, and don't want me to reach out to the local news, blogs, hell, hire a skywriter that you guys pushed me out because I stood up for womankind, then . . ." I shrugged. "Welp, let's just say things will get sticky for you."

"Sticky?" Rhonda asked.

I folded my arms and leaned back in my seat. "Gorilla Glue sticky."

Tony, who'd been silent during my exchange with his minions, tapped his long, manicured nails on the table. "You want us to pay you based on what? A handshake? I don't think so."

"I'll sign the confidentiality agreement, modified, of course. I'll agree to refrain from posting negative comments on social media and giving negative interviews. No-go on discussing my experience on the show. As a matter of fact," I reached for the papers in front of Rhonda, "I'll just review this with my lawyer"—*i.e. Sienna.*

Tony nodded. "Review the contract, send your changes, and we'll go from there."

"You can't be serious!" Franklin jumped from his seat.

"She's right." Tony nodded to me. "The former owner should've had her sign the NDA. I'm not saying I agree to your terms, Ms. Williams, but I'll review your changes with *my* attorneys."

I stood and grabbed the entire tray of green tea bags, because I'm *that* damn petty. "Gentleman, lady." I nodded to Tony and Rhonda.

"Rumpelstiltskin." I winked at Franklin. "Didn't think I

would figure out your real name, did ya?" I said to the troll of a man. "Y'all have a good day. Tell Jamie I wish her good luck."

I pasted on a smile, gave them a jaunty wave, and twirled on the balls of my feet. My smile didn't waver, not when I told Sheila that I would no longer work for the station, nor when I said my final goodbye to Greg. Only when I closed the door to my car did I scream.

"Fuck!" I slammed my palm against the steering wheel. I could only pray they'd give me a year's severance and that I snagged a book contract before the severance ran out. After my hissy fit, I smoothed back my dreads, took a calming breath, and turned the key in the ignition.

"So?" I paced the floor of Sienna's living room. Her one-bedroom apartment didn't give me much space to pace. I bent over and grabbed the vodka tonic Sienna had offered me when I arrived and downed half of it.

Sienna fiddled with the pen cap while she reviewed the NDA. Her legs were crossed, and the heels of her shoes tapped on the bottom of her chaise lounge sofa.

"I'm glad you didn't sign this." She flipped to the next page and scribbled something lawyer-y on it. She patted the open seat beside her without looking up. "Sit."

I slumped into the seat, hands over my face. "Sock it to me."

She lowered the NDA and pried my fingers from my face. "You have to understand that they ultimately want to protect their rep, their culture, which is fine. But the nondisparagement clause in this NDA really ties you up. I mean, you cannot write your book if you sign this. See here." She pointed to a paragraph and read it out loud. "'You shall not at any time, directly or indirectly, disparage the Company, including making or publishing any statement, written, oral, electronic, or digital, truthful or otherwise, which may adversely affect the business, public image, reputation, or goodwill of the company.'"

"Okay," I nodded. "So what do I do?"

"Don't sign it." She shrugged as if her answer was simple. "You don't work there anymore."

"But I want the money. I *need* the money."

"Okay then," Sienna massaged her temples. "Then we'll modify the language. I can ask them to reword, make it clear that you won't speak poorly of the station but you will discuss content related to the callers. So nothing that would impact the station's rep." She sighed. "It's gonna be tough because it could be argued that speaking of the listeners' experiences violates the agreement. They really need to remove the nondisparagement clause. This isn't my area of expertise, Keith would've been good at this, but—"

"We hate Keith."

"We sure do." She gave me a firm nod while the corner of her lips turned into a funny frowny face. "I have a friend, Lorraine, from law school who I can ask. Another thing that's going to be difficult is the time limit. They're asking for four years."

"That's insane."

Sienna bobbed her head. "I can probably knock it down to a year. Can you work with that?"

"Yeah, I think so. It takes about a year or more to publish."

"I hate to do that, but I think it's the only way we can get you a full year's severance. But we may need to get creative."

"Creative?"

"Call their bluff. You haven't signed an agreement. Outside of money, you have nothing else to lose. They do. They just fired a popular radio host who stuck to her morals. The press would eat this up. Not to mention social media. This could go viral. You've got all the power here, Raina." Sienna squeezed my hand. "Don't let a few bucks scare you away from standing up for what's right. I'll help you, too, if you need the money."

"No." I shook my head. "You've helped enough." I nodded down at the legal bullshit the station gave me.

"All right." She gave me a small smile. "I'll call up Lorraine, get her feedback. You sit tight."

A few days later, Sienna met me at the parking lot of the station.

"You ready?" She nudged my shoulder with hers.

"Hell no." I stuffed my keys into my purse and pulled the strap over my shoulder.

"It's fine." Sienna wore a cocksure smile. I hadn't seen her like this before—her eyes sparking, a Mona Lisa smile on her face. "We're just going to have a conversation. We'll say a few legal terms, empty laughs, a few well-timed *hahs*, and then we'll come to an agreement."

"But what if they decide to give me nothing?" I asked as we walked toward the front of the building. I stopped in front of the revolving doors. I hadn't been through the front since my interview.

"Hey." Sienna put a hand on my shoulder. "I know you haven't seen me in action, but I'm pretty good at what I do."

"But you said this wasn't your area of law and that—"

"I've done the research. I won't let you down," she said, her voice slow and steady. "Trust me."

"I do." I had no choice. I couldn't afford a contracts attorney. Sienna was doing this for free.

She turned me toward the revolving door and pushed me in. I shuffled to keep up as the doors turned. We walked into the station, conference room F again. I was starting to associate the letter with "Fired" and "Failure" and "Fuck!"

"Sienna Njeri," she purred and offered her hand to everyone seated at the table. Everyone introduced themselves. I stood near the door, not sure what to do.

"Coffee? Tea?" Mr. Rossi offered my friend.

I eyed the green tea packets. Depending on how the meeting went, I might swipe some more.

"No thank you." Sienna smiled and took a seat. She turned and looked back at me, her winning smile still in place. Only I could see her eyes and the message she sent: *Sit your scary ass down.*

I scurried to the seat next to her.

Rhonda wasn't present, but Franklin sat at the end of the table. Flanking the station owner were two men, one in a blue suit, the other in a red and white plaid shirt with khakis. Franklin had added a brown blazer to his usual Kmart attire. *Classy.* I mentally rolled my eyes.

Something squeezed my leg, and I jumped. Sienna gave me a quick smile. Fire lit her eyes—so much her skin glowed.

She slid the manila folder that contained the legal documents. "Gentlemen, I'll get right to it. My client, Ms. Williams, will not be able to sign this document as it stands." Her voice was confident, light, not at all combative, but firm. "I do hope we can come to an agreement that is mutually beneficial."

"Is this a particular part of the agreement that concerns Ms. Williams?" Mr. Khaki Pants addressed my friend.

"Many parts." She shook her head. "But the nondisparagement clause has to go."

Khaki Pants shook his head. "It's imperative to keep this, and it's a reasonable request." He flicked his brown eyes toward me, then back at Sienna. "The language was added to ensure your client doesn't impugn the reputation of the station."

"And while I understand, Mr. Anders, my client should have the opportunity to speak about her experience and the advice she has given to her fan base. This"—she pointed to the papers—"would essentially bind her to silence. For *four years.* How, then, will she be able to take on another job? This precludes her from leveraging her own experiences elsewhere."

She sighed and leaned back into the chair. "There is no way around this. It simply has to be struck or at least modified."

"Hmm. I don't think—"

"Mr. Anders." Sienna put up a hand. "I hate to interrupt, but I do want to cut to the chase. Ms. Williams doesn't have to sign this NDA. Nothing is stopping Ms. Williams from going online or to the media to discuss how the station treated her unfairly."

"Now that's subjective, Ms. Njeri." The Anders dude interrupted. "Your client verbally attacked a listener."

"She *defended* a woman and her family. She stood up for what she believes in—morals, fidelity, family." She ticked off the points with her fingers. "The press and social media would eat this up."

"If your client wants her severance, she'll need to sign it." Anders leaned back in his chair, hands folded across his potbelly.

"She'll make up that money from press appearances. *National* press." Sienna shrugged. "She does not need your money."

Yes, the hell I do!

I shut my mouth. Sienna was on a roll, and from Mr. Rossi's reddened cheeks and stuttering Stan, the lawyer to his left, the tides were changing.

"So, this is what we can agree to." Sienna pressed her hands against the table. "My client will not speak ill of the station. She will, however, discuss her experience with listeners. She will not refer to names or time periods. She will not mention anyone at the station by name. She will agree to a time limit of one year, not four. One year in exchange for one year's pay. That's fair." Siena sliced a hand in the air. "Either make the changes or we walk." She leaned in and tossed them a tight smile. "And we talk."

Damn. My girl was in her element. Warmth filled my stomach as I watched my sister, my mastermind, shine in her craft. She was unicorns and rainbows, glitter and star fire. A law goddess, a defender of the defenseless. You get the point. She's my #WCW.

Sienna stood and smoothed down her bone-colored pencil skirt. "We'll give you a few minutes to discuss. Ms. Williams and I will sit in the lobby for . . ." She looked down at her gold watch. "I can spare thirty minutes. If you need more time, let us know. We'll get back to you at our earliest convenience."

She waved me toward the door. "Gentlemen," she tossed over her shoulder, and then we strode out the door.

"Damn, girl" I whispered to her. "You did that."

"I know." She gave me her open palm, and I gave her the high five she deserved.

Thirty-five minutes later we had our answer. They would change the contract, I could write my book, and I wouldn't be broke as hell. Well, at least for the next year.

"Congratulations." Cam clinked his wine glass against mine. With his other hand, he gave me a fist bump. "You're glowing, baby."

His compliment stoked the energy and confidence and fire that burned inside me. "Thanks, Cam." He was right, I was glowing, and I had great reasons for the change.

Tony and his team of merry lawyers had agreed to my demands. The severance gave me time to figure out my next move. And right after my severance victory, I was offered a contract to write my book, tentatively titled *Rainstorm.* Thankfully, my brilliant agent worked out the NDA details, and the book wouldn't be out for a year and some change. Which brought me to dinner by candlelight with my fine-ass man in a three-piece suit, seated in front of me.

"So now that you'll be a world-famous author, what's your next move?"

"Next move?" I twisted one of the tendrils that framed my face. "I dunno. I'm just happy I have money in the bank and can breathe easy on this mortgage."

Cam grabbed my hand, intertwining his pecan-sandy skin with my dark chocolate. I smiled at the contrast and looked at him. My breath nearly caught at the love I saw in his eyes.

"You know I'll always take care of you."

That's what my daddy used to say, too. "I know, Cam. I just don't want to have to depend on you. This relationship has to be equal, otherwise—"

"Otherwise, you think I'll run away in the middle of the night like your coward father."

I took a deep gulp from my wine glass. "Trust me, it wasn't the middle of the night. The sun was shining, an otherwise ordinary day."

"That's beside the point, Raina. What I'm trying to tell you is that I've got you. Soon, *very soon*, you'll see."

I squeezed his hand, leaned over, and kissed it. "I know you love me, baby, and I love you. You don't have to prove anything to me."

"Maybe I want to." He gave me a cocky grin that sent a flood of heat to my lady parts.

A stick-thin man sidled up to our table, soprano sax in hand. With a dramatic flair, he inserted the instrument into his mouth and softly played smooth jazz in the background.

"What's all this, Cam?" I waved at the musician.

Cam laughed, but it was forced, nervous. He licked his lips. "Baby, you know I love you, right?"

My attention darted around the restaurant. Thanks to Kenny G going ham on the sax, we were snagging the attention of other dinner guests.

"Cameron?" My pitch went Minnie Mouse high. "What are you doing?"

Cam took a deep breath, stood, and walked to my side of the table.

"What's going on?" I whispered, now anxious.

He dropped to his knees in front of me. "Raina, I love you. You're my first thought when I wake up in the morning and my last before I sleep. I knew you were the one for me when I first met you, and for the past six years I've been waiting for you. I know I've asked you a few times before, and I know now you were just waiting for the right time, for everything to come together."

Was I? No, I'm pretty certain I told him I wasn't ready for marriage anytime soon.

"Raina, baby." He reached inside his jacket. A ten-pound boulder landed in my stomach. He pulled out a ring box.

Fuckity fuck fuck fuck!

"Will you do me the incredible honor of being my wife?" Warmth filled his eyes.

Thunderclaps rang in my ears—no, it was my heartbeat. This man, this wonderful man, had asked me to marry him. *For the fourth time.* But as awkward seconds passed, the warmth in his eyes grew dim, cold.

"Oh, no," I heard someone whisper.

"Say yes!" someone else hissed.

How could he do this to me? To us? I took a deep breath, ignoring the crowd that stared at the train wreck, offering no sympathy or help, just undisguised pleasure at witnessing our demise. "Cam, baby, I—"

He stood, dropped the hand he'd so lovingly caressed a second ago. The absence was so startling, I clenched my hand for heat.

"Listen, baby." I stood. "I'm not . . ." I leaned closer to whisper, "I'm not ready yet. Everything is so topsy-turvy right now."

Kenny G was hitting a high note in the background. I threw him a venomous look and gave him the cut signal. He finally got a clue, took a freaking bow, of all things, and strode away.

Cam threw a hundred-dollar bill and a few twenties on the table. He rushed out of the restaurant. Trailing behind him, I darted through a maze of tables and scrutiny.

Once we stepped outside, Cam didn't have a choice but to slow down at the valet stand. He couldn't very well leave without his car. He cut the line and slid the short and stocky valet his ticket and a twenty-dollar bill. "Make it quick and I'll give you another twenty."

A tall Asian man stepped toward Cam. "Sir, I was next in line." Despite the calmness in his voice, his tensed shoulders and twisted lips showed his irritation.

"See that woman beside you?" He pointed to me. "I asked her to marry me. She said no. I need to get the hell out of here."

The blond companion beside the Asian man gasped and grasped the slender man by his bicep. "I'm so sorry, honey. Of course you can cut in front of us." She swung her gaze in my direction and gave me a what-the-hell look.

Seriously, this woman was judging me? Cam could be a contract killer for all she knew.

I walked the short distance to stand beside my so-called *jilted* lover. "Really?" I hissed under my breath. "You're gonna embarrass me in front of strangers?"

"You mean like you embarrassed me in front of everyone in the restaurant?"

Cam's silver Audi swerved into the turnaround. "Let's go," he said without looking at me and strode to his car.

Good. He's not so angry that he'd leave me stranded. I dashed to the car. The blond woman stared at me, this time shaking her head. I shot the nosy woman a nasty look. Granted, she probably didn't see me because the windows were tinted, but it gave me an odd sense of satisfaction.

That woman didn't know my story. She didn't understand that it was just a matter of time until a guy showed his true colors. Marriage didn't mean happily-ever-after. Exhibit A: Kara and Darren. The fool was dragging my friend through the wringer with his therapy sessions that didn't seem to work. He was quiet before, but I'd noticed after an awkward triple date with Nikki and James last week that he'd barely spoken to anyone. Kara had dropped at least fifteen pounds, maybe more. So, no, marriage did not equal happily-ever-after, fuck you very much.

Cam blasted the music, a silent message to shut the hell up and ride. A dull throb had formed behind my eyes. I massaged my forehead as I thought through what got me to this point.

I'd never promised him anything, and I'd been up front with my stance on marriage. *Damn, Cam.* The man always wanted me to give more than I was capable of, wanted to strip me bare until I was raw and vulnerable. Been there, done that, and at the tender age of eleven years old, I promised myself to never let a man hurt me again. My sperm donor of a father taught me that hard lesson.

After a short drive, Cam parked his Audi in our garage, yanked out his key fob, and jumped out of the car.

Scrambling to grab my purse and phone, I rushed behind him. Despite the drama from tonight, I didn't want to lose him. Cam was rarely in a bad mood, and when he was, I could usually tease him out of it. *Not this time.* I didn't have a plan, or the time to formulate one.

"Cam!" I shouted as he strode through the breezeway connecting the garage and house. I nearly tripped on my shoes to keep up. Kicking off the death-trap heels, I followed him into the house. "Dammit, slow down!"

Thankfully, he stopped to deactivate the alarm. He swung around to face me. "What, Raina?"

"We need to talk."

"You're not going to talk your way out of this."

"I don't want to talk my way out. I want to fix this."

"Fine." He folded his arms across his chest. "I want to get married. You don't. What else is there?"

Patience, Raina. "My view on marriage hasn't changed since you asked me a few months ago. I'm not sure why you asked me in public, of all places."

"Few months?" He gave me an ugly look that curled my stomach. "I asked you a year and a half ago."

I racked my brain. When he'd asked, it had been a few days before Thanksgiving . . . the year before. *Damn.* "Okay, so it's been a while, but we haven't had a formal discussion about it since then."

"Not from my lack of trying. My God, woman, what do you think we've been doing this whole time? We bought a fucking house together with how many bedrooms?"

"F-four." I cleared my throat. "Four bedrooms."

"We're using one bedroom. What did you think we would have three extra bedrooms for?"

I shrugged. "An office for me—"

"Your attic is the office. Still have three rooms left."

"You've always wanted an exercise room, and then your man cave. Th-that's two rooms. The third is for guests."

He shook his head and laughed, but it wasn't a warm, fun Cam-laugh. It was alien, scary, hard. I didn't know this man in front of me.

He wagged his finger at me, pacing the floor. "You know, my friends said you were playing me. That you were flighty as hell. Told me to get out while I can. But what did my dumb ass do? Buy a damn house with you."

"That's not dumb, Cam. Like you said, we're investing in our future."

"We don't have a future!" He waved his arm about the room. "We can never make this house a home because you're too damn scared that you'll be hurt again. So, your dad left you. You aren't the only child that grew up fatherless. Stop using that shit as an excuse and fucking grow up."

I snapped my head back. "Grow up, huh? So, what, we can be married for five to seven years and then start hating each other? Oh, and have kids and use them as leverage or hurt them in the process? You see what's going on with Kara and Nikki. Do their marriages seem like fun and fucking rainbows?"

"Married or not, you can't avoid conflict. I don't know why I have to tell a radio therapist this shit. Dig deep and give yourself the advice you like to dish out."

"Fine. I'd tell me to find a man who isn't stuck on the idea of marriage because it's a piece of fucking paper. An *expensive* piece of paper. God! Why can't you just be happy with what we have?"

"Because I love you. I want to marry you. And if, God forbid, something happens to me, I want to make sure you're taken care of. Because I want to have kids and raise a family with you." He was yelling by the end, a vein throbbing in his neck. Like a balloon losing its helium, his body folded and then slumped against a wall.

"Cam . . ." I reached for his face. He slapped my hands away, and pushed off the wall.

"I can't—I can't do this. We can't do this."

Fear quadrupled my heartbeat. This was it. I knew the day would come, but not like this.

"You've gotta go."

"W-what?" Water drowned my lungs, swooshed through my chest, and clogged my throat.

"You need to leave. Be gone by the time I return from my trip. Three days is plenty of time."

The dull headache from earlier had turned into a full-on migraine. A tingle shot through my fingers and gave way to numbness. "But I helped you with the down payment and the mortgage for months."

"I'll give you the money back. I've been setting aside the money. Silly me, I thought we could use that for our wedding."

I reached for him again, this time grabbing his hand. "Don't do this," I whispered, unable to speak loudly. My voice was fragile, my throat tender.

"I'm not doing anything. It's you." With a firm grip, he pushed away my hands.

My knees buckled until my ass hit the floor. I scooted against the couch, tucked my legs in, and rocked. He knelt beside me. We stared at each other, his eyes wet but resolved. He wasn't changing his mind. This was it. I knew it.

They all leave.

"Three days," he repeated. His voice was not unkind but matter-of-fact. He stood and left the room. The stairs creaked under his weight.

A tear escaped. Tears were okay if no one saw them. I licked my lips, tasting the salt, remembering the last time I'd tasted them.

Twenty-two years ago.

Daddy was leaving, this time for good. Ma followed him, wringing her hands and pleading with him to stay. "What about us?" she'd asked him for the umpteenth time.

"I told you, Vanessa. It's over." The finality of his tone seemed to push Ma over the edge. Slumping on the floor, she gripped her thin cotton dress and wailed. Daddy looked over her, scanned the house, and then walked out the door. I jumped from my hiding place and rushed outside. Daddy loved me. He wouldn't leave me with Ma. She was too timid, too weak, always begging. Daddy said he and I were two of a kind. I was his special girl.

"Daddy!" I yanked the door and tackled him from behind, wrapping my arms around his waist.

Suitcase in hand, he continued to walk, the tips of my Keds dragging along the pavement. "Stop it, Rae."

He never called me just Rae. I was always his Rae of sunshine. The good-luck charm he hugged when he returned from his casino trips and needed a spot of luck.

"C'mon, baby. Stop this." He finally reached his Caddy. Unwrapping my arms from around him, he hustled to the trunk and threw in his suitcase.

I folded my arms across my chest. Despite the beautiful sunny day, goose bumps formed along my arms. I tilted my head back, staring at the sun, waiting for him to stop me. Daddy always joked that I'd go blind. Waves of heat attacked my vision, forcing me to blink away the moisture that had formed.

He sighed, snagging my attention and giving me much-needed relief from the sun. He leaned against the car and opened his arms. I ran into them, breathing his scent in deeply. "I knew you wouldn't leave me, Daddy," I whispered fiercely against his stomach.

He pushed me back. A grin broke across his handsome face. "Guess what?"

"What?" I smiled back, wiping away the tears that had trickled down my cheeks.

"You're gonna have a little brother." He tapped my nose. "Like you've been asking for every Christmas."

"A little brother?" I clapped my hands together. I didn't understand why Ma was so upset.

"Ma never said—"

"It's not with your mama." The smile dropped from his face. He shifted his weight and knocked his knuckles against the roof of the car. "I . . . I've got a new woman. Her name is Denise. You'll like her. She's a real sweet woman."

I folded my arms again. "O-okay. Is my little brother going to live with us?"

"No, baby. But you can come visit. Real soon. We just gotta get Junior's room together." Daddy's voice was weird. The same weird that made my stomach feel funny when he smelled like rubbing alcohol and yelled at Ma to give him more money. Then he'd calm down, get on his knees and beg and plead until she gave in. After that, we wouldn't see him for a few weeks.

What about us? Ma's voice echoed in my mind. I took a step back and shook my head. "You hurt Ma. Y-you're leaving us."

Daddy didn't answer. Just walked to the driver's side of the car. The window on the passenger's side was rolled down. I stared at him. We stared at each other until he looked away.

The engine vrooming, his car jerked forward and then sped from the curb. I returned to the house, slumped on the floor next to Ma. She was hiccupping now, no more tears, but her lower lip trembled. Twin black mascara lines streaked her cheeks. Cedar and cinnamon and allspice filled my senses. Ma's prized potpourri basket, something she'd made herself, was toppled on the floor.

Eyes focused on the ground, I plucked at the dark and hardened stain on the sticky, brown carpet.

The sound of my nails scrapping against the hardwood floors brought me to the present. Cinnamon and spices lingered in my memories, in the air.

Fighting for breath, I inhaled and forced myself to breathe. I'd survived Victor Williams, and I'd survive Cameron Jefferies.

Ma lived a few miles outside of Atlanta, so I'd stay with her for now. She wouldn't mind. She hated being alone. With a plan, I continued to rock myself. Exhausted from the day, I leaned against the sofa and closed my eyes.

A creak woke me from my slumber. I took in my surroundings, grabbing the pillow on the bed.

Cam.

He must've carried me to our room. Wishful thoughts and

wistful memories sped through my mind. I conjured up my father's face, the last look he gave me before he sped his blue Caddy out of my life. My father's face transformed into Cameron's, the memory still fresh when he knelt in front of me, looked me in the eyes, and told me to leave my home. Squeezing my eyes shut, I turned off my heart and gave up the ghost of our relationship.

CHAPTER 10
Lost Ones—Kara

Heavy rain crashed against the window. Streaks of lightning split like rivers, igniting the sky. I loved a good downpour with wind, thunderbolts, and dark clouds. You couldn't ignore a storm; you either sped up to get the hell out of the way or slowed down because you couldn't go anywhere.

When I woke up in the morning, I spotted the gray clouds rolling across the sky. I knew I had to hurry so I could get the hell out of the way. Today was a special day, an anniversary. The day Mama passed away.

Passed.

It sounds as if she passed a test or passed a car on the road. Pass sounded like a choice, but the cancer didn't give her much of one. Cancer robbed her of her future, yanked away her energy, and took her life. Cancer was a *taker*.

Today, like the year before, I put flowers on her grave. When I got to the cemetery, I'd spotted Father Frank hovering over Mama's grave. I dare say she was his favorite parishioner. Mama had always volunteered for community outreach, dragging Tracey and me, and occasionally Daddy, along.

The flat cemetery gave me nowhere to hide.

"Kara Jones." Father Frank had a light tilt in his voice, giving away his Irish upbringing, despite his being in the States since I was a little girl. He waited patiently by the grave, knowing my destination.

"Father Frank." I sighed heavily.

"I miss seeing you at Mass. I've seen Tracey fairly regularly, even your father."

"I've been busy studying." I looked him dead in the eyes, lying to his face.

Despite the outright lie, Father Frank kept up his affable expression. "Ah, the wine test. One of Jesus's finest miracles, I say." He smiled, stretching his ruddy cheeks.

"Yes, because in a matter of seconds, Jesus was able to pick the grapes, crush and ferment, and then allow it to age. Sounds feasible."

He placed his hand, a hand I once found comforting, on my shoulder. "But now you must put them all away: anger, wrath, malice, slander, and obscene talk from your mouth." He quoted the Bible.

"Ask and it will be given to you; seek and you will find; knock and the door will be opened to you," I quickly fired back, shrugging away his embrace. "I asked, begged, pleaded for Mama to get well. Didn't happen. I sought God, but couldn't find Him. I knocked—no I *banged* on the door!" I yelled, breathing heavily. "No answer."

"He did answer, Kara, but it wasn't what you wanted to hear. The cancer was aggressive. By the time Carla found out, it was too late."

"Right. He can turn water into wine but He can't remove the cancer from my mother?"

"Kara—"

"He can't save my marriage! He can't make my husband love me." The blasphemy in my harsh words scraped against my spine, a coldness crawled over my skin. Taking a deep breath, my eyes sought Father Frank's kind brown ones. I softened my tone but not the content. "Save the scriptures, Father Frank. I know God exists, I just don't much care for Him. Now, can you leave me in peace to speak to my mother?"

He took a step back, disappointment etched on his face. "With your dear mother gone, and . . . and Darren, you think you're alone, but you're not. He will show you, if you just open up and listen."

I blew a tired breath. "I don't want to hear it, Father."

"Go in peace, child. I'll continue to pray for you."

Or not. I took a few steps closer to my mother's grave, then lowered myself to the ground. Before my feet were a dozen red roses on the grave. An odd choice, but Daddy was trying to be romantic. Tracey, my sister, hadn't been by yet, but I knew she'd give Mama purple hyacinths. I lowered my white lilies in front of the headstone. If Darren were here, he'd given her sweet peas, because Mama used to call me her sweet pea. I talked to Mama and then returned home, bogged down by thoughts of her and Darren.

I couldn't believe Darren didn't remember Mama's anniversary. Last year, he took off work and held me until I cried myself to sleep. No judgment, just silent strength. Later, he'd driven me to the cemetery where I whispered to the stone slab, updating my mother on the past year, or reminding her of a funny time we'd shared. After I spoke to her, Darren talked to her, too, low and serious, as if he were asking for advice. I never asked him what he said to Mama, and he never shared.

Mama loved Darren. She'd told me once that I was the light in his sky. I don't know if Mama would love him now. On days like this, I wish I could pick up the phone and call her. What advice would she give me? The weeks before she died, she gave me lots of advice.

In bouts of lucidity from the medicine, she'd opened her warm gold eyes. They stood out against her skin, ashen and slick with sickness. Despite her poor health, she'd gift me that famous smile of hers and drop me a pearl of wisdom. "Don't go out in public without clean underwear."

"Yes, Mama." She'd said that since I was a child. I didn't get it then and I didn't now. Who in their right mind would go out in dirty underwear?

"You have a little girl; don't you force her to get a relaxer like I did to you and Tracey. You've gotta teach 'em early to love the hair and the skin they're in."

"All right, Mama. Promise."

In the last few days of her life, she'd gotten deeper, more serious. Her breathing was raspy and light. I had leaned in to listen to her soft, wise words as her life began to wane.

The last story was about her regret. She'd gotten pregnant with me in college. Daddy, a midlevel executive, had met my then coed mama at a friend's birthday party and swept Mama off her feet. He'd been gallant, and after just six months of dating, they were married. Soon after, they had me. Unfortunately, she had to drop out of school and place her dreams of being a teacher on hold. I frowned when she told me that.

But she hadn't. Her face softened. "I've no regrets about having you, sweet pea. I could've done both. But your father . . ." She licked her dry lips. "Your father wanted me to stay home. He didn't see why I needed to teach when he made enough money for the both of us. I listened to him, but I shouldn't have." She squeezed my hand. My heart grew. I never knew the story of why she returned to college at age forty-five, but I respected the hell out of it. Daddy had put up a stink from the time she'd enrolled. But Mama smiled and continued along, doing what she intended to do.

"And you see he came around. He was smiling ear to ear and clapping the loudest at my graduation, one of the happiest days of my life, outside of having you and Tracey. I had to prove to myself I could do it, that I could go after what I wanted."

Mama had gotten a job straight away after college, working in Fulton County, where she proudly served as a teacher for eight years. Until cancer.

"Don't let anyone take away your dreams, sweet pea. Not anyone, you hear?"

"Promise, Mama." That time, my tone wasn't dutiful. I meant it. I'd never forget Mama's earnest expression. Remembering her last days, I blinked away the moisture. That's why I couldn't give up on my dreams. Not for Darren. Not for anyone.

I pressed my forehead against the window, trying and failing to shake off the lingering remnants of the memory.

My thoughts volleyed back to Darren. He still had sessions with the counselor, Dr. Fuckboy, as Raina called him. Not that it was doing Darren any good. The man baked all the comfort food for a twelve-year-old—cookies and pies and Rice Krispies treats. He was obviously going through some things he didn't want to share. In a rare moment, Darren had told me that Dr. Fuckboy had tasked him to write a letter to his grandfather about his feelings.

Maybe I should read the letter?

No, it wasn't right. He needed to process his feelings. But it was so damn hard to go on not knowing what he was thinking or the state of our marriage. And today of all days, I needed my husband.

Just one peek. It won't hurt. I glanced at the oven timer. *Three p.m.* He wouldn't be home for another three hours at least. I had time.

Decision made, I crept down the creaky steps and then clicked on his computer. The black screen turned bright blue, signaling the computer was on. I logged into his email and typed in his predictable password, his name and date of birth. *I'm in.*

I gripped the mouse. This was wrong. A heaviness settled in my stomach, and something poked at my conscience. But it'd been four months. Four long months of blank stares, no kisses, no comfort.

I had to know. Searching for Dr. Fuckboy's name, I found an email. The subject line: *Letter to my grandfather.*

> *Grandfather Jeff:*
>
> *I'm writing this letter because I'm at a crossroads in my life. I understand my parents' death was tough for you. You lost your son, your only child, and on the very same day gained a toddler. I'm sure at the time I was a handful, and I appreciate you and Grandmother taking me in. But sometimes I felt unloved. You wanted me to be seen and not heard. Smacked me when I was a nuisance, and you and Grandmother flew all over the world, without a thought for your grandson.*
>
> *Were you running away from me? I get it. When I look in the mirror and compare myself to Dad's picture, I see that I reminded you of your son. But your choices, your decision that it hurt too much to love me, heavily impacted my life. So much that I don't how to decipher what real love is.*
>
> *When I was ten years old, my babysitter, Shanti, touched me. No, she raped me. I must accept the fact that no matter how much I thought I loved her, she, being in her twenties, had no business engaging in a sexual relationship with a child.*
>
> *But then one day, she left and was replaced by Mrs. Grierson. Not a trace of Shanti. Over the years, I've often wondered if you really knew or if she felt guilty and decided to leave.*
>
> *All I know is that I was distraught. The one person who I thought loved and cared for me abandoned me. Just like my parents.*

Just like you.

And here I am, twenty years later, and I don't know what love is. I don't even know if I love my wife, or if I ever did.

I don't expect you to acknowledge this letter, but I'm told it's a step in the right direction. I need to move on. I need to heal.

Sincerely,
Darren

Like a jagged blade, the words on the page stabbed and twisted in my gut. If I didn't move, it wouldn't hurt, I illogically reasoned with myself. I clutched the edge of the desk, an effort to not feel for the wound and stanch the blood that I was sure poured from my belly.

Struck mute, I stared at the screen, my attention zeroing in on a particular line. *I don't even know if I love my wife, or if I ever did.*

The words stung—no, they burned. Blazed a fiery path through my veins, incinerating my lungs, eviscerating my heart.

Breathe. Think. He's in pain.

I'm in pain.

Mama. Squeezing my eyes shut, I played the make-believe game I'd done as a kid. I was curled in Mama's lap, and her candy-cane sweet scent filled the air. My head rested on her bosom, while her soft and sure hands stroked my hair. "What should I do, Mama?"

"Put yourself in his shoes," Mama whispered.

I knew he had a tenuous relationship with his grandparents. His grandmother had died before we'd met, and Darren rarely spoke to his grandfather. But I never knew about the sexual abuse. My heart hurt for the sad and confused boy that still lived inside him.

Tears slipped down my cheeks, blurring my vision. Everything made sense now. When I first met him, we were inseparable. It was as if he were love-starved. And anytime we'd get into an argument, he would freeze up, as if he expected me to leave.

His face! He never let me touch his face. Could be the abuse from that fucking babysitter, and if I ever got my hands on the woman, I would douse her with gasoline and burn her alive.

Or it could be the abuse from his grandparents.

Physical, mental, and emotional abuse.

Bile filled my throat, pushing and squeezing and demanding to be released. Unable to hold it back, I stumbled into the bathroom and vomited. Pressing down the handle, I mutely watched my breakfast of tea and toast flush down the commode.

How did I not know?

The dull light in the basement bathroom flickered like a D-list horror flick. I caught my reflection in the mirror and stared at the brokenhearted phantom. Looking away, I grabbed a paper towel and wet it under the faucet. After wringing it out, I pressed it against my neck and cheek.

Coldness seeped into my bones, so deep, I shivered.

How do I do this? How can I help? Should I tell him I know?

Eyes bloodshot, hair swooped into a tangled bun, the phantom blinked back at me and gave me no answers.

I mindlessly climbed the steps and drifted back to my window seat.

Staring, rocking, waiting. I sat there for I don't know how long, but then I heard the soft purr of Darren's Camaro. A spark of hope ignited in my core as I imagined Darren dashing through the house, confiding in me about his past.

He opened the door and I held my breath, waiting for this droid that had replaced my husband to disappear.

Straight away, he strode to the fridge, grabbed a few cookies he'd baked, and clomped downstairs to his man cave.

My heart sank so low, it dragged me like a moored anchor. "I can't believe this," my scratchy voice whispered as I blinked away tears.

My attention snapped to the wedding album on the coffee table, and I reached for it. On the front cover, was a picture of us. A young, handsome Darren smiled from ear to ear. I was looking up at him, adoration clear in my eyes.

I don't even know if I love my wife, or if I ever did.

I squeezed my eyes shut, burying the emotions. Maybe he didn't know how he felt, but this was beyond my feelings. Someone violated him as a child, something he'd never addressed until I forced him to go to counseling.

Fresh tears welled in my eyes, and my hand stilled on my husband's face. It was my fault. I did this. Pressure seized my chest, a million pounds pressing down, cracking me open.

It was only fair. I'd cracked him open, too.

And all the good and bad bits of our relationship seeped out.

The way he'd instantly go to the shower after we made love and then fully clothe himself, socks included.

I'd thought it was quirky, but maybe he was hurting or coping?

My attention zeroed in on the wedding picture. Darren's sweet, shy smile when he told me that he hoped our daughter had my eyes. *"You're the love of my life, Kara."*

Am I? Maybe he just wanted to be loved. I squeezed my fist, waiting for the anger to surge. Waiting for the feelings of betrayal. I knew it was selfish, and I could be self-centered at times. My husband had been raped and I didn't know how to help him.

But . . .

But. I would allow myself this moment. Just one moment.

Then I could figure out a way to be good partner. A better friend. And somehow, push aside my feelings and be a great wife, at least until he healed.

The pressure moved on from my chest and settled deeper, somewhere that couldn't be touched.

It was dark clouds and torrential rains. It was stomach-clawing starvation and a dry, unquenchable thirst. It was never-ending cold.

The cold turned to ice and shattered. Not for myself. For my husband. For the men and women who'd been betrayed. For those who struggled to make sense out of a senseless world.

God's handiwork. He let this happen: Death. Death of a dream, death of innocence. Why did he allow this evil?

Why, why, why?

A stampede coming from the basement caught my attention. "You read it."

"What?" I jumped guiltily from the couch, wiping my tears with the back of my hand.

He stalked closer, backing me into a wall. He grabbed my shoulders, his grip squeezing my body like an angry anaconda.

"Why?" he asked, his voice furious.

I shook my head, unable to look him in the eyes. He gripped the underside of my jaw; I had no choice but to focus on his ravaged expression. "Why, Kara?"

"I don't know—"

"Why? Kara!"

"I don't kn—"

"You do know. Why did you snoop? Why didn't you let me figure this shit out?" The volume of his voice increased with each question asked.

"B-because . . ." I drew a deep breath.

"Why. In the hell. Would you do that?" He loosened his grip.

"Because you don't talk to me!" I wrenched away from his body. This time, I escaped. "Do you know what today is?"

His hands cradled his head as he shook it from side to side. "Mama."

He jerked his head, his eyes grew wide. "Shit, Kara, I—"

"I was missing Mama and I . . . I needed her advice and I talked to her. Like really talked to her today and I pretended that she was holding me. I asked her to help me and then it hit me, really hit me, that she wasn't ever gonna answer me. So I looked for my own answers. I knew about the letter and, yes, I violated your trust. I'm sorry but . . . why?" I whispered the question. "Why didn't you tell me?"

I pointed to my chest. "About *her*? About your g-grand-parents?"

Darren stared at me, his eyes bloodshot. He walked to the couch and slumped in his seat. "I thought I was over it. I took a few therapy sessions in college, got it off my chest, and I thought I was cured. But . . ." He clenched and unclenched his hands. "I'm not. The doc got into my head, asked a bunch of questions about my childhood, and the dam that I'd been holding back just broke."

He sighed and leaned back. "Now I have all this shit out in the open, scrambled so much I don't know what is right or wrong, up or down. I'm like Humpty fucking Dumpty, and I can't find the pieces to glue my shit back together."

That made sense. He was a droid. He didn't talk, didn't touch me. Maybe because everything had risen to the surface.

"Is he helping?"

"Is who helping?"

"Dr. Fuc—I mean Dr. Harrison. Is he helping you?"

He shrugged. "I don't know. I don't feel good. I'm trying to keep myself tight at work, but by the time I get home, I feel like I'm going to burst. I'm confused about a lot of things, and that letter was just a way to figure them out."

"Do you love me? Have you ever loved me?"

Shoulders slouched and shaking with emotion, he whispered, "I don't know. I honestly don't know."

"How can you not know?" I sighed. "I get that you're confused, but I love you so, so much, and it hurts that you don't feel the same way."

"I. Don't. Know. I honestly don't know." His voice broke.

Tears slipped down his face. He cradled his head, covering his face.

I lowered myself on my knees to kneel before him. I wanted to touch his face, but I knew he'd flinch.

"What can I do to help? Tell me what to do, and I'll do it."

"I just need some time." His voice was muffled under his hands.

"By yourself?" The sound of my voice was small and injured. "Or . . . or with me?"

The falling rain filled the silence. I don't know how much time passed, but it seemed like forever.

"Without you," he finally answered. His red eyes took me in. "Just for a little while."

I shook my head and stood. I cleared my throat, which was thick with emotion.

He blinked rapidly. "I'm so sorry, Kara. I wish I could make myself feel better. I wish I were normal."

"You just need to let yourself heal and figure out what you want. And I love you enough to let you go."

CHAPTER 11
Wine and Cookies—Nikki

"Isn't this supposed to be a send-off? A farewell party?" Hands on my hips, I looked at my sad-ass friends, looking like ambassadors for the Mary J. Blige my-man-did-me-wrong club. Earlier tonight, we'd all caught up on our man troubles, myself included.

Raina blew into her noisemaker and twirled her hand in the air. Kara shrugged, while rocking herself. Sienna, surprisingly, was the only peppy one in the group. She had taken her broken engagement in stride. I suspected a certain campaign manager was giving it to her on the regular, but she'd claimed she was on a man-free diet.

Bending over, I smacked the wobbly table in front of me, determined to grab their attention and break up the pity party. "C'mon, ladies! I'm leaving in two days, and I need to have some fun! I ditched my family for you." I poked out my bottom lip, attempting to look cute and pitiful like Bria often did. Apparently, it wasn't working for me, based on the eye rolls and dismissive waved hands.

Tonight was supposed to be a fun girls' night in. Sienna had volunteered her new place, an apartment in the historic West End, and we had claimed the community rooftop.

"You're right. Let me get out of my feelings." Raina rotated her head and shook out her hands as if she were about to dive into a pool. "I don't need Cam," she said, voice shaky. "I'll be just fine."

Not without help. "You know what? I was gonna wait till later, but I think we all need this now." I reached into my bag and yanked out a Ziploc bag containing my special-made treats. "Cookies!"

Sienna crossed her legs and leaned closer, inspecting my bag. "What kind of cookies?" she asked in her trademark cross-examination voice.

"Only the best kind."

"*What*. Kind?"

"Chocolate chip."

"*And?*" She arched a brow.

"Herbs. Of the green variety."

Sienna gave me a wide-eyed look. "Jesus, Nik. You're gonna get me kicked out of my apartment. I've only been here a few months."

"No you won't. And it's not like we're smoking a blunt. We could all use a cookie."

"I'll take a cookie." Kara's alto voice broke the stare-off between Sienna and me.

"What?" Sienna snapped her head toward Kara.

"I'll take a cookie. And wine, please." Kara cleared her throat. "The Cabernet Sauvignon."

"Fuck yeah!" I pulled out a stack of plastic plates. "You deserve *two* cookies after what you've been through."

Kara smiled, took the plate, and then took a large bite of the cookie.

"Slow down there, champ. This is a marathon, not a sprint." I shook my bag of cookies. "Raina?"

"Girl, you don't have to ask me twice. But I'll take just one.

I've gotta get up and write tomorrow morning. I need this book advance so I can get out of my ma's house ASAP."

"You can stay with me." Kara chimed in, still munching on her cookie. "I've got a spare bedroom, and besides, Darren is moving out in a week or so." Kara's voice lowered to a pathetic whisper.

Too bad the weed didn't work fast enough to alter Kara's mood. "C'mon, chronic."

"What?" Kara asked.

"Nothing." I wasn't supposed to say that aloud.

Raina rolled her eyes, most likely on the same crazy wavelength as me. "Kara, I will happily take you up on your offer. I appreciate Ma's help, but I'm tired of her asking me about Cam."

Sienna sighed. "I'll have one, too." She reached out her hand.

I decided not to give her shit and gave her a cookie instead.

"Turn up the music, girl!" Raina yelled to Sienna.

"Any requests?" Sienna asked, digging into her carryall bag for her portable speakers.

"'Hotel California'!" I yelled, breaking off a small piece of the cookie. Although I was ready to party, I had a long day tomorrow, and I wanted to have my head screwed on straight for the last night with my hubby and babies.

"No, ma'am." Sienna shook her head. "We need Ms. Badu."

I shrugged, popping a piece of cookie in my mouth and then swallowed. "I can get down to some Erykah."

After a few songs, everyone was feeling loose. "On and on and on and on . . ." Raina and I danced and sang to each other. Kara, with a silly smile on her face, shimmied in her seat.

Raina slapped my shoulder with the back of her hand. "Look at Sienna's high ass."

A bubble of giggles rose in my throat when I saw Sienna, patting her hands against her chest and slow winding in a circle.

"Here goes the African princess, he-heeeee!" Kara slurred from her seat.

This time I full on laughed. Whenever Sienna got drunk or high, she'd get super in touch with her African roots. The second-generation citizen hadn't set foot on the Motherland.

"Both of them are high AF," Raina snorted.

"I'm not high AF, I'm high as fuuuuuck!" Kara twirled a hand in the air and then studied it for a full minute, as if it were a sculpture at an art museum.

"Slang lesson, Kara," Raina yelled as if she were at a football game. "'High AF' means 'high as fuck.'"

"Oh. Then you're right!"

It could be argued that all three of them were high AF.

Raina stumble-walked to her seat. She slapped her thigh. "We gotta start. It's time for the mind meeting. Meeting of the minds." She snapped her fingers. "No, that's not it."

"Meetings of the masters!" Sienna yelled, still dancing in the corner.

"Mastermind meeting," I supplied. "Damn, y'all can't hold your liquor or your high."

Raina rolled her eyes. "Whatever the hell. You know what I meant. Anyway, let's do it." Raina slapped her leg again, as if her hand were the gavel in the courtroom. "I'll go first." She drew a deep breath. "So, fuck Cameron Jeffries with his three-point-five-kids, having me chained to a stove, barefoot, breast-feeding a little crumb snatcher ass."

Well, damn. "Um, I'll try not to get offended by your lack of enthusiasm for motherhood."

"Girl, you're a cool mom. You're going on tour with your ex while your husband takes care of your kids. Winning!" She raised her hand for a high five. The guilt that warred at me before turned on full blast.

"I'm not abandoning my kids. I'll be back in a few months."

"Girl, yeah." Raina lifted her glass to her mouth. "We know that."

"Okay, what about the book stuff?" I asked Raina.

"My second round of edits is due to my agent in a few weeks. Book will release early next year." Raina waved a hand like it was no big deal. "You know what I *won't* be doing next year?"

"What?" Kara asked.

"Fooling with Cam's ole baby-soft ass. Maybe I'll go on a book tour in another country, find me a fine-ass man, and have a fling." She tilted her head and sipped her wine. If there was a class offered in the art of being petty while drinking wine, Raina would be a gold-certified instructor.

"Right!" Kara encouraged her. "This time next year, I'll be touring the world. I'll be a master Somm and work as an ambassador for a vineyard."

"Oh, and you can have a fling with a guy named Francois!" I teased Kara. "Nothing gets you over a guy faster than being underneath another one." I nudged Sienna. "Ain't that right?"

"Please. I do not have time to get into another relationship." She crossed her long legs. "Is Chris fine? Yes. Does he have me clamping my legs together every time he gets too close and I smell his cologne? Yes. Does watching his strong hands fly across the keyboard and watching his chest heave up and down under his suspenders give me hot flashes?"

"Yes!" Kara, Raina, and I answered for her.

"Right?" Sienna nodded as if we could follow her direction. "But, anyway, I'm too busy running for office—"

"And ruining Keith's life," Raina cut in.

"Yep!" Sienna popped the "P." She shrugged. "Chris wants me to walk the straight and narrow, to stick to the facts and focus on my strengths as a leader. I'm cool with that, but I still want to drag that asshole through the mud."

I shook my head. "What happened to my sweet and inno-cent friend?" My tone was teasing, but I was concerned for my girl. She had gone from sweet girl Rihanna circa 2005 to the RiRi we all know and love today.

Sienna sipped her wine. "I'm just tired of doing the right thing. Besides, relationships are a scam. Especially with these triflin'-ass men in Atlanta."

"Not all men are trifling. My husband, for example." Though he was acting like an asshole at the moment.

Sienna shrugged. "Fine. Not all men. But most men are con artists. They steal your youth, your optimism. They steal your power. Not only from the women they are cheating on, but from the ones they are cheating with."

"Sienna," I interrupted.

"No, think about it," Sienna interrupted. "When someone cheats on you, what's your first thought? What's the first thing you do?"

I tapped my fingers on my thighs. "Google how to shank someone without killing them. Look up the jail time in case he presses charges. Which he better not."

"Watch a few *CSI* episodes." Raina shrugged. "I need op-tions."

Kara raised her hand. "I think about what's wrong with me. I compare myself to the other woman."

"Exactly." Sienna sliced her hand in the air. "Am I too skinny, am I too fat, in my case, I put weave in my hair because Keith said she had long hair and a big booty. How crazy is that, huh?" Her voice rang in the air. "And in the end you change yourself to look like someone else. You change yourself for a man after *he* did you wrong. That's the biggest scam of all. I lost myself and I lost my power with him, and I want my power back. I used to be strong, confident. And I'll be damned if I give another man a piece of me."

She shook her head. "I sat on my virginity and didn't give

it up until I met Keith and what did he do? Tossed it away. Tossed me away." She pointed to her chest. "I've always wanted to go into public office, I told him straight up when I first met him, and he agreed. But then he and his precious family convinced me to set aside my desires and stand by my man." She snorted. "What a damn joke. So, yeah, I want to tell all. I want all the women he's ever dated or plans to date to know he's a scumbag. And quite honestly, if his dick fell off, I wouldn't shed a tear."

"I get it," Kara whispered. "I so get it." She cocked her head. "Listen to the song."

We all went silent, listening to "Bag Lady" by Erykah Badu.

"That's who we are," Kara continued. "We take on all the baggage from other people. Our jobs, our men, our family. They pile it on until *our* backs break. And what do we have to show for it?"

"Not a damn thing." Raina shook her head. "We've gotta let that shit go!"

"You're right." I pointed to Kara. "James is still giving me hell about going on tour. Yes, I'm a mom, but I'm not dead. I can do both."

Sienna nodded. "And you'll show James you can do it. You have to show men, show the world, that we shouldn't have to be the ones to sacrifice everything. It's time for our men to pull their own damn weight."

Sienna lifted her wine glass. "To dumping the baggage."

We lifted our glasses, answering Sienna's challenge. "To dumping the baggage!" we toasted.

"I'm gonna miss you, Mommy."

I scooped up my baby girl and squeezed her tight. "I'm gonna miss you, too, Bria-bree."

James, stiff in his body and lips, held Junior tight. My mother's arms were crossed. I settled Bria on the ground.

"Give Mama a hug, baby boy." Reaching for my baby, I met resistance from James. I damn near had to pry my son away from him.

JJ wiggled in my arms. He wasn't quite sure what was going on, but he swung his head from me to James, as if his toddler radar told him that Mommy and Daddy were not okay.

The horn blared from behind me in three long, dramatic honks. "Move your ass, Hardt!"

Fucking Trent. My ex was determined to drive a wedge in my marriage. I knew it. Hell, even my former best friend and drummer, Davey, had warned me to stay away from the flirty front man.

Bria tugged the hem of my sundress. "Ooh-weee! He said a bad word, Mommy."

"That's the least of her worries," Mama not-so-quietly mumbled under her breath. James did his best nosy-church-lady impression with a mouth twist and a whispered, "Mm-hmm." All that was missing was a small green New Testament Bible gripped in his hand.

"Guys, please." I looked down at the kids, who volleyed their attention around the three of us like we were in some sort of weird tennis match. "Mama, can you look after the babies for a minute? I need to speak to James."

Mama nodded. "C'mon, precious." JJ leaned close to reach for Mama, and Bria grabbed her other hand.

"Let's talk over there." I jerked my head toward the back of the bus. James followed me to the back, still stiff, and still the asshole he'd been for the past three months.

"Babe." I turned my back toward the harsh rays from the sun, forming a visor with my hands. "I don't want us to leave on bad terms. Can we, can you . . . ?" I licked my dry lips. For the first time in a long while, I was nervous.

"Can I pretend that I'm happy that you'll be spending day and night with your ex?"

"No, it's not like that." I shook my head. "It's business. I'm hanging with Davey, Drew, Ethan, and the roadies, but I won't be spending personal time with Trent."

"Right, Nik."

"I'm serious. I love you, only you. And besides, Trent will be too busy with his skanks to be thinking about me."

"Jealous?" His brown eyes glinted.

"Are you kidding me?"

He shrugged. "I just don't have a good feeling about this, Nik. I feel like . . ." He sighed, taking a few steps back. "I feel like I'm losing you."

"Never," I harshly whispered above the lump in my throat. "Don't you trust me? I'd never, ever cheat on you." I stepped closer. "You've gotta know that."

"I do. I trust you. But sometimes with the band, you don't make the best decisions."

I snapped my head back. "That's not fair. The last time I was in the band was ten years ago."

"And you were wild, crazy. I loved that about you, but now . . . now things are different. We have a family. We can't just go barhopping all weekend. We can't break into someone's lake house and go skinny-dipping at midnight or smoke weed for a Sunday Funday."

I grimaced, remembering the cookies I'd taken to girls' night. Whatever. Weed didn't have an age expiration date.

"And why can't we? Just because we have children doesn't mean we can't have fun. Sure, we have to be responsible, and we can't act willy-nilly, but we can plan fun trips with just us or with our friends. We have your parents and my mama—they adore our kids."

James stared at me for a moment and then sighed. "Come here, Nik." He opened his arms. "I love you, baby. Just promise me you'll be safe. Be smart."

"I promise," I whispered into his chest, tears pressing

against my eyelids. "I'll call you and the kids every day. I've got to teach Bria the rest of the song. I'll be back for the talent show."

"Okay." He squeezed me tighter. The python squeeze across my chest that had plagued me for the past few months loosened. We were finally breaking through the icy fortress that had surrounded our marriage. I stepped back, taking him in. Fear and love swirled in his honey-brown eyes. We stared at each other, nothing else said, but I knew that he loved me and I loved him. We had a beautiful family, and maybe he wasn't convinced at the moment, but we could have it all.

Another rude honk from the bus interrupted our moment.

James rolled his eyes and shook his head. "Let me walk you to the front of the bus." He grabbed my hand. I gave him a shy smile, that old yet familiar feeling of excitement and uncertainty filling my chest.

On the way to the front, I caught a glimpse of Trent making kissy faces in the window. James gripped my hand tighter. Arriving at the door, we walked onto the bus, pausing near the driver's seat.

I needed to make a statement to James, to Trent. I was a married woman, this was business, and I was following my dreams. No silly-ass feelings of jealousy or slutty exes would get in my way. "Kiss me," I demanded.

His lips, strong and soft at the same time, pressed into mine. Good gracious, this man made a move on my heart.

After he kissed the soul out of my body, he wrenched himself away. It felt as if I were carving out a piece of my heart.

James cleared his throat and walked me to my seat. "Davey!" he yelled over my head. "Take care of my girl."

Drumsticks in hand, Davey stopped mid-twirl and saluted James. "Ten-four."

"Masters." James nodded to Trent, who was slumped over with his guitar in hand.

"Yeah?" Trent shook the shaggy blond bangs from his eyes, an amused expression on his face.

"Twenty-seven."

Trent shrugged. "Is that supposed to mean something to me?"

"That's the number of bones in your hand. Touch my girl and I'll break all of them."

Davey snorted and Drew full on laughed.

Drew leaned over his seat and patted Trent's shoulder. "Dude. If I were you, I'd keep that guitar in your hands. That way you'll be covered."

"Fuck off," he growled at Drew, but stared at James. "Can we leave now?"

I nodded and hugged James. "Kiss my babies again for me."

"Goodbye, baby." He walked backward, his eyes never leaving my face.

"Not forever. Just for now," I whispered.

"Just for now," he agreed. Finally, he turned and walked off the bus.

"Yippee ki-yay!" Trent whooped. "Time for Nikki Hardt to play."

I shook my head and pushed the window down. I leaned out and yelled, "I fucking love you, James Grayson!"

James stopped in his tracks, turned around, and grinned. "And I fucking love you, Nikki *Grayson*."

I winked and gave him a grin.

A little farther out, my mom, Bria, and JJ waved.

"Bye, babies! I love you. Be good!"

Bria rushed toward James's open arms. "Bye, Mommy!" she yelled and then wiggled out of my hubby's grip. The driver cranked the engine, and the bus leaped forward. Bria jogged beside the bus. "Love you, Mommy."

"Love you to the moon and back, precious."

"Forever and ever?"

"Forever and ever!" I waved and she waved until we couldn't see each other anymore.

"We love you, Cleveland!" Trent shouted into the mic.

The crowd yelled their approval. Thank goodness the audio equipment cut through the screams. Tattered Souls had a strong following, more than I'd first thought. Davey had assured me it wasn't always like this, but rather the viral sensation with adding me to the band.

"Did you guys enjoy our girl Nikki?"

Louder cheers and whoops exploded from the crowd. I raised my guitar and then took a bow. The crowd began to chant my name. The energy from the audience gave me a buzz on top of the one I had from my three vodka shots that I'm sure I sweated out during the concert.

The band and I did one last wave and the lights switched off, a signal to our fans that the show was over.

"We. Are. On. Fucking. Fire!" Trent grabbed my waist and twirled me around.

I laughed like a maniac, still high from the gig. "Put me down, Trent!"

"Fuck yeah!" Drew grabbed a bottle of water and sloshed it over his purple Mohawk.

Davey and Ethan brought up the rear and bumped arms with each other, the same shit they'd been doing since we first formed the band.

Trent lowered me to the ground with his hands on my ass.

A flare of anger hit my chest. "Watch it, Masters. My husband meant what he said about breaking your precious hands." I speed-walked to the green room and pushed open the door. Trent was hot on my trail, and the rest of the band soon followed.

"Yeah, yeah. He's so tough shuffling papers around for his rich clients."

Davey snorted. "You didn't say that shit when he was in front of you a month ago. Don't get all brave now." Davey squeezed my shoulders and walked to the bar. Drew and Ethan, who'd settled on the love seat in the room, kept quiet, as usual.

"Whatever, man. What trouble are we getting into tonight?" Trent slapped Ethan's shoulders. Long, dark hair tied in a man bun, full beard, and sea green eyes, Ethan got a lot of attention. He had an insatiable appetite for men and women, and I dare say he may have surpassed Trent's whorish tendencies. Panties and boxer briefs were permanently wrapped around his fans' ankles. Occasionally, at the same time.

Ethan rubbed his hands together, a mischievous twinkle in his eyes. "Did you see the brunette with the huge tits?" He mimicked the size with his hands a foot away from his chest. "I'd motorboat the fuck out of 'em."

"Yesss. I was hoping you were in the mood for women tonight!" Trent gave Ethan a high five. "There was this blond chick beside her. Killer face. Decent rack."

"Please spare me the details of your orgy." I grabbed my phone, which was charging on the glossy vanity cabinet with a large mirror.

Trent leaned down, his eyes focused on me in the mirror. "Just say the word and I'll dump Ethan and those chicks for you."

"I like my vagina disease-free, thank you very much."

Trent's cheeks reddened. "I got checked out before we toured."

"And you've fucked at least a dozen women since we've been on tour."

"So you noticed." He waggled his eyebrows and made a beeline to the mini-fridge.

I rolled my eyes and focused on my phone. James had sent a goofy pic of himself and the kids at the park. JJ had lost a tooth and stuck his tongue through the opening. I rubbed a hand over my chest.

"Drink, Nik?" Trent asked over his shoulder.

"Yeah."

"I got ya." Trent returned with a plastic cup filled with a heavy pour of vodka and a splash of cranberry juice.

"Just how I like it." I saluted him and tossed back my drink.

"Another?" he asked.

"Yup!"

One, two, three . . . five. I lost count of the drinks I'd consumed. Didn't matter. My alcohol tolerance was legendary, and this former stay-at-home mama still had it.

Still, the drinking didn't stop me from thinking about James and the kids.

I glanced at the clock. It was only eleven at night, and I was in the same time zone as Atlanta.

Send me a pictuuure. A dirty one.

I ended the text with a winky smiley or whatever the hell it was. After a minute or two of silence, I sent him another one.

Hello???? You there? I need a picture of you naked! If you don't send one in zero-point-eight seconds I'll hate you forever.

Still no answer.

OMG. I hate you.

Just kidding, I love you. A lot, a lot. I must love you a lot because Trent is always tryna get in my pants. But I always say NOOOO!

James finally replied back.

What??? Are you drunk?

I snorted.

Am I drunk? N-O.

I typed back my response. What did he think I was? An amateur?

Yes, you are. The last couple of texts you've sent me have been belligerent. I'll talk to you tomorrow. Please be sober.

I focused on the last word and rolled my eyes.

Technically I wasn't *sober*, but I wasn't operating a vehicle, upchucking, or running around with my clothes off. I'd done that a few times in my younger days. I was way past that stage.

I loved James, but he was being a hater.

Our band manager, Julia, opened the door. "Time to meet the VIPs."

"Or as we like to call 'em, fresh meat!" Trent laughed and followed the manager out of the room.

God, these guys were the worst. Mostly Trent and Ethan. Drew was quiet and sweet and had a girl back home. Davey wasn't a saint, but he was selective with his bed partners.

I followed the band to the VIP room and sat at the end behind a long, scuffed-all-to-hell table. The boys had a large clump of fans surrounding them.

"Of course I'll sign your tits." Trent winked at the girl, then looked at me.

"Such an ass," I whispered under my breath.

"Yeah, he is." A tall black woman with long, gorgeous twists that framed her face appeared in front of me.

"Oh, hey. Sorry! I didn't notice you. Do you, um, want an autograph or something?"

She shook her head, her twists moving with the headshake. "Or something. I'm actually a new fan . . . because of you."

"Really?" I raised a brow. Not that I wasn't talented, but I was the new kid on the block, lucky to get a head nod from the groupies. The guys tended to be chattier, but I couldn't tell if it was because they enjoyed the music, were trying to entertain themselves while their wives or girlfriends hit on my bandmates, or if they wanted in my pants.

"Yes, really. I'm Monica, by the way." She laughed and stuck out a hand.

I found my manners and shook her hand.

"Anyway, I'm a traveling music blogger and reviewer, and

since you joined the band, I plan to follow you guys around to a few cities. I would love to interview you and the band, but I want to focus the piece on you. It's not every day you see an African American woman leading a rock/alternative band."

I put my finger over my mouth. "Don't let Mr. Trent Masters hear you say that. He might lose his egomaniac mind." I pretended to shudder. "Anyway, I'd love to do an interview. I need to run it by our manager, Julia, but—"

"I already pitched her the idea, and she's down for it." She waved at Julia.

Julia gave me a wide smile and thumbs-up. I wasn't sure why she was excited about a blogger following us around, but since Monica was a sister and seemed to genuinely like our music, I was down for it. "What's the name of your website?"

"RockHop.com. I cover all music, but mostly hip-hop, R-and-B and rock. I have a few contributors, but I write most of the content. It's fairly new, only been around for a year."

"Okay, I'll have to check it out, Monica." A niggle of recognition wormed in my brain.

"Wait a minute. Are you *the* Monica Davis, music critic at *Rolling Stone* magazine?"

She shrugged. "The one and only. So, true confession, I'm doing the full-on series of articles on the blog and then a feature piece for the magazine."

"Okay." That's why Julia was all over it.

"Great! Your manager told me you guys were heading on the road tomorrow at ten. I'm actually going to ride with you to the next city. I can get a feel of you and the band in your natural element."

Trent walked past us, a girl on either side, followed by Ethan.

I shook my head. "Buckle up, Monica."

* * *

I grabbed the weed from Drew's outstretched fingers, took a puff, and then passed it to Davey. Monica waved away the smoke cloud and continued clacking along on her laptop. For some reason, Monica was enamored of our band and decided to tag along for the remainder of the tour. Her readers had enjoyed the initial write-up about me and our unique rock-and-soul sound.

The label had been impressed as well and paid her to follow us until the tour was over in a month.

Ethan, seated beside Monica, palmed her breast and sucked her neck.

"Cut it out, Ethan."

Monica had been trying to hide their fling. Monica was well aware of my amorous bandmate's hoe-ish tendencies. After she'd confirmed he was STD-free—she forced him to take a test—they went at it like rabbits.

It was damn uncomfortable. Trent, in particular, hated that his best bud was boo-ed up, but Davey and I also suspected he was upset I wasn't giving him the time of day.

Trent and I wrote music together, played together, sang together, got high and drank together, argued together—all the things we had done when we were a couple—minus the sex.

Guitar in hand, I hummed a tune I'd been fiddling with all day. The words were being shy, so it seemed like I had to pluck them from the sky and scramble them around to make sense.

The alarm beeped and buzzed on the small side table.

"Dammit." I reached over and cut off my alarm, then resumed my strumming.

A little over an hour later, I finally achieved the soothing buzz I usually got when I had a solid song in place. "Done!" I passed my notepad to Trent. "Check it out and pass the dutchie." I sang the famous song.

I placed the guitar back in my case. Thankfully the bus

pulled to a stop. We had a gig in Reno, and tonight we got to stay at a decent hotel.

Monica closed her laptop and rubbed her eyes. I took a puff of my blunt and sighed. "Want a hit?" I asked, knowing she would say no. She didn't drink or smoke.

She shook her head, looked at her watch, and then froze. "Weren't you supposed to call your husband and kids tonight?"

My heart sped up. "No, I don't think so. I set the alarm this time, so I wouldn't—"

"You mean the alarm you turned off?"

"Shit!" I checked my phone. I had two missed FaceTime calls from James. It was ten thirty p.m. on the East Coast—well past my kids' bedtime, but I could probably catch James.

"Dammit! I am the worst mom and wife ever." I scrambled for my phone.

"Why don't you get settled into your room and give him a call?" Monica squeezed my hand. She knew how hard I struggled to be a mom yet maintain my rock-and-roll schedule. After we settled into our rooms, I rushed to dial James.

After a few rings, he picked up the phone.

"Hey, baby!" The nervous tremor in my voice couldn't be contained. "You're up."

"I'm in bed," he said, his voice cold and clipped.

"Oh, okay. Caught you at a bad time, huh?"

"If by bad time, you mean *bed*time, then yes. It's a bad time."

I chewed my bottom lip. "Yeah, I'm sorry about that."

"I'm starting to hate that damn word."

"What word?"

"Sorry."

"Sor—" I caught myself. "Apologies, baby."

A heavy breath rattled through the receiver. "That doesn't

hold up, Nikki. Our child, your mini-me, waited an hour past bedtime because Mommy promised to call this time. She's nervous as all hell about her talent show, and there's a riff in the song she doesn't have yet . . ." He sighed. He sounded tired, resigned. "Look, I'm out of my depth here. I'm just going to hire someone to help her with another song."

"No, you don't have to do that."

"Yes, I do. You're too busy reliving your youth to give a damn about your family."

"That's not true!" I paced the worn carpet of my hotel room.

"Have you been drinking?"

"What?" I stopped pacing. "Why do you ask me that every time we speak?"

"I dunno, Nik. Maybe because your words are slurred half the time." His voice had turned putrid.

"No, I haven't been drinking." Much. I had two or three shots of whiskey. One to loosen myself up for songwriting, and the others after I came up with a fucking awesome pre-chorus and tweaked the hook.

"Knock, knock!" I heard a light rap from the door.

"Who the fuck is that?" James's deep voice commanded.

Shit. I do not need this right now. "Not sure." *Total lie.* It was Trent's thirsty ass, trying to get into my panties for the umpteenth time. That man was gonna get his ass kicked one day, *by me*, not my husband.

"One sec!" I yelled at the door. After pressing the mute button on my cell, I rushed to the door and then cracked it open, the chain lock still in place. "What in the hell do you want, Trent?"

"I'm not sleepy."

"Then drink warm milk or count some fucking sheep. I'm busy." I slammed the door in his face.

I turned off the mute button and put on my sweet voice. "Hey, baby. I'm back."

He didn't respond.

"You there?"

"Yeah." He sighed into the phone. "Look, I'm beat. I'll talk to you whenever you decide to make the time."

"Oh. Okay. Well, I'll call you tomorrow, before the gig. I promise I'll have a long conversation with Bria."

"She doesn't want to talk to you."

"What do you mean? You just told me she waited up for me. Of course she wants to speak to me."

"She told me to tell you that she doesn't want to speak to you anymore."

"She doesn't mean it, and, besides—"

"I got the distinct impression that she does mean it."

"I'm still calling her tomorrow." I could hear the determination in my voice. My baby loved me. She would forgive me.

"Fine."

"Kiss my babies for me."

"Sure."

"I-I love you."

"Good night." He hung up.

"Dammit!" I smacked my palm to my forehead. I loved the music and being onstage again. Deep in my heart, getting a taste of this life, I knew that I could never *not* perform or create music again. I loved the energy, penning the perfect song. The high when I hit a note that had the crowd screaming for more.

Another knock sounded at the door.

Fucking Trent Masters. The man was driving me crazy. I jumped from the scratchy cover on the bed, marched to the door, slid the lock, and yanked it open. *"What?"*

Monica raised a hand. "Girl, my bad! I'm just checking in on you."

My anger dissipated and I stepped back to let her in. "Sorry. I thought you were Trent."

"Say no more." She walked into the room. "So, you talked to James."

"I did."

"And?"

"And he doesn't get it." I flung my hands in the air. "He doesn't see me busting my ass writing music, the hours upon hours of practice, and the energy it takes to perform. He has it in his head that I'm drinking all day with the band. Not to mention Bria, my baby girl, doesn't want to speak to me anymore." My chest squeezed. "Anyway, I know when you met me, you thought I was some superwoman, but in reality, I'm a hot mess."

Monica chuckled. "Girl, I know that."

"Huh?"

"Spotted it a mile away. The first night I met you, you drank like a fish and smoked like a chimney. I'd originally planned on doing an exposé, but then . . ." She sighed. "Then I got to know you. And I couldn't do it. But, girl, you've got to get it together. You're a mess."

"So I drink a little and smoke weed." I shrugged. "That's rock-and-roll."

"A little?" Monica tilted her head. The look she gave me—twisted lips, hands on hips, and a *don't play me* glint in her eyes, reminded me of Mama.

My cheeks burned. "Seriously, I'm good. Trust me. I've been around alcoholics."

Monica clapped her hands together. "Okay, then tell me this: Would you feel comfortable drinking this much if your husband and babies were around? Imagine Bria watching you stumbling around—sweaty and drunk and high."

I didn't imagine myself, but I remembered Daddy stumbling around the kitchen, making a mess, toppling over chairs and breaking dishes.

Heat prickled my neck. I loved Daddy so much. He was a genius. He had a good heart. He was the best daddy in the world when he didn't have a bottle clutched in his hands.

"No," I finally answered, shame weighing down my voice. "I wouldn't want that."

"That's the first step." Monica nodded. "Can I give you some advice?"

I snorted. "You ask me now?"

She remained standing, hands clasped in front of her. Waiting, I guess, for my answer.

I nodded.

"As much as I love the band, love—I mean *like* Ethan, you may need to leave them." She shrugged as if she hadn't suggested that I ruin my career and go back home.

"Leave them?"

"Yep." Her eyes serious. "For your own good."

I threw my hands up. "I can't go back to being a stay-at-home mom. I'd die of boredom."

"I'm not suggesting that."

"Then what?"

"Do it on your own."

"Do what?"

"Music. Listen, the music is good, and you guys are on fire, there's no denying that. But you could have a stellar career without the guys. Ethan's said it, the label knows it, and Trent damn well knows it. The size of the crowd has nearly doubled because of you. They aren't chanting Trent's name as much anymore. They're shouting for you."

I tapped my heels against the carpet, considering her observations. At the beginning of the tour, I was just a glorified backup singer, but now, we were playing more of my songs. Just last week, the record label tried to get me to sign on permanently.

"Let's be real," Monica continued. "You don't seem to like the traveling part. You light up when you sing, but more so when you write lyrics and compose the music. That's where your talents lie."

"So, I should just go solo? What about Davey, Ethan, Drew . . . Trent?"

"They survived without you before, they can do it again. They have an audience, a solid following. They may never make it to the Rock and Roll Hall of Fame, but they're hot and make good music. With strong management, they can make it work for the long haul."

"Still, I've written like five songs for them. I'd feel bad to just leave them high and dry."

"You can still write the music. Just don't record the songs and perform. For your career, work with a smaller or indie label where you can have more freedom in your contract."

"You are so right!" I rushed to hug her. "You are my new best friend. Thank you, thank you, and thank you!"

She chuckled. "You're welcome."

I stepped back from her embrace.

"But, um, one more thing."

"Yeah?"

"You really need to lay off the drinking. I . . . I hope you don't take this wrong, but I do think you need some help."

Embarrassment flooded my cheeks. "I think I—"

"I'm speaking from experience." She reached in her pocket and pulled out a purple and gold-plated medallion. "Three years sober. I was hesitant to join you on this tour. I was afraid of being tempted, and it's been hard. Damn hard, but I've been going strong." She rolled the coin in her fingers. "I know I dumped a lot on you, but when you're ready, we can talk."

Monica paused at the door. "I know everything seems overwhelming right now. And the addiction, it wraps its scaly skin around your body and squeezes and chokes and robs the life out of you." She exhaled, a faraway look in her eyes. "You feel like you can't move, can't breathe." She refocused on me. "But you can fight it. You can win, and nothing is sweeter than a clear mind and a clear heart."

CHAPTER 12

Good Girl Gone Bad—Sienna

Whoever said revenge is a dish best served cold is an effing liar. My revenge is a piping-hot plate of petty, and I'm loving every millisecond of it. And the ladies had happily joined me in my plot for retribution.

Raina patted a sticker with my name and campaign logo on her chest. "I can't wait to go door-to-door to campaign for you." She passed a sticker to Kara.

Chris strode into my living room, clipboard in hand. He waved over Kara and Raina, who'd sat on the suede couch across from me. I stood to join them.

Chris shook his head. "Sienna, you keep practicing for the debate next week. I'm just showing Kara and Raina where they'll be canvassing."

"Canvassing." Raina clapped her hands together. "I feel so official."

Kara gave me a weak smile. Although she looked perfectly put together on the outside—starched black slacks and a cotton button-down shirt—a cloud of sadness cloistered around her, like a bad aura. My heart went out to her and Darren, and I wished I could've been there for my friend. If only she would let me in.

She ignored my calls and would only respond with one- or two-word text messages. Until today, none of us had met up since Nikki left a month ago.

Raina had given me big eyes when they'd arrived at Chris's place. I knew that look. We needed an intervention. Usually, I was the one who could get things out of Kara. I'd tried to approach her a few minutes ago, but Kara just whispered, "Later." I'd give her the weekend, but after that, I was going to invade her space until she exorcised her feelings about the separation from Darren.

"Okay, you'll be going here," he pointed to the sheet, "and here."

Kara nodded. "Got it. I'll put it in my phone's GPS."

"Great." Chris pulled back the clipboard. "Have you reviewed what you'll be saying? I emailed you the talking points last night."

Raina raised her hand. "About that . . . love your talking points, but I'd like to spice it up a bit."

"Spice it up?" Chris's tone turned to the trademark take-no-bullshit voice.

Raina was not deterred. "Yeah. I think we should talk about why they should vote for Sienna—"

"Which is what I've done." Chris cut in.

"And not vote for Keith."

"I'd like to hear it," I yelled from the couch.

Chris gave Raina a hard stare.

Raina glanced back at me. "The candidate has spoken, so I'll take that as a yes . . . Okay! Here's a good one." She cleared her throat and turned on her late-night radio voice. "Did you know that Keith sits down when he pees?"

Kara coughed, and a surprised laugh spurted out of her like an old engine. "Good grief, Raina."

"It's true." I shook my head. "I thought that was weird."

"It is weird." Raina looked back at me and nodded. "Anyway, I'll give them a chance to respond. Most likely with, 'Really! That's fascinating. What else should we know about our councilman?'" Raina lifted a finger to Chris, who opened his mouth to interrupt.

"Then I'll say, 'Did you know that your councilman has athlete's foot . . . not only on his feet but also on his penis?'"

Kara cackled. "Raina, you're too much."

"Enough!" Chris's voice rose over Raina's chatter. "We will not insult Davenport. That is not how you win people over, and that is not how I win campaigns. Stick to the notes. No exceptions."

Raina sighed. "Fine, fine." She nudged Kara's shoulders. "Let's get out of here."

Kara cracked a smile and Raina gave her a big smile back. I suspected Raina had no intention of saying those things about Keith. She had probably noticed Kara's mood and attempted to make her feel better with a few immature jokes about my ex.

After they left, Chris turned his attention to me. "Please tell me you have normal friends who can help out?"

"Afraid not. Besides, being normal is overrated."

"Sure it is." Chris nodded to my yellow legal pad with notes. "Let's practice. This," he pointed to my temple and then my heart, "is how we beat Davenport."

The cheater, formerly known as Keith Davenport, paced to my left, shucking and jiving for votes.

The crowd was fairly large for a debate, and I knew why. They wanted fireworks. Drama. I'd heard the whispers. "What happened to Keith and Sienna? They were so cute together."

Chris had encouraged me to embody Michelle Obama's famous motto: *When they go low, we go high.*

I'd discovered that I wasn't quite as forgiving as the former First Lady. While I didn't plan to announce that Keith was a lying, cheating scum of the earth, I was mentally throwing my ex weapons of mass destruction.

"Focus on your personality," Chris had advised while we waited in the green room. "You know these people and you care. That's your strength."

I snorted. "Yes, I care. See where that got me."

"A great relationship with the Neighborhood Planning Unit, coffee dates with the president of the West End Neighborhood Association, first-name basis with involved citizens—"

"Okay, okay," I raised a hand, "I've got it."

"Do you?" He crossed his arms and tilted his head. He cocked his head a lot around me. A crease between his eyebrows usually meant he was frustrated. Whenever the crease was absent, he was thinking, assessing. In this instance, he frowned.

"You don't realize how beloved you are. Keith won the last race because voters knew *you* would keep him accountable. And you tried, but you can't do his job for him. And, sure, people will ask what happened between you two, but keep it above the belt."

I gave him a fake-serene smile. "I'll keep it classy." Besides, my friends and parents were here. While the ladies would get a kick out of it, Mama would be horrified if I embarrassed her, though I'd never done anything of the sort.

When it came to Keith, Baba would give me a thumbs-up. He'd never hid his hatred for my ex.

"The race needs to be about the people and how you will improve your constituents' lives, not about a woman scorned. Don't waste my time with your 'I am woman hear me roar' bullshit."

I rolled my eyes, deciding to ignore his last insulting statement. Sometimes Chris's straight-shooter ways were harsh. I was *mostly* used to him. "Of course I care about the people. I'm just—"

"You're just what?" He stepped closer, towering over me. His sturdy hands rested on my shoulders, comforting and strong.

I softened a bit under his expert touch. "I'm angry, okay?" My eyes lifted to study his, to scan for judgment. There was none, and in that moment, I decided to reveal the core of my heated resentment. "I have a right to be angry, too. I won't pretend that I'm not hurt or that I'm miraculously healed. I have a right to process my feelings."

The pressure from his fingers deepened slightly. His curved lips flattened into a thin strip. "No one out there will give a damn about your feelings. The ones who do are here for a show." He released my shoulders. "Key stakeholders want to know three main things." He raised his fingers to tick off the points. "They want to know who you are, what you stand for, and what you'll accomplish. Stick to the facts, be yourself, and you'll win."

"I hear you," I said.

"Good." He relaxed his tense stance and gave me a rare smile. "Now go kick his ass."

I gave him a winning smile and left the green room. I spotted Raina and Kara in the center of the crowd and gave them a quick wave. Kara waved back and Raina gave me a thumbs-up. My parents sat toward the back of the room, both of them wearing wide and proud smiles.

Keith was chatting it up with the moderator. From the goofy-ass grin on his face, I could tell he was laying on the charm. Martha was a middle-aged white woman with three kids, and by the looks of it, she wasn't swayed by his all-teeth-and-no-soul smile. After a few minutes, we got started.

"Ms. Njeri. As the contender, you'll go first. What is your vision for the TrailLine?"

I gave Martha a wide and genuine smile. I was passionate and proud that the city had rejuvenated and leveraged 1,000-plus acres of green space.

"I love the direction the TrailLine is going. It's fantastic because our residents and tourists are enjoying the trails. But we need to make a major push on the transit elements, which means connecting the streetcar to the TrailLine. Specifically, we need to incorporate the changes that were floated up from the Georgia Department of Transportation and then begin the rollout of the next phases to expand the route along the full length of the line. We also need to pay close attention to other cities, like Portland, that have a successful model for streetcars." I offered a few more ideas and facts, getting a couple of head nods and a quick grin from Chris.

Keith basically spouted off the same message with a story about his experience at the TrailLine that was supposed to be funny but fell flat. You could hear a pin drop outside of Keith's droning voice. I hated his voice, hated the way he lied to his constituents about his plans. Hell, half the things he'd proposed had been my idea. And that was the crux of my problem: We basically had the same plan because I had created the strategy.

We received a few more questions about taxes and public safety, and an hour into the debate, I knew I'd edged him out by giving genuine responses and a straightforward way to solve issues within the district. There were few claps and lots of silence after Keith's responses. I was kickin' ass and takin' names; I felt damn good going the Michelle Obama route. I snuck a glance at Chris, who smiled at me. Not just a smile. A dangerous one—hot, potent, daring. A smile that conveyed that if there weren't seventy-something people in the building, a camera crew, Keith, and a moderator, he'd give me much more than a smile.

"Okay, this is the last question for our candidates. Mr. Davenport. What is your stance on police shootings as they relate to black lives?"

I perked up and attempted to hide a smile. Keith and I hadn't discussed this subject. After the recent shooting of a young black man within the district, racial profiling had skyrocketed into a hot topic. I reclined in my seat and, for the first time, willingly looked at my opponent.

Keith cleared his throat and steepled his hands. "As a black male, the shooting of Devon Jordan in my district particularly hit home for me."

Right. I mentally rolled my eyes. Keith grew up in a predominantly white neighborhood and could count his black friends on one hand—his pinkie and his thumb. Not that his neighborhood had any bearing on race relations, but the man had no desire to connect with his community.

"I've had many conversations with citizens and leaders of this fine city. As much as I'd love to push the issue, this type of thing, making a real effort at police training and reform, would have to come from the mayor. It's truly out of my hands." He lifted his hand in a "don't shoot" gesture, the absolute wrong movement, given the topic.

Just keep digging, Keith. I rubbed my hands together like a greedy miser collecting a debt.

"Also, we have to own up to our mistakes. I can't help but think if the young man had stayed at home, refrained from smoking an illegal drug, this incident could've been avoided."

People shot from their seats. "What in the world?"

"Are you kidding me?" a young black woman yelled from the crowd.

"Everyone, please, settle down," Martha yelled over the crowd. "Mr. Davenport, are you finished with your points?"

"I want to wrap this up by stating that I am on your side. I will meet with the mayor and the police force to come up with a viable solution."

"Ms. Njeri, can you please give us your opinion?"

"Absolutely." I leaned into the mic. "As a public defender, I have a front-row view of the justice system. My clients are lucky enough to be alive but unlucky in that they were arrested. Many of my clients have expressed that when approached by the police, they were often told that they fit the profile of a criminal. This is just another way to criminalize blacks and widen the gap of economic disparity. Jail time, fines, the impact on employment and other opportunities can ruin people's lives. I am so damn tired of our young men and women being targeted. We have to take steps to end inequalities in Atlanta's criminal justice system, and I am committed to pushing this through. The way we solve this issue is on a state and on a local level. It's not just up to the mayor to act." I looked at Keith, narrowed my eyes. "We have to stop criminalizing petty things like panhandling and drinking alcohol in public, or sending people to jail for parking tickets. And for goodness sake, we have to take care of those who have mental issues and struggle with substance abuse. They deserve help, not jail time. These are just a few ideas, but not all-encompassing. We, the city council, and you, the citizens, can demand change. The police force is enacting the will of the democracy. Together we can make an impact and form a better bond between our community and the police force that protects us."

A thunder of applause followed my impassioned speech. People rose from their seats again, but this time in support.

"So naïve." Keith's sharp voice cut over the crowd. He leaned closer to me, a hand gripping the back of my vacant chair. "You think drug abusers and criminals should just run rampant in our city?" The bitterness in his tone stank like weeks-old trash.

The crowd went quiet, save for one woman that I was pretty sure was Raina, who whispered, "No, he didn't."

Yes, he did. Gripping the mic in my hand, I took a cleansing breath, rolled my shoulders back. In my peripheral vision, I saw Chris scoot to the edge of his seat.

"I'm not naïve, Mr. Davenport. I *care* about our citizens, and I'm not suggesting we let drug dealers run rampant. But up until last year when the city decriminalized marijuana, you could face up to six months jail time. God have mercy on residents outside of the city proper."

"Caring doesn't make things happen, Sienna." He got his tone back under control. This time it was mild and condescending. "Perhaps you're out of your depth here. But I would like to state, for the record, I do care."

"Do you now? That's certainly a change."

"What does that mean?" He stood, his palms down on the table.

"Did you or did you not refer to my clients as poor, unfortunate souls? Did you or did you not once tell me that they weren't worth the hours I spent poring over discovery to try to win their cases?"

"Oh, oh. Girlfriend went there," someone shouted from the crowd.

"Well, hell, he went there first," someone in the first row yelled back.

Keith adjusted his tie and then licked his lips. "Sienna, I said no such thing."

"Candidates. Please stick to the topic," Martha lightly admonished. "Let's not make this personal."

"My apologies, Martha." I straightened my skirt and tossed her a strained smile.

"Sorry," Keith mumbled under his breath.

Martha nodded, although her eyes brimmed with amusement. "Sienna and Keith, please present your final remarks."

Keith begged for votes. I tried to pivot and get my Michelle

Obama on, but I could tell the crowd wasn't buying it. The good news: They seemed to like my message. The bad news: Our lovers' spat may have discredited us as serious candidates.

After the debate, I was accosted by my parents. Kara and Raina looked like they wanted to come over, but I shook my head. I would never live it down if they heard my mother lecture me about controlling my temper.

"Sienna." Mama grabbed my elbow. She had a strong grip, despite her petite frame. Baba was close behind. My parents maneuvered me to the back of the room. Mama nodded as people waved. On the outside, she was all smiles, but on the inside, I knew she was boiling mad. Mama didn't tolerate us cutting the fool in public. It didn't matter that I was in my thirties, had a good job and paid my own bills.

I had definitely cut the fool with Keith, of all people. I sighed and readied myself for the verbal lashing I deserved.

Finally away from the crowd, Mama dropped her smile. "Sienna, dearest, what in the world were you thinking? Arguing like a . . . an elementary student with that man." She squeezed her slender hands together, again, I knew this was an effort to not swing her hands widely like she usually did when lecturing one or more of her seven kids.

"I . . ." She waved at Baba. "We are so disappointed that you—"

"Speak for yourself, Winnie. I, for one, am proud of our little girl."

Mama tutted. "Busar."

"Oh, stop it, woman. I saw you fighting a smile when she went toe-to-toe with that spineless rat. Our daughter has always fought for her fellow man, and we raised an exceptional woman. The only time she got in trouble is when she defended her classmates from bullies and when she boycotted McDonald's after that ridiculous documentary."

I smiled. That was the turning point of me becoming a vegetarian. I'd been a junior in high school and had convinced a few other students to picket the McDonald's near our school. I was convinced McDonald's was the cause of all things unhealthy, and I wanted to save our little town in middle Georgia. The police had been called, but luckily my parents came by and forced me home.

"Today," Baba continued, "and for the first time, our daughter stood up for *herself*."

"You are right." Mama smoothed her hands over her gorgeous bright orange dress. "I just wish she would've done this in a non-public manner. There are other productive ways of getting your point across, young lady."

A blast of hot energy hit my back and the back of my neck prickled. *Chris.*

"Mr. and Mrs. Njeri." He smiled at my parents and shook their hands. "I need to steal your daughter." Chris turned his attention to me, and his smile dropped. Raw energy electrified the air around us.

Mama must've felt it, too, because at some point, she'd drifted closer to me, her hand now on my shoulder in a protective Mama Bear manner. "My Sienna was a little spirited, but there's no need for . . . whatever it is you plan to say to her."

Chris nodded. "I assure you, Sienna is safe with me. But there is much your daughter and I need to discuss. It's what we typically do after each event." He modified his earlier spitting-mad tone and somehow had switched to competent counselor.

"Oh, good." Mama sighed. "Well, he is your campaign manager, after all." Mama patted Baba's potbellied stomach. "I need to get your Baba some food. His stomach was growling the entire time." She attempted a small joke.

Baba was oddly silent during this exchange. He just looked at me and Chris with a highly amused expression on his face.

After we said our goodbyes to my parents, Chris placed a hand on the small of my back and then guided us out of the building to his car. He clicked the alarm to his car, opened my door, and then walked to the driver's side. He quickly reversed his car and sped out of the parking lot.

"Chris—"

He unclenched his hand from around the shift and raised his hand "Don't. We'll talk about it once we get back to head-quarters."

I scrunched my nose. "And where is headquarters?" Techni-cally, we didn't have a building. We were in the process of lo-cating a building, but so far, it'd been at Chris's office in his condo.

"My place."

"I—"

"Quiet, Sienna. You showed your ass today, and you aren't going to talk your way out of this. For the next forty-eight hours, your communications manager and I will have to tap-dance our way out of that shit show. I need peace. I need to think. I need *quiet*."

I gave him quiet.

Chis tugged his tie off and then went for his cuff links. He waved toward the buttercream suede sofa. "Sit."

I tilted my head and narrowed my eyes. So, yeah, I might've gone the middle-school playground route with Keith, but that didn't mean Chris could be a jerk.

"Excuse me?"

"Sienna." He clenched his jaw. The skin beneath his sandy brown goatee stretched with tension. "Please, take a seat." Chris strode to the kitchen.

"All right, then." I smoothed my black pencil skirt and sank into his couch. A clinking sound grabbed my attention. I couldn't see him from where I sat, but I could guess he was making himself a whiskey neat, as he typically ordered and slowly sipped during our weekly schmoozing obligations.

While he poured himself a stiff one, I took in the tall plants in the corner and the elegantly decorated living room. A small glass sculpture rested on a side table. Art—by the looks of it, a mixture of African and French-style canvases—decorated his wall. Stylish, but not pretentious. Just like Chris.

My attention was snagged by something that definitely didn't fit into his obviously expensive yet tastefully decorated condo.

Ignoring Chris's earlier request to sit down, I was drawn to a picture framed in a dried-macaroni frame. In the photo was Chris, who looked to be in his preteens, and a white woman who looked to be in her late thirties. They were standing in front of a yellow house that had lots of long windows and a pointed roof.

"My mom." I felt a warm tickle from his breath along my neck.

Taking a few steps back, I clutched my chest. "I didn't hear you."

"I didn't want to be heard." His gaze seared me, the same one he'd given me at the debate that nearly made me combust.

"O-okay." I turned away and swallowed, an attempt to get moisture to my suddenly dry throat. I focused back on the picture. "Nice frame."

"Thanks."

The room grew quiet again. I wrapped my arms around my middle and continued to stare at his mother, a brunette with striking blue eyes and laugh lines around her mouth. She clutched Chris to her side, her head resting on his shoulder. Chris wore a goofy grin, and surprisingly, he didn't have a look of disdain like most preteens would have when their moms got too mushy.

"She's pretty."

"She was."

Was. I turned to face him again, at a loss of what to say. *Is he still hurting?* "I'm sorry," I whispered.

"Not your fault. It's been a long time."

"How long?" I couldn't help but ask, not at all expecting Chris to share.

"She died soon after that picture was taken. Car accident. We lived in a small town outside of Paris. That day," he pointed to the picture, "we took a day trip to Paris. Exploration day, she used to say."

"You're French."

"French American."

"You speak French."

"*Oui, madame.*"

And my ovaries exploded. Of course this incredibly sexy, smart, and sometimes sweet man spoke one of the sexiest languages in the world.

"Oh, um, that's neat." *Neat? No, that was hot. Definitely hot.*

I ran my fingers through my curls, an attempt to get a hold of my libido. "I didn't realize . . . you don't seem to have an accent."

"I moved to the States after she died to live with my dad and his family."

"Really? So you have, like, half brothers and sisters?"

"Yeah, but I don't consider them half. They're full and we're close." He set down his drink on the coffee table. "Enough about me. Let's talk about you."

"M-me?" I huffed and squared my shaking shoulders. *Get it together.*

I wasn't some trembling virgin. And although Mr. Sexy decided to turn up the heat, whether consciously or not, I wasn't playing his game. As a vegetarian, I was on a meat-free diet in both respects.

Keep it professional. "Look, I apologize for my behavior today. I just got so heated and, well, I didn't think things through. If you want, I can draft up a statement."

"You will?" He stepped closer, his eyes becoming a deep swirl of blues and browns.

"Yes. Um . . ." His ambrosial, *manly* cologne twisted my senses and jacked up my heartbeat as if I'd been hit with a dose of adrenaline. "Yes, anything you want."

"Promise?" He leaned closer, cupping my face.

"S-sure. I mean, within reason."

His lips grazed my earlobe, followed by a soft nip. "I want you."

"You do? I thought you were mad at me."

He leaned back, still cupping my face. "As your campaign manager, I'm pissed. As a man, a man who's been attracted to you since day one and fought his attraction every second you were in my space, a man who tried to respect your decision to marry a man not worthy of you, who finally has the opportunity to come for you when you gave Keith his walking papers, I was turned on. He's an asshole, and you put him in his place. I've tried to keep my attraction contained. This is completely unprofessional, but . . ."

"But?" I leaned in closer, my head tilting up to stare into his serious eyes.

"But fuck it." He followed up his declaration with a kiss. It was the permission we both needed. We rushed into action. Me unbuttoning his dress shirt. Chris reaching for the zipper of my skirt and tugging the shirt out of my skirt.

He murmured something hot and sexy in my ear, something foreign that caused a flood to rush between my legs. "Say that again," I commanded.

"Tu es mon fantasme devenu réalité," he whispered, tugging off my shirt.

"What?" I asked, breathing heavily and seriously turned on. "What does that mean?"

"You're my fantasy come true."

I unclasped my bra, grabbed his hand, and led *him* to *his* bedroom.

I was feeling bold, being someone's fantasy and all. I needed this—to feel desired and special and attractive. And from the hot and heavy look on Chris's face, he'd meant every word. I walked to his bed, turned to face him, and then slowly sat down. I crawled backward, still facing him. "Touch yourself. Show me how much you want me."

He smiled, but that hot look was still in his eyes. Reaching down, he unabashedly stroked himself.

Panting, I opened my legs wide, slid my finger down to the vee between my thighs, and touched myself.

He continued to pump himself. I threw my head back, unable to handle the intensity of the moment.

"Eyes, *mon chéri*," his deep voice commanded, pulling me back to his sexy gaze. "Don't come."

I nodded my acquiescence, well past the ability to form words.

He stalked to the nightstand. A crinkle of foil sounded and then he slid the condom along his length.

Dipping a knee onto the bed, he gripped my hips and drew me closer. "I want to taste you, touch you. But I cannot. Too close," he grunted, a pained expression on his face.

When he slid deep inside me, I gasped. He was big, so big he filled me up.

And he filled something else up that I had no intention of thinking about at the moment.

"*Je suis chez moi,*" he said, thrusting deeper and staring into my eyes.

"Translation?"

"Tell you later." He stroked me again. I shuddered at the pleasure and gripped my legs around his waist.

"Chris!" I yelled as he continued to pound me with such precision, such beauty, a tear rolled down my cheek.

But Chris was wrong.

This wasn't quick. It was long, artful, and painstakingly thorough. He touched my body, my soul. This was something I'd never experienced.

When I squeezed my eyes shut, he commanded me in that deep and patient voice of his. "Look at me. Don't cut me off," he said right before he took us over the edge.

Still inside me, Chris caressed my cheek with his calloused thumb and kissed me deeply.

He rolled off and walked to the connecting bathroom. Like magnets, my eyes were drawn to his muscular ass. I sighed wistfully when he shut the bathroom door. I rolled over to the other side of bed, aka the wet spot.

Nibbling my lips, I thought through my plan.

Should I leave? No, maybe I should wait, thank him for a good time? Dang it! What did single, unattached people do after just having sex? I was half a decade out of the game.

Just wait for him. We're still working together, I think. Oh shoot! What if he doesn't want to work together? Or what if—

My mini freak-out was cut short. Chris returned with a serious look on his face. His brows creased. *Apparently, I pissed him off. Maybe I should've left.*

"Why are you way over there?" He lifted the covers, got in bed, and then jerked me to his chest.

"Oh, I wasn't sure. I didn't know if you wanted me to leave or—"

"We'll have some major problems if you attempt to sashay your sexy ass out of my house."

"Oh, well, that's good then."

"And a new rule. When we're in bed, you're by my side."

I smiled at Chris's bossiness. That's a rule I could get behind. I sighed, relieved. "I like that rule. Keith never, well, he didn't like to hold me afterward. He said I was too hot."

"Another new rule." His voice dropped to frigid tempera-

222 / SHARINA HARRIS

tures. "Don't mention Keith's bitch ass while in bed with me. Out there in public and for business, sure. But that's it. He isn't like me, and I'm damn sure not like him."

I squeezed his bicep and snuggled against his chest. "I'm sorry, that was dumb of me. I won't mention him, in um, bed again."

"Good."

"So, there will be an again?" I tried but failed to contain the hopeful tone in my voice.

"Damn right," he rumbled. "Give me ten, twenty minutes, we'll do another round."

"Twenty minutes?" I lifted my head. "That doesn't happen in real life." I snorted. Only in books. The romance books I used to love reading until Keith shattered my heart.

"I already confessed you were my fantasy come true. You think I'm waiting hours to get my fill again?"

"We shall see," I teased and patted his chest. "We shall see."

It's important to note that I did see. All. Night. Long.

SEPTEMBER

CHAPTER 13

O Sister, Where Art Thou?—Raina

"You sure you don't want to stay with me?" My mother's big brown eyes peered at me from across the breakfast table.

I shook my head, scooping up my corn flakes and feeling like a big fat loser. *Single, in my thirties, living with my mama.*

"I'm sure, Ma. Kara already has a room ready for me. It'd be rude not to move in." *And I'll lose my damn mind if I have to tell you for the umpteenth time that I'm fine.*

"All right then. I just want to make sure this is what you really want. I just want you to be happy. You seemed *really* happy with Cam—"

"Ma," I groaned and dropped the spoon in my nearly empty bowl. "I don't want to talk about it. Why do you keep bringing him up?"

"Why don't *you* want to talk about him?" She dug in.

Ma had never had a real backbone, so it surprised the hell out of me that she decided to have some steel in her spine now.

"Because we're over. Because he wanted things from me that I couldn't give him. People break up all the time, every day, in fact. And when people end relationships, it's viewed rude as he—I mean, as *heck* to bring it up."

"Sorry. I live alone, so I must've lost my manners over the years," Ma said in the most unapologetic voice I'd ever heard in my life.

I stood and emptied the milk from my bowl into the sink. "I'm going to my room to write. Please don't—"

"Interrupt you," she interrupted me. "I know."

I left the kitchen and returned to my box-size room. Ma had downsized, but I was damn lucky to have a room, even kid-sized, to crash in. I needed to save all my coins for my career change. Being a writer ain't easy.

I sat in front of my desk, shook my head from side to side, and did a few exercises I knew some actors did before a scene. Doing this relaxed my mind and my fingers, and I was able to zone out and hit my daily word count.

My plotting board sat propped against the dresser. The yellow trifold board looked like a seventh grader's science project with its array of sticky notes scribbled with my outlines for each chapter. My manuscript, a series of humorous essays, was turning out well. Today's entry would be about the bougie friend who studied abroad for one summer and came back speaking another language like she was a native.

My old college friend had spent a year somewhere in Latin America. Homegirl came back with a wavy brown sewn-in weave and started rolling her R's like there was a gun to her head. I chuckled at the memory. Plot in place, I was on a roll and nearly finished with the chapter about being true to yourself when the doorbell sounded.

A flash of irritation zipped through my body, but then I remembered that this wasn't my place.

"Raina!" Ma's voice was high-pitched and weird. "You've got a, um, visitor."

"A visitor?" I mumbled under my breath. "Be there in a minute!"

I saved my work and pushed away from the desk, wondering who it could be. It wasn't my girls—they knew how bad I felt about being at home. So if we did anything, it was at their house or somewhere in the city.

Is it Cam? My heart sped. It had to be him. Outside of my girls, no one else knew where I lived. He'd shipped a few of my knickknacks to Ma's place. She had watched me open the small box, giving me a sad, commiserating smile.

I balled my fist and jerked open the door. I was *not* like Ma. I wouldn't fall to the floor and beg a man who didn't want me to stay.

Rounding the corner, I stopped short. He wasn't Cam but a young man in his twenties. Tall and muscular, with broad shoulders, wide-set eyes, and a nutmeg brown complexion. He looked familiar, but I knew I hadn't met him before.

Ma stared at him as if she were staring at a ghost. Her breathing was erratic, and she grabbed her chest as if she were experiencing a heart attack.

"Ma? You okay?" I rushed to her side, in front of the door. "Is he bothering you?" I kept my eyes on Ma, completely ignoring the young stranger who *seemed* harmless from his nervous smile. But the way Ma reacted, I knew it wasn't the case.

"No. I, I'm fine. This young man is here to see you." Ma's smile was strained. "I'll give you some privacy."

I gave her a what-the-hell-don't-leave-me-alone-with-a stranger look. Which she totally ignored.

Ma stepped away from the door. "I'll just be in the other room." She jerked her head toward the kitchen, which was steps away from the dining room.

"That's fine, Ma." I waited for her to walk the short distance behind the wall, pretending for the stranger but knowing that she would be able to hear us.

"Who are you?" I crossed my arms, cutting the bullshit.

"I'm Victor . . . Junior."

Victor Junior. My brother? The news slammed into me like a heavyweight wrestler.

"J-Junior?"

He nodded, his eyes serious, his expression tense. "Call me Vic."

I stepped back from the door and then waved at the patchwork couch. "Sit." I took my own advice and flopped on the recliner. So many things sped through my mind. My father was an asshole who'd left his wife and kid brokenhearted. Was my father's spawn different? Did my father tell Junior he was his ray of sunshine? Did they play catch? I bet they did. Dad loved football, and Junior was jacked. He probably hadn't missed a day at the gym.

Heart pounding, I breathed deeply, trying to grab hold of my radio personality persona. She was cool, calm, and collected. I needed her serenity, needed her to block the painful memories that swirled like a Georgia cyclone in my head.

He put up the Vulcan salute and formed a V with his hand. "I come in peace."

"I thought that meant live long and prosper."

"Yeah, that, too." He gave me a half smile.

I couldn't help but smile back. My brother was a charmer. *Just like Daddy.* Straightening my back, I cleared my throat and began my interrogation.

"How did you find me?"

"Dad wrote you a few months ago. I found a returned letter with your address. I figured you weren't keen on emails or letters, so I tracked you down. I, um . . ." He paused, scratching his head.

"You, um, what?"

"I met your boyfriend, I mean ex-boyfriend, Cameron. He

seems like a really great guy. He invited me in, sat me down. H-he told me about you."

"What did he say?" I leaned in closer, my hands gripping my knees.

"That you were funny as hell, used to be a radio host, but I knew that because I googled you. He said you're writing some sort of self-help book that'll be on the shelves next year. He said you were gorgeous, not that I cared because I'm your brother and, um, he showed me a picture of you."

Good to know my things weren't tossed in a burn pile.

I relaxed in my chair.

He was silent for a few beats. I waited him out, hoping Cameron had further expounded on my wonderful virtues and beauty.

"So why did y'all break up?"

"None of your business, little brother." I waved at him. "He just gave you my address?" I asked, changing the subject.

He nodded. "Yeah, he said that you needed to resolve some issues."

I rolled my eyes. "Right. Why have you decided to meet me after all these years?"

"I didn't know you existed."

An arrow pierced through my armored heart. After all these years, my father's aim was still true.

"I . . . I'm sorry. I didn't mean it like that. It's just that Dad—"

"Victor," I interrupted. My voice was Alaska winter cold. "I call him Victor."

"Right," he continued. "Victor and Mom never mentioned anything. Mom died a few years ago, so I can't interrogate her, but I asked Dad, I mean, um, Victor. Anyway, he was really sorry about it. He's been trying to reach you over the years, but he said you didn't want to see him again."

"He's right. I don't. Don't get me wrong, it's been a shock, but a good one meeting you. You were innocent in all of this. Your mom and your father were not."

"Look, I get where you are, and I don't know how else to say this, but I really wish you would consider changing your mind. Dad—Victor is dying."

"How?"

"Emphysema. He's in the last stages. He can barely breathe."

I could barely breathe. Fighting against my panic, I drew in a deep, life-affirming gasp.

"H-he . . ." I cleared my throat. "Okay."

Daddy.

I swallowed the surge of emotions that rose in my near-frozen heart, threatening to spill over in tears and curses and unwanted memories.

But they came anyway. Daddy was tall, strong, *vibrant*. Tight fro, impeccably dressed unless he'd just returned from a gambling bender. And he was funny, so funny he'd made my cheeks stretch and my stomach tighten from laughing. And when I had Daddy's attention, I felt like the center of his world.

When he left, I felt as hollow as an empty well.

"It's okay if you're upset. It's okay to feel hurt." My little brother's tawny eyes were patient and kind, and it pissed me off.

"Oh, fuck me, of course he is!" I jumped from the chair.

"Huh?" He shifted in the chair to properly stare at me. His eyebrows were near his hairline.

I threw my hands in the air, anger spreading like steam in a shower. "He's dying. And now he wants me to crawl after him and forgive his dying ass. Well, no, thank you." I pointed to my chest. "And now there's a ticking time bomb to speak to him, right? That's why he's been trying to get in touch with me."

Vic, cool as a summer breeze, shrugged. "Life is shit sometimes. You just gotta roll with it."

"And what does your barely twenty-year-old ass know about

life? And PS, you don't seem to be overly bothered by Daddy Dearest being near death's door."

He raised his index finger. "I'm twenty-two. Graduated from Georgia Tech on a full ride, an academic scholarship. Mom was a functional alcoholic, which was ultimately the reason she died from liver cirrhosis. Dad drank, not as much as Mom, but he could toss them back. I'm sure you remember. And, of course, he gambled away our money. I learned early on that if I wanted to eat, I had to earn it myself, so I ran drugs for a gang that had a soft spot for me."

Well, damn. Maybe Daddy being out of my life was a blessing.

He clenched his jaw. "So, yeah, life can be shit."

"Sorry. I thought for sure he'd play catch with you or something."

"What?"

"Play ball. I always imagined he'd magically became a family man after he left me and Ma."

"We played . . . once. I graduated high school and he realized that I was leaving and most likely not coming back home."

"Where is home?"

"Now, Atlanta. Then, Birmingham, Alabama."

Dang. We now lived in the same city and I never knew. Guilt hit me like a stack of bricks. Vic had been abandoned, had to depend on a gang to survive. If I had connected with Daddy, I could've taken care of my little brother at some point. At ten years apart, I could've been his guardian.

"I'm sorry. Apparently, you've had a hard life. I'm sorry Victor wasn't a better father to you. For what it's worth, he was really excited about you. He had such pride in his eyes when he told me I was getting a little brother."

"You knew about me?" he whispered, his tone no longer soothing and calm, but tense and angry.

"I . . . I did. And you'll never know how sorry I am. Especially now that I know that you were all alone."

He shot me a look that made me check myself for exit wounds. "I've done my job. I told you about him. Up to you how you want to move forward."

He stood and turned toward the door.

"Wait!" I yelled just as he reached for the door.

"Yeah?" He turned to face me.

"I'm sorry for not reaching out to you. But it looks like you turned out well despite our father."

"Yeah . . ." He gripped the door handle. "But it would've been nice to have a sister." He opened the door and closed it. It wasn't a slam or a bang, just a sad and final closing.

"Shit, shit, shit." I rushed back to my room and searched for my phone.

"Raina," Ma yelled behind my closed door.

"I'll talk about it later, Ma. Give me some time." I found my phone on my desk.

"Okay, baby. I'm here when you want to talk."

I waited until I heard her walk away and then I typed in a message, surprisingly not a group chat with my girls, but to Cam.

Just met my brother. Freaking out. WTF???

My hands shook as I pressed the send button. A few minutes later dots danced on my screen. "Oh my God, he's texting me back."

Yeah. He seems like a good dude. Sorry I didn't warn you but . . . you tend to avoid anything related to your dad.

"You're damn right." I blew a breath, still rocked by the news. Cam sent another message.

Don't worry, I checked him out before I gave him your information. Plus he looks like your father.

"Looks like Daddy?" I didn't have any pictures of him anywhere.

How do you know how my father looks?

**Your mom has a photo of him. I noticed it when we
helped her move into her apartment.**

That was Ma. Forever a fool for love. I shook my head and
replied.

Did he tell you Daddy Dearest is dying?
**What? No, he didn't. Just said he had something to
tell you and that he wanted to find you. I'm sorry,
Raina.**

"You're sorry, huh?" I muttered to myself and tossed the cell
on my bed, and then I threw myself on the bed. If he wanted to
be sorry, he should apologize for kicking me out of our home. I
didn't need Cam's sympathy.

Or love.

I was exhausted. I squeezed my eyes shut, praying for sleep
to drag me into a soundless void, but it wasn't to be. Instead,
thoughts of my dying daddy, lost brother, and jilted lover
haunted my dreams.

After a night of shitty sleep and shittier dreams, I had an
epiphany. I was a big sister. And just because Vic Jr. was an
adult didn't mean that I couldn't be there for him.

Granted, I wasn't the model of a successful life. I was jobless, homeless, and manless. But I could still be there, at least
emotionally, for Vic.

The issue was I needed his number. An even bigger issue,
my ex most likely had it.

I had a weak moment yesterday by texting Cam, but I didn't
need to make it a habit.

"Just say hello and ask the man for your brother's number.
Stay strong," I coached myself as I pulled my phone from the
charger.

Hey. How are you?
Good. What are you up to?

I tapped my lips, thinking through a nonchalant response.
Currently debating title names for my book.
What are the options?
***Woman to Woman* or *What Grandma Jean Taught Me*.**
Definitely Grandma Jean. I wish I could have met her.
Me too. She would've liked you . . .
I finally got to the point of the text.
So I didn't have a chance to get Vic's number. Do you happen to have it?
I released the breath I didn't realize I'd been holding in. Cam replied back with the number and added:
I'm proud of you. I know reaching out to your brother is hard and your father dying can't be easy . . . anyway just know that you're in my thoughts.

A stampede of wild horses thundered in my chest. Cam was miles away. I hadn't seen him in two months, but still I bloomed like a thirsty-ass desert flower under his praise. I thought through my next message. I needed to convey maturity, yet resilience. I wasn't sad. I was a woman about town. Not in reality, but Cam didn't need to know that.
Thanks, Cam. I appreciate your support.
"Should I add a smiley?" No. I shook my head. No smiley. A smiley was flirty and sweet.

I sent the text, rolled over, and screamed into my pillow. I hated this shit. I needed to move on with my life.

I called Vic, and it was awkward as all hell. From his starched voice and cool tone I could tell he was still pissed about the whole ignoring his existence thing. I didn't blame him. There was no excuse once I became an adult.

But I would own up to my mistake, and here I was, in a coffee shop near his job downtown, waiting for my brother with sweaty pits and shaking fingers gripping my coffee cup.

I spotted Vic as soon as he entered. He was all business casual in a nice blue shirt and navy blue slacks. I waved my hand in the air and he nodded, making a beeline toward me.

I stood. *Hug or handshake?* I debated with myself during the few seconds it took him to reach me.

I stretched out my hand, smile strained and heart smashing against my rib cage. "Hi."

"Hey." He clasped my hand and gave it a jerky shake.

I cleared my throat, and he released my hand. We both hurried to sit down.

"So thanks for, um, taking my phone call and for agreeing to meet me." I gripped my mug again. The heat from the cup gave me a small dose of comfort and confidence.

He rested his chin on his clasped hands. "Why did you call me?" His voice was still cool, but his eyes seemed curious.

"I would like the opportunity to get to know you. And I want to apologize for not reaching out to you over the years. I've thought about it, and I can admit that I resented you and your mother."

He nodded. "I can understand where you're coming from. Thanks for being honest."

His tone was thawing, and I relaxed my grip from around the cup. "Okay, so why don't we tell each other about ourselves? It seems that you know a few things about me from Cameron, so why don't you start?"

"All right. I'm a gym rat."

I snorted. "Naturally." I waved at his toned physique.

"Yeah, but it wasn't always that way. I was skinny and short as a kid. Didn't hit my growth spurt until I was seventeen. Coach in high school cut me every year but then begs me to try out my senior year. I told him to kiss my ass."

"You didn't?" I leaned forward and smiled. I could hear the pride in my voice. I totally would've said the same thing. Not out loud, but under my breath. Ma or Grandma Jean would've slapped the taste out of my mouth if I disrespected an adult.

"Well, I didn't exactly say 'kiss my ass.' I just told him I wasn't interested."

"Tell me more."

He went through a laundry list of things. We didn't have much in common, but I didn't care, I was desperate to somehow make up for twenty-something years in twenty minutes.

After a few minutes, we finally found something we had in common: music. My brother loved all genres, like me. I told him about my Mastermind group and how Nikki was on tour with her band. He promised to look her up.

Vic looked down at his phone. "Oh, shit. I gotta go. I've got a meeting in fifteen minutes." He stood and grabbed his messenger bag.

"Of course." I pushed back my chair and stood. "I'd like to hang out again."

A small smile curved his lips. "Sure, Rae-Rae."

I snorted, feigning annoyance at the nickname. "Looking forward to it, Vickie Junior."

"Touché." He smiled.

"I'll give you a call. Maybe tomorrow?"

"Sure. If you aren't busy, we can do lunch this weekend. Or I can show you my place." He seemed a little unsure.

"Trust me, I'm not busy. I'll call you, and we'll do lunch."

I relaxed back in my seat, a victorious smile on my face. I had done it. I'd swallowed my pride, and now my brother and I were on our way to forming a relationship. It was all thanks to Cam. He didn't have to point Vic in my direction, yet he did.

I wanted to thank him.

No, I wanted to *see* him.

Giving into my desires, I grabbed my phone and called him. After a few rings, the voicemail came on. I hung up, too nervous to leave a message.

Hey. I met up with Vickie.

Vickie? He quickly texted back.

Oh. So he ignored my call. I mentally waved away the on-slaught of humiliation that surrounded me like a dense fog.

Vic Jr. My brother . . .

Oh, yeah. He mentioned you guys were hanging out today.

"What? They're talking now?" I yelled. An executive-type dude scooted his chair away from me. Whatever. We lived in Atlanta. Plenty of people walked around talking to themselves.

You guys talk?

Yeah.

Like on a regular basis?

My thumb nearly broke the send button on the screen. Irritation tingled my scalp. It felt like a swarm of mosquitoes danced on my head. I don't know what I was more jealous about—Cameron forming a bond with my brother, or my brother feeling more comfortable talking to my ex.

About?

Sports, video games . . . you.

Oh. That's okay, then. A wide grin spread across my face. Cam talked about me. I knew he missed me, missed us. It was just a matter of time before he got over the whole marriage thing.

That's cool. So . . . wondering if you're free next week? I'd love to catch up.

I leaned away from the table, high on optimism—like I'd just had a good cigar and a great glass of Scotch.

I don't think that's a good idea. I'm not ready to talk yet. That's why I didn't pick up the phone.

The steady hum from the coffee shop disappeared.

Not ready to talk. He doesn't want to hear from me.

A sharp pain burned my chest.

I studied the message again, and my eyes zoned in on a word: *yet*. He wasn't ready to talk yet.

"I'm not giving up on you, Cameron."

* * *

"Damn, how much stuff do you have?" My brother swiped his brow and leaned against the moving truck.

I smirked. "What's the point of having all those muscles if you can't use them to move your big sister's most precious treasures?"

After we had lunch a few weeks ago, I casually mentioned I was moving in with Kara the following Saturday. Vic had volunteered to help in exchange for a six-pack of beer. I tried to give him money but he adamantly turned me down. My brother thought I was dirt poor. The just-graduated civil engineer thought he was balling and refused to let me pay for lunch. It was damn embarrassing, and I needed to make money from this book, pronto.

Vic gulped from a water bottle and then exhaled. "This was not the type of thing I'd imagined we'd do when I discovered I had a sibling."

"Sorry to burst your bubble. But the advantage of not knowing me when we were kids is that I didn't dress you up in my Barbie's mannequin clothes. Mr. Puff Puff, my poor neighbor's dog, God rest his soul, couldn't walk right after I stuffed his paws into Barbie's plastic heels."

My brother laughed tiredly. "I don't know what's more ridiculous, the dog dressed in drag or his name."

"Definitely his name." I punched his shoulder easily. Somehow, my brother had quickly carved out a space in my heart, and I cared again. He was smart, charming, and a little geeky and shy, but that totally worked for him. Best of all, he was the complete opposite of our father. *Thank God.*

"Raina!" Kara yelled from the porch of her home. "Can I start organizing your closet?"

I gave her a thumbs-up. "Go crazy."

"She's cute." Little brother gave Kara a head bob and a slow smile I'm sure he thought was sexy.

"She's old. Avert your eyes, young'un."

"I can't promise that." He shook his head. "Anyway, I think you're good to go. I don't do the unpacking stuff, so I'll see you next weekend."

"A whole week?" I poked out my bottom lip. "What are you up to?"

"I'm visiting Dad. You want to come?" he asked me, and it was not his first time.

"Nah." I shook my head. "I've got to get my stuff unpacked. Plus, I'm on deadline."

"Sure, you are." He gave me a tight smile. "Well, it's a standing offer. I go to the hospice every Sunday, but this time I'm staying for a few days."

"Got ya. Text me when you return."

"Okay." He hugged me. "Bye, Rae-Rae."

Just two weeks into living together, Kara and I were circling each other like starving alley cats. After fifteen years of friendship, we realized how much we didn't know about each other. I thought Kara was extreme with all her competition and wine obsession, which got on my nerves at times, but now I missed it. Brokenhearted Kara was pathetic. It was like seeing a blind newborn kitten struggle to get out of a basket.

She went to wine practice or whatever the hell she called it, worked at the restaurant, where she'd cut her hours in half so she could focus on her studies, and then returned home to study flash cards. Which was what she was doing now.

I needed to break this shit because her boring ass was seeping into me. I got up, ate, wrote, watched Netflix, and slept.

I flopped on the love seat beside Kara. She continued to

thumb through her notes and turned over the lined five-by-seven cards, muttering nonsense.

"Boooooooo!" I cupped a hand around my mouth for good measure. Homegirl needed a strong wakeup call.

Kara jumped, tossing her precious stack in the process. "What's wrong with you?"

I didn't answer her initially. We stared at each other, unease between us.

"We're friends, right?"

"Um, yeah." She rolled her eyes, as if the question was ludicrous.

"Right. Damn good friends, but we aren't *best friends*, would you agree?"

"Agreed. Sienna is my best friend." Her tone was matter-of-fact.

"And Nikki is mine. And our girls are living their lives like it's golden. We," I waved a hand between us, "are not."

And in times like these when your life is turned upside down and your main girl is indisposed, i.e. a rock star, you expanded your horizons. I refrained from voicing my thoughts. Didn't want Kara to think she was chopped liver. "We need to get to know each other. Hang out, just the two of us."

Kara nodded. "I can do that."

"So . . ." I clicked my tongue against the roof of my mouth. "What do you like to do for fun? Not the marathon stuff, like what do you do to relax?"

Kara restacked her cards and then placed them on the ottoman in front of us. "I like to hike. I enjoy reality TV and Disney movies." She mumble-rushed the latter confession.

"Excuse me?" I perked up, not expecting that answer. "*You* like Disney movies."

"Yes." She gave me a weary look as if she was preparing for me to judge her. "Mama and I used to snuggle up and watch them all the time. Even as adults." She smiled, but her eyes were distant.

I thought it was cute, interesting, and I was a little sad that I didn't know that about my friend.

"Okay, why don't we try something new that each person likes. I'm not an outdoors person by any means, but we can try hiking or watch your favorite cartoon."

"They're animated movies, but sure, we can do that." She gave me a small smile. "What do you like?"

"Watching movies, *adult movies*," I lightly teased. "Love hitting the cigar bars, trying new restaurants, and going to festivals." I shrugged. "So, what are you doing now? It's the weekend. We could start today by watching your favorite movie."

A smile broke across Kara's face, and I swear, a little light flickered in her eyes. Damn, she needed this.

"Sure!" She stretched. "Let me take a quick shower and we can get started."

She stood and then made her way toward the stairwell.

"What are we watching?" I yelled at her back.

"*The Little Mermaid*." She jogged up the stairs.

I instantly regretted my suggestion. "Wonderful."

The following week, Kara and I did something I liked. I smoothed my little black dress that hugged my curvy frame. I sat on the footstool in front of my mirror, reached for my lotion, and slathered a good amount on my legs. A dab of perfume, which was pointless because we were going to smell like smoke as soon as we entered the cigar bar, and then a swipe of lipstick, and I was ready.

Leaving my room, I yelled for Kara while walking down the stairs, "You ready?"

"Yeah. Let me grab my earrings."

After a few minutes, Kara joined me downstairs. We were no longer circling each other like alley cats, and I dare say, we were closer. Last Sunday, we hiked Stone Mountain. I bravely battled mosquitoes and pollen while Kara twirled around like one of her Disney characters. She said she got her best smells in during a hike, which helped her identify and describe wines more easily.

Wine was wine. Bitter, sweet, good, and sometimes gross.

We took a car service from our phone app to the Midtown area.

As usual, the popular cigar bar was male-dominated. We got a couple of outright stares and a few head nods from acquaintances I'd met during previous visits.

One of my favorite servers greeted us by the door. "Hey, Raina. Long time no see."

"Yeah, Daisy, it's been a while." I gave the tall blonde a hug. "Got any good tables for me and my girl?" I nodded toward Kara.

"For you? Always." She smiled and waved at us to follow her. "Is this okay?" She guided us to a tallboy table with large, square chairs.

"Absolutely," I told Daisy.

"Works for me," Kara agreed behind me.

"Great. I'll get your friend a cocktail list. Raina, you still want the dark and stormy?"

"You know it."

"Do you have a wine list?" Kara asked, settling herself into the chair.

Daisy nodded. "I'll grab the menu and be right back."

"So, this is my spot." I proudly looked around. Just a few feet away, a preseason football game was displayed on mute. We were seated adjacent to the cigar room. The speakers overhead blasted neo soul music.

Daisy returned with my drink and a menu for Kara. She ordered some fancy-ass wine I'd never heard of while I vibed to the music. I handed my credit card to Daisy. "We can start a tab."

"The first round of drinks are free." She jerked her head to a group of men playing dominoes at the corner table near the door.

"I'm sure Cam wouldn't mind a little freebie," Daisy joked.

"Oh, um, we aren't together anymore."

"Oh!" Her blue eyes looked genuinely aggrieved. "Well, I'm sorry to hear that. You two were always so . . ." She shook her head, as if she finally remembered her manners. "Well, anyway, enjoy the first one from the guys. Let me know when you're ready to select your cigars, unless you brought some from home."

"Nope. Come back in a few minutes and we'll be ready to go back to the cigar room to make our selection."

Daisy gave me another pained look and then escaped as if the hounds of hell were on her heels.

"So that wasn't awkward at all." Kara broke the silence.

"Right," I sighed. "Obviously, this used to be me and Cam's spot."

"Then why did you choose this place?"

I tapped my fingers on the table. "Cam and I did a lot of things together. If I avoided every place that reminded me of him—of us—I'd be a hermit. I've got to get back to living." I narrowed my eyes at her. "Speaking of living, you need to get your ass back out there."

Kara rolled her eyes. "I don't have the time. I study, work, then study some more."

Daisy returned with Kara's wine. Kara skipped out on the sniff and shake routine she usually did with every glass of wine she drank, and gulped down the drink in two swallows.

I signaled Daisy and pointed to Kara's empty glass. "Another."

We didn't say anything, just listened to the music and absently watched the game. Daisy returned with another round of drinks, and soon after we picked our cigars. I had a good buzz going by drink number two and a third of the way through my Cohiba cigar.

Kara broke our easy silence. "I'm sad, Raina," she softly confessed. "I'm thirty-three, and I'm separated from the man I thought I'd spend the rest of my life with. And I don't know how to help him. The only friends I have are you, the girls, and my wine group. The wine group is debatable. They're a bunch of obsessive psychos."

"Worse than you?"

"Yesss," she hissed. "So if I'm walking around like ghost lady, I just . . . I don't know what to do. The only thing I can focus on is this exam in a few months. And the crux of it all is that I'm terrified of this test."

"Girl, as much as you're studying, you will ace it."

"That's the problem. I'll ace it and then what? What's next? I love my career, don't get me wrong, but I want to have a life outside of expounding on wine complexities." She tugged the ends of her recently hacked hair. "I wish I had my life together and could move on like you." She waved in my direction. "But to be honest, when Darren cracked, so did I. And I don't have anyone to hold me up."

Kara had mentioned on our hike that Darren was going through some traumatic issues that stemmed from childhood. Kara decided to fall back, as he'd asked of her, but she was devastated that he hadn't wanted her help.

"I'm not fine, either," I confessed.

Kara snorted. "You don't say." Her lips tipped at the corners, forming a small smile. "Girl, I know you aren't okay. But you're doing better than me. And you have that little hottie brother of yours helping you along the way. Speaking of, what's up with that? How come you never mentioned you had a brother to the girls? Does Nikki know?"

"No. Just a dark family secret Ma and I never discussed. When Daddy left us, he ran off to start another family. He got some other woman pregnant, then sent the divorce papers through the mail."

Kara gasped. "That bastard." She leaned forward. "Tell me. Tell me everything," she encouraged.

"Well, *that bastard* is dying." I shook my head. "My brother didn't know about me. He found a returned letter Daddy had sent and confronted him. So, of course, Daddy Dearest's last wish before he leaves the earth is to reconnect with me." I shrugged. "I guess he wants my forgiveness."

"Are you going to give it to him?" There was no judgment in Kara's voice, just curiosity. I hadn't realized until she said it, but I needed someone to listen, to not lecture me about forgiveness.

"Don't know for sure, but I'm leaning toward no. If I see him, it's for my brother. Or to show him that I flourished despite his abandonment. My intentions are not pure."

"What is he dying of?"

"Last stages of emphysema, and he doesn't have long. No more than two or three months." I tore my cocktail napkin into smaller pieces. "What do . . ." I cleared my throat. "What do you think I should do? What would you do?"

Kara gave a husky laugh. "We aren't the same person, Raina, you know that."

"I do. But I still want your opinion. You don't sugarcoat things. Nikki, despite her gruff exterior, would tell me to forgive. I think she would see her father in mine. Sienna, despite her bad-girl phase, is an optimist."

"True." Kara nodded.

"So? How about it?" I asked. "The floor is yours."

"Okay, here goes. And no sugarcoating. But if I were you, I'd do it. And it's not because my mama died and there's an ache in my heart that will never go away." She took a sip of her wine, then continued. "Don't do it for him. Do it for *you*. You

246 / SHARINA HARRIS

need a resolution and, girl, no offense, but you've got major daddy issues."

"Well, damn. At least lube me up with Vaseline before you—"

"Stop." Kara waved a hand. "You're doing the sarcastic defensive thing. I'm giving the opinion *you* asked for."

"By all means, continue." I grabbed the lit cigar from the ashtray, inhaled, and took a long puff. With my lips, I formed a smoke ring that danced around Kara's head.

She frowned and coughed, but the ring of smoke didn't deter her.

"When your father dies, so does your opportunity to heal. But if you talk to him, you can move on in your life. Namely, your love life. You need to be able to see a guy for who he is, not worry he'll leave like your dad."

I knew Kara was right, and I knew her answer before she gave it to me. Guess we knew each other better than I had originally estimated.

"So, I think I screwed up a little with Cam."

"Sure, you did." Kara nodded. "But you shouldn't let him off the hook. He knew where you stood regarding marriage. And, honestly, I think with time, a *looong* time, granted, you would've gotten to that place. He forced your hand, and he lost. You both lost. To be honest, I think you guys should try again. You could work it out."

"You think so?" My voice sounded small and unsure.

"I know so. That man loves you, and you love him. Everything else will take some work, but it's fixable."

"For what it's worth, I think Darren loves you, too. He's just confused."

"I wish I knew, but I honestly don't. You didn't see the empty look he gave me every night before he rolled over to his side of the bed. Like I was a stranger. A stranger he wasn't particularly fond of." She took a pull from her cigar. "God only knows how things will pan out."

I reached over and squeezed her hand. "I'll hold you up."

"What?" Kara tilted her head.

"You said that you didn't have anyone to hold you up. But I can. You aren't alone. We're in this together, no matter what." I lifted my glass to clink with hers and to seal the vow I'd just given her.

"Alone, together," she repeated. It sounded silly as hell, but it was meaningful. Kara and I were no longer semifriends who tolerated each other.

Daisy came back to the table with fresh drinks on her tray. "Another round from the gentlemen in the corner."

"Nice." I grabbed my drink and lifted the glass in the air, giving the men a silent thank-you.

I looked at Kara. "What do you say that we pause on being *alone together* and go flirt with the cute guys across the room?"

Kara nodded. "Dibs on the redbone with the baby face."

"You always liked them light."

"Not true. Remember Patrick from college? Definition of tall, dark, and handsome."

"Yeah, he was fine. All right, you can have the wannabe Drake and I'll take Wesley Snipes circa nineties."

We stood from our seats.

"Wesley Snipes looks the same as he did back then," Kara whispered as we approached the men. "His black ain't crackin'."

"I know, right?" We gave each other air high fives.

For the remainder of the night, we laughed, played dominoes, or bones, as they called it, and flirted. It was fun, the most fun I'd had in a while. We exchanged numbers with the guys and promised to call.

Kara and I giggled and swayed as we waited on the curb for the car service to pick us up.

"Are you calling Drake?" I asked her, wrapping my arm around her shoulder, more so to keep my balance.

"No. I need to pass this test and then, I don't know." She shrugged.

"You don't know?"

"I don't. Being out tonight, it was everything. I lived in the moment. Didn't think about my test, or fret about Darren, or try to guess what region the wine came from. I flirted with a guy, I hung out with my girl, and I'm tipsy! I guess . . . I guess what I'm saying is that I appreciate tonight." Her voice grew softer. "I'm content, and I don't want this feeling to end. I don't need to base my happiness on a title or a man. I need to live fully in these moments."

"Well, damn."

"Too deep for a Saturday night?" She winced.

"No, what you're saying is perfect. I needed to hear that."

Kara shook her head. "No, you didn't. Despite your breakup, you haven't missed a beat. You have an agent, a book deal. Nothing to sneeze at."

"And you are, too." I squeezed her shoulders tighter.

"No, I'm a zombie. I have no passion, no purpose."

"No, you're doing great. Your mama passed away less than two years ago, and now you're separated. Life has given you a lotta bumps, so give yourself some credit. And despite it all, you're going after what you want."

She nodded. "I love what I do. I just don't want my career to define me."

"Then don't. Like you said, live in the moments."

"Fine. I'll live in the moment, and you need to be brave."

"Brave?"

"Your daddy. Cam."

"Where do I begin?"

"I have faith in you, Raina. You'll figure it out."

I needed to, because although flirting shamelessly with good-looking guys into the wee hours of the morning was fun, I only wanted Cam. I didn't know how, but I needed to get him back.

After we returned home, I rushed to my room upstairs and texted him.

I held my breath as I typed,

Hey. Miss you. Can we meet up? Please?

After ten minutes of staring at the message, I pressed send. I stared at the phone until I fell asleep.

A few hours later, midmorning, I woke up with a start. Scrambling for my phone, I found it underneath my pillow.

Heart slamming against my chest, I pressed my phone screen open.

I can't, Raina.

I huffed, then typed: **Why?**

He didn't answer right away, in fact, it took two long hours before a response.

I'm not ready. And I don't think you are, either.

CHAPTER 14

The Night My Life Began—Kara

"Talk to me," I whispered into the wine glass. The dark liquid sloshed in the cup, my fingers wrapped around the stem.

"This wine has black pepper. Violets grown in the area. Southern region of France. Year: 1998."

Martin, one of my study partners, sighed and rolled his eyes. "What? No."

"No?" I asked, feigning surprise. The wine wasn't talking to me today. I sat the glass on the table. "Which part?"

"You tell me." Martin's hard, beady eyes drilled me. I didn't blame him. My mind wasn't on wine, a bad thing given we were just two months away from the exams.

I'd taken my conversation with Raina seriously about enjoying my life. I blew off a few study sessions and called up some of my tennis buddies. Despite my rustiness, I got my Serena Williams on and waxed my opponent's ass like she was Sharapova in a Grand Slam. Anyone who loved tennis knew that the tennis phenom seemed to take extreme delight in whupping her ass around the tennis court. The high from winning jumpstarted something in me. Tomorrow I planned on signing up for a 5k.

"Kara?" Martin's voice, now impatient interrupted me.

Eduardo, my other partner seated beside me, bumped my knee. His brown hands rubbed my shoulder. "Taste it again. Tell us the story." He picked up the glass and lifted it to my lips. The gesture seemed harmless, but his sensual brown eyes sparked with something intimate, dangerous.

I cleared my throat. "I've got it." I sniffed and closed my eyes.

"Take your time." Eduardo's lovely Spanish accent teased my senses and clouded my thoughts.

"Yes," Martin hissed. "Take your time. We've got all night."

"Shush, Martin," Claudia admonished.

"The fruit is . . . elusive. Very mature but bitter and complex. From age and time. Hints of chocolate and leather. Vintage. 2005. Napa."

Martin inclined his head and then focused his attention on Claudia.

Eduardo rubbed my shoulder. "Great job, Kara. Vintage can be tricky."

"Yeah." I munched on a tortilla chip and washed it down with sparkling water with lemon. After a few sips, I swirled it around to remove the chalky taste in my mouth.

"I had to beg Roddy to let us try it," Eduardo whispered, his voice conspiratorial.

"So, you're the one I should blame."

"Blame?" Eduardo's smile gave way to dimples. The man was gorgeous and knew it.

"You should be thanking me. That was a gift. I taste it, and I want to cry." He lifted his fingers to his mouth and kissed them, like a chef giving a dish praise.

I couldn't help but laugh at Eduardo's earnest expression.

"Don't you wonder what happened during this time? We are drinking history, the heart and soul of the year. How, I wonder, did they tame the plant that doesn't want to be controlled?"

"Listen to Shakespeare over here." Martin snorted at Eduardo's musings.

Eduardo raised a hand. "To be or not to be an asshole like Martin. That is the question."

Despite the insult, Martin, Claudia, and I laughed at the joke. One, because Eduardo waxed poetic about wine nearly ever study session, and two, Martin was indeed an asshole, unapologetically so. But he made the people around him stronger, tougher. You were on your A-game because you knew one day Martin would be one of the greats.

Eduardo and Martin were frenemies, and each would jump at the opportunity to embarrass the other. While Martin excelled at tasting, Eduardo was a master at regions and history. Our fourth partner, Claudia, was proficient at the service part, despite her seemingly punk rock appearance.

"Okay, Martin's turn." I pushed the test flight in front of him. He went through the paces and surprisingly got the last one incorrect. A softball one at that.

"Sorry, Marty boy, but the last one was incorrect," I informed him.

"Was it?" He mimicked the same tone I'd used before.

"Yep." Eduardo nodded, after leaning over and verifying my printed-out answer bank.

Martin sighed and folded his arms like a five-year-old. "And what do you two know? Both of you failed. Kara failed twice already."

Three times, but who's counting.

"True enough." I ground my teeth. "It doesn't change the fact that you guessed incorrectly. I know the pressure is getting to you, but don't take it out on me."

"The pressure is getting to me?" He laughed, leaning back in his seat. "The only reason you're in this group is because Roddy begged us to let you join. Sure, you were a great asset initially, but for the past three months, you've been a dud. Look at your clothes, they are hanging off you. If anyone is buckling under pressure, it's you."

Eduardo raised a hand. "Don't go attacking her because you got an answer wrong."

"You know it's true. Hell, we all talked about kicking her ass out a few weeks ago when she blew us off because of a headache. Give me a break."

The headache was the day I'd played tennis and then afterward, Raina and I went clubbing. I had no regrets. I needed to have fun, to forget Darren and wine and the pressure of this test.

Butthurt Martin continued his rant. "Why in the hell should we keep you around anyway? You don't have what it takes. What happens if other things in your life go wrong? Huh?" Martin asked in a bratty voice.

I threw my head back and laughed. God, how I wish it were just about this damn test. I'd give my kidney for that to be the only reason.

"Oh, shit," Claudia whispered. "She's cracking up."

Martin shrugged. "Some people can't hack it."

"Oh," I stopped laughing and focused on Martin. "Oh, how I wish it were that simple. I'm separated from my husband. I've gotta put my house on the market, and I'll be starting my life over again. So I apologize if I'm not a ray of fucking sunshine, but yet here I am. I'm studying my ass off. And last I checked, I've aced all taste tests and regions pop quizzes with the exception of today. When Claudia calls me late because she works nights at the restaurant, I comply. Martin, when you lost your regions map that outlined the history of wine, who did you call?"

"You," he quietly agreed.

"Right. So, Martin, you can kiss the darkest part of my ass, which, I'll have you know is in the southern region where the sun don't shine." I grabbed my bottles of wine and packed them in my roller bag.

"Wait!" Martin called, as I prepared to leave the study group in divalike fashion. As far as I was concerned, everyone here could kick rocks.

Well, except for Eduardo, who stuck up for me. Plus, he's hot.

"Why?" I asked Martin as I stretched the handle to pull the bag behind me.

"I was wrong. We should've asked what was going on. This journey is hard and lonely. My girl just broke up with me last month because she said I love wine more than her."

Claudia chuckled. "You kind of do."

"Shut up." Martin smiled, not at all denying the accusation. "Anyway, I was wrong. And you're right, I'm stressed, and I shouldn't have taken it out on you."

"I'm sorry, too," Claudia added, as she tucked a purple-streaked strand behind her ear.

I'd heard my mentor Roddy scream many times for Claudia to dye her hair a respectable color if she expected to work at a five-star restaurant. Claudia sighed and continued. "This is my third time around, too, and I broke up with my girlfriend last year because of this damn test."

"I didn't realize you're a lesbian." Martin scrunched his brows. I could get the confusion. They'd been flirting nonstop, even when Martin had a girlfriend.

"Bi," she said, giving him a saucy smile.

"Forgive us?" Eduardo, asked sliding his hand over his buzz-cut hair.

"Sure." I moved my bag back into the corner. Instead of us going back to studying, we swapped war stories about how our poor significant others had to deal with our craziness.

"My girlfriend's little girl sniffed everything. She would set up her juice boxes, swirl, and spit the juice in a bowl. It drove

Jenny crazy. And everything tasted like apple or grape juice."
Claudia snickered.

"My ex's friends used to call me Rain Man," Martin confessed.

We all laughed. Martin had the tendency to recall wine in a robotic and matter-of-fact voice.

The night went on with more ribbing. It felt good to laugh deep from my belly, gut-splitting laughter. I'd relegated the group to business only, but now I realized I'd missed out on friendship.

My eyes caught the time on Martin's oven. "I can't believe its two o'clock in the morning. I need to get home."

"Me too." Eduardo looked down at his watch. "Let's walk out together. We've got a long trek back to our cars."

Martin lived in an apartment in Midtown with zero parking, so we had to park on the side streets nearly a block away. I didn't want to walk alone in the city at night. It was a relief to leave with him.

We gathered our bags and bottles. "Bye, Claudia. Bye, Martin." I waved and walked out the door.

"Tonight was fun, huh?" Eduardo slowed his long-limbed pace to match mine.

"It actually was." I heard the surprise in my voice. "I didn't realize how—"

"Cool, awesome, and amazing we are?" he supplied.

"Yeah. I guess I was so caught up in my personal drama, and focused on passing the test, I forgot how to make friends— well, outside of my girlfriends."

"Oh, yeah. Is that the one you went to the cigar bar with the other weekend?"

I stopped my steps. *How in the heck did he know about that?*

"I follow you on social media. You posted the quintessential smoke ring picture online."

"Oh, I . . ." I cleared my throat. "Didn't realize you followed me." I resumed walking, picking up my pace.

He laughed and squeezed my shoulder. "I'm following you, not stalking you."

"Oh, well, yeah I knew that." I laughed, too, as we neared our cars. "And shut up." I nudged his shoulder. "I'm just not used to whatever this is that I'm doing."

"Being single again?"

"Not quite single and not quite divorced. We're separated."

"Damn, I'm sorry about that, Kara." Eduardo's chocolate eyes reflected sincerity. "Any chance for reconciliation?"

"Kind of hard to reconcile when you don't speak." I shrugged.

"That's tough."

"Yeah." My voice shook. "We were nearing our seven-year anniversary. Didn't even get to the itchy part." I leaned against my car, swiping at an errant tear.

"Hell, maybe one day you'll find someone that you'll get to seventy years with," he said, smiling.

I shuddered, imagining myself at a century old. "I'll settle for fifty. And thanks for talking and walking me back."

Eduardo nodded and jerked his thumb toward his car. "See you later?"

"Every Tuesday, Thursday, and Saturday."

He nodded, turned on his heels, and walked a few steps toward his car. He stopped, turned and speed-walked back to me. With a look of determination on his handsome face, he cupped my neck and kissed me. The shock of his soft lips against mine popped my mouth open. After a few beats, I relaxed under his expert tongue.

Eduardo broke away. "Damn, you taste like . . . like strawberries. I thought you'd be bitter."

"Bitter?" I jerked back. "Why? Because I'm going to be a divorcee?"

"No. From the wine."

I licked my lips, my heart racing. But as expertly as he kissed, something was off. Wrong. I slammed my back against the car. "W-what . . . What was that?" I fingered my bruised lips.

"I'm sorry." He stuffed fingers through his hair. "You're tough and extraordinary and beautiful. And you standing there, looking fragile and fierce at the same time, I just had to kiss you."

"Look, I'm not even divorced and I—"

"I know. I knew as soon as I charged over to kiss you that it wasn't the right time. But I had to take my shot." He gave me a small smile. "See you later?" He repeated his earlier question. But I knew this time it meant something different. He wanted to make sure we were okay.

"Every Tuesday, Thursday, and Saturday."

I stared at my phone, hands sweating and shaking, as I had been for the past thirty minutes. My mouth went hot and dry, so dry the swallow I forced had scratched my throat.

Can I swing by later today? I have a few things I need to get from the basement.
Darren.

I wished I could run into Raina's room to get her advice, but she wasn't home. She already had a full day planned with her brother, going to Six Flags, of all things. I shuddered thinking about the lines and thousands upon thousands of people.

"You can do this." I wiped my hands on my summer dress and responded.

Sure. What time?

I asked so I could get the heck out of Dodge. I needed to see Robotic Darren like I needed a hole in my brain. I already had a huge hole in my heart.

There were dancing dots on the phone screen. He was responding quicker than I had anticipated.

I'm a few minutes away, if that's okay?

My heart stuttered and plopped on the ground. I wasn't ready for this. I wasn't ready for him. I hadn't spoken to the man in months. No talks of divorce proceedings or *I miss yous.* Just radio silence. I didn't know what to do or say. From the research I'd done online on how to support a partner who'd been sexually abused, the biggest factor was to be supportive and give them time to process their feelings.

I bit my lip and paced the floor. What in the heck did he need from here anyway? He took everything, rented out a storage unit up the street. The day he left was the most emotional he'd been since starting his sessions with Dr. Fuckboy. He hugged me, albeit awkwardly, and promised to continue to pay half the mortgage. I didn't know where he'd been staying, and I didn't ask. I'd been too torn up to form a coherent sentence.

I rushed to the mirror, taking a quick scan of my appearance. When one goes through a divorce, one wants the soon-to-be ex–significant other to do a double take—and not from pity.

The summer dress that used to hug my curves hung from my body like a burlap sack. And speaking of ugly bags, they were present and accounted for under my eyes. My hair was smooth and together thanks to my earlier salon appointment.

Pulling open my vanity drawer, I grabbed and then scattered makeup on the counter. I swiped the foundation stick across my face, focusing on the bags.

"Problem solved." I smiled at myself in the mirror. I dabbed on a clear gloss that tasted like strawberries.

"Damn, you taste like . . . like strawberries."

A wave of guilt stopped me. The kiss was soft, gentle, reverent. And though the feelings weren't there for Eduardo, I was secretly thrilled to feel wanted.

The doorbell rang. I was surprised. He had a key, and he'd paid well over half of the mortgage. He could walk in if he pleased, but I knew he did this to prepare me, prepare us, for the reunion.

I gave myself one more glance in the mirror and then rushed downstairs. I slowed midway down. *Calm down. Keep your expectations low, deep-blue-sea low.*

I counted my breaths; I was at thirty by the time I arrived at the front door. After keying in the security code, I opened the door.

Darren, back against the brick entryway, rubbed a hand over his scruff. There were patches of hair just below his cheek and along his jawline, a thick 'stache that I wasn't all too sure I cared for. His normally short hair was long with a light curl. After my long perusal, his coffee black eyes caught mine. I gasped at what I saw.

It wasn't blank, but active. *Alive.*

The small light of hope I'd had and pretended that I hadn't, extinguished. Outside of the gruff and scruff, he seemed to be healing. *Without me.* Maybe he truly was better by himself. He didn't need me. I was the crutch, and without me he was flying.

Good. Good for him. A smiled curled on my lips and yet, at the same time, my heart fell somewhere around my toes.

"Are you going to let me in, Kara?" His deep voice pulled me out of my weird headspace.

"Of course," I flattened my voice, grabbed my dignity and stepped back. Darren walked into the house and somehow invaded my space.

"I'll be upstairs. Just lock up and activate the code before you leave." I could feel his eyes, hot on my back. Grabbing the banister, I hopped on the first step and dashed all the way up.

I shut the door to the bedroom. Like an old lady, I lowered my tired body to the bed, closed my eyes, and slumped against my pillow. I made it. I survived the encounter. Was it awkward? Yes. Hell, yes, but I needed to see him. I needed the closure.

260 / SHARINA HARRIS

I hummed the power ballad from one of my favorite movies by Disney, "Let It Go."

Fitting. I felt cold and alone, but I needed to find my inner strength. I didn't have the worst voice in the world, and the lyrics soothed me.

"Hey."

I startled from my position, my eyes flew open. "W-what . . ." I cleared my throat. "What are you doing here? In my room." Technically, our room, but, hell, he left. So, I was claiming it.

"I forgot something in here."

I narrowed my eyes. Everything was clear of Darren—I made sure of that—but I didn't have the desire to call him on it. "Fine. I'll go into another room while you look around." I rolled out of the bed.

"Why do you keep running away from me?"

I paused at the door. "What?"

"You keep leaving."

I turned around. "I'm giving you space."

"You're giving yourself space."

"What if I am?" I bristled at his accusation. "You asked me for time. I'm giving it." I sighed, looked at the ceiling. "How are you? You look good."

"I'm doing well. Much better than before. I'm working through a lot of things."

"Good." I licked my lips. "I guess time away from me is a good thing." I cleared my throat, gearing myself up for the next question. "So do you want a divorce? Is that why you're here?"

He flinched as if I'd stuck him with a shank. Still, he didn't answer.

Neither of us had hired an attorney. I'd been playing the waiting game, determined for him to make the first move to end our marriage. "Why haven't you filed the papers yet?"

"Why haven't you?" he parroted.

"I asked first."

He sat on the bed and patted the space beside him. I shook my head. He was right, I needed space from him.

He took a deep breath and nodded, as if conceding to my decision.

"I don't want to do this anymore."

My body rocked from the verbal slap, and my stomach curled into itself. *I knew it.* We weren't going to make it. "If you can't do this," I whispered, my throat suddenly raw, "then file the papers. Let me go so you can continue healing. You can find someone who can support you, someone you love."

"Allow me to clarify." He stood. "I can't do this, be apart from you. I changed counselors. I realized he wasn't any good, and I received a recommendation from one of my coworkers. They could tell I wasn't myself, and Dr. Caine, she's great."

"You're healed?"

"Working on it. I'm not there yet, but things are clearer now that the fog is gone."

"Why are you here, Darren?"

"I'd like for you to come to one of my sessions with Dr. Caine. I'll be happy to answer any questions you have, and Dr. Caine will provide some structure, make sure we have a constructive conversation."

"I don't know, Darren . . ."

"Please. Give me another chance. I love you, Kara. Always have and always will, but I was lost."

He came closer until he backed me against the wall. It was everything I'd wanted to hear, but something fell flat. I couldn't believe what he said. Maybe I needed to go with him for, at the very least, a resolution. Just like I'd told Raina she should do with her father.

"Fine. I'll come to one session."

"Thank you. I think this will be good for us," he whispered. His breath grazed my cheek.

He stepped back, giving me much-needed space. "I'll call Dr. Caine on Monday and send you the details."

I nodded.

"Okay, I'll give you some space." He turned toward the door.

"Don't forget your *stuff*."

He turned around, eyes dancing. "Don't worry. I got what I came here for."

Darren's new counselor's office was different from Dr. Fuck-boy's. There was no fancy waiting room, just an entryway and open office. Behind a desk sat a white woman in her late fifties or early sixties with snow white hair, a pair of purple glasses perched on her nose.

Darren was already seated on an overstuffed brown sofa. He stood and wiped his palms on his jeans.

He met me halfway to the couch and placed a gentle kiss on my cheek. "Thanks for coming, Care Bear."

I nearly flinched at the name. He hadn't called me his Care Bear in years. "Hey," I whispered to him.

"Hello, Kara." Dr. Caine greeted me. "I'm so pleased you agreed to join us." Her voice was soft and conversational. "Would you like some water, coffee, or tea?"

"Water would be nice." I was usually a tea person, but I needed something cold for my parched throat.

Dr. Caine nodded and pulled out a bottle of water from the knee-high fridge near her desk.

I grabbed the bottle, then settled on the couch. My back hit the knitted rainbow-color throw on top of the sofa.

Dr. Caine gave me a motherly smile. "Comfortable?"

"Yes," I lied and nodded. I was as comfortable as wearing a pair of itchy wool pants. And who in their right mind could be at ease with a woman who planned to air out dirty laundry?

She reached for a pen and yellow legal pad. "I suggested that

Darren invite you to counseling. Over the past few months, he's come a long way. I think we'll be able to have productive conversations that will lend context to Darren's past and how it's shaped his outlook on relationships." She paused and waved to Darren. "Why don't you get started?"

He nodded and turned to face me. "Kara?"

"Yes." I smoothed nonexistent wrinkles from my chinos.

"I want to apologize for the pain and confusion I caused you. I never meant to hurt you. Through my therapy, I realized my unresolved issues impacted our marriage. I want to tell you about my past, if you're open to it."

I nodded. "You know that I am. What hurt me the most is that you didn't feel you could trust me to share your burdens."

Darren wiped his hands on his jean-clad thighs. He lowered his head and took a deep breath, as if centering himself. Tapping his feet against the hardwood floor, he hesitated a few more seconds, then focused on me.

"You know about my sexual abuse and a little about my upbringing. I grew up in a cold home. I knew my childhood wasn't typical, so I was determined to find someone I could love and be loved in return. It sounds crazy, but even back then I knew what I wanted. I dreamed of and craved love. I just didn't know how to do it. It wasn't natural for me because I didn't grow up in a loving environment. And to make matters worse, I never healed from my childhood scars." Darren rubbed his thighs again.

After seven years together, I knew his tells. He was stalling, but this time, I wouldn't rush him to speak his truth. I leaned back into the sofa, twirled the crocheted blanket that rested below my shoulder, and tried to stay in the present.

The past hurt, the future was hazy. Despite my sobering thoughts, somewhere in the deep recesses of my heart that I thought had gone cold, a flare of desire heated my chest.

Darren cleared his throat and gave me a strained, here-goes-nothing smile. "I married you too soon—I shouldn't have done that, knowing that I hadn't addressed the past." He went on with more details and told me about a time when his grandmother left him in a car for hours when he was five years old. Another *American Horror Story*–esque anecdote about his grandfather locking him in a dark room when he didn't do as he was told—usually something small, like not eating all his vegetables or not cleaning his room. As a result, he was afraid to confide and connect with others.

No wonder he was so withdrawn. Video games became his friend. The internet raised him.

He sat back, quiet for a few moments. I knew he was giving me time to digest his words.

Dr. Caine spoke up. "Kara, how do you feel about what Darren has shared?"

My hands were ice cold. I rubbed them together without building much heat. I was relieved that Darren had shared, but I was also terrified.

Unlike Dr. Caine, I wasn't qualified to deal with his baggage. And as selfish as it seemed, I wasn't sure if I wanted to. This was a man who didn't know himself or his feelings.

Still, this was a strong effort on his end, and I needed to handle him with care. "I'm glad you were able to talk to me about this, Darren. I can tell you've come a long way. I want you to know that I love you. But . . ."

"But what?"

"It seems like you're still sorting through your issues. There is still a lot of confusion on your end."

"Kara." Dr. Caine tapped the pen to her pad. "What do you think he's confused about?"

"He grew up in a home without a lot of love. He has a lot to process," I hedged, not wanting to completely voice my concerns.

Darren reached for my hand. "If you think I'm confused about loving you, I'm not. Let me make this clear: I love you."

Love. He was the first to say "I love you." Had Dr. Caine helped him enough to know what love was? I wasn't all too convinced.

"Why?" I asked.

"Why what?"

"Why do you love me? Do you need me or do you love me?"

"Both," he quickly replied.

"So, you need me."

"And I love you."

"Love or *in love*?"

"Both."

I shook my head. "I don't know. You said in that letter to your grandfather that you didn't know what love is." I shook my head. "Maybe you love this life we've built, and you love me as a friend. But I cannot believe that after just a few months, all of sudden you see the light."

"I do love you, Kara." There was frustration in his voice, which added to my frustration. "I was processing. I was reliving the memories of what happened to me. And being in that dark place made me question everything I'd done in my life. The decisions I'd made were made by someone who was broken, and I didn't trust myself. But then I remembered when we first met."

The night we met, I was shadowing Roddy at a restaurant. One of Darren's friends had graduated with a master's in business. His family and a few friends were celebrating.

"I couldn't keep my eyes off you," he continued. "Everything slowed down, my heart nearly jumped out of my chest. And when you spoke to me in that husky, sexy-as-hell voice, asking me what I wanted, it took everything in me to not say *you*."

I looked away, my cheeks blazing.

"I was determined to get your number. I'd never in all my life chased a woman before."

The party he'd sat with had stayed until closing. I'd been doing my end-of-shift duties, counting the wine bottles, properly storing the opened ones.

"I had to get your number that night because I knew damn well I wouldn't be able to afford to come to the restaurant again, and I couldn't risk coming and you not working that day." He smiled. "Then I scared you, and you dropped a bottle of wine."

I remembered the wine slipping from my fingers. But I hadn't been scared. Not like he thought. I was scared at my heart nearly bursting from my chest when I saw the way his eyes tracked my movements. The way he licked his sensuous lips. The cologne he wore turned me on so much that I breathed out of my mouth to resist the temptation that teased my olfactory system. After the second time I returned to their table, it took extreme effort not to turn into a puddle of lust.

"Why are you doing this?" Tears filled my vision. I turned to face the counselor. "Why am I here?"

Dr. Caine nodded to Darren, and I returned my attention to him.

"Dr. Caine asked me about my happiest memory ever. I immediately thought of that moment. And she said, there you go." When he exhaled, I smelled the mint in his breath.

"I didn't get what she was saying at first. I asked her what she meant, and she told me to figure it out. I go home and I'm lying in bed, staring at the ceiling, thinking about my best memories. Every time, you're the star. And then it hit me: That was the night my life began. I love you. Down to the soles of my feet, I love you. I want more memories with you. I want us to top my happiest memory."

I stood from the couch. My head spun, wariness and optimism doing a torturous tango.

"All right." Dr. Caine's voice broke me from my trance.

"Kara, do you have any more questions for Darren?"

I shook my head. I was overwhelmed. "Not right now."

"This was a good start." Dr. Caine leaned back in her chair. "Kara, would you be willing to come to another session? Perhaps next week? Tuesday, same time?"

The walls were closing in. *No, this is too much, too soon.*

"Yes." I agreed despite my internal struggle.

"Wonderful." She clapped her hands together. "Next time you'll get to talk more, and we will discuss your expectations for each other."

I met with Dr. Caine and Darren the following Tuesday and every week following for the next six weeks. I finally got used to speaking in front of the therapist. She was the nonjudgmental, approachable auntie I never had. Each time we met she greeted us with a smile.

Somehow the counseling transitioned from Darren to us. Not all the discussions were pleasant or productive. Darren had disclosed his feelings about my tests and how I'd become withdrawn after my mother's death. It hurt to hear about my shortcomings, but I knew it was true.

We had an exercise where we told her two things we were grateful for. Darren always mentioned something about me. I teetered between work and friends, but at this past meeting, I'd said, "Grateful for our conversation. Grateful for our openness."

We had just left our appointment with Dr. Caine. Instead of rushing back to my car with a strained smile and wave at Darren, I lingered in the parking lot. He walked me to my car. One hand rested on the roof, the other was inches away from my shoulder. My body shivered from his closeness.

"I think we're making some good progress. Don't you?" Darren's deep voice broke into the quietness of the night. His finger trailed along my bare shoulder.

"Yeah." I gave him a breathy response. My skin tightened and tingled under his touch.

He lowered his face, his lips now against mine. "Kara?"

I licked my dry lips. "Yes."

"Can I kiss you?"

I nodded, unable to speak or breathe or think.

He inched closer, his lips now over mine. He kissed me slow, deep, reverently.

Like Eduardo.

Electric currents jolted my body. I pushed away from him. Guilt and confusion spun within me. I was out of control.

Which was why I did something stupid. "Eduardo," I whispered. *Don't do it!* "I . . . someone kissed me."

"You're dating?" He stepped back, waves of pain emanating from his body.

"No. I couldn't . . . I can't." I shook my head. "I'm sorry, I'm just confused. But I . . . I didn't think it was good to kiss him, then kiss you."

"I thought you said someone kissed you."

"He did. I stopped him. Well, after a few seconds." *God, someone stitch my mouth shut.* I felt like Jim Carrey in *Liar, Liar*, like I was compelled to tell the truth.

"Did you like it?"

Did I? I liked the intimacy. I liked feeling wanted.

"I was more so caught off guard."

He shook his head, squeezed his eyes shut. "Do you like him? This Edward guy?"

"Yes. No. I like him as a friend. He cares, and it feels good to be cared for. But I don't *like-like* him like that." I shrugged. "I don't know why I told you."

"To make me jealous? I get it. I deserve it."

"No, I don't want to hurt you. I just—"

"It's okay. I appreciate your honesty and communication. That's what we're here to do, right?"

"Yeah." I clasped my hands together, looking everywhere but at him, too afraid that he'd regret the beautiful moment we'd had.

"Hey." He now stood in front of me. I hadn't even heard him move. "Things haven't changed for me. Do you . . . still love me?"

I nodded. "I love you. I'm just not sure if you truly love me, too. I know I shouldn't have read that letter. Sometimes I could kick myself for doing that to you, but I can't get those words out of my head. And . . . and if you don't love me, that's okay, too. I can still be there for you. As a friend."

And it was true. I wanted Darren to succeed. But when it came to a romantic relationship, I just wasn't sure. Sometimes love wasn't enough. Damn, I hated when people, actors, would say things like that in a movie. Everyone deserved a happily-ever-after, and if the love was there, people could work it out. Or so I thought.

Real life is messy and complicated, and hell if I knew what to do.

"I'll give you all the time you need." He leaned down and kissed my forehead. "But know this. I'm not giving up on us. Not ever again. And I'll earn your trust. Even if it takes the rest of our lives, I'll happily prove my love for you every day." He backed away, moving toward his car. "See you soon, Kara."

CHAPTER 15
Hold On—Nikki

"The wheels on the bus go round and round," I sang to myself, staring mindlessly off in space as our tour bus drove toward the entrance of the motel. We were covering the central part of our tour and were now moving south toward Memphis.

Before the tour began, James had planned to fly in and stay for two nights. But no such luck. My mini-me had stuck to her guns and no longer wanted to speak. I mean, WTF. I go off for a few months and everyone hates me. James and I don't speak, but he does daily texts to see if I'm alive.

To check if I'm drunk.

The conversation with Monica had sobered me a bit. I still drank, still smoked, but there was this consciousness that hadn't been there before. An angel on my right shoulder, telling me there was another way, and the devil on my left reminding me how good it felt to be faded.

They were both fucking nuts, but the angel drove me crazier. The divine messenger made me dig deep, remember why I started drinking in the first place.

And I'd finally remembered it was one night that Daddy had stumbled in, smelling like a distillery. Mom came out of bed mad at the world and told him to shut the hell up because I was sleeping and had school in the morning.

The next morning before I went to school, I confronted Daddy. It was the first time I'd been mad at him.

"Why do you drink so much, Daddy? You know it upsets Mama." I didn't want to confess the truth. It upset me, too.

Daddy's cheeks blazed. He shoveled corn flakes in his mouth, munching, stalling, or maybe he was thinking. Then he finally responded, "It shuts it out, baby girl."

"Shuts what out?"

"The world. The voices. The voice that says you aren't good enough to get that record deal. And when you get the deal, it quiets the voice that taunts that you can't make the sales. And then sometimes, sometimes I feel too much; the good, the bad, the ugly from this world. I've gotta shut it up to numb myself. Make sense?"

I nodded. It did make sense. When Daddy first taught me to play the guitar, I'd get this feeling—it would swell up, making me feel big and small at the same time. Big, because I was creating something wild, bold, and beautiful. A gift that was mine and unique. And small because what made me so special that I could be fortunate enough to share it with the world?

I saw how Daddy and his musician friends struggled.

It was a war, a beautiful war, and sometimes you needed armor to protect yourself. Now I was starting to realize that booze wasn't armor and, in fact, made me weak. But it was steeped so deep in my system I didn't know how to let the poison out.

And I was scared. Scared for me, scared for my husband, scared for my babies.

"Memphis, here we come!" Davey yelled beside me, pulling me into a hug.

"You excited?" He smiled, his blue eyes dancing.

I shrugged. "Why should I be excited?"

"Oh, I don't know. We're coming up on the last leg of the tour, and I know you miss your family. Besides, you've been writing some kick-ass songs and I can't wait to get back to the studio and record."

The good thing about my angel and demon, whom I'd lovingly named Angie and Denny, was they talked a lot. To me and to each other. The constant push and pull for my immortal soul resulted in some deep shit, if I do say so myself.

"You made a decision yet?" Davey twirled a drumstick in his hand.

I opened up my notepad and yanked the pencil from behind my ear. I doodled a bit, hearts and rainbows and musical notes.

"C'mon, Nik." Davey stilled my busy hand with a gentle squeeze. "You know I'm here for you, right?"

I nodded. Davey was a brother for life. He wouldn't begrudge any decision I'd make.

"You know I want you with us, but I've got eyes, you know."

"Yeah, they're blue," I attempted to joke.

"I mean I *see* you. See the way you use drinking to self-medicate. See that you check your phone every five minutes when we aren't onstage. And I see the heartbreak on your face when you can't say good night to your kids. That you can't settle shit with James."

He jerked his head toward Trent. "And I see the way that fucker looks at you." He shook his shaven head. "He wants you and James to fail. That's why he's keeping you high and drunk. But you know better, Nik. You've gotta be stronger than him. Fuck!" He slammed the stick against his thigh.

"What?"

"Just realized something and, no, I'm not gonna tell you. You've gotta figure this shit out on your own." He stood. "I'm getting a drink."

"Oh, can I have—"

"A fucking Gatorade."

I sighed, heat flaming my cheeks. I wasn't that far gone. "I was going to ask for cranberry juice. That's it. Geez, Davey."

"What the fuck ever, wino!" He shot me a killer grin. It slightly softened the fact that he thought I was a raging alcoholic.

"If the shoe fits." Angie's sweet voice popped in my head.

"Screw you, Angie," I whisper-hissed.

"You aren't supposed to curse at angels."

"And you aren't supposed to be an asshole, yet you are."

"Truth hurts." Her voice held a nah-nah-nah-boo-boo lilt to it. "And don't put the vodka you've got hidden in your blazer in the juice."

"I wasn't gonna do that," I whispered, still doodling.

Angie harrumphed. "Keep it up and you'll be one of those sad episodes of *Unsung* where the artist didn't get a chance to reach their potential because they died too young." Angie's buzzkill voice was low and serious.

"We've all gotta die." Denny finally popped into the conversation. "Might as well have fun doing it."

"You've got to die for your sins to live again," Angie whispered and drifted like a faint voice on the tail end of the wind.

I stopped my doodles. "You've gotta die to live again."

"What's that?" Monica asked. She'd initially sat at the front by Ethan. Now she sat across from me on the bus. I hadn't even heard her because Denny and Angie were taking up my headspace.

"Just being a psycho and talking to myself."

Troubled heart, why do you let your sins weigh you down? So heavy, you despair. Can't you see the life that you lead will end in death?

Troubled heart, why are you crying? You just have to believe. Give it up, give it all, get it all.

I slouched back in my seat and smiled. Angie had given me a good nugget. More words flew through me like a strong gale of wind. I just had to hold on, pick out the good parts, and stand strong.

Warmth filled my core. The good kind. The kind I hadn't felt in a long time. And it was better than the warmth that whiskey gave me. The armor that Daddy had unconsciously given me was cracking. Not much, just a little. Something was unfurling in me; with each stroke of my pencil, something shifted in my soul. This song was for me. A love letter to myself. And, no, I wouldn't heal overnight, but I knew, like this song, I had to give it a try. Each day would be a battle, but one day it wouldn't.

"Good luck with that," Denny's voice held a small tremor.

"Fuck you, Denny," I said, writing the final words to the song.

"Yeah, fuck you, Denny," Angie parroted.

"What kind of angel are you?" I shook my head, closing my song book.

Angie sighed. "You know I've gotta be a little cray-cray to deal with you."

We were two songs away from finishing out the set with a racy song that had Trent working the stage, slick with sweat. The Memphis crowd was live, vibrant with pure rock-and-roll and the band fed off it. But now we were coming to a close. Davey signaled the slowdown with his drums; Drew followed suit and slowed it up with a new song I'd composed before we went on the road. And then I noticed *him*.

Maybe it was the trick of the lighting, or maybe it was by design, but it seemed as if a spotlight illuminated James, making him stand out from the crowd.

I nearly stumbled in my two-step I'd been doing across the stage, nearly slipped the chord on my guitar. Catching myself, I walked stage left, swapped my acoustic for electric, and sat on a stool. The tune was slow, bluesy. Sad, yet sexy. About someone who wasn't ready for love. Someone who wasn't ready to love themselves. Denny and Angie had been busy again. I flicked the plectrum, making the guitar cry—no, making my *soul* cry.

Focused on my husband, as if we were the only two people in the room, I told him what I couldn't put into words.

> *My world was darkness until I laid eyes on you.*
> *Heart caught on fire, oh, the things I would do to you.*
> *I'm spinning and twisting in the whirlwind that is you.*
> *Pinch me, I'm dreaming, I'm falling into you.*
>
> *I wasn't ready for you.*
> *I wasn't ready to love you.*
> *Wasn't ready to love myself.*
> *My heart belonged to another, my soul bound to the liquid fear.*
> *Can't hold the light you bring. Can't break the darkness over me.*
> *Still, foolishly we jumped and drowned together.*
> *Till I pulled you down,*
> *Pulled you down, down, down.*
>
> *Catch our breaths, you're breathing again.*
> *Go back to shore, I can't let you back in.*
> *Leave me be, let me drown.*
> *Don't let me pull you down, down, down.*

I couldn't read James's expression from so far away, but I'd said what I had to say. After I sang the last of the lyrics, I exhaled into the mic. Thunderous applause followed, as they chanted *Nikki! Nikki!*

Tears leaked from my eyes. I wanted to keep hold, stay in this moment, and somehow make the world of music and my home life meld into one. I thought we could have it all, but I was beginning to realize that it was bullshit. To get more, you had to give less elsewhere.

My soul was split in two, because in my heart, I knew James was making a stand. He wasn't here to smile, clap, and support me from the crowd. I had a feeling he wanted me to choose.

Somehow, I got it together. Finished up the last song of the night and marched off the stage.

"Did you see your guy out there?" Davey smiled.

I cleared my throat, stiffening. "Was that you? Did you ask him to come?"

He nodded, taking in my stance. "Bad move?" His voice was slow, careful.

"No, I'm happy, I just . . . I just hope he's here to reconcile, not to break up."

Davey threw back his head. "Break up? Are you serious? That guy loves you. Didn't take too much to convince him to get his sorry ass out here." He chuckled low again. "And you're well past the point of *breaking up*. You're married, have a mortgage, two kids, and a minivan."

"SUV," I quickly corrected him.

"Same difference. Go get cleaned up. I'll distract Trent so he doesn't get his faced wrecked by your man. See you in ten."

"I didn't bring anything. I figured we'd do the handshakes, VIP gig, and then head back to the hotel."

"Got you covered, sis." He walked to his backpack and threw my bag with toiletries over, then tossed me a Tee and my stonewashed jeans.

"How in the hell—"

"Had a little help from Monica. Now go get changed." He gently pushed me toward the hallway.

"Why, thank you. I've always wanted my very own fairy god-mother. I thought I'd get an old white lady, but a bald white guy will do." I leaned in and gave him a quick peck on the cheeks.

"Such a little asshole. Save those sweet words for your man." He shook his head. "I'll see you later."

I nodded and headed for the women's bathroom. The venue was sweet, decked out with a college-style communal bathroom. After taking a shower, I swiped on some deodorant and slathered myself with lotion. I took a quick glance in the mirror, then hurried back to the VIP room.

The guys worked the room with our fans. Monica was busily typing away on the computer in the corner, ignoring the men and women who sniffed after her lover. She was a confident woman, and Ethan was firmly under her spell, if the not-so-secret glances he snuck her way meant anything.

I finally spotted James, eyes guarded and focused on me. I gave him a shy wave, then tugged the hem of my shirt. *Get it together, Nik. This is your husband, he still loves you. I think.*

Taking a deep breath, I walked to him, jerked my head toward the exit. "You want to go someplace quiet? Have a talk?"

"What about your fans?"

There were a few people looking my way, some curious, probably wanting to say hey or good show or what the hell ever to me. I couldn't concentrate on them, only on James.

"They can wait." I reached for his hand. "Follow me. I know a place." I gave him a confident smile, so unlike the unsure girl I was feeling like on the inside.

The place I knew was our dressing room. There was nowhere else we could go and have privacy.

"Are you staying for the night?" I asked, waving at him to sit. He sat on a pea green couch that looked the color of vomit. Despite the unsightly backdrop, I drank James in. He went straight to my head like an oak-aged whiskey.

I stood, pacing the floor.

"Not sure. But I'm here."

"Because Davey called you."

"Because I needed to see you."

"You needed to see me?" I licked my lips. "Why?"

"Your eyes. I wanted to see if you were . . ." He sighed. "I wanted to see if you were happy without me. Without us."

I laughed. Husky and barren and sad. So fucking sad. "And what do you see?"

"I see a woman who's scared. Scared of herself, scared that she'll lose it all."

I stepped closer until I stood between his knees. "And will she?" I cleared my throat, repeating my question in a whisper. "Will she lose it all?"

"Depends." He shrugged, folding a long leg across his knees. His toffee brown eyes intense on mine. "Do you love me?"

"Duh."

His lips turned up at the corner. "Our kids?"

I rolled my eyes. "Double duh."

He chuckled. "Then . . . then we'll figure out a way."

I straddled his lap, cupping his face. "Miss you." I grazed his lips, teasing him, teasing us.

He sucked my lips, and with his tongue implored my mouth with a kiss. Years later and this man still rocked the hell out of my world.

"You love me?" I whispered against his lips.

"Triple duh."

"Hell yeah, you do." I leaned in for another kiss. Angie was dancing around my head, thrusting her hips and shaking her ass.

"So you're okay with me being in the band?" I smiled against his lips.

James groaned. "Baby, I won't lie . . . I don't think I can handle the band."

Angie stopped her happy dance. "Ruh-roh," she said in a Scooby-Doo voice.

"Baby . . ." I sighed against his ear. "You've gotta trust me."

James leaned back, his eyes serious. "I trust you. But, baby, you've got a problem. Several. Drinking and Trent."

"Okay, so I'm working things out. Maybe I don't have to stay with the band. But I need time to talk to management and the label."

"How much time, Nik? The tour is almost over, right?"

"Yeah, but then we're thinking of doing a big media splash. Maybe if I transition slowly? Like one or two more songs before I leave? I don't want to piss off the bigwigs, ya know? I want to do this right."

"This is crazy, Nik." James shook his head. His tone switched from sensuous croon to seriously pissed. "I feel like you don't want to come home"

"Nikki!" I heard the most irritating voice on earth sing. Trent stumbled into the room.

James gripped my hips. "Thought you knew a *secret* place?" he mumbled while the band filed into the room.

Davey, Drew, and Ethan came over to slap James's back.

"Good to see you, my man," Davey greeted James. The drummer gave me a shit-eating grin. "Told you he still loves you."

"You thought I didn't love you?" James gave me an incredulous look. "You aren't someone who I could easily fall out of love with."

"Got that right," Trent muttered. But in a small-ass room, it didn't take much to hear anything. By the squeeze on my waist and hot breath on my neck, James had heard the obnoxious comment as well.

"Did you just say that shit in front of me?" James's deep voice nearly growled.

I locked my knees around him before James could jump from the seat and cash in on the promise to break our lead singer's hands.

"Chill, Trent." Drew slapped the front man's chest.

"Yeah, man, chill the fuck out," Davey said, his voice hard and cold.

" 'Scuse the fuck outta me, but this is *our* tour." Trent's voice was slurred. "And this is our room." He waved his arms about. "I can do whatever I want."

Was this how I sounded and acted when I was drunk?

Angie's voice popped in my head. "Yes, dear. You aren't exactly a walk in the park. Not to mention, you're rude, obnoxious—"

"Shut up." I cut her off.

"What?" James asked.

"Let's go back to the motel." I didn't even want to try to explain how my subconscious had manifested as Angie and Denny.

James squeezed my neck. "I got us a room at the Hilton."

I nuzzled his cheek. "Thank you, baby."

"You used to call me baby," Trent grumbled. This time, he wasn't trying to be obnoxious. There was a thread of regret, jealousy.

I stood from James's lap and grabbed his hand. I didn't know what to say, but I felt sorry for Trent, despite his asshole ways.

"Well, um, catch you guys on the bus. Noon, right?"

"Noon," Ethan whispered back, squeezing Monica tighter to his chest.

"Bet he doesn't fuck you like I did."

The air was sucked out of the room. All was quiet. My hands wrapped around James's bicep, but I couldn't stop him, couldn't grip him tight enough. He crossed the small room and jabbed Trent twice in the jaw.

"James, stop it!" My voice was shrill, desperate.

At the sound of my voice, the guys unstuck from their seats and rushed into action. Davey grabbed James. Drew and Ethan dragged Trent to the corner of the room.

Julia, the band manager, rushed into the room. "What's going on?"

"Nikki's psycho husband just attacked me." Trent rubbed his bruised jaw.

Julia's blue and serious eyes scanned me and then James. "You both need to leave."

"Not Nik." Trent's tone held a stubborn note. "The asshole beside her."

"Oh, shut the hell up, Trent." I turned around to face him. "You taunted my husband and you nearly got your ass beat. Be glad it wasn't your hands. You need to man up and get over it." I walked to his corner of the room and pointed my finger in his face. "Get. Over. Us."

"Is this how it is?" James's garbled voice grabbed my attention.

I turned to face James, took in his squeezed fists and heaving chest. I needed to get my man out of here. Pronto.

"It's no big deal, baby." I rushed back to my husband. I reached for his jaw, stroking it. "I can handle it."

"What if I can't?"

My eyes stung at his confession. My new life and my old one had finally come to a head. "Maybe I—"

"JJ cries for you at night. Bria is acting out. They miss their mama. Meanwhile, you're touring with your ex, who harasses you."

"James." I sighed deep.

"It's true, Nikki, and you know it. He has no regard for our marriage—hell, no regard for you. And since you've been with the band you drink, you smoke . . . to be honest, a part of me came here to see if you'd be sober."

I took a step back, hurt by his confession. "I-I'm not as bad as you think I am. I'm trying," I whispered. "I know I have a problem, and I haven't been drunk in nearly two weeks."

Damn, that sounded pathetic. Not even two whole weeks.

"That's good, Nik. But it's not enough. Your kids need you. I need you." James took a deep breath. "I can't do this, baby. I'm trying, but I'm drowning. We're drowning."

I flinched at his words. He'd heard the song. He got it, and he knew I was pulling him down.

"I can't stay. I've gotta go."

"N-No, baby. Don't leave. I choose us. I choose you."

"No." Julia stepped toward us. "You have three more weeks in this contract. Otherwise, you'll renege."

"Now is *not* the time," Monica's hard voice cut in.

"He'll be fine for a few weeks." Julia shrugged. "Handle your drama, then."

"She's right." James lowered his lips, kissed my forehead. Why did this feel like goodbye? "I'll see you soon. We'll talk. But I can't be here."

"But our room . . . at the Hilton."

"I won't be good company. I need some space, all right?"

His eyes showed regret, but I knew he was resolved in his decision. He turned, leaving the room.

I whipped around, facing Trent. "How. Fucking. Dare. You!" I ran across the room, smacking his cheek.

"Fuck, Nik!" he yelled, grabbing his cheek. No one helped him. With the exception of Julia, everyone looked disgusted.

"Do you enjoy it?"

"Enjoy what, you little psycho?" he asked, stroking his face.

"Hurting me?" I slumped against the sofa. "We didn't work out. We're history, and we're that because of you. You pushed me away because you couldn't keep it in your pants. You broke my heart. But now I'm better. James makes me happy."

"Give me a break." He chuckled without feeling. "When I saw you again, sitting out there, tears in your eyes when you saw us, you didn't seem so happy. You wanted to be onstage. You weren't happy being the perfect little wife and mom. You hate your life."

"No." I shook my head, although there was some truth to his assessment. "I love my husband and kids."

"But you hate your life. Otherwise, why do you drink and smoke? Because you're a tortured soul. Like me."

"Maybe you're right. I don't fit the mold of suburban mom and wife, but I love my family. I'll figure it out." I grabbed my bags. "See you guys back at our motel." I pushed open the door and rushed out of the building.

"Nikki!" Trent yelled after me.

I sped up, although I had nowhere to go. I hadn't called a car service and the bus would wait for the entire band.

"Hey!" He finally reached me, jerking me around by my elbow.

"What, Trent? What else do you possibly have to say? You just ruined my night, possibly *my life*. What the hell do you want from me?" I screamed. "What is it?"

"You!" He raked his hands through his hair. "I want you. Always have and damn it, I always will."

"Oh, stop it, you're just—"

"No, Nik. I'm serious. When you left the band, left me, I was lost. Spinning out of control. Boozing and shooting up."

"Have you considered that you just have a substance abuse problem? That's got nothing to do with what happened to us."

He shrugged. "Somehow, I got my act together when we got the record deal, but it didn't feel right without you." He rubbed his heart. "I just kept thinking about you. The way we played music together. The way we made love. You know me inside out and I know you, too."

"You *knew* me, Trent. I've changed."

"Have you?" He widened his eyes. "You're still a brilliant lyricist and you sing like an angel. You party, drink. You're still rock-and-roll."

"Fine. I'm *trying* to change. I've been so busy trying to be cool, to shed the suburban mom rep, that I've lost myself."

"You aren't a suburban mom. Fuck driving a minivan and PTA meetings. You're too talented for that. You deserve more. Not some bullshit white picket fence, saddled with two-point-five kids and a husband."

"Watch it, Masters. My family isn't a burden." And they weren't. They were wonderful. I enjoyed dropping my kids off with sing-alongs. I got to teach my baby girl how to play guitar. JJ liked to bang on things, and I planned to teach him how to play drums. I wasn't the best, but Davey could fill in once JJ advanced.

And James, my God, he was everything. And despite the hot mess I could be—sarcastic, a little crabby, and let's be real, an alcoholic—he stuck by me, while protecting the kids.

Even now, he came to my show, despite his reservations to support me. He was willing to swallow his pride so that I could live out my happiness. I didn't deserve more. I already had it. My talent wouldn't go anywhere. I could do this alone. Without the band. Without my ex.

A smile broke across my face. "I've already got it all."

He gave me a small, sad smile. "The *all* isn't me."

"No." My tone was sharp at first. But taking in my ex, his disheveled appearance and bloodshot eyes, I knew that in his own way, he did love me.

I leaned in to kiss him on the cheek. "Let's finish out this tour. You need to move on."

Twelve years ago, I would've been over the moon for Trent's undying love. But now, he wasn't even in the same galaxy as James and my kids.

CHAPTER 16

Don't Let Me Be Misunderstood—Sienna

I wrapped my arms around Chris. He continued to smoke, facing the breathtaking Atlanta skyline at dawn from the balcony of his thirty-sixth-floor condo.

"Sienna," he said on a sigh, his bare chest heaving with the action.

"Can't sleep?" I whispered, an attempt not to wake the neighbors or disrupt nature's soft chirps and buzzing. I nuzzled my cheek against his firm back.

I'd been sleeping until I rolled over and felt the cool sheets under my fingertips. Only a few months together, and I couldn't sleep without his strong arms wrapped around my middle.

"My mind is busy."

"What's up? Maybe I can help."

He drew in another puff. "Just thinking through your last debate with Keith next week. I want to make sure you drive our message home before ballots are cast."

"Hey." I stepped back and gently tugged his shoulder.

He turned, a lit cigarette between his thumb and forefinger.

I grabbed the cancer stick and broke it, as was my usual pattern. Chris was accustomed to it, but usually, he put up more of a fight.

"Gonna quit this someday."

"What?" I jerked my attention to his eyes.

"Not today, but I'll try. For you." The honesty in his blue eyes jump-started my heart.

I knew breaking the habit wasn't a walk in the park, but he wanted to try. *For me.*

"I'd like that." I smiled. "Not because I'm trying to control you but because I lov—I mean, like you. A lot. A whole lot." I spread my hands wide.

"You *like* me, huh?"

"Yes. I definitely like you," I agreed, nodding.

"I like you, too." He smiled, his eyes teasing and glinting in the soft light.

"The debate." I quickly changed the subject, not at all ready to go *there* with Chris. I'd decided to take this relationship, whatever this was, turtle-crossing-the-road slow. "We've gone over the talking points, I've been out in the community, we've raised the money, and I'm ready. I won't let you down." I shook my head. "Not like last time. No more lovers' spats."

"I should hope not." He leaned against the rail, taking me in. "Besides, he's no longer your lover. That would be me." He pointed to his chest.

I lifted my head. "Right. Speaking of lover . . ." I stepped closer, crowding his space. "Come to bed. I'll put your mind at ease."

He lifted me, cupping my ass. "I more than like you," he whispered against my lips. I shivered, wrapping my arms and legs tighter.

"How much?" I dared him to say more.

"Let's go to bed. I can show you how much in there."

He walked us back inside the condo and showed me just how much.

* * *

"I'd like to order a poppy seed bagel, please." I smiled at the young woman behind the counter. "Oh, and a medium coffee, no sugar or cream."

After I got my order, I settled at the two-seater table in the back, then sipped my coffee, I smiled, staring aimlessly out of the window. I needed peace, away from Chris's nervous energy and the nosy but well-meaning questions from my coworkers and friends. Surprisingly, the small café that I'd frequented over the years had always given me calm. I was so close to achieving my goal I could taste it. Sure, I had a battle ahead, but I was so ready to fight for what I wanted.

My phone pinged, signaling an email. I was tempted to disconnect, but with weeks until the election, I needed to stay on top of communication.

I opened the email, though I didn't recognize the name or the email address.

I scanned the email and gasped. "Holy. Shit."

Keith had been a bad boy, a *very* bad boy. I leaned back, stunned. Stunned and thinking what I should do.

I needed to tell Chris, stat. This email changed everything. I slung my purse on my shoulder and hustled out of the coffee shop. The bad girl in me rubbed her hands together. The debate was just two weeks away, and this would make a splash. I finally had the bastard by the nuts.

I tossed the printed documents in front of Chris.

"What is this?" He smiled up at me from his desk.

"Just read it."

He crooked his finger. I leaned down, knowing he wanted a kiss. After a quick smooch, he grabbed the pages and moved them to the corner of his desk. "All right."

I backed away. "Can you read it now?"

"Right now?"

I nodded. "Yes! Right now." I snickered. "You won't believe it." I settled into the seat in front of his desk.

Chris chuckled. "Fine, sunshine." He reached for the papers, a bemused smile on his face. After reading the first page, he frowned, flipped through the others. After a few minutes, he was done.

"Damn." He rubbed his face. "He's trying to force a county vendor to contribute to his reelection?"

"Apparently, he's trying to blackmail him. He wants two hundred thousand dollars."

Chris whistled. "So I see. He really is an asshole."

"He's a liar and a cheater and, good grief, I can't believe I loved him. I was going to marry that crook."

"Yeah, you dodged a bullet on that one." He shook his head, eyes still on the papers.

"Right!" I jumped from my seat. "And how stupid does he have to be to send threats via text and email?"

"He's not stupid. He just feels powerful, invincible." He sighed. "I noticed it only after a few months of campaigning. It's like he enjoys playing with fire. Women, money, power—it's all a rush for him." He looked up. "Do you have any idea who sent this to you?"

"No. The email and name are anonymous."

Chris nodded. "How do you plan on using this information?"

"I'm not going to bring it up during the debate, of course!"

Chris sighed. "That's a relief. I don't want another crazy debate with you two."

"I wouldn't do that to you. I'll be discreet. I can have someone reach out to a paper and plant the bug in their ear."

"What?" His voice was sharp.

"I . . ." I sat back down, licking my lips. "You don't think it's a good idea? This could ruin him, change the tide, and I'll be a sure win. According to the latest polls, we're pretty close."

"You're still ahead and on your way to win, Sienna. You don't need this." He tossed the documents back on the desk. A few loose papers fell on the floor. "I can't believe this."

"Believe what?"

"Believe that you would stoop so low to win."

"I'm not stooping low." I pointed at the pages on the floor. "Stooping low is when Keith threatened to leak news about that man if he wouldn't contribute to his campaign. I'm simply passing along the info to the right people. I don't see how that's so bad," I said, my voice defensive. I couldn't believe Chris was acting so uncool about this. He was a campaign manager, for goodness sake. Surely, he could see how this could work in our favor.

"You don't see what's so bad, that's what the issue is." He pulled his dreads back from his neck. "A year ago, you wouldn't have even considered this."

"A year ago, I was a fool."

"Not a fool. Sweet, kind—"

"Weak."

"No, strong."

"I am *not* that girl anymore."

"You're my sunshine."

"No, I'm not anyone's sunshine. I'm just me. A woman who gave her heart to the wrong man. A woman who was dumb enough to turn down a well-into-six-figure job to be a freakin' public defender. A woman who used to let people take advantage."

"I disagree. You're just lost."

"Then I like being lost." This time I crossed my arms, mirroring his stance. "And maybe I don't want to be found again." I stood. "Look, I've gotta go."

"Are you going to leak this?"

I shrugged. "Maybe I will, maybe I won't. It's a solid strategic move, and God knows who else he's been threatening. We could be helping people with this info."

"Is that your primary objective? To help people?"

"I'm helping myself right now, and considering the time and effort I gave to Keith, I'm feeling pretty damn good about it."

His nostrils flared. He clenched his jaw and hardened his eyes. "Don't go down this path, Sienna. When you adopt a shark mentality, everything that once seemed black and white, and right and wrong, gets mixed together in shades of gray."

"I've got to go."

"Promise me you'll think about what I said."

"Fine."

"And that you'll give me the courtesy of a call before you do anything."

"Yes, Chris. You're my campaign manager, I haven't all of a sudden lost my sense of professionalism," I said between gritted teeth and pivoted toward the door.

"No, just your moral compass."

The debate was tonight, and although I was prepared, I was still at work. I'd planned to take a half day, relax, and review the talking points in my head, practice controlling my gestures in the mirror.

I'd called Chris a few days ago. He asked if I made a decision, I said no. He said he didn't want to be associated with my campaign until he knew for certain I wouldn't leak the information.

I told him *Bye, Felicia* and promptly hung up the phone.

My phone rang at the desk. Rubbing my tired eyes from the hours of discovery I'd been reviewing, I picked up the phone. "Sienna Njeri."

"Girl, you are inspired."

I instantly recognized the voice, my reporter friend from high school. "Hannah Montana," I said. Though her name was

Hannah Corver, she was a dead ringer for Miley Cyrus's famous Disney character. "As much as I enjoy random compliments, I have no idea what you are talking about."

"I just read the exposé on Keith. I'm guessing you slipped the info to Chuck Archer?"

"No . . . that . . . that wasn't me."

"It wasn't?"

"No."

"You sure?" Hannah's voice was suspicious, the cadence of her question slow and exaggerated.

"I wouldn't lie, Hannah." I clicked on my computer and searched for Keith and the reporter's name.

City Councilman Keith Davenport threatens county worker for campaign funding.

"Oh. My. God." I smiled. "I wonder who leaked this."

"I dunno. But I'm not surprised that Keith has enemies."

"Well, it wasn't me," I said again.

"I believe you. You would've admitted it by now. I'm surprised you didn't see this earlier."

"When was it published?" I looked at the time of the article to answer my own question. Seven a.m.

"It was in the papers this morning, and they released it on their blog at the same time. Crazy, huh?"

"Very." I shook my head.

"Well, looks like the election is yours. You should celebrate."

"I'll think of something," I airily replied. "Anyway, I've got to wrap up this case, switch gears, and then prepare for this debate."

Hannah snorted. "If the snake shows up. If I were him, I'd gracefully bow out."

"Right. But Keith is a special kind of evil. Never say die."

"We'll see," Hannah said, but her voice reflected doubt. "Let's connect soon. Maybe after the election, once things settle?"

"Sounds wonderful."

Someone knocked on my door. A tall, skinny man in khaki pants and a polo shirt waved from outside the glass door. I motioned him to come inside.

I spotted a small white box in his hand.

"Delivery," he said unnecessarily.

"I'll let you go," Hannah said in my ear. "Bye."

"Can you sign, please?"

I glanced at his shirt. He worked for a local courier service. "Sure."

"Thanks." He placed the box on my desk. "Have a good one."

"You too," I said to his back. Curiosity piqued, I lifted the lid. Inside was a broken cigarette on top of a folded piece of paper. *A letter maybe?*

Unfolding the paper, I recognized Chris's handwriting, and under the paper the clipping of Keith's article.

My heart tripled. *No. He can't believe I did this. I told him I would give him a heads-up.*

> *You're wrong. People do change. I can no longer work*
> *on this campaign, though. You don't need my help.*
> *Congratulations and best of luck.*
> *—Chris*

"Congratulations? Best of luck?" Red-hot lava surged through my veins. "Oh, heck no!" I tossed the broken cigarette back into the box and then shut down my computer. "He doesn't get to break up all symbolic-like while I'm at work," I muttered to myself.

After grabbing my personal belongings, I hurried out of the office building, dashed across the street to the parking lot. I dialed Chris while my heels clacked across the paved lot.

"Hey, you," I whispered breathlessly into the receiver. "Got your *care* package. Just wanted you to know that it wasn't me.

I did not leak that stuff about Keith. Now, I can't say that I'm not happy and I wasn't tempted, but still . . ." I took a deep sigh. The phone beeped and the connection died. No matter. After twisting the ignition, I sped through the bumpy parking lot, straight to Chris's condo.

I jogged up the stairs as fast as I could in my four-inch heels, took the elevator, and then banged on the door like the police doing a drug raid. "Open up, Christopher!" I knocked again. "I know you're in there. Open up."

Chris swung open the door. "I do have neighbors." He didn't step back to let me in but instead, leaned against the doorjamb. "What is it that you want, Sienna?"

"What happened to 'sunshine'?"

He crossed his arms over his chest.

"I didn't do it!" I blurted. "I didn't set Keith up."

"Look, I know that you and Keith have history, but I'm not interested in being in the middle of your war. I chose to work with you because I thought you cared about the people."

"I do."

He shrugged. "Then why are you at war with him? Is your revenge that important?"

"It's not about revenge!"

"Did you or did you not say that you wanted to drag him through the dirt? That you wanted him to hurt like he hurt you?"

"Okay, so maybe it started off that way. But I've always wanted to run for public office. I've always wanted to serve."

"You expect me to believe that just this weekend, you gave me the very same information that someone else leaked to the papers?"

"Yes. And I expect you to believe it because you know my character. If I told you I didn't do it, then I didn't."

"It had the same details in the article, Sienna."

"And I am maintaining my innocence!" Heat spread through my cheeks and traveled down to my toes. I took a deep breath to calm myself. "Look. I'm not going to argue with you in the breezeway. Why don't I come inside and we can discuss this?"

Chris shook his head and shuffled from side to side. "No. Now is not a good idea."

"Why?"

He jerked his head back toward the door and then turned back to face me. "It just isn't a good time."

"Chris! I'm starving! Feed me," I heard a whiny voice call from inside.

"Really?" I took two steps back.

"It's not what it looks like."

He reached for my arms, but I stumbled away.

"Sienna, I have my—"

"You have a side chick, mistress? Or am I your side chick?"

His head jerked back as if he'd been slapped. "I would never do that to you. You know that."

"But I guess we're broken up. You sent me that stupid cigarette and everything, so technically, you didn't cheat. Unless you were two-timing us both."

"Even if that's the case—"

"Chris! C'mon!" the whiny female demanded again, her voice coming closer. The woman popped out her head. She was gorgeous. Smooth brown skin and curly short hair that accentuated her elfin features. "Oh, h-hello? Didn't realize you had company, Chris." Her eyes held a glint of mischief.

"Goodbye, Christopher." I stumbled down the stairs. My heart squeezed so tight I thought I was having a heart attack. I wanted to stop, bend over, and let the pain wash through me. Chris's betrayal reopened feelings I'd pushed dormant.

But like a sleeping volcano, they had awakened, spewing flames, hot lava, and cinders.

"No more," I promised myself. I jumped into the car and

sped away. A ping from my phone snatched my attention. I glanced down at my phone.

Keith Davenport Drops from the City Councilman Race.

I shook my head and tossed the phone into my purse. I'd won by default, but I knew in my heart I would've won fair and square. I should be happy, ecstatic even. But my victory had been spoiled by Chris's betrayal. No matter. I would dedicate my life to the constituents, to making my city better. And I would never, ever open my heart up again.

I played with my plate of spiced rice, tomatoes, and lettuce, minus the stewed meat that the rest of my family had eaten. Mama and Baba, as well as my sister Farah and my brothers Joshua and Edwin, were seated around the large oak dinner table. The rest of my siblings were out of town or lived elsewhere. Otherwise, when Mama mandated dinner with family, everyone scrambled to attend.

"Sienna, stop picking at your food and eat," Mama admonished from across the table.

My sisters and brothers snickered. Instead of responding to their juvenile behavior with my usual response of sticking out my tongue, something we'd all done as kids and continued as adults, I shoveled down the rest of my food.

I felt like such a fool. After Keith, I'd vowed to never get myself worked up over a man. Now here I was, depressed as all get-out because Chris had proved the age-old truth that men couldn't remain faithful.

Now he had the audacity to blow up my phone. I didn't need an explanation, I just needed him to leave me alone.

Dinner ended, and I began my chores of washing dishes and clearing the table along with my brothers and sisters.

"Sienna." Baba tapped my shoulder. "When you're done with the kitchen, meet me in my study."

After I finished with the dishes, I headed to Baba's study. It smelled of worn leather and lemon oils. Ten years ago, it smelled of leather and tobacco. After my campaign for his lungs, he finally quit his bad habit of smoking.

"Sit, binti." He gestured at the maroon chaise that reminded me of something that would be in a therapist's office. "What troubles you, daughter?"

"I—" I sighed, not quite sure how I wanted to play this. Did I really want to go crying to my dad about a man?

"Tell me it isn't that spineless rat, Keith."

I laughed, despite my melancholy. Baba had come up with the nickname when he'd heard Keith give a speech at our home church. Keith had gone on and on about his Christian upbringing, which both Baba and I had known to be false. Later that day, Baba told me to watch out for him.

Baba didn't know about Keith's philandering, but I suspected he had a hunch.

"No, Baba. It's Christopher." He was the real rat. Building me up, telling me he more than liked me, and as soon as the first storm of our relationship hit, he ran away into the arms of another woman.

"Ah. Now that's a man's man."

I grunted. "Does a man's man accuse you of leaking a story about your ex, break up with you via a dramatic symbolic broken cigarette, then the very same day have another woman in his home?"

Baba's coffee brown eyes widened. "No."

"Sadly, yes." I nodded.

"Did you give him a chance to explain? What did he say?"

"I drove to his house to confront him. Saw that . . . that woman myself."

"So he admitted that he'd moved on?"

"No." I shook my head. "He said that 'it's not what it looks like.' Just like Keith did before. Just like a man." I groaned. "Why do guys think we're so stupid?"

A weird look flitted across Baba's face. He wanted to say something but decided against it. "What did the woman say?"

"Nothing much. Just that she didn't realize someone was here. She didn't look particularly bothered. Just inquisitive." Her eyes had danced and she seemed overly interested and giddy, like I was some sort of alien species she observed under a microscope.

"Not every man is Keith, my daughter. Everyone deserves a second chance."

"I'm not giving another cheating man a second chance."

"And I agree. But you don't really *know* if he has cheated." Baba stroked his salt-and-pepper goatee. "I'm shocked he hasn't tried harder."

"Oh, he has." I'd blocked his phone number and email. I told Baba how he'd tried to bum rush me at work. Thankfully the public defender's office had security, and I'd asked them not to let him back to my office. My apartment was gated with a security guard. After he smashed my heart to smithereens, I quickly took him off my guest list.

Baba nodded, looking not at all impressed. "Oh, my daughter. Has this man hurt you so much that you are afraid of living?"

"Chris hurt me, but I'm—"

"Not Chris. Keith, the rat. I sat back while you hardened your shell. I was so happy you redirected that fierce energy you had for others to yourself. But now, daughter, you trust no one. You just sat here and told me, your father, that men are no good. I was the first man to love you. Have I not shown you what love and trust from a man means? Have I not treated your mother with love and respect?"

"You have, Baba. I'm sorry I've disrespected you."

He shook his head. "This isn't about my pride, this is about maintaining your conviction."

"For me?"

"For humanity. As much as people like to pretend, especially men, you can't compartmentalize your feelings. It spreads everywhere. Don't let Keith or Chris or any man change who you are."

"And who am I, Baba?"

Baba smiled. "Who you've always been. You're just a little lost."

Lost. Chris had said the same thing to me. Was I lost? Or was I just evolving? Was it so bad being the new Sienna?

"I see you have a lot to think about, so I'll let you be. I do have one request."

After I hurt my father with my thoughtless words, I was willing to donate my kidney to spare his disappointment in me.

"Anything."

"Talk to Chris and Keith. Resolve your hurts and fears. Then let it go in whatever form that means. Promise me you'll do this."

I didn't need to hear their tired excuses. I didn't want to see them, to unlock all the unwanted and ugly feelings I'd barricaded within me, but I couldn't deny my father's request.

"Okay, Baba. For you, I will."

NOVEMBER

CHAPTER 17

Papa Was a Rolling Stone—
Raina

"Thanks for cooking dinner!" Although I was enjoying my freedom at Kara's, I missed Ma's home cooking. My mouth salivated at the spread before me in Ma's kitchen. Collards, lima beans with bacon, fried pork chops, and mac and cheese.

"Thanks for the cupcakes." She waved at the red velvet cupcake I'd placed in the middle of her dinette table. "Now dig in."

I grabbed the empty flower-power plate and then zeroed on the plates and platters of food on the kitchen counter. "I can't believe you cook all this food every Sunday, and for fun." I muttered the last part as I scooped mac and cheese onto my plate.

"What else am I gonna do? I'm fifty-six. I'm not trying to go out to the club or anything."

"Then go out to eat." My mouth watered at the crispy fried pork chop.

"I love to cook, unlike you. Just you, food, and a good movie are all I need."

The hot sauce was already waiting for me when I returned to the small table in the dining room. "Thanks, Ma."

"I know how you love your hot sauce. It's gonna eat up your insides one day."

"Until then . . ." I liberally shook the hot sauce on my food, except for the mac and cheese. That would be gross.

After she said grace, we dug in. Halfway through the meal, my phone rang. My little brother's picture popped on my screen.

Ma looked down at the phone. I lifted my eyes to meet hers, checking her reaction to the disturbance from my brother.

Ma shrugged. "He's your brother. I understand."

I picked up the phone and left the kitchen, going back to my old room.

"Hey. What's going on?"

"He doesn't have much time, Raina." Vic sighed. "He's dying. You need to come soon."

I nibbled and then licked my lips. "How soon?" My voice croaked.

Vic blew out a breath. "A few days, maybe. Today or tomorrow would be better."

"It's that serious?"

"He's only holding on because I told him I'd try again with you."

"That's not fair, Vic." I paced the floor. "I'm not ready for this. I'm not ready to see him again."

I'm not ready to forgive.

"Like I told you before, life can be shit sometimes. This is one of those moments. He wasn't father of the year. I know that, he knows that, and you know too. But if you have it in you, dig deep and come to Birmingham. Go to the hospice and give a dying old man peace of mind. He wants to see his baby girl all grown up. He can't stop talking about you or writing on the damn dry erase board they gave to him to use when he loses his breath."

"Well, I wanted to see my daddy when I was growing up, but guess what? It didn't happen!" I yelled.

"Raina," Vic rumbled, his voice ragged and rugged. He seemed to be losing patience. "Can you please, please just come? For me? I don't wanna . . ." He sighed, softening his voice. "I don't want to do this alone."

Alone. I knew all about that. Regret and shame washed over me. I couldn't leave my little brother alone to see his father dying. To make funeral arrangements and contact family and friends to notify them of his passing.

Damn, damn, damn!

"Fine, little brother. I'll do this for you. Not for him. Sorry to sound heartless, but he doesn't deserve closure."

"When are you coming?" Vic's voice was higher, optimistic even.

"I'll leave early tomorrow morning."

"Cool. I'll be here."

"Good. I've gotta go pack or whatever."

"Yeah, pack for a few days, maybe a week."

"You're pushing it, Vic. Didn't say I'd stay the entire time."

"Yeah, but do you really want to drive back and forth?"

"I plan to show my face, say 'Hi, you can die in peace, and have a good afterlife.' I'll come back to help you with funeral arrangements."

"C'mon, Raina. You aren't working full-time, and my job is being flexible, but it's been hard lately. They want me to come into the office soon."

"Fine, Vic," I bit off. "See you tomorrow."

"Thanks, big sis. Glad I'm not doing this alone."

"I know. I'm glad you're not alone." I sighed and melted a bit. It wasn't his fault our dad was a dying asshole.

"Bye, Rae-Rae."

"Bye, Vickie." I clicked the end button. "Dammit!" I yelled, flinging my cell on the bed. "Motherfucker!"

Ma knocked on the door. "Hey, baby. What's going on?"

I leaned against the wall. "Victor Senior isn't looking so good right now."

Ma nodded, sadness overpowering her still youthful features. She'd overhead that Daddy was dying from when Vic and I first met. "So, you're going to see him. To say goodbye." It wasn't a question. It was as if she knew I'd eventually cave.

I nodded.

"I knew you would. You're a good girl." Tears in her eyes, she leaned in and hugged me. "I know this is hard for you. You were a daddy's girl, and as much as you hate him, you love him just a little more, don't you?"

Tears clogged my throat. "I dunno. Maybe."

"You do." Ma stepped back, looking at me with tears and pride shining in her eyes. "Because I felt—no I *feel* the same way." She squeezed my shoulders. "It's okay to love someone. Even when they don't deserve it."

"I hate that I feel so weak, so silly. I wish I could remove my feelings and throw them away."

She nodded. "Because with all this love comes pain when they've done you wrong. It's hard to separate the two."

"When did you get so wise?"

Ma laughed. "Your grandma and I may not have gotten along, but she raised me, and some things stuck. Now, let's get back to dinner. I want to try that fancy cupcake you got me."

Chills scraped my spine when I crossed over the Georgia border into Alabama the next morning. I zoned out and sped until I reached Birmingham. I grabbed my cell and dialed Vic. "I'm here, little brother."

"At the home?"

"No, but I just entered the city. GPS says I should be there in twenty minutes or less. Who should I ask for when I get there?"

"They have your name. Just sign in and mention his name."

"Cool. See you soon." I cut off the call before he could shower me with more gratitude. I didn't want it. In fact, I was slightly miffed that I was in this situation. I wanted to confront Victor on my own terms. I couldn't exactly curse a dying man out.

I finally arrived in front of the hospice, Summerhill Homes. The facility was nice enough, and it sat perched atop a hill that made me wonder why in the hell they would put an old folks' home that high. Poor orderlies. Oh, and old people, too.

The sign was slightly faded, but the landscaping was lush. Mixes of different color flowers I couldn't name and bright green bushes made the outside welcoming. But once I entered the building, I knew it couldn't mask the stench of death. Antiseptics, soiled clothes, and bleach assailed my nose.

"Raina Williams here to see Victor Williams," I told the college-aged boy at the desk.

He pointed to a clipboard on the desk. "Sign in and I'll radio our facilities coordinator."

After I signed in, I lingered in the hallway. Not quite sure what to do with myself, I thrummed my wiggling fingers against the wall in the hallway and hummed a little, nothing in particular but something to quell my need to run away and never come back.

"Ms. Williams?"

"Right here." I raised my hand like an elementary school student being called to the principal's office.

"C'mon back," the woman in purple scrubs said. "Your brother and father are waiting for you."

"Oh, Victor, um, Senior isn't asleep?" I glanced at my cell phone. It was just eight a.m.

"Nope, he's wide awake. He's been so excited he could barely sleep last night."

"Awesome." I followed the caretaker down the hallway. Soft

music and televisions cut through the eerie silence that had met me at the front of the building.

My gladiator sandals squeaked against the linoleum flooring until we finally arrived in front of the door.

"Knock, knock!" Her voice was slow and bright, the perfect impression of a kindergarten teacher. "Mr. Williams, your daughter is here."

Daddy lay tucked under covers in bed, a breathing tube under his nose and the oxygen tank on the side of the bed.

His nutmeg skin had paled. When he gave a tired wave, I noticed large veins protruded from his hand.

"Raina." His voice was weak, shaking and vibrating with emotion.

"Hey." I gave an awkward wave.

Vic smiled from his chair and then stood. "Good to see you, Rae-Rae." He gave me a hug.

He waved at his chair. "Take a seat."

"Oh, I'll get another one. I don't want to take yours."

"That's okay. I'm about to head out soon anyway."

"What?" I turned away, my back to Daddy, who was staring on in interest. I lowered my voice to a whisper. "I thought you were staying, too."

"I'll be back after work tomorrow. They want me to come in for the day. I need to wrap up a project."

"And you can't do it from here? Your father is dying." Sure, it was a low blow, but I couldn't be here by myself. I wrung my hands.

"Not cool, Raina," he whispered. "I've been here taking care of the old man. I need you to do me a solid. If you don't want to talk to him, fine. He can't talk that much anyway. Just read a book, watch TV, and kick up your feet. Relax."

"Sure." I narrowed my eyes. "Because watching your father die at a hospice is just like a weekend at the spa."

Vic twitched his lips. "Sarcasm doesn't become you."

"Nor you." I rolled my eyes.

Daddy wheezed from behind me. Looking up to the ceiling, I sighed and then looked back at my brother. "Fine. I'll handle it. Go to work. I'll see you tomorrow."

"I knew you wouldn't let me down. And Cam said you'd give in."

Of course. He and Cam were still bosom buddies or whatever. Despite the mention of my ex, my heart lifted. Someone depended on me. It felt nice. I punched his shoulder. "Yeah, yeah. Get out of here."

For the past few hours, Daddy had slipped in and out of sleep. When he was awake, he stared at me, as if committing me to memory. Tears would gather and I'd look away. I hadn't said anything to him yet. What was there to say?

Daddy wheezed again, grabbing my attention away from the rain pelting on the window.

"Come." He waved at me and then patted the bed.

"Um, I don't know about that, old man."

"Need to tell you something. Not over there." His breathing was labored.

"All right. All right." I settled in bed next to him. From the other side, he grabbed a small whiteboard.

Writer? He wrote in a shaky script.

I nodded.

Read to me.

"You want me to read what I've written?"

He nodded, smiling.

I sighed, shaking my head. "Um, I don't know. I'm still making edits, so it's a little rough."

He pointed to the board again, silently demanding that I read to him.

"Okay." I wasn't sure why he wanted to hear my ramblings, but for some reason, I couldn't deny his request. Oddly, I was proud. Proud that he would know that I had grown up to be a writer, despite his neglect.

I pulled the tablet from my backpack and powered it up. "Okay, I guess I'll start from the beginning."

For the next hour, I read my book out loud. Daddy smiled huge and even laughed a few times, losing his breath. I would stop when he did.

He grabbed his whiteboard. *Keep going.*

"I had a whiteboard, too, at my old job at the radio station. I used to be a radio personality, and I would play hangman when I had crazy callers."

Listened to every show.

I snorted. "Sure you did."

He nodded earnestly and erased the whiteboard. *Jeffrey the Cat.* He pointed to the board and smiled, then erased again.

"Oh, the song dedication to the cat. Good times. Okay, so you listened to my recent work."

Girl. Suicide.

"H-how? How did you hear about her? That was back in college." Nadia had sent me an email a few months ago. She and her husband had just found out she was preggers with baby #3. She'd also sent a family picture. I was so happy for her. She had healed and started a new life with a good man, de-spite losing her mom, father, and sister in a car accident when they were on their way back home from a visit with her in col-lege.

I listened to EVERY show.

I smiled, believing him this time. I kept on reading.

Two days had passed. Somehow, we got into an easy flow. I read for an hour. Daddy even gave me feedback on occasion, as much as he could—changing a word here or there.

A knock on the door interrupted my reading.

"Hey, Vickie!" I greeted my brother when he popped his head into the door. An athletic bag was slung over his shoulder.

He gave me a two-finger salute. "Rae-Rae." His eyes drifted to Daddy. "What are you guys up to?"

I lifted my reader in my hand. "Reading my soon-to-be *New York Times* best seller."

"What?" Vic walked into the room and sat. "I've been begging you to let me read your book."

"I wasn't ready."

He lifted an eyebrow and waved toward Daddy. "Obviously you are."

"Fine. I'll send it to you tonight."

Vic sighed, leaned back in his seat, and closed his eyes. "I'm beat. I'll just listen for now, like Pop."

"Fine." I turned my attention back to my dad. Tears shone in his eyes.

"Chapter Eighteen: The Girls with No Booties are always the main ones trying to twerk."

Vic's eyes flew open. "Really?"

"Really. Sit back and learn something, young one."

I read the chapter to lots of laughter—from Victor—and wheezing—from Daddy. A few nurses came in to ask about the commotion.

"All right, Raina." Vic shook his head. "I have to admit that it's good. Who knew you'd break down self-esteem issues so thoroughly?"

"I aim to please. People hate being preached to. You have to make it funny and relatable. I got to do that a bit on my radio show, but I love writing. I get to explore and delve as deep as I want and not worry about commercials or offending the FCC."

Vic stood and stretched. "I'm hitting up the vending machine. You want anything?"

"Reese's Peanut Butter Cups if they have them."

Victor grinned. "You love those, too?"

I nodded. "Loved them since . . ."

Memories flooded me. Daddy returning home with a pack of Reese's. If he hit it big that week, he'd bring home a king-sized pack.

Daddy swallowed from the bed, jerked his head down.

"Yeah," I whispered and looked away. "I love them."

Vic dropped his smile and then reached for my shoulder for a comforting squeeze. "I'm gonna make a quick call, too. I'll be back—"

"Take your time. You've left me by myself for two days." I shrugged and lifted my tablet. "Just know that you're missing out."

He grinned, waved at Daddy, then left the room.

"Okay, just me and you again. And lookee here, only two chapters left."

Daddy nodded, as if to say "go on."

"Chapter Nineteen: The Girl . . ." I stumbled a bit on the title. "The Girl Who Doesn't Know How to Love."

I took a deep breath and read. This chapter was for women like me, issues a mile long and dragging baggage any which way they can. I'd occasionally look up from my passage. Daddy was tired, his breathing more labored. I was surprised he'd lasted this long. I finally ended the chapter.

You know how to love.

"Do I?" I shook my head. "You were the first man to break my heart. I don't think it's been the same since the day you left us."

Sorry. Want to be good. But bad. You love Junior.

"He's hard not to love." I grinned. "And yes, I love him. Love my mom. Love y—" I stopped myself from the confession. I didn't want to torture him, but I couldn't give him power over me again. Words were powerful. If I gave in, told him I loved him, he could break my heart again. This time it wouldn't be his fault. He'd break my heart when he died. I couldn't afford another crack.

"Chapter Twenty: The Girl Who Became a Woman." I read the last chapter and sighed, still looking at my book. "Well? What do you think? Am I destined for stardom?" I hadn't asked for his opinion, didn't want to until I was done reading the book.

"Proud," his scratchy voice whispered. He struggled to breathe.

I looked up, peered over the top of my brightly lit screen, and smiled.

Daddy pulled in another breath. He winced. His brown eyes reflected his pain. He looked at me, *really* looked at me, as if he were burning me into his memory, etching me into his soul.

My heart stuttered. I knew, suddenly I knew.

He was ready. He wanted to leave this world, but he held on. I knew then why he lingered.

"Daddy, I love you. I forgive you."

He blinked rapidly, breathing heavily again, and gave me a near-imperceptible nod.

I stood, leaned over his frail body, and kissed his forehead. I smoothed the roughened grooves with the back of my hand. "I'll take care of Vickie. He won't ever be alone. Promise."

"Love you," he whispered. He continued to stare at me until the light dimmed in his eyes. With one last breath, he died.

The monitor flatlined into a steady whine. A nurse rushed around me, stood over him, and then closed his eyes. He'd died in peace, with his children, surrounded by love. More than he could ask for, I know he'd say, but he got it. And I was proud I was able to give him closure.

Victor rushed into the room, took in Daddy's lifeless body, and gulped deep. I opened my arms and he rushed into them. Hot tears splashed on my cheeks, cascaded down my shoulders.

312 / SHARINA HARRIS

"I don't have parents anymore." Victor's voice shook.

"No, but you've got me. And your big sister has a lot of making up to do." I squeezed his torso.

"We've got each other, Raina."

I nodded. "We do. And one day we'll grow our family. You'll have kids and so will I. They'll be cousins and best friends. Maybe we'll live beside each other."

"Now you're taking it too far."

I laughed and sniffed. "Okay, but five miles tops. You can't be too far away."

"I can deal with that. But you'll have to ask my wife first."

"She'll love me." I stepped away from his arms. I turned and took in the nurses' worried faces.

"It's okay. We're okay." I side squeezed my brother. "Vic, you call all of his friends and family, and I'll make arrangements with Nurse Penny."

Victor pulled out his phone, avoiding Daddy's body in the bed. "You sure?"

"I've got this. You handle the calls and let me know if you want help with that, too."

The funeral director parked the hearse. He cleared his throat. "Ready?" His voice felt like a warm cup of chamomile tea, soothing and just the right temperature.

I steadied Vic's bouncing knee with my hand. "Yeah. We're ready."

The church service had gone by in a blur. There wasn't much of a crowd. Most of his gambling buddies had died, which left a sprinkling of family I hadn't seen in years, a few of Vic's friends, Sienna, Kara, and Mama.

Now we were at the grave site. Surprisingly, Daddy had wanted to be buried in Atlanta, by his parents and the sister who died before I was born. Vic had seemed bothered that he wouldn't be laid to rest by his mother, but he hadn't put up much of a fight. I think Vic needed to move on as much as I had.

The funeral director opened my door. Carefully, I placed my heels on the concrete as he assisted me out of the car. My brother stepped beside me. I reached for his hand and took a deep breath. "Don't let go."

He squeezed my hand and nodded. We marched forward, the small crowd already in place. I smiled and nodded at Sienna and Kara, and my mouth popped open in surprise when I spotted Nikki. She gave me a soft smile, yet her eyes told me *girl, what the hell?*

I gave her a quick nod and then my attention went to Ma, who stood by my friends. She, too, gave me a sad smile and then blew me a kiss.

A tap on my shoulder startled me. Fixing my lips into a smile, I turned to graciously accept the condolences that were sure to follow.

"Hey."

My breath caught. "C-cam?" My body shook from the impact. It had been months since I'd seen him.

"What are you doing here?"

His dark eyes swirled with emotion. "You text me nonstop, but you don't when your father dies?" He seemed confused, uneasy.

"You didn't seem to be interested in seeing me, so I . . . I didn't want to bother you. Anyway . . . thanks for coming here for Vic Junior."

"You're never a bother, Raina. And I'm here for you, if you'll have me."

Tears streamed down my cheeks. Damn, this entire time I hadn't cried about Daddy's passing, but this man, my soul mate, swallowing his pride to take care of me had me sniffling like a proud mama on her daughter's wedding day.

"No pressure," Cam whispered "I just want to be here for you."

I hadn't realized how long I'd been staring at Cameron. "I'll have you," I whispered. *Forever.*

Cam smiled and blew a relieved breath, then he grabbed my hand.

Vic snorted. "You knew damn well she was gonna *have* you."

"Shut up, Vickie." I bumped his shoulder with mine.

"Yeah, yeah. Let's go sit down." With Cam and Vic on either side, we settled in the three seats in front of Daddy's final resting place.

Everyone took a seat. The program was short and sweet, as Daddy would've wanted. The funeral director gave us roses and we tossed them on the casket.

"Ashes to ashes, dust to dust," I repeated after the preacher.

"Goodbye, Daddy. Love you."

Cameron flinched beside me. We turned away and walked toward the car. Vic speed-walked in front of us. I knew he was trying to give us space. I stopped in my tracks. "I love you, you know."

"I know you do, Raina. I love you, too."

"I know this isn't the most romantic spot to confess, but I want it all with you. I want to be your wife, I want kids, I want to be yours. For always."

Cameron shook his head and looked around. "Only you would propose grave side."

"Oh, I'm not proposing. You have to ask me again."

"Nope." We walked to the car. He opened the door and we both slid in.

Cam resumed the conversation. "You have to propose. I want candles, some R-and-B slow jams, and it wouldn't hurt if you wore lingerie." He leaned in and whispered, "Or nothing at all."

"Trying to grieve over here." Vic stuck fingers in his ears. "La la la la. You two are disgusting."

I tilted my head back and laughed. Today I'd told my Daddy goodbye for the last time. This time he didn't leave on his own accord. I'd forgiven him, forgiven myself, and in the process gained a little brother and devoted boyfriend—soon-to-be husband, once he proposed. My heart was full.

Chapter 18
Cleaning House—Kara

I attacked the counters with all the vigor I could muster, as if the few crumbs and invisible microorganisms personally insulted me. I started my war against germs at six a.m. Raina had stumbled down the steps, taken in my cleaning frenzy, crossed herself as if warding off bad spirits, and hurried back upstairs.

I stopped midwipe when my cell buzzed against the table. I looked at the screen and picked up the phone. "Hey, Dad."

"Hey, sweet pea." His voice was light, soft, and slurred.

He's drunk. "Dad." My voice broke. A stoic man, my father usually kept it all inside, but on anniversaries and birthdays, a crack appeared in his steel armor.

"Ya know what today is?"

"Yeah," I whispered. "Mom's birthday." I tossed the dish cloth in the sink and settled on the barstool by the counter.

"I got a rum cake, her favorite. Even put the candles on the damn thing, all fifty-seven of 'em. But I couldn't . . . I can't blow them out." His voice shook. "If I do, she'll go away."

"Daddy. She's already gone."

"I feel her, Kara. I know she's with me."

"No, Dad. She's gone." I said it more firmly, not only for

him but for myself. Daddy grieved, like I'd been doing for the past few weeks before I had my awakening. He was living half a life since the heartbeat of our family died.

The phone beeped. I glanced down at my screen. *Darren.*

"Decline." I hit the button. I knew that he wanted to comfort me, but I needed to focus on Daddy.

"What's that, sweet pea?"

"Why don't I come over?" I asked, changing the subject. "I can cook us something nice. Chicken, yellow rice, and plantains? Mama loved—"

"No."

"No?"

"No. I don't want you to come over. No, I don't want you cooking nothing your mama ain't around to eat."

Ain't around? I shook my head at Dad's denial, that is, until I remembered that Darren had suggested the very thing last year and I pushed him off. I couldn't bear doing something Mama enjoyed without her here.

"Okay. Are you going to visit her gra—I mean, visit her?"

"I already did this morning. Talked to Father Frank, too." He dropped his despondent tone and switched to authoritative, though he was still slurring his words. "Said he saw you a few months ago."

I stopped swiveling on the barstool. "We spoke." My voice was clipped. "Is Father Frank sticking around today?"

The church was located just down the road from the cemetery. Father Frank often floated around caring for the grounds, although the church paid someone to do it.

But he shouldn't be. It was a Tuesday, which meant volunteer day at the halfway house downtown. At least that was his schedule a few years ago, when I used to go down and volunteer with him. Although I was getting better, I still wasn't ready to add God to the mix.

"No, he said he had some errands to run. He told me to tell you and Tracey hello. Are you going to say hello to your mother?"

"Of course I am."

"Right," he whispered. "Gotta go."

"Daddy?" I cleared the croak from my voice.

"Yes, Kara."

"Blow out the candles. Mama wouldn't want you to linger. She'd want you to heal, or at least try."

"I'm trying, baby. Every day I'm trying."

"I know, Daddy. Me, too. I'll give you today. But maybe I can come over this weekend? I'll see if Tracey can swing by, too. We don't have to eat Mama's favorite foods, but maybe we can just talk."

"We never talk about it." His voice wasn't negative, but contemplative.

"*Not* talking about it doesn't seem to help, does it?"

"You and Tracey are doing okay." His voice grew stubborn. "And don't worry about me, I'm just a brokenhearted old man."

"You're not old, Dad, and we all have broken hearts." I spun in my chair, now facing the window. "Tracey is hopping from man to man, looking for love in all the wrong places. Darren and I are separated . . . when Mama died, we all became a little lost. But I've been trying hard lately, and I swear I'm getting better. That's why I think we should talk."

"And talking about your mama being gone makes you feel better?"

"I'm not saying I have the answers, but Mama would want us to try."

Dad sighed over the phone. "When did you get so wise?"

"I hit rock bottom, Dad. All I could do was look up and think."

The phone receiver rattled as if Dad were going through a wind tunnel.

"Dad? What's going on?"

"I blew out the candles."

I parked the car in the church parking lot. Today was beautiful, a perfect tribute to Mama's born day. Though it was cold, the sun kissed my skin, dashing away the chilly weather.

The grass hadn't taken on the dull brown tint that other yards had done. No shoots of weeds or unsightly plants marred the manicured grounds. I wasn't surprised, Father Frank was faithful in making sure the grounds were well-kept.

I walked along the winding path, flowers in hand, so lost in thought I didn't see Darren until I was nearly at Mama's grave. Darren was seated, a blanket and picnic basket on the side of Mama's headstone.

Darren had arranged food on top of the blanket. He watched me, his expression relaxed save for the intensity in his eyes. My skin blazed under his scrutiny.

"What are you doing here?"

"Care Bear." His deep voice reached out and soothed the fiery path his gaze had caused.

I battled my lungs to pull in air. "How long have you been here?"

He shrugged. "Few hours." His voice was nonchalant, as if it were perfectly normal to stalk your almost-ex-wife at her mother's grave.

"You're a determined man."

"I made us some sandwiches." He waved to the brown wicker basket without addressing my comment.

"You made us a picnic . . . at Mama's grave?" I wanted to laugh at the absurdity.

"You always cry when you come. It's never cleansing, never healing. I wanted to make a good memory. We can eat, think of good things. Make it beautiful."

"Things like?" I asked, not quite sure I was committed to leave my melancholy behind.

"Like how your mama would say everything was her jam. Remember how she hopped from her seat and then started swaying her hips to the beat, doing that wiggle thing with her shoulders?"

I giggled and then mimicked the dance. Mama was from the islands, but she had zero rhythm. "Aww, shoot. This. Is. My. Jam!"

"And remember when we first moved in together? Your mama dragged you to Mass, and after church, pushed you to the front of the line to talk to Father Frank?"

The melancholy vanished, replaced by hysterical laughter. Mama's Caribbean accent would grow thick when she was riled up. *Father Frank, please pray for my firstborn's eternal soul. She'll be waiting for you at confession next week.*

I bent over from laughter. "I looked Father Frank straight in the eye and said that I'd been living in sin and enjoyed every minute of it, and asked if he wanted to hear all about it."

"His face was beet-red!" Darren shook his head. "He told you to go in peace, and then ran away from your poor mother."

Our laughter continued until we looked at each other. He was doing that looking-into-my-soul thing again. Something hot and potent blanketed the air, and then I felt it. An invisible string, a tether tugged at my heart. I shook my head, literally shook it, as if to signal this thing called love to cool it.

Darren raised his eyebrow, a smirk forming along his lips. He patted the blanket. "Want to sit down? Join me in my creepy picnic?"

The tether tugged not-so-gently again. "Yeah, you can't be the only weirdo eating PB and J sandwiches in a graveyard." I lowered myself to the ground.

He passed me a sandwich wrapped in plastic. "For you."

"Thank you, good sir." I took the proffered food.

After unwrapping the sandwich, I looked down at my lap, avoiding Darren's eyes. Heat zipped through my bones. I could feel his stare on my face, my breasts. I wondered if he could see how hard my heart pounded beneath my chest.

I took a bite, swallowed, then found the courage to look up. Like magnets, my eyes found his.

"Kara . . ." He sighed, reverent. Worshiping.

"Yes?"

"Are you okay?"

"Why do you ask?" I wondered if he could read the confusion on my face.

"Today is your mother's birthday. I need to make sure you're okay."

"I am." I nodded. "Really, I am. And I talked to Dad today. He's still taking everything hard, but he, Tracey, and I are going to talk more."

"Really?" A small smile formed on his lips.

He'd always encouraged me to talk to my family, but I wrapped my grief around me like a cocoon and was too engrossed in my pain to see anything else. *To see him. To see his pain.* "Why didn't you ever tell me?"

"About what?" He dropped the smile.

"About your past and what happened to you as a child."

He sighed, shook his head. "I was ashamed. Men, we don't talk about stuff like that. If you have sex with an older woman, it's like a rite of passage."

"Not when you're a kid. How old were you?"

"Ten."

"Ten." I shook my head. "That's rape." The word was foreign and tasted sour on my tongue.

"I know that. I always knew, but I was confused. She was the only person to show me affection and touch me, though inappropriately."

He bit into his sandwich. "Then I found Dr. Caine, and I've been talking to Father Frank, too. He helps me with the spiritual aspect. Made me realize the Big Guy upstairs actually cares for me."

"Good, I'm glad. I'm happy for you."

His eyes sought mine again. "Kara, I love you."

I looked away and twisted the plastic in my hand. *Does he?*

Even after our counseling, I was still unsure, still thoroughly confused. But despite my dark thoughts, my heart leaped just a bit, as if it wanted to be closer to Darren.

"I know you've been working on yourself, and that's great. But you said it before . . . you don't know what love is."

"I do."

"You don't. Or maybe you do? But I can't afford to be your experiment. I need a man who loves me. Scratch that, loves me and *knows* it."

"I'm your man and I love you. So much that it hurts looking at you, knowing the pain I caused by my actions, or rather inaction. Let me prove myself."

"Fine." I waved at him. "But, first, tell me what love is?"

He frowned, but not in irritation, as if thinking through his answers. "I can't give you a definition. It's complicated."

"I need you to try," I whispered, looking at Mama's grave. "Help me understand why you didn't love me."

"It's not that I didn't love you. I just . . . my heart wasn't turned on all the way. Back then, I loved you in a limited way. I was just bumping along in life. I didn't believe in God, but you went to church and I wanted to make you happy. I didn't love my job, but I was good at it and made good money. I didn't have any passion. Not real passion, like you do for wine. I saw your light and it shined brightly. And I was drawn to it like a moth to a flame because everything around me was dark. You are my firefly. You guided me out of my darkness. Back then I drained your light. And when your mother died, your light dimmed. I saw it, recognized it, but I didn't help you out of the darkness. I know I love you because I want to make you happy. I want to be your partner, the person you rely on. When I think of you, my heart speeds. I'd die for you. I know it hurts for me to say this, but back then, I didn't love you unconditionally. I didn't understand the full range of love. It's like I was operating in black and white, and now I see color. I see you."

My heart clanged like an old church bell. My body shook so much I had to clench my stomach to stop the shakes. But it didn't stop the hope from growing in my core because, damn, he moved me. *Moved my heart.* I wanted to bury myself in his arms, but something held me back.

"What do you love about yourself?"

"Me?"

"Yeah, you."

"I like my drive to make myself a better person. I like my relationship with God. I read and studied the Bible, and I realized that a part of me never forgave God for taking away my parents, for leaving me with loveless grandparents, and for allowing *that* to happen to me, an innocent child."

"How did you move forward? How did you forgive Him?" I leaned forward, hoping he could give me the answers I needed.

"I realized that I knew nothing."

"Huh?" I asked, underwhelmed by his answer.

"I'm looking through a keyhole. I won't ever truly understand God's ways, and for a guy who considers himself intelligent, it kind of pissed me off. Honestly, I asked Father Frank the same question."

I rolled my eyes. "And what did *His Immenseness* say?"

"To lean not on my own understanding but know that God is good, just, loving. And that He gave us a gift of eternal life. I just have to open my heart to accept it."

I rolled my eyes. "How trite."

"More like impossible. It was kind of hard for me to do, to love Him when I didn't love myself. So, I started to just read anything I could get my hands on about hearing from God. And then one day, I did."

"Oh, yeah? What did He say?"

"It wasn't anything He said, just a feeling. Of love. Like my heart got unblocked and I could feel and hear and see clearly. Everything just clicked." Darren stretched his legs. "And you know me, I wasn't talking for months. But I had an epiphany. God gave us a heart, a brain, consciousness, and intellect to be able to get back up and try again. He never promised us a perfect life, but He gave us the means to survive." He grew quiet after his statement.

I remained silent. I didn't know what to say, how to follow up his aha moment. I was happy, *truly* happy he felt better, but I wasn't ready to forgive . . . Darren or God.

"Do you believe in Him, Kara?"

"Yep. Never stopped believing. Which is why I'm pissed. I know He's supposed to be with me." I tapped my heart. "But I'm not ready to accept some corny thing about understanding the will of God. My mom was kind and good and . . . and she was just living her dream as a teacher. She deserved better. Deserved more time to enjoy her life, deserved more time to meet her grandchildren. She would've been an awesome grandmother. But no. He," I pointed to the sky, "yanked my mother's life away."

Darren nodded, his eyes compassionate, patient. "So if you believe, then you believe in eternal life, right?"

"Yes," I hissed, slightly agitated that he didn't address why God took Mama away.

"Then you know that she didn't die. She's living, more fully than we can ever imagine."

A breeze fluffed up my hair. Goose bumps formed on my forearm, and I *swore*, I swore I could feel her, as if she were sitting beside me.

"One of the main things I realize is that we aren't meant to live life alone. We were built to love and be loved. And to love, unconditionally, is to accept things about ourselves and each other: the good and bad and ugly. To love without boundaries or conditions. I couldn't love you the right way because I was blocked."

He pointed to me. "But you put conditions up, too. You stopped loving God because you think he's mistreating you. But everyone lives and everyone dies. And now, you're convincing yourself that you don't love me because you think I never loved you."

I lowered my head. Shaking my head. *Not true. Not true.*

I loved him so much that every day without him felt heavy and worthless. It didn't matter how many victories I'd won in my life. I was losing the most important thing in the world: my husband.

He remained silent. Maybe he was letting me digest my part in our destruction. But then he spoke. "Just . . . just try to remove those limitations of what you think life should be and how love should be expressed."

His voice shook as he lifted my chin to meet his eyes. "I love you. Your drive, your ridiculous victory dance. The way you twist up your nose when you smell cheap wine. The way you give your girls shit when you think they messed up. And the way you support them when they're low. I love everything about you, and all I'm asking is that you love me as I am. An imperfect man. A man with a lot of scars and skeletons, but a man who loves the hell out of his woman. A man who'll love you for the rest of his life, if you let him. Let me in. Let *Him* in, and every day, we'll show you just how much we love you." He held out his hand and I took it, needing comfort. "Let me help you, Kara. I don't know all the answers, but I know Mama Carla wouldn't want you to feel this way. You aren't alone in this."

He pulled me close into his arms, warmth seeping from his body. Gathering me closer, he whispered, "My biggest regret was not being there for you. For allowing you to slip into the darkness. When you needed me, I wasn't there and I didn't know how to be someone else's light. I failed you. I should've followed you into the dark."

I leaned into his chest and cried. Cried for us, cried for Mama, cried for Dad and Tracey.

Cried for me.

"I love you, Kara. He loves you, too. And you love Him. Let go of your anger and let Him in."

His word seemed to untighten and loosen the bands of fear, anger, and sadness across my chest. I exhaled, gasping for air as if I'd broken the surface of choppy water.

A ball of energy warmed me from the inside, percolated through my pores, and ignited my body. It was as if I were coming to life after a long hibernation.

I felt it. I felt *Him.* "Well, I'll be damned," I whispered to myself, realizing that Darren was right.

Darren leaned back, looking in my eyes. His eyes brightened at whatever he saw in me. "Told you."

"Yeah," I whispered, overwhelmed by emotion. "You did."

I moved away and pushed off from the ground, full of boundless energy. "Can you take a few days off for a road trip?"

Darren, still seated, looked up questioningly. "Where to?"

I reached out my hand. ""St. Louis, Missouri."

One week later, Darren drove eight hours to Saint Louis. He held my hand the entire time, never letting go. Not even on the fast highways or the winding back roads or in the bumper-to-bumper traffic.

He drove us to the Four Seasons, checked us in, gave me space to study, and then the next day waited in the lobby while I took my exam.

Half an hour later, I floated out of the exam room. I saw him before he saw me.

He paced the floor, glancing at his watch. He held a bunch of flowers behind his back. Before my exam, he'd tried to pin a white heather flower on me for good luck. I had declined because we weren't allowed to wear anything that could throw off our senses.

"Darren?" I called across the lobby. Some of the patrons and staff at the Four Seasons rolled their eyes. I was buzzed. I was happy. I didn't care.

He rushed toward me, grabbing my elbows. I swayed a bit.

"Did you…" He looked at my chest, pointing to the small, round pin. "You did it?" A wide smile spread on his face.

"I did it." I grinned and twirled. "Twenty-five minutes. Six glasses of wine. I'm a mother-effing-master!" I yelled again.

He pulled me to his chest and hugged me tight. "Baby, I am so proud. So damn proud. And your mother would be, too."

"I know." I bit my trembling lips.

"Let's go celebrate. I got us reservations to a really nice restaurant." He grabbed my hand and led me to the entrance.

"What if I hadn't passed?"

"I knew you'd pass."

I stopped walking. Daren looked at me.

"How did you know?" I asked.

He shrugged. "You were so focused and confident. I haven't seen that look in a while and well...I believed in you because you believed in yourself."

I looped my arm through his and sighed deep and content. "Guess I'm back in the game."

"You just pulled a Michael Jordan and left the game for a little bit. But as soon as you returned, you found your way back."

"Hmm." I said, making the comparison in my head. Like MJ, I'd lost a parent, switched directions, and then returned back to the game I loved. "Guess I did."

CHAPTER 19
I Ain't the Same—Nikki

Sipping my coffee, my latest vice that had replaced booze, I scanned the small crowd dressed in all black.

"So . . ." I waved to the gathering, cup in hand. "Did anyone know about Raina and her daddy? I always assumed the stork dropped her off on her mama's doorstep."

Sienna shook her head. "No idea. Didn't know about her brother, either." She bit her lips and her eyes watered. Knowing Sienna, she was upset that she hadn't realized her friend was going through hell while we skipped through a field of daisies and forgot about everyone, Kara included.

Kara nodded. "Yes. Raina told me about it."

I found my head twisting in Kara's direction like the girl in *The Exorcist*, with no control over the motion. The guilt I felt for abandoning my friends was replaced with a little green fella, better known as jealousy. "What in the entire hell?" I had expected her to say an emphatic no. Raina, my bestie in the whole wide world, had not said a damn thing about her father.

"Now, now. Let's not forget you were too busy drinking and gallivanting to be there for your friend." Angie's know-it-all voice popped into my head.

"Shut it, Angie," I muttered to myself. But she was right. I should be grateful someone was there for Raina. I was a shit friend. I didn't even know her father was dying, much less that they had reconciled, and hell, I didn't know she had a little brother, either. Raina hadn't told me on purpose. The girl had skeletons, not that I could judge. I had a walk-in closet full.

"It was recent." Kara's voice pulled me back from my self-reflection. "I met her brother, Vic Junior, when he helped her move into my place. Things just piled on her at once, but trust me when I say that she is doing well, considering all that has happened in the past few months." She squeezed my shoulder. "You don't have to feel guilty about anything. You've got a lot going on."

"Yeah. Don't we all." I squeezed her hand on my shoulder. *I'll be a better friend.* I mentally added the vow to my ever-growing list of things to improve. Wife and mother hovered at the top of the list.

Kara seemed to be on the mend, too. Sure, she was still rail thin from her recent weight loss, but she looked healthier. Brighter. Darren came behind her, an orange juice in hand. He wrapped his arms around Kara's waist, whispered something in her ear, and handed her the plastic cup.

Kara smiled, turned in his arms to face him and touched his face. Darren grinned and kissed her lips. Kara had given me and Sienna the lowdown on what happened between them nearly an hour ago while Darren went to the restroom. She explicitly asked me not to give him shit, and I didn't. Sienna, of course, agreed without much pushback. She even did a few awws when Kara told her about the graveyard picnic. But best of all, and yes, even better than their reconciliation, my girl passed her test. Her red and gold pen gleamed against her black dress.

Despite my happiness for my friend, the little green man appeared again; this time, he danced on my embattled heart. I missed my husband and had no idea if he wanted to fix our marriage. I hadn't seen him since Memphis. Our conversations afterward had been stilted, generic, not at all us. I was ready to clean house, *my house*.

Thankfully, the band had a small three-day break before our last push for the tour. In less than an hour, I planned to hit the road for Bria's talent show today.

I glanced at Sienna, who looked at Kara with an expression much like I imagined mine had been. Happy as all hell for Kara, but a bit forlorn. *I wonder if it's about Chris.*

"Congrats on your win, Sienna." I lifted my coffee cup to her.

"Yeah," she said, her voice unenthusiastic. "Kind of easy to win when your opponent is a douchebag."

"You would've won anyway." And I wasn't blowing smoke up her ass. I'd been keeping tabs on her campaign online. I wish I would've been there for the infamous debate. "What did Chris say about it?"

"Christopher?" She snorted, a frown marring her face. "He can go jump in a lake with cement blocks tied around his ankles."

"That's specific." Kara raised her eyebrows.

"I've been gone too long." I shook my head. "What happened?"

"Hey, ladies!" Raina walked into the middle of our circle, her bodyguards Cameron and her younger brother flanking her.

"Well, hello there, best friend. So great to see you." I gave her a look that conveyed that I better get all the tea spilled and pronto.

Raina smiled and gave me a small nod. "I want to introduce you to my little brother, Vic Junior, aka Vickie."

"Vic is just fine." Raina's brother rolled his eyes.

"Vickie," Raina ignored her brother's comment, "please meet my friends Nikki, Sienna, and you already know Kara."

"Hello, Nikki, Sienna." He stretched out his hand for a shake and we obliged.

"Beautiful Kara," he said in an overly familiar tone.

Darren squeezed Kara tighter to his side.

Vic noticed the small splay of possessiveness as well and smirked. I snorted. He was a little shit stirrer, just like his big sister.

I gave him a wink and then focused on Raina's other body-guard, Cameron. That asshole had caused my friend heartache. Sure, it was because he wanted to spend the rest of his life with her, but he knew she had commitment issues. He should've been more patient. But, no, he had to kick my girl out of *her* home. He had no idea how much courage it took her to buy a house with him.

"Cameron Jefferies." I dropped the sweetness in my voice and squeezed the Styrofoam cup of coffee. "I'm assuming you're here because you pulled your head out of your ass, got over yourself and your life, and—"

"Hey, now." Raina lifted her hand. "Don't scare him off already. I just got him back."

"Don't worry, baby. I'm not going anywhere." He hugged Raina to his side but gave me his attention. "I promise I'll take care of our girl. You can drop your weapon."

I looked down at myself. "I don't have a weapon."

He nodded to my cup of coffee. "You're gripping that cup like you're ready to toss it on me."

Damn if it didn't look like I was about to launch it at his face. But my hand didn't relax its grip or aim.

"Chill, Nikki. We'll talk soon, but Cameron here will be asking me to marry him again. And, spoiler alert, I'm accepting." She grinned.

"Woman, I told you that it's your turn to ask me," Cameron damn near growled at her, but I could tell he was joking.

"Oh, you didn't mean that." Raina waved him off. "I'm thinking a summer wedding no more than a year from now."

"Way to plan your wedding at our dad's funeral." Vic shook his head, his tone teasing as well.

Damn, these siblings were strange.

"Alrighty, then." I relaxed my arm. "I'm guessing I'm missing some context clues as to why you guys aren't—"

"Crying? Sad?" Raina supplied.

"Morose?" Vic added.

"Sure," I agreed. "All of the above."

Raina nodded. "Daddy is at peace now. I've forgiven him, and I had the chance to form a relationship with my little brother." She lifted her face to kiss Cameron. "And I've got the best guy in the world. I can't pretend I'm not happy right now. Daddy would want me to be happy."

My heart lifted at my friend's serene expression. This time, there was no jealousy. If anything, it gave me hope for my situation.

Shit! I looked down at my phone.

"Guys, I've gotta go. Bria's talent show is in a half hour."

"Ahh." Raina nodded. "That's why James isn't here."

I don't know if he would've come anyway.

I kept my thoughts to myself. Ironically, I didn't want to bring down the mood at a funeral. "Yeah, Bria had to arrive early for the last rehearsal." I gave my friends hugs.

"Raina, I'll call you soon." I pointed to Kara and Darren. "Congrats, guys."

"Hey!" Raina pointed between her and Cameron. "What about a congratulations for us?"

"Yeah, yeah. I'm happy for you. Go, team!" I pumped a fist in the air.

I turned to face Sienna. "Let me know if you need Louella again."

She nodded. "Maybe this time I'll break some knees."

"Jesus, girl. What happened?" Raina tilted her head.

I left before Sienna could launch into her story. Much as I wanted to know, being there for my baby girl was more important.

I tapped a beat against the steering wheel, a recurring tune in my head that needed to be played to exorcise my nervousness.

I was beyond nervous, I was afraid. Afraid JJ wouldn't recognize me. Afraid Bria would reject me. It had been three whole months since I'd seen my babies in person.

James and Mama knew I was coming, but I'd asked them to not tell Bria. I didn't want her nervous, looking over her shoulder and listening for every door opening or slamming shut.

"It'll be fine. JJ loves you." I took a deep sigh. "Bria loves you, too." I was a new woman, and I intended on striking a balance between being a good wife, mom, and artist.

Hadn't figured out all the details yet, but I knew that I didn't need Tattered Souls to be successful. I had a handful of songs that were perfect for me, and I knew they'd be a hit once I cleaned them up.

I turned into the school, parked, and hustled to the auditorium. It was just five minutes before the show.

Meegan, the PTA queen, sat regally at the ticket table. A Cash Only sign acted as a backdrop. I patted my pockets. Damn, I didn't have a ticket or money.

"Sorry, Meegan," I said, as I approached the table. "I don't have a ticket, and I don't have any cash on me right now. I promise I'll give you the money after the show."

Meegan lifted a shoulder, accompanied by a go-to-hell smile. "Sorry, Nicole. This is a fundraiser and we don't take IOUs. You must have a ticket or cash. Twenty dollars, to be exact."

I took a cleansing breath. "Remember, you're turning over a new leaf. You're a new woman now," I muttered to myself.

"What's that?"

"Surely, Meegan, we can work this out?" I glanced down at my phone. "There isn't an ATM nearby, James's phone is off, and the show starts in two minutes."

"Sorry," Meegan said, but her tone said she was anything but. "No can do. Cash or ticket." Her voice hardened at the end.

"You're being ridiculous." I heard a strident voice behind me.

I sighed and turned. Of course Mama would find me outside and take the PTA queen's back.

Mama slapped a twenty-dollar bill on the table. "There." She put her hand on her hips. "And let me tell you something, Miss Thang. If *my child* would've missed *my grandchild's* first performance because you've got something stuck up your ass, it would've been me and you, young lady." She pointed at her chest, then directed her finger at Meegan.

I smiled. *You tell her, Mama.*

Meegan angrily tore off a ticket stub. "Enjoy the show."

"Let's go, baby." Mama jerked her head toward the double doors. "I saved you a seat at the front, but we've got to hurry."

While Mama walked toward the door, I turned around and shot Meegan the bird. Two fingers because Meegan was a bitch.

Meegan gasped. "Unbelievable."

"So I've been told." I spun around and followed Mama into the auditorium. Guess I hadn't changed that much. Well, I'd changed where it counted. Family, being true to myself and all that jazz.

The auditorium was completely dark save the bright white spotlight. Mama and I made our way to the front and settled in our seats near the edge of the stage.

A little girl with blonde pigtails hop-skipped onstage and recited an Easter Sunday–esque speech.

"Where is JJ?" I whispered to Mama.

"With a sitter," she whispered back. "You know that boy can't sit still for long."

"Good call." Hopefully JJ would grow out of that once he got out of the toddler stage, but I doubted it. I think he got that annoying trait from me. I fidgeted in my seat, bored to tears.

After the little girl finished her poem, a boy, a few years older than Bria, most likely a fifth-grader, sang "You Are My Sunshine." His voice was a dead ringer for Alfalfa from *The Little Rascals.*

God save me from talentless kids.

"He's nowhere near as good as my Bria," Mama whispered to me.

"I know, right?" I whispered back, giving her a low five.

"Two more kids, then Bria is next." Mama grabbed my hand. "She's ready. You did good."

I shrugged. "I can't take the credit." I cleared my throat from the guilt clogging it. "I wasn't there to help her finish the song."

"But you helped her learn music, taught her to play guitar and sing. And, honey, the girl shines bright when she sings. Like I said, *you did good.*" She nodded and looked straight ahead. Mama hummed, something she usually did when she was nervous.

I smiled and squeezed her hand. "Dare you say music isn't the devil?"

Mama shrugged. "It's fine. Long as she doesn't end up like your daddy, God rest his soul. You turned out okay."

"Two compliments in a day? Be still my beating heart."

"Child, hush." Mama slapped my hand, but even in the dim light I could see a slight curve on her mouth.

Maybe absence does make the heart grow fonder.

"Next on the stage, Bria Grayson singing 'I Will Survive.'"

Hope that isn't a silent eff-you to me. God knows what James was thinking these days. Despite my reservation for the song subject at hand, I clapped and whistled.

The spotlight was on Bria, who stared at her feet. She wore a cute disco outfit with flowers embroidered at the hem of the bell-bottoms. The piano teacher, who thought she was Beethoven in another life, ran up the scale of the famous song, cuing Bria to sing.

But she didn't. Bria continued staring at her shoes, a death grip around the mic.

"Oh, no," Mama whispered beside me.

The piano teacher was undeterred. After a few more seconds, the pianist started up again, but baby girl was still frozen. I finally spotted James backstage, near the piano. He looked as if he was about to storm the stage and save our child from pain.

On the third cue, I shot from my seat. I sang the opening line about being afraid, being petrified, added some flair, and put my hand on my forehead and looked away, doing a perfect impression of a brokenhearted woman.

I stole a glance back at the stage. The piano teacher was following my lead. I pointed to Bria, pretending this was part of our routine.

My baby beamed, grabbed the mic, and started to sing. She strutted up and down the stage, working the crowd. I nodded to the piano teacher and returned to my seat.

Bria's voice was clear and strong. She was clearly the most talented kid so far, and I wasn't being biased. Some people in the crowd stood and clapped with the beat, while the more conservative ones rocked in their chairs.

I, of course, was dancing in the aisle, and so was Mama. I saw James backstage and blew him a kiss. He smiled and pretended to catch it.

After her performance, I hustled to the side of the stage. Bria spotted me and then hopped off the stage into my arms.

"Great job, Bria-bree."

"Mommy!" She squeezed my neck. "I thought you weren't coming."

"I wouldn't miss this for the world." I rocked her back and forth. "And you killed it. I knew you would."

"I got scared, and I was sad."

"Well, that just makes your performance more amazing," I whispered, walking her farther backstage so as to not disturb the next act.

"How am I amazing?"

"Because despite your fears, you went for it. A lot of people can't do that. A lot of people aren't brave."

"Even grown-ups?"

I lowered her to the ground. A clutter of small square chairs were stacked in the back along the wall. "Especially grown-ups." I sat on one of the chairs and gathered her onto my lap. "You know, I'm not really that brave, well, until recently. When I was your age, I knew I wanted to be a singer. But then I stopped."

"Why, Mommy?"

"I was scared that I wasn't good enough. I made excuses, blamed other people because I got resentful."

"What's resentful?"

"Mad." I sighed. "At other people. But for no good reason."

"You were mad at Daddy?"

"No, baby."

"Me? JJ?" Her voice was small and unsure.

"Of course not. It's a long story, but it was my fault. And I apologize for how I treated you. You, Daddy, and JJ are the best things that have ever happened to me, and I'll never ever let you go again."

Bria squeezed me tighter. "Good, Mommy. Because I missed you. And I was tired of being mad at you."

"I was tired of you being mad at me, too."

Bria giggled against my chest. I breathed in her fresh cotton clothes, the smell of coconut oil in her hair. She smelled like my baby. She smelled like home.

"I'm tired of being mad at you, too." James's voice jerked my attention. Bria hopped off my lap and rushed her daddy, giving him a big squeeze.

"You did great, baby girl."

"Thank you, Daddy."

I stood and then rushed him like our daughter, wrapping my arms around his waist.

"Love you, Nik," he whispered against my hair.

"Love you more."

"Not possible."

"Is so."

"Eww." Bria made gagging noises, but the grin on her face gave away the fact that she was happy her mom and dad were happy.

"I'm sorry I left you hanging." I squeezed him tight again, snuggling against his chest.

"It's okay. You had to lose yourself for a while so you could figure things out."

"I quit the band."

He exhaled. "Not gonna lie, I'm happy about it, but how do you feel?"

"Happy, sad, a little lost, but optimistic."

He leaned away, grabbing my chin. "Look, I know music is as important to you as breathing. And, baby, I want you to breathe deep. So, I *insist* that you follow your dreams. And to support you, I've decided a few things."

"What's that?"

"Well, I don't love my job. And, honestly, I do taxes, which can be seasonal. How about I quit my job, work part-time and help out at home with the kids while you pursue music? We'll have to cut back and downsize, but as long as we're together I'm happy."

"W-what?"

"I'm quitting my job so you can be my sugar mama." He smiled. "I'm gonna be a good trophy husband, and I promise to keep my body tight."

I snorted. "We don't have to downsize."

"We don't?"

"Nope." I popped the *P*. "I'm writing songs for Tattered Souls and a few other bands on the record label. And . . . I'm doing a solo album. They sent the numbers over and, baby, not saying we're rich, but I'm making a little more than your salary."

"Hot damn. I married up."

I narrowed my eyes. "You had already married up."

"True that." He laughed, and the vibration that rumbled in his chest warmed me.

"So, we're doing this?"

"No doubt, baby. Where you go, I go." He waved at Bria. "We go."

His voice dropped to a whisper. "We need to talk about your drinking. Not now, but maybe later when—"

"I'm handling it, babe. I signed up for local," I looked around and dropped my voice lower, in case of eavesdroppers, "AA meetings. I also joined an online support group the other day. It'll be good for me while I'm on the road."

James exhaled and pulled me tighter. "That's my girl. I knew you'd figure it out."

"I'm trying. It's going to be a long road." I nuzzled his chest. "I need you to have patience with me."

He kissed my forehead, then gave me a bright smile. "You've got it."

"They're about to announce the winners!" Mama whispered from behind us.

From the tears in her eyes, I knew she'd overheard our conversation.

James scooped Bria in his arms and then took my hand. "Let's go, girls. You too, Mrs. Hardt." He jerked his head toward Mama.

She smiled and joined us. We gathered near the stage as one of the teachers made the announcement. They were now up to the top three winners. Pigtail girl had been announced as the runner-up. No mention of Bria's name. I was not at all nervous. My baby was the best.

"And the winner of Baywood Prep's Talent show is . . . Bria Grayson!"

Bria ran onstage and accepted the gold trophy and red ribbon. Without prompt, she took the mic from the teacher, who looked shocked. "This is dedicated to my mommy. She's a rock star and the bestest mama in the world. And one day we're going to sing on a big stage, even bigger than this one, and see the entire world."

I heard a collective "aww" from the audience.

I wanted to run onstage, hug and kiss my daughter, but this was her moment. I thought I needed other people to worship me to be happy. But here, with Mama, James, and my baby, and once we got home, JJ, my life was pretty damn good. Happiness wasn't thousands of miles away on the road with a band, nor was it in the future.

Happiness was in this moment. Happiness is now.

CHAPTER 20

Ghosts of Lovers Past—Sienna

"Congratulations, Sienna." A deep, husky voice that used to hit me in all the right places greeted me from behind. Now, instead of a shiver, my body wracked in revulsion. I'd honored Baba's request and reached out to Keith. Instead of meeting in public, I'd invited him to meet at my office. Total power play on my end, but I needed to be on my territory. I had a lot to say.

"Ah, my eleven o'clock. You're prompt as always," I said without looking up from my desk, summarizing notes for my defense strategy.

"I have to tell you, I was surprised to hear from you after all this time. And well played on the blackmail thing. Didn't know you had it in you."

I stopped typing, eyes now on Keith. He rubbed his hands over a scruffy beard. It was a good look on him, not that I would be telling him anything complimentary. Besides, he didn't compare to the man who had haunted my dreams for the past month.

"What now?"

"Didn't think you had it in you. To drop that story to the reporters."

"Oh, the thing where you were stupid enough to blackmail a county vendor? *That* story."

"Yes, Sienna," Keith hissed. "That one."

I shrugged. "Wasn't me. Now, I didn't ask you here to trade barbs. I want to make peace."

"It wasn't you." His question wasn't a question but rather a disbelieving statement.

"That's what I said. I've won the election. I don't have to lie about it now, which I already told you when you blew up my phone with those weak-ass messages. I. Didn't. Do. It. Frankly, I'm tired of you and others who think I would stoop so low."

I mean, I *had* deeply considered going there, but then I regained my conscience.

His brows furrowed. "So who did it, then?"

I pushed away from my desk and pretended to look at the door. "Did I have Detective or PI written across my door when you walked in?" I asked, losing my patience. "How in the world am I supposed to know that information?"

I raised my hand as he opened his mouth. "Never mind. I'm not entertaining this conversation."

"You damn well are entertaining this conversation."

I tilted my head. "Excuse me?"

"You destroyed my home, destroyed my reputation, and destroyed my career. My family thinks I'm a disgrace because of the investigation. You need to help me fix this."

"I don't need to do a damn thing but stay black and die. And I don't plan on dying anytime soon. But let me drop some knowledge on you. The reason why your place was wrecked is because you wrecked me. You cheated on me left and right, and each time I found out, I wondered why it was so easy for you. You, who claimed to love me above all else, how could you hurt me like you did? How could you give that intimate piece of you to someone else? I could never, ever, do that to

344 / SHARINA HARRIS

someone I loved." I blinked away tears. "You have no idea what you did to me. You destroyed my self-esteem, my belief in love, and now I'm so screwed up I don't believe in love anymore." I blew out a shaky breath. "And yeah, I ran against you for revenge at first, but the city council position was *my* dream, Keith, and I deserved to see it through. If you dig deep, you know that you don't enjoy serving others. Not unless your dick is involved."

"There's no need to be crude."

"Yes, there is. You're a thirty-four-year-old man-child. Up until now, your mom and dad have preened over you since you made poo in the toilet. There's nothing wrong with supporting a kid, but you are so far up your own ass, I'm surprised you remember to breathe."

I gripped my desk. "Now, as far as who sold you down the river, I suggest you make a list of people you've wronged over the past few years. Take your time. I know it's been a few dozen others who've been mowed over courtesy of Keith Davenport, But you can scratch my name off the list. Matter of fact," my voice raised, "scratch me out of your life."

He looked as if he'd been sucker punched. "I really screwed up."

"Monumentally."

"I had it all with you."

"And now you don't. Look," I grabbed the back of my neck, massaging out the tension, "thank you for coming. I wanted to get this off my chest. Besides, Atlanta is small, and I'd like for us to be cordial if we see each other in passing."

"I came for other reasons. I'd like to be forgiven. To see if we could go back. But now I see that we can't."

"I can give you forgiveness and closure, and by God, for the next woman that you pledge your troth to, treat her like a queen."

"What about you?"

"What about me?"

"You said you don't believe in love, but trust me, Sienna, you still do and you love hard. Your love is one of a kind. I was lucky to have it."

"I think I've got it covered, Davenport," Chris said, leaning against my door, appearing like the ghost of lovers past. *How long has he been there?* Chris was my twelve o'clock, and he was early.

"Guess I'll let you two hash it out." Keith stuffed his hands into his trouser pockets and rushed out.

"Chris! How long have you've been here?"

"I couldn't wait to see you. I sat in the lobby intending on waiting until noon, but then I saw Keith and, well . . . I gave you time to say whatever it is you wanted to say." He shrugged.

"And I also wanted return this." He lifted the check I'd written and dropped off in the mail, and tore it into pieces. The ripped paper fluttered to the floor. "I don't want your money."

"Why?" I folded my shaking hands across my lap.

"Because I love you, and it hurt me that you wanted to pay me off. Like I was a business transaction."

"Well, I would've explained my actions if you hadn't broke it off without speaking to me. Not that it matters. You've moved on."

"I haven't."

"You have. I saw it. No offense, but I'm not the dumb broad anymore that lets a guy cheat and pretend like he's gonna change."

"The woman that you saw, she's my sister."

"That's a good one. I didn't get that excuse from Keith."

He pulled his cell phone from his pocket and pressed the screen a few times. "Here."

There was a family photo on the screen. I immediately recognized the beautiful woman from his condo. Beside her were a man and another young woman who looked identical to her. Standing behind them was Chris, and flanking him, an older man and woman. Upon deeper scrutiny, I noticed they had the same nose and smile.

"So what." I shrugged. "The other day, I read an article that reported people are attracted to those who resemble their parents or themselves." I pointed to the picture. "Like so. You should check to see if you aren't distant cousins."

He did his sigh-slash-forehead crinkle thing. "We aren't distant anything. We are brother and sister." He tapped the phone screen and zoomed in.

"Well then . . ." I straightened my shoulders. "Why didn't you tell me while I was at your place?"

"I tried, remember? But you rushed off and then blocked me out of your life. I knew how you felt about cheaters, and I didn't want you to feel like I'd done that. Not for one second. I sent you emails, calls, texts, and I tried to talk in person."

"Why?"

"Why what?"

"Why did you break it off with me that way? Why were you so angry about the story leaking?"

"Because . . ." He stepped into my office and settled into the chair in front of my desk.

"Because?"

"When I was younger, just starting out in my career, I fell for one of my clients. She was an older woman, by about fifteen years. Smart as hell, sharp, shrewd. Just what I *thought* I liked in my woman. She was running for mayor, up against a seasoned politician, and she was in the fight of her life. But then someone anonymously dropped some very sensitive information about her opponent."

I leaned in closer. "How sensitive?"

"The man was undercover."

"As in, in the closet, gay, undercover?"

"Yeah. He had a wife, two kids in high school, the other in college. Married for twenty-plus years."

"Damn, that sucks. He was living a double life."

"Yeah. I remember when she came to me with the information, said this was the perfect way to shake up his good rep for being honest and trustworthy, which was something she struggled with in the public perception. She was an attorney."

I bunched my shoulders. "Not all attorneys are bad. I hate we have that rep."

"Excuse me, a high-powered attorney for insurance companies."

"Well, I can understand how citizens felt like she wasn't for the people." I cleared my throat. "Go on."

He nodded. "I felt uncomfortable about it. My uncle on my father's side came out later in life, and it was tough on him. But he did it freely and on his own terms. I advised her not to, but I didn't press it. She told me I was too soft for politics and if I wanted to make it, I needed to win by any means necessary. So, I backed off. Let her do her thing."

I could guess the rest. "The shit hit the fan, huh?"

Chris rubbed a hand over his face. "One week later, he killed himself. She won, but at what cost? She destroyed an entire family. And, sure, he was shitty to do that to his wife and family, but there could've been another way. She didn't have to smear him publicly. Outside of his indiscretions, he was a good man from a political standpoint. He did a lot of good, helped a lot of people during his tenure."

I sighed. "So when I came to you about Keith, you were reliving it all over again. No wonder you were so dramatic about it."

"I wouldn't use me and dramatic in the same sentence. But concerned, yes. I didn't want you to end up like Sylvia." He sighed. "And the way you looked, how you smiled when you presented me with the information." He shrugged. "Just seemed like I was repeating history. I couldn't stand by and see another life destroyed. Even if Keith is an ass."

"Keith is too in love with himself to go that route."

"You never know. People have invisible scars, depression, mental illness. Sometimes they can't see a way out. I don't want to be the person who pushes someone over the edge. I want to lift people up. I'll never be charismatic, or a great public speaker, or someone who inspires motivation from people. But I know how to recognize talent, people who can make a difference. I try my hardest to make sure the good ones are the decision-makers. And I—"

"You what?" I asked, choked up by his admission.

"I want to do things to make my mother proud. She was a good person. A really good person to the core. Like you."

"You were wrong about what you said earlier."

"Which part?"

"That you don't inspire motivation. I'll admit, I got caught up. I was a little lost in my quest for revenge. I was so hurt and angry and tired of being run over. I wanted him to hurt. But in the process, I dragged the district into my drama. I shouldn't have done that. I swear, since I was elected, I've been focused on the right things."

"I know you have. I've been keeping tabs."

"Why did you try so hard to get back with me? Before you overheard my and Keith's conversation, you were still under the impression that I leaked the story."

"I couldn't stay away." He stood, walked behind my desk.

"What are you . . ."

He lifted me from the seat, swapped our positions, and then sat me on his lap.

"This is my office, Christopher."

"You're still the boss," his husky voice whispered in my ear. I clamped my legs and willed my body to stop mid-shiver.

"I know you still believe in love, Sienna, because it's what I feel for you and what you feel for me."

"You love me?"

"I do. From the moment I first saw you, I knew you were the one. And damn if I wasn't crushed when I found out you were committed to someone else."

"That must have sucked." I gave him a shy smile.

He snorted. "I'm not the unrequited love type, so I felt pathetic. I pushed you away. Tried to avoid you as much as possible. Even when I knew Keith wasn't the man for you."

"It may not have been love at first sight for me, but I saw you. I just pushed down my attraction because—"

"You're a good woman. You didn't let your mind go there."

"But when I *finally* saw you," I sighed, "I was a goner, too."

"When did you see me?"

"When I hunted you down at the Mayor's Ball. You were smoking a cigarette, pissed off and cold, but too proud to admit it."

"I saw the determination in your eyes. That, plus that sexy dress you were wearing, sent me over the edge. I had to get away."

"And I was determined to find you." I stroked his face.

"I'm glad you did." He squeezed my hips.

"So, are we official? Facebook official?" I joked.

"We are heart and soul official. You've always had it, even when I wasn't there." He cupped my cheek. "There's no going back now."

"I don't want to." I leaned in, kissed him once, twice, teasing and licking until he took control and devoured me.

"Happy?" he whispered against my lips.

I hadn't put myself first in a long time. And through heartache and trial by fire I became confident, content, self-contained. *Happy.* I couldn't love Christopher fully until I learned how to love myself.

I nodded, my smile spreading like sunshine. "Ecstatic."

EPILOGUE

Something New

One Year Later

Raina

Nikki was rocking it out for the small crowd of one hundred–plus people. It was small potatoes for her these days, but she was doing me a favor. An arm wrapped around my middle.

"Best day ever?" Cam's warm breath sent shivers down my spine.

"Yes. Best. Day. Ever!"

"Even better than being a *New York Times* best-selling author?"

Getting that accolade was one of the best feelings in the world. I stayed on the list for eight weeks. I was damn proud of myself, and my agent was bugging me about the next book, which I didn't plan on touching until after my honeymoon. Writing full-time, plus marketing and book tours, took a lot of my time. Luckily I was with a man who accepted the crazy that came with my career.

I turned around in Cameron's arms. "We officially belong

together. Under the eyes of friends and God. I'm buzzed and we're partying and I look gorgeous. Of course it's even better than being a *New York Times* best-selling author."

Kinda.

He twirled me around. "And your ass looks gorgeous in that dress."

I wrapped my arms around him and giggled against his chest. Life was good. After Daddy's funeral, Cam had tried to convince me to move back in with him. Surprisingly, I declined and moved back in with my mother. My grandma's sage advice about not shacking up with a man before marriage haunted me. And while I knew in my heart the reason why we didn't work out the first time was my hang-ups about men leaving me, I wanted to do it right this time around.

So here we were, dangerously in love, dancing to my best friend's hit song. I blew her a kiss and she gave me a wink, then dashed across the stage to work the crowd.

"You need more champagne!" Kara thrust a flute in front of my face.

"And you need more beer!" With the other hand, she gave Cameron a beer.

We took our beverages. I sipped and continued to dance on Cam.

"Time for the garter toss!" Kara yelled and pumped her now-empty fist in the air. She grabbed my hand and hustled me to the middle of the floor, while Nikki made the announcement. The singer cued the band, and a bass guitar blasted across the speakers.

Nikki pointed at me. "Look at her." Nikki sang to me and shimmied across the stage to "She's a Bad Mama Jama."

My husband strutted across the floor, lifted my dress, and then slid his hands up my thigh.

"Keep it PG, Cameron!"

Kara

I gave the TSA agent my passport.

"Where are you off to?" the old lady with snow white hair asked, her tone affable.

"Italy." I smiled.

"Oh, that's nice! For vacation?"

"Work orientation." I gave her a bright smile. "I'll be there for a few months. I'm an ambassador for a vineyard." I smiled again, happy with myself. Normally, I would've given one-worded responses to a virtual stranger, but counseling had done me some good. That and finally passing the Court of Masters Sommeliers.

"That sounds like fun. My husband and I are going to Italy next year to celebrate forty years together." Her hands shook as she stamped the booklet. "Have fun."

"Thank you."

I trudged through the rest of the line. Thirty minutes later, I was ready to board. I glanced at my watch, hopeful my companion wouldn't be late.

"Hey, beautiful."

I dropped my carry-on bag and turned at his voice. I threw myself into his arms.

Darren's company had given him the green light to work remotely for a month. It wouldn't be the entire time I would be staying, but I appreciated that his job gave him the option.

Darren lifted me from the ground, spun me around, and then kissed me. I giggled happily in his arms. If someone would've told me a year ago that we would be stronger than ever, I would've laughed then cried at the cruel joke. The entire time Darren and I had been estranged, I was so focused on us recalibrating, getting back to how we used to be. Thank

God it wasn't how we used to be. We were broken, otherwise we wouldn't have had our issues.

Now we were stronger, something new. We had plans to continue our counseling sessions with Dr. Caine via Skype while I was abroad.

Darren had drastically changed for the better. But I won't lie, sometimes I had nightmares of our tumultuous year before, and fear would creep into my thoughts of him going back to that dark place. He seemed to know every time my thoughts drifted to black. Instead of comforting me with words, he'd gather me in his arms and hold me until the shivering stopped. Our counselor encouraged to me to live in the present. Fear was based on things that occurred in the past, but if I lived in the now, where every day was new, I could achieve happiness. Happiness is a choice. Most days the choice was easy, but sometimes it was hard. Darren squeezed my waist, a worried look on his face.

"I'm good, baby. I'm glad you're here."

He lowered me to the ground and kissed me senseless. The boarding call cut our kiss short.

"Time to get on the plane."

"Ready?" He smiled down at me and then grabbed my carry-on.

"Yes!" We walked down the corridor to the business class section, settled into our seats, and Darren asked for wine. Staring into each other's eyes, we clicked our glasses together.

Nikki

"Why do I need to learn math? I'm just gonna play music anyway." Bria furiously erased an equation that, according to her tutor, was wrong.

My baby hated math, which drove James, the numbers-loving

accountant, crazy. He was holding out hope that JJ would take up the helm, but JJ seemed to concentrate more on banging drums with Davey than counting numbers.

"Sorry, Bria-bree, but rules are rules. You want to travel the world with Mama, you've got to keep up your studies."

"No fair. Daddy doesn't have to study."

"Daddy's been in school longer than most since he received his master's, and then Daddy paid the bills, kept you clothed and fed. Daddy gets to do whatever the heck he wants."

"Darn straight." James smacked me on the lips. "Now I get to be Mama's trophy husband."

"And you're doing a wonderful job, babe." I laughed. He was doing more than that. In fact, he'd taken over the duty of becoming my manager, which thankfully worked out for us. He'd studied the music industry and helped me avoid the many pitfalls that plagued new artists. James also had a network of fraternity brothers in the industry who helped us out when were out of our depth. My man was a shark and I loved it. Even Mama helped out and took the kids for a few weeks when they needed a break from the road. It was truly a family business.

"Two more shows and then we're done." James looked at the calendar on his phone.

"I. Can't. Wait. I'm not leaving home for at least a month." I sipped on my strawberry banana smoothie.

"Well, you have to do *The Tonight Show* in a few—"

I placed a finger over his lips. "Shush. Let me dream."

"It'll be a quick trip. We can make a fun weekend out of it. Just me and you. Your mom said she'll stay with the kids. My frat brother Jake is out of town that weekend and will let us stay at his condo on the beach."

I smiled. "You're going with me?" I knew he loved going home as much as I did, so I figured with the quick TV gig, he'd stay at home with the kids.

He grabbed me close and whispered against my lips, "I already told you, Nikki. Where you go, I go."

He kissed me amongst the symphony of *ewws* from our kids. We ignored them as usual.

"I love you, James."

"Not as much as I love you, Nikki Grayson."

Sienna

I cut the red ribbon and stepped back. The crowd around me clapped and whistled.

"Ladies and gentlemen, I want to thank you for allowing me to be a part of this momentous occasion. The streetcar expansion project has always been a dream of mine, and I'm so pleased that we can offer this option to Metro Atlanta residents. My husband and I," I pointed to Chris, "have had the awesome opportunity to ride the streetcar, and I encourage everyone from tourists to residents to check it out. Thank you!"

Chris stepped beside me and steered me away from the crowd. "Great job as always, Madam Councilwoman."

"Thank you, First Man," I replied with the nickname he'd given himself since I was in public office. "Ready for that surprise?"

"Yes. I'm still mad I couldn't seduce the surprise out of you."

My body flushed as I remembered the sexy French words he'd whispered in my ears while bringing me to orgasm. "Sorry, but it's too important."

I grabbed his hand and guided him to the flower section of the community garden where we'd planted two red tulip flowers right after we were married.

Chris had proposed one month after we reconciled, and we were married two months later. He didn't want a long engagement and neither did I. We were ready to start our lives together as husband and wife as soon as possible. "Check out our flowers."

"Looks like something else has been planted and it's sprouting. Who the hell planted something in our plot?"

"I did. For us."

He lowered himself for a closer look at our plot, then looked at me. Understanding dawned in his eyes.

"You're . . ." He stroked the soil.

"Pregnant," I finished, nodding.

My breath caught at the emotion swirling in his eyes.

"Baby, I'm so happy." He rushed to me, then stroked my belly, and lowered himself to his knees. *"Salut, mon precieux. Je suis ton papa."*

He stood and gave me kisses on my collarbone, cheek, and then lips, whispering *"je t'aime."*

"Je t'aime you, too," I whispered back.

"Aussi." He jokingly corrected my French, which I often botched for his amusement.

"Let's go home." I gave our community garden one last look, thanking God for my journey. If it hadn't been for my friends insisting we resume our Mastermind group, I would've been married to the wrong man, stuck in his shadow. I lifted my face, and the sun's rays caressed my cheeks. Happiness took courage. The path to happiness had been a series of twists and winding roads, but it'd been worth it because I found love—most importantly, love for myself. If I were any happier, I'd burst.

I took Chris's hand and rested the other on my stomach. "If we have a girl," I whispered, "I'd like to name her after your mother."

The look my husband gave me made the happiness that nearly burst at the seams grow even more.

My mistake, I had room for just a little more.

Connect with Us

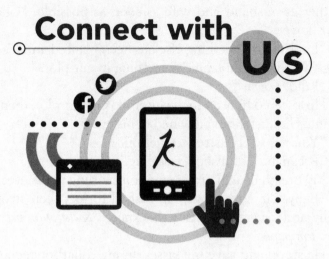

Visit us online at
KensingtonBooks.com
to read more from your favorite authors, see books
by series, view reading group guides, and more.

Join us on social media

for sneak peeks, chances to win books and prize packs,
and to share your thoughts with other readers.

facebook.com/kensingtonpublishing
twitter.com/kensingtonbooks

Tell us what you think!

To share your thoughts, submit a review,
or sign up for our eNewsletters, please visit:
KensingtonBooks.com/TellUs.